* * *

The Rass Campaign

Book Four of the Battles of the Republic

* * *

By James Rosone
and
Brandon Ellis

* * *

Illustration © Tom Edwards
Tom EdwardsDesign.com

* * *

Published in conjunction with Front Line Publishing, Inc.

Table of Contents

Chapter 1:
Edge of Formation

Late 2098
RNS *Poseidon*
Stargate 352-NHW

Three Orbot battleships closed like the Grim Reaper himself, their obsidian hulls nearly invisible against the void. Commander Ripley Willis Lee sat in his captain's chair on *Poseidon*'s bridge as Admiral McKee's order echoed through the fleet communications: "All ships… damn the torpedoes, ahead full speed… let's kill 'em all! McKee out!"

"You heard the admiral," Lee barked. "Ahead full speed! Rhom, fire at will. All guns, lasers, and missiles! Let's kill 'em all!"

The *Poseidon*'s weapons erupted. Magrail rounds and missiles streaked across the blackness of space toward the retreating Zodark formation. A heavy battleship at the rear of their formation took the brunt of the assault. Tungsten penetrators punched through its aft armor. Missiles detonated against its hull plating. Around it, Zodark frigates and cruisers scattered, but the damage was done. Its engines flickered and died, the battleship dead in space while its companions fled deeper.

The Republic fleet surged forward, fifteen warships strong, led by the massive *George Washington*. McKee's dreadnought looked like a steel mountain compared to the rest of the Republic fleet. Alongside them, the battered Primord armada stretched across space, their vessels' armor scarred and bruised from the initial Zodark onslaught after they'd first sped through the stargate. But, the good news? Their weapons still worked, which brought Lee to the most important conclusion of all. Combined with that of the Republic forces, their firepower could crack worlds. And defenses.

"Range to lead Orbot, two hundred thousand kilometers and closing," Ensign Mark Baldry reported from sensors.

Lee tensed as the Orbot ships continued forward. Their initial vector looked like they were heading straight for *Poseidon*.

"Sir," Lieutenant Lewis Reynolds said, breath catching. "Their course projection… they're still maintaining direct intercept with us."

Three Orbot battleships coming right at us, Lee realized. Then something shifted on the main screen.

"Sir," Ensign Mark Baldry called out. "They're adjusting course, but they're still coming for us. We're the most exposed target."

Lee's stomach dropped as he studied their position relative to the fleet. The three Orbot battleships continued their approach, but now he could see their tactical thinking.

"Our position on the fleet's edge makes us the easiest target to isolate," Reynolds announced. "They're trying to pick us off."

Three Orbot battleships against one heavy cruiser—not great odds. These enemy vessels were some of the most advanced warships in the galaxy. And they wanted the *Poseidon* specifically.

"Well, aren't we popular," Lee said grimly.

Being on the edge of formation makes one a better target, genius, he told himself.

But it also meant he could serve as an early-warning system for the fleet.

"Maintain current course," Lee ordered. "We're staying out here on the flank for now."

"Sir?" Reynolds questioned, glancing back from his navigation console.

"Any Zodark or Orbot trying to hit the main formation from an unexpected angle has to get past us first. We're the picket ship now. Screen the fleet's vulnerable flank while *George Washington* and the others concentrate their firepower forward."

"Aye, Captain."

The central holodisplay flickered as long-range sensors locked onto the approaching vessels. The massive ships emerged from the darkness of space, each one stretching across thousands of meters, their black hulls almost camouflaged by the dark expanse. No exterior lighting marked their approach. None at all. Just three obsidian giants bearing down on them.

"Look at the size of those things," Baldry muttered from his sensor station. "I'm reading weapon ports all along their hulls. Torpedo tubes, energy projectors, fighter bays."

"Commander," Lieutenant Lucia Rodriguez said. "Zodark fleet is falling back. They're repositioning behind the Orbot formation."

Lee studied the tactical display with growing concern. The enemy was using their cybernetic allies as a spearhead, letting the Orbots absorb the initial engagement while the Zodarks maneuvered for advantage. At least, that was how it appeared.

The tactical holo updated as hundreds of smaller contacts began separating from the three massive ships, spilling from the Orbot flight decks like metal piranhas.

"Fighter launch detected," Baldry announced. "Hundreds of automated craft inbound."

"Starfighter launch from *George Washington*," Tactical Actions Officer Connor Rhom announced. "Several more ships deploying Orions."

The tactical display updated as starfighters streamed from Republic vessels. These drone fighters were fast, agile, and trained by the best the Navy had. They'd need every advantage possible against the automated Orbot fighters.

"Sir," Lieutenant Commander Noriko Sato said from her command seat, "damage control teams report ready. All departments standing by."

"Make sure they stay that way," Lee replied. "We're about to find out what these Orbot ships can really do."

The first salvo came from the Orbots and Zodarks. Plasma torpedoes raced toward the Republic formation, their warheads glowing. Behind them, Orbot and Zodark energy beams reached across space.

"Sir, I count fifty-six plasma torpedoes inbound," Rhom said, his eyes locked on the tactical display. "Eighteen are tracking directly for us."

Tension coiled in Lee's chest. "Evasive maneuvers," he ordered. "Reynolds, keep us on this vector but give those torpedoes room to miss."

Lieutenant Lewis Reynolds manipulated his navigation controls. The *Poseidon* banked to port. Around them, the Republic fleet scattered into defensive patterns while maintaining their advance.

"Sir, our evasive maneuvers have carried us more outside the fleet's defensive envelope," Reynolds reported, checking his navigation display with growing concern. "We're drifting farther out from the formation's edge. Three thousand kilometers from our assigned position."

Lee cursed under his breath as he studied the tactical plot. In avoiding the torpedo barrage, the *Poseidon* had maneuvered even further away from the protective umbrella of overlapping point-defense fields that kept the fleet's ships mutually supporting each other. Out here on the periphery, they were exposed, vulnerable, and exactly the kind of target enemy commanders looked for.

"Rhom!" Lee said. "PDGs online, now!"

"Already on it, sir!" Rhom worked over his console, bringing the *Poseidon*'s point-defense network to life. "All sixty PDG turrets coming online. Proximity fuses set to maximum sensitivity."

The tactical display erupted in contacts as the ship's sixty quad-barreled 30mm turrets swiveled toward the incoming storm. Each turret could spit out devastating barrages of high-explosive rounds, and with sixty of them working in concert, they could throw up a wall of steel and shrapnel.

"PDG network active," Rhom announced. "Tracking solutions locked. Permission to engage?"

"Light them up!"

The *Poseidon*'s hull came alive with gunfire. Sixty turrets opened up simultaneously, their quad barrels cycling at maximum rate. The 30mm rounds screamed out at the approaching torpedo swarm. Each projectile carried a programmable proximity fuse that Rhom had dialed to hair-trigger sensitivity.

The space around *Poseidon* filled with explosions as the PDG rounds found their targets. High-explosive charges detonated in bright flashes. Clouds of shrapnel blasted in all directions. And, to make it all worthwhile, the plasma torpedoes ran straight into this wall of destruction.

"Direct hits!" Rhom shouted over the thunder of gunfire. "PDGs are shredding them!"

Plasma torpedoes died in rapid succession, their warheads detonating prematurely as shrapnel tore through their guidance systems. All eighteen tracking *Poseidon* simply disintegrated.

"Adjusting proximity settings," Rhom said. "Tightening the spread, increasing detonation range."

The PDG turrets continued their deadly work, tracking individual torpedoes. Rhom's modifications to the proximity fuses paid off. Big-time.

"Outstanding work, Rhom," Lee said as the last torpedo died in a spectacular explosion. "PDG network efficiency?"

"One hundred percent, sir," Rhom replied. "All turrets operational. Ready for follow-up salvos."

Thank God for that, Lee thought to himself.

"*Poseidon*, this is McKee. Fall back into formation immediately. You're too exposed out there. Close to within defensive range of the fleet."

"Understood, Admiral. Rejoining formation now." Lee looked at Reynolds. "Reynolds, bring us back into formation. Close to within five hundred kilometers of *George Washington*'s starboard quarter. We need to get back under the fleet's defensive umbrella before the next wave."

"Aye, sir, adjusting course to rejoin formation," Reynolds replied. The *Poseidon*'s engines hummed as they accelerated back toward the main body of the fleet.

"Orions engaging enemy fighters," Rodriguez reported. "Squadron leaders report contact."

On the tactical display, blue and red dots swarmed together. The Orions were outnumbered three to one, but they had something the automated fighters lacked—human instinct.

"Rhom," Lee called to his weapons officer. "Target the center Orbot battleship. Full magrail salvo."

"Aye, sir. Solution locked. Firing!"

The *Poseidon*'s twin-barreled magrails roared. Twelve tungsten-carbide penetrators streaked across space at ten percent light speed. Lee counted the seconds, his eyes on the tactical display as tension knotted his shoulders.

The rounds struck the Orbot ship dead center. Sparks cascaded from the impact points, but the vessel held. No breaches. No secondary explosions. Just superficial damage to the black armor, pieces of it twirling into the void.

"Minimal damage," Rhom reported with frustration. "Their armor's tough as hell."

"Damn it," Lee cursed under his breath, not loud enough for anyone to hear. Across the fleet, other Republic ships were learning the same lesson. The *George Washington*'s massive guns hammered the lead Orbot with enough firepower to level a city. The enemy ship shrugged off the assault and kept coming.

Lee studied the tactical holo. The Zodarks were using the Orbots as a shield, letting their allies absorb the Republic firepower while they positioned for return fire.

"Admiral McKee's adjusting formation," Rodriguez said. "All ships, prepare for close engagement."

The main fleets maintained their separation while the starfighter battle raged between them. Republic Orions twisted through swarms of enemy fighters. Explosions blossomed where automated fighters died, but more kept coming.

The *Poseidon* shuddered as enemy fire found its mark. Not plasma torpedoes this time, but smaller weapons from the Orbot's secondary batteries.

"Minor damage to forward sections," Sato reported. "Hull integrity holding. No critical systems affected."

"Engineering reports all green," Chief Engineer Boyd MacGregor's voice came through the comm. "These Orbot bastards hit hard, but we're built harder, sir."

Yes, we are, Lee thought.

"Sir," Reynolds said, "enemy fighters are breaking through our screen. Some are heading for the capital ships."

On the main screen, Republic fighters weaved desperately through enemy fire.

"Orbot battleships are starting to pull back," Rodriguez reported. "Long-range sensors show them adjusting course."

Lee frowned as pieces clicked together. Something felt off. The Orbots had engaged for fifteen minutes, absorbed tremendous punishment, and now they were changing tactics. Had they accomplished what they wanted?

"They're going after stragglers," Lee realized aloud. "Any ship that drifts too far from the fleet's protective envelope. Classic predator tactics."

"Sir," Baldry said. "The Rass defense platforms are fully operational now. Energy readings are off the charts. These things are packing more firepower than intelligence estimated."

The tactical display shifted, showing long-range sensor data from the inner system. Planet Rass hung in space like a blue-green jewel, but it was surrounded by something that made Lee's stomach drop. He'd seen them in the tactical briefings before the invasion, but seeing the orbital defense platforms in real time was quite different.

Dozens and dozens of them.

Lee then realized—because he'd do the same if he were in their shoes—that perhaps the Orbots were targeting isolated ships and buying time for those platforms to reach full power. It was the stalling move he'd pull to get his defenses ready before the main fight.

"Enemy fighter formations breaking up," Baldry announced. "Orion squadrons are cutting through their ranks."

"Good," Lee said, though his mind was on the weapons platforms rapidly coming online.

The retreating Orbot battleships soon rendezvoused with the Zodark fleet. Together, they formed a defensive line between the joint Republic and Primord force and planet Rass. The skirmish was over, but the real battle was just beginning.

"All ships," McKee's voice carried across the fleet frequency. "Re-form on *George Washington*. We've got a fleet to destroy."

The Republic and Primord armada pulled back from the engagement zone, Orions returning to their carriers while damage control teams assessed casualties and damage. The *Poseidon* had taken hits, but nothing critical.

Lee studied the holodisplay showing Rass and its defensive grid, his jaw tightening with each new contact that appeared. This wouldn't be simple. The Zodarks had turned their prize into a fortress that could hold off entire fleets, and the reality of it was bigger than he'd realized.

"Signal from Admiral McKee," Rodriguez said. "All ships, set course for Rass. Form up on George Washington for assault approach."

"Reynolds, set course for Rass," Lee commanded.

The lieutenant complied. "Course laid in, sir. ETA to Rass orbit, seventeen minutes at current speed."

Lee stood from his command chair, his hands clasped behind his back as he stared at the main screen. Seventeen minutes to assault the most heavily defended planet he'd ever encountered.

"Sato," Lee said, quietly but with steel in his voice. "Make sure all departments are ready. What we just went through was the warm-up act. We're going to need every advantage we can get."

His executive officer nodded with shared understanding. "On it, sir. We'll be ready for whatever comes next."

Lee hoped it would be enough. Because, looking at those orbital platforms, he had the sinking feeling they were flying into hell itself.

Chapter 2:
Dividing Forces

Late 2098
RNS *George Washington*
Nearing Planet Rass

Rear Admiral Fran McKee pressed the comm button as the last Zodark vessels raced toward Rass. "All ships, this is Admiral McKee. We're entering the assault phase. Enemy forces are retreating to prepared defensive positions around Rass."

On the *George Washington*'s bridge, tactical officers tracked the scattered enemy formations on the main display. Each Zodark group headed for different defensive sectors around the planet. McKee couldn't let them consolidate their forces, not when she had momentum.

The main viewscreen showed Rass in the distance, its orbital platforms dotting space like deadly jewels. McKee had seen too many assaults fail because commanders got cautious at the critical moment. Not today.

"Ma'am," the tactical officer said, "enemy formations are breaking into four primary groups. They're making for predetermined defensive positions around the planet."

McKee nodded grimly. The Zodarks had a plan. "Show me the platform distributions."

The display shifted, highlighting orbital defenses in different colors. Red for heavy laser installations. Yellow for torpedo batteries. Orange for mixed-weapon platforms. Far too many of them.

"Admiral," the electronic warfare officer called out, "we're detecting massive energy buildup from those platforms. They're powering up for coordinated defensive fire."

McKee studied the tactical readout. Intelligence had underestimated the defensive grid's capabilities. Those platforms could beat up her fleet if she attacked piecemeal. "We hit them simultaneously across multiple sectors. Force them to divide their attention."

She opened the fleet channel. "All ships, this is Admiral McKee. We're dividing into battle groups for coordinated assault. I want those orbital platforms neutralized before they can achieve full operational status."

McKee pulled up the sector assignments on her command screen. "Captain Lee, you'll take tactical command of Battle group Four. Frigates *Polaris*, *Bolt*, and *Ranger* will serve as your screen, with cruisers *Duncan* and *Oceanus* as your heavy units. Your primary mission is orbital platform suppression in grid reference 12-Alpha."

"Understood, Admiral," Lee's voice came back as confident as ever. "Battle group Four will eliminate the orbital platforms."

"Position your force in the middle screening formation," McKee continued. "You'll have tactical flexibility while staying clear of the initial defensive salvos. Those platforms pack enough firepower to gut a battleship."

She assigned the other battle groups their sectors, watching her fleet reorganize on the main holo. The coordination had to be perfect. Any hesitation would let the Zodarks establish killing fields around their strongest positions.

"Ma'am," the communications officer said, "Admiral Stavanger is requesting fleet disposition. The stargate needs to be secured for incoming reinforcements."

McKee had been expecting this. "Signal Admiral Stavanger. Half the fleet stays to defend the gate. We can't leave our exit route undefended, especially with troop transports inbound."

The tactical situation was more complex than a simple assault. Enemy reinforcements could emerge from FTL. The Zodarks might try to retake the stargate while her main force attacked Rass. She needed to maintain a strategic reserve.

"Admiral," the sensor officer called out, "those three Orbot battleships we engaged earlier have taken up defensive positions in high orbit around Rass. They're coordinating with the orbital platforms."

McKee gnashed her teeth. Those same Orbot ships that had shielded the retreating Zodark fleet now dug in around Rass, supporting the Zodark defense. "Analysis of their new positions?"

"They're positioned to provide overlapping fire support with the orbital platforms. A layered defense."

The enemy was using the Orbots as a spearhead while the Zodarks maneuvered behind prepared positions. McKee had to respect their coordination even as she planned to destroy it.

"Tactical," she said, "break down those enemy vessel types. I want specifics on what my battle groups are walking into."

"Majority Zodark vessels as expected, but those three Orbot ships change up the equation. More concerning is that Zodark star carrier. Intelligence estimates it's carrying two full fighter wings."

McKee grimaced. A star carrier meant hundreds of enemy fighters could swarm her formations. Combined with orbital platforms and Orbot battleships, the space around Rass was going to become a killing field.

"ETA to weapons range?" she asked.

"Fifteen minutes to optimal firing positions, Admiral."

Fifteen minutes to coordinate the most complex assault of her career. McKee studied the enemy positions one more time, noting how they'd positioned their strongest assets to cover several approach vectors.

"All battle groups," she announced over the fleet channel, "commence approach to your assigned sectors. Expect heavy resistance from orbital defenses and coordinated fighter attacks. Execute Operation Saber on my mark."

She opened a private channel to her communications officer. "Prepare a drone for transit back through the stargate. Once we engage those platforms, I want ground assault forces notified to begin their phase."

The next few minutes would determine whether they maintained momentum or walked into a carefully prepared trap. McKee watched her battle groups form up, knowing thousands of lives depended on the decisions she made in the coming engagement. In truth, across the galaxy, perhaps billions would be lost if they didn't take this planet back for the Prims.

"Admiral," the tactical officer said, "stargate is activating behind us. Republic reinforcements incoming."

Although McKee maintained a passive expression, she smiled inwardly. *Perfect timing.* "Signal the incoming ships. Defensive positions around the gate until further orders. We're about to find out exactly what the Zodarks have been building here for three centuries, and in person."

The *George Washington*'s engines rumbled as the great ship accelerated toward Rass, leading her fleet into one of the most heavily defended systems in Zodark space.

Chapter 3:
Middle Screen

Late 2098
RNS Poseidon
Nearing Planet Rass

"Stargate's activating," Baldry said from sensors. "Multiple contacts emerging."

Far behind them at the shimmering gate, three Republic battleships materialized. Two dozen frigates followed, spreading out in defensive formations as their engines spun up to full power to put distance between themselves and the gate rather than clustering near the exit point.

The added firepower would no doubt shift the battle's momentum. More ships kept arriving. The stargate flashed again, disgorging thirty-two Primord cruisers and battleships. Their weapons immediately came online.

"Fleet composition update," Rhom said. "We now outnumber Zodark forces five to one."

Lee nodded. The math was brutal and simple. Hopefully this meant the Zodarks would get their butts handed to them, and it wouldn't be pretty.

Good. So damn good, Lee thought. *And twelve minutes to optimal firing range.*

The Orbot and Zodark retreat was textbook. Disciplined formations maintaining support while maximizing their speed toward Rass, where they now floated in orbit. They waited. No stragglers. No hesitation.

Observing this, instead of a huge, dangerous chase, Admiral McKee had ordered fleet deceleration. All ships had reduced to half speed to re-form battle groups and gather themselves.

Lee understood immediately. With the enemy in full retreat, pursuing at maximum speed would stretch the fleet out and leave individual ships vulnerable to ambush. Better to consolidate their overwhelming numbers, ensure proper formation discipline, and approach Rass as a unified force. The Zodarks and Orbots had fallen back to prepared defensive positions where they could make their stand on favorable terms.

"Admiral McKee is coordinating with Admiral Stavanger," Rodriguez said, her head in her console's interface. "They're dividing forces. Half the fleet stays to defend the gate. The rest will eventually join us as the assault group for Rass."

It made perfect sense. They couldn't leave their exit route undefended, especially with hundreds of Republic troop transports about to transit through the gate. The Zodarks might try to retake the stargate while the main force was busy at Rass. McKee was too clever to fall for that trap.

"Assault force composition," Rhom said, reading from his displays. "Six cruisers including us, *Argo*, and *Polaris*. Two battlecruisers. Six frigates. And the *George Washington* as flagship."

Lee's expression hardened. Planet Rass. A strategic Primord world the Zodarks had seized three hundred years ago, turning it into a fortress system. The planet bristled with orbital defenses, a massive starbase, and three Orbot battleships and the remnants of the Zodark fleet. This stargate battle had been the warm-up act. Rass would be the main event, and it would get ugly. Damn ugly.

"Admiral McKee's sending a communications drone back through the gate," Rodriguez said. "Authorization for the ground assault forces to begin their phase of the operation."

The real war was about to start. The Zodarks had turned planet Rass into a killing field complete with orbital weapons platforms, defensive satellites, and enough firepower to turn attacking fleets into scrap metal.

"All ships, maintain formation," McKee's voice crackled through the fleet communications. "Continue course for planet Rass. Time to take back what belongs to our allies."

Lee had no illusions about what waited for them. The Orbots and Zodarks would fight like cornered animals, throwing everything they had at the approaching fleet. It would be brutal, bloody, and decisive. But after three centuries of occupation, the Primords deserved their world back. They'd do this for the alliance, the Galactic Empire. For Earthers. For all those subjugated and enslaved by the enemy… the Zodarks, the Orbots, and all those other species forming the Dominion Alliance that Lee hadn't met yet.

"Rodriguez, patch me through to the crew," Lee said.

"Channel open, sir."

Lee keyed the shipwide communications. "This is the captain. We're heading for Rass to finish what we started here. The Zodarks are going to throw everything they've got at us. But we've got something they don't—each other, and the biggest damn hearts in known space. Stay sharp, stay focused, and we'll see this through together. Lee out."

The Republic fleet had formed up around the *George Washington*, fifteen warships carrying enough firepower to level continents.

On the main viewer, the Zodarks had established their defensive positions around Rass, exactly where intelligence had predicted they would make their stand—positions they'd had three centuries to perfect. The Orbot ships, a surprised guest to the operation, took flanking positions, their obsidian hulls gleaming against the planet's azure color.

"Sir," Rodriguez announced, "Admiral McKee is transmitting battle group assignments."

Lee moved to Rodriguez's station as the tactical data streamed across her displays. McKee's voice came through the comm.

"Commander Lee, you'll take tactical command of Battle group Four. *Polaris*, *Bolt*, and *Ranger* will serve as your frigate screen, with cruisers *Duncan* and *Oceanus* as your heavy units. Your primary mission is orbital platform suppression. Those defense stations need to be neutralized before the main assault."

"Acknowledged, Admiral," Lee replied. "Battle group Four will eliminate the orbital platforms."

"Position your force in the middle screening formation," McKee continued. "You'll have tactical flexibility to respond to emerging threats while staying clear of the initial defensive salvos. Those platforms pack enough firepower to gut a battleship, so keep your ships moving."

Lee studied the tactical assignments flowing across Rodriguez's screen. The formation made sense. His battle group held the middle screening formation between the fleet's forward elements and the main body. A tactical sweet spot. Close enough to respond to threats, far enough back to avoid getting chewed up by the enemy's initial salvos.

The massive Republic and Primord armada stretched out ahead and behind them. Today, that three-century occupation of Rass would end.

"Engineering to bridge," MacGregor's voice crackled through the comm. "Reactor's running at ninety-two percent efficiency. Drive systems are holding steady, but I'm seeing some fluctuation in the port fusion manifold."

Lee keyed the comm. "How long can you maintain current power output, Mac?"

"Six hours at this pace, maybe eight if we dial back the acceleration by five percent. The Primord vessels are keeping up, but their power curves are different. More… organic, if that makes sense."

"Copy that. We won't need six hours. Keep me informed of any changes."

"Aye, Cap."

Lee walked to his command chair and stood behind it. There, he studied the sensor readings flowing across multiple displays. Everything about the *Poseidon* represented the marriage of human engineering and Altairian technology. Sometimes a nice tactical fusion, sometimes an awkward political compromise. He glanced at Reynolds's navigation display, noting their distance to Rass—280,000 kilometers and closing.

Lee sat in his captain's chair. *Nine minutes until optimal firing range.*

Ensign Baldry hunched over the sensor station, his instruments showing an increasingly intense picture of the space ahead. Baldry was a young officer. Eager. He still had that Academy shine that combat still hadn't worn off yet, which was strange. It should have mostly vanished by now. His displays flared with new contacts as he adjusted the sensor gain. "Sir, I'm detecting active targeting sweeps from Rass orbital space. Multiple sources. Energy signatures are spiking across the defensive grid."

"Witkowski," Lee called to the electronic warfare station. "Target those orbital defense platforms. I want their targeting coordination disrupted before they can achieve solid firing solutions."

"Aye, sir. Retargeting to planetary defense grid. Focusing jamming on their fire-control networks and targeting data links. At this range, I can introduce significant delays in their targeting solutions and degrade their point-defense accuracy."

The specialized EW equipment aboard the *Poseidon* gave them some advantages that pure Republic or Primord vessels lacked. Their hybrid systems adapted to both human and alien electronic signatures, allowing them to disrupt enemy communications in ways other ships couldn't match… yet. It was one of the reasons Admiral McKee had positioned them in the middle screen. They could hit the enemy where others couldn't reach.

"Witkowski," Lee said. "Status on our jamming?"

"Holding steady, sir. Their targeting solutions are degraded but not eliminated. I'm introducing random delays and false returns."

Hundreds of *Vulture*-class interceptors accelerated toward the Republic and Primord fleets, closing fast to five them a pounding. New contacts appeared every second.

"Fighter screen incoming," Rhom reported. "Estimate a hundred and fifty plus Vultures launching from the Zodark carrier and escort vessels. Time to intercept… three minutes."

McKee's voice burst across the fleet's main communication channel. "All ships, this is Admiral McKee. We're entering the next phase of the assault. Expect heavy resistance from orbital defenses. Battle groups will maintain formation and execute Operation Saber on my mark. Fighter squadrons, prepare for immediate launch upon entering combat range. This is what we came here for. Make every shot count."

Lee immediately switched to his battle group's tactical frequency. "All ships, this is *Poseidon*. Prepare for Operation Saber implementation. Focus fire on designated orbital platforms per your target assignments. Watch for friendly fighters in our fire lanes and maintain formation discipline."

The orbital defenses opened fire in coordinated volleys. Space filled with energy bolts, turning the final approach to Rass into a gauntlet of destruction. Plasma torpedoes streaked toward the fleet. Laser beams burned through the vacuum.

"Evasive maneuvers," Lee ordered. "All ships, maintain formation but execute random course changes. Don't give them predictable targeting solutions."

The *Poseidon* shuddered as near misses from plasma torpedoes detonated from perfect PDG strikes, all close enough to rattle the hull. Rhom operated his tactical console like the professional he was as incoming torpedoes appeared on his point-defense grid. "Point-defense guns engaging," he said.

The *Poseidon*'s 30mm quad-barrel point-defense guns and laser arrays again swiveled and fired in bursts, intersecting the incoming plasma torpedoes. More brilliant flashes erupted across the starboard quarter as the defensive fire found its marks, vaporizing all but a handful of torpedoes before they could impact the hull. Emergency lighting flickered as power systems compensated for electromagnetic interference from the explosions.

"Damage report," Sato called.

"Minor hull scoring on the port side," came the reply from damage control. "No penetration. All systems nominal."

"Sir!" Baldry's voice remained controlled but tense as he stared at his sensor display. "New contacts launching from the far side of Rass. Another group we hadn't detected. I'm reading… massive fighter launch, sir… another hundred-plus Vultures inbound. That's over two hundred and fifty fighters heading straight for us. Time to intercept… ninety seconds, sir!"

Chapter 4:
Whiskey-Six

Late 2098
Stargate 352-NHW
RNS *Gallipoli*

The briefing room aboard the RNS *Gallipoli* reeked of coffee brewed too long. Lieutenant Naomi Love sat with her crew in the third row as Commander Rhett Granger approached the holographic display. The tactical readout of Rass glowed in blues and greens.

Today, the Republic would help take this planet back. Love grinned at the thought—then frowned at the realization that there would be those who wouldn't make it back. That was always a terrible feeling. And with war, it would never change.

"Ladies and gentlemen," Granger said, "Admiral McKee's fleet has successfully engaged and neutralized primary Zodark defenses around Stargate 352-NHW. It gives us our operational window for planetary assault."

Chief Brian Ford sat beside Love. Second Lieutenant Caleb Green took notes on his tablet, stylus moving fast. Petty Officer Second Class Marcus Torres, their gunner, watched the display with ridiculously focused attention. Love almost grinned at how locked in Torres was, but she was starting to get used to it.

Love studied Torres's face as he took in the briefing details. The eager-to-prove-himself attitude was gone. It had since been replaced by something steadier, and a hell of a lot more reliable. That boxing tournament a while back had definitely helped. So had their talk in *Jack* while chomping down on donuts. Torres wasn't Williams, and never would be. But he was part of the crew. That was what mattered.

Why the hell did Williams die? Love thought. *Why'd you do that to me, Williams?* She pinched her thigh to get those horrible, unwarranted thoughts out of her mind. In truth, she was getting over her old crew member. Day by day, the sting indeed lessened gradually. She just hoped she'd never forget the man, and all he had done for them, and for the Republic.

"Mission overview," Granger continued, manipulating the holographic display. "Second wave transport operations will commence once McKee's fleet and the rest of our allies clear a corridor to Rass, then the *Gallipoli* transits to the planet. Primary objective is deployment of Republic Army to designated landing zones across Rass's northern continent."

The display zoomed in to show forest coverage, rolling hills, and river systems in blue—terrain that would provide cover for friendly forces and deadly ambush positions for entrenched Zodark defenders.

"Transport crews will deploy assault forces according to operational schedules. Crew assignments are posted on your tablets now. Mission-specific briefings will follow this general overview."

Love checked her tablet. Alpha Company, Second Platoon. Sixty-four soldiers total. Primary LZ designated Whiskey-Six, a clearing in heavy forest approximately two kilometers from Alpha Company's primary objective, a Zodark defensive installation.

"Intelligence assessment indicates moderate to heavy ground-based resistance," Granger went on. "Zodark forces will be deeply entrenched, and their orbital fire support will have been eliminated. However, they'll maintain surface-to-air missile capabilities and energy-based anti-aircraft weapons throughout the operational area when we get there."

A pilot from her squadron, Wolfpack Three, a man named Lieutenant Heath Hodges, raised his hand. "Current threat assessment for Orbot support units?"

"Confirmed presence of biomechanical cyborgs. The Orbots. Expect unconventional attack patterns. These aren't your typical organic defenders."

Love made notes on her tablet. Orbots meant serious trouble. Although she had only seen them on holos, and not in person, she'd be happy never to lay eyes on them. The lower portion of their bodies resembled mechanical spiders with half as many legs. Their upper bodies were mostly organic, mostly using conquered species fitted with cybernetic implants. Some looked like Primords, others like Sumerians, Tully, or even Altairians. With their mechanical arms and neural interfaces, their bodies had been turned into weapons.

"Weather conditions on Rass are currently favorable," Granger continued. "No significant atmospheric disturbances expected during our operational window. However, terrain conditions may be significantly altered by the time you reach your assigned LZs. Zodark

bombardment of suspected landing zones will most likely be…
extensive.”

The briefing continued for another thirty minutes, covering
communication frequencies, identification codes, extraction protocols,
and casualty evacuation procedures—the mundane details that kept
military operations functional when everything inevitably went
sideways.

“Stargate transit begins in exactly forty minutes,” Granger said.
“Individual crew briefings commence immediately. Equipment final
checks begin following your mission-specific briefs. Questions?”

Only silence came from the assembled transport crews.

“Then get our people there, and back home. Dismissed.”

****

Love gathered her crew in Briefing Room C-7, a smaller
compartment equipped with secure communication links and detailed
tactical displays. She pulled up their specific mission parameters as
Ford, Green, and Torres settled around the conference table.

“Transport designation Four-Five.” She activated the
holographic display. “Alpha Company, Second Platoon’s our first drop.
Sixty-four Republic Army personnel with full combat loads.”

The tactical display showed their assigned drop zone
coordinates above Rass. High-altitude atmospheric entry followed by
deployment in the target zone.

“Primary DZ is Whiskey-Six.” Love highlighted the
coordinates. “HALO deployment at thirty thousand feet, combat spread
across a two-kilometer dispersal pattern. Secondary rally point
Whiskey-Eight, approximately one kilometer northeast through this
valley system. Tertiary option Whiskey-Nine, two kilometers south
along this ridgeline.”

High-altitude drops gave the troop transports better survivability
against anti-air but put the troops at greater risk during descent. It
wasn’t always a winning scenario, but it was strategic. Better to HALO
in on a planet heavily defended than risk a direct hit on an entire
Osprey during an attempted landing, thus eliminating not only the
transport and its pilots but also every trooper inside.

Love continued, “Republic and Primord probes show Zodark
anti-air coverage is concentrated at lower altitudes. HALO insertion

gets our people through their defensive envelope before they can react effectively.”

Torres raised his hand. “What’s our specific engagement protocol during troop deployment?”

Interesting question. But the kid was new, so Love gave him a pass. It should be something he already knew, had experienced, but again, in her mind this guy was still rather green.

“Suppress and evade. Your primary job is keeping Zodark interceptors off our back while our passengers make their jumps. Ford will coordinate all defensive fire with squadron elements.”

“Rules of engagement parameters?”

Love’s jaw tightened. Williams would have known the ROE cold before walking into this room. “Cleared hot on all confirmed Zodark positions. No firing into unconfirmed targets under any circumstances.”

Green looked up from his tablet, where he’d been calculating flight vectors. “Estimated flight time from launch to drop coordinates?”

“Approximately eight minutes from *Gallipoli*’s launch bay to Whiskey-Six once we’re in Rass airspace. Navigation will be entirely on you, Green. Expect heavy electronic jamming and sophisticated countermeasures.”

She manipulated the display to show their planned flight path— a high-altitude approach maintaining maximum ceiling until the final descent into the drop zone, using speed and altitude to minimize exposure to Zodark defenses.

“Extraction protocol assumes Alpha Company will secure rally points after landing,” Love said. “If they need emergency extraction, we’ll coordinate with other squadron elements for pickup operations under whatever conditions exist.”

Ford gave a nod. He’d been through enough hot insertions to understand the very real risks of HALO operations.

“Passenger manifest includes one TASC unit,” Love noted, checking her datapad again. “Led by Lieutenant Blake Cooper, call sign Coop. He’ll be coordinating close-air support with Admiral McKee’s fleet elements if the situation becomes complicated.”

The name registered immediately. Cooper had been a drone pilot aboard the *Gallipoli* before transitioning to forward air control duties. He had a solid reputation, and was known for being a hotshot ace turned into the conductor of an orchestra of weapons. He'd had the hots for her when they'd first met, and God willing, he had forgotten all about that—and no doubt he had. Combat sometimes shook a crush out of an individual, and she hoped it had violently shattered Coop's crush.

"Medical considerations," she went on. "Alpha Company has their own medics for immediate battlefield casualties. Serious wounded will be extracted to the field hospital being established at Whiskey-Prime via dedicated medevac assets."

Ford looked over at Torres. "You've done the HALO support training, right? Different procedures than standard insertion."

"Yes, Chief. Practiced it extensively during advanced flight training," Torres replied.

Torres had that look now. Focused. Ready. No more constant suggestions about procedures. No more references to his last unit. Just solid work and attention to detail. Love had seen what happened when new crew members came in too cocky or too anxious. Torres had been both when he'd arrived. But that was before the fight. Before the punishment. Before their crew had finally become a crew.

"Good. The timing's more critical," Love responded. "Troops exit in rapid sequence, so we need to maintain precise altitude and airspeed. Any deviation could scatter the drop pattern. So, any questions specific to our mission parameters?"

"Ammunition allowance for defensive operations?" Ford wanted to know.

"Standard combat load. Additional ammunition belts secured in the weapons locker. Resupply available from fleet assets if we expend our initial allocation."

Love studied her crew's faces. Ford looked ready, but then he always did. So many combat operations had taught him to manage pre-mission nerves effectively. Green appeared characteristically calm. Torres, on the other hand, looked alert and professional, with focused energy.

"You're doing fine, Torres," Love said. "HALO operations are complex, but you've got the training. Trust your preparation."

"Thank you, ma'am. I'm ready for this."

"Final briefing point," she said. "Today, we'll be making multiple high-altitude runs under increasingly heavy fire. Stay sharp, stay flexible, and remember that our primary job is getting our passengers to their drop zone safely."

She closed down the tactical display. "Equipment checks begin immediately. We have twenty minutes until the *Gallipoli* transits through the stargate and into the Rass system."

In the flight bay, Love led her crew back to their Osprey, *Jack*. Mechanics swarmed over spacecraft, performing final checks on engines and weapons systems. Pilots reviewed flight plans one last time while loadmasters coordinated jump manifests.

Their bird occupied Bay Seven. Love began her external inspection while her crew scattered to handle their specialized responsibilities.

Up the ramp into the troop compartment, the first thing that caught anyone's attention was the plaque bolted securely to the starboard bulkhead: "*Vivere Pugnare Alium Diem.*"

Live to Fight Another Day, she said to herself.

Words that had kept her crew breathing through three major campaigns and more close calls than she wanted to remember. Every soldier who rode in her bird touched that plaque—a ritual that might be mere superstition, but one they all believed in. Williams had touched it on Intus, right before he'd saved her crew. The plaque hadn't kept him alive. But his sacrifice had kept the rest of them breathing.

Love climbed into the cockpit and settled into the pilot's seat. She started the comprehensive preflight checklist that by this time in her life, she could perform in complete darkness. Fuel systems, engine diagnostics, navigation computers, life support backups.

The worn photograph caught her eye. Jack's face smiled back from the instrument panel, edges softened from constant handling. She pressed her finger to her lips, then touched his picture gently. Another ritual, another piece of protective superstition.

Through the cockpit window, she could see other crews preparing their birds throughout the massive hangar bay. Mechanics crawled over engines while pilots conducted their own inspections.

Her comm system buzzed and Ford's voice came through. "Preflight weapons check complete. All systems showing green across the board."

"Copy that, Chief."

Green's voice followed. "Navigation systems verified. Communication arrays tested and encrypted. Ready for mission operations."

"Good work."

Movement in the hangar bay drew her attention. Republic Army soldiers were checking their jump gear and parachute systems, preparing for HALO insertion. It was Alpha Company, judging by their unit patches.

That was when she spotted Coop. He moved through the crowd, no longer the somewhat awkward drone pilot she remembered. Now he wore the specialized radio pack and targeting equipment of a TASC— Tactical Air & Space Controller, one of the elite controllers who bridged the gap between Navy firepower and Army operations, mostly responsible for coordinating precision fire support between ground forces and fleet assets.

War changed everyone. Pushed them into new roles, forced new responsibilities. Cooper looked older, more serious. The boyish charm remained, but tempered by the heavy responsibility of calling in fire missions to save friendly forces or causing catastrophic collateral damage depending on his precision—and with that, who knew how many close friends he'd lost along the way? It changed a person, more so than even those who'd lost those closest to them would like to admit.

She remembered his nervous attempts at conversation during the Intus campaign. The way he'd lingered awkwardly after briefings, trying to work up the courage to ask her for coffee. He'd been sweet in his own way, but she'd had absolutely no room for personal complications then.

Still didn't.

Cooper headed toward her Osprey with a squad of Alpha Company soldiers, Second Platoon. He paused at the base of the ramp, checking his jump gear. Altimeter, reserve chute, radio frequencies, targeting designators, backup communication systems.

She watched Coop through the monitor. Up the ramp, he touched the plaque. Just another passenger. No complications. No personal entanglements. Just like everyone else, she was responsible for getting him to his drop zone safely.

Green settled into the copilot's seat, running his own detailed diagnostic sequence. Navigation systems, communication arrays, backup protocols. Everything had to be perfect.

"Torres is looking solid," Green observed, watching the crew chief through the internal feeds. "Williams would be proud of how he's stepped up."

Love watched Torres through her holo feeds. The kid was methodically checking jump safety protocols and emergency procedures. Professional, thorough, no wasted motion.

"He's earned his place on this crew."

"Williams always said the best crew chiefs were the ones who cared about getting everyone home."

Torres had that same dedication Williams had shown, so it seemed. Personal attachment got good people killed, but professional competence and crew loyalty kept people alive. She'd learned that lesson far too many times.

The speakers crackled to life. "All second wave personnel, prepare for passenger briefing and final equipment inspection. Repeat, all second wave personnel to assigned stations."

Alpha Company finished their jump preparations and Cooper sat near the front with his radio gear.

As the soldiers secured their gear and checked their parachutes, the door guns were loaded, ammunition belts were properly seated, and backup supplies were stored in the weapons locker. Everything was ready for whatever reception committee waited at thirty thousand feet above Whiskey-Six.

"Remember," Ford said to Torres over the comms, "during HALO ops, we maintain stable flight profile while they exit. Suppressive fire only if we encounter interceptors. Your job is monitoring jump conditions and calling out any safety issues."

"Understood, Chief."

"And keep an eye on wind speeds during the drop. If conditions change, call it out immediately so the jumpmaster can adjust. These guys are depending on us for accurate deployment."

Green nodded approvingly. "Good guidance, Chief. Torres, you've got good instincts. I can feel it. Trust them out there, all right?"

"Yes, sir."

Through the dash screen, it looked like Torres absorbed the team's instructions quite well. But, like all things, looks could deceive. Only time would tell how he'd react to the pressure of troop deployment in a battle zone.

"All hands, prepare for stargate transit," came the announcement over the radio. "Transit commences in five minutes. All personnel secure for dimensional transition."

The *Gallipoli* shuddered slightly as her engines reached full power. Through the hangar bay's atmospheric barriers, Love could see the massive stargate growing larger as they approached. A ring of exotic technology defying understanding, capable of folding space across impossible distances and created by an alien race they'd barely any knowledge of, with technological capabilities better than anywhere they'd seen from species to species. To this day, no one could replicate these stargates.

"All stations, final systems check," she announced over the intercom.

"Weapons systems all good," Ford reported.

"Navigation and communications ready," Green confirmed.

"Jump bay secure, all safety protocols verified," Torres added.

Love nodded, settling back in her pilot's seat. "All stations ready for stargate transit."

"One minute to transit," came the announcement over the comms.

Turning up the troop bay volume, Love could hear some of the soldiers running through final jump checks and reviewing their descent profiles. Even experienced veterans found stargate passage unsettling. The human nervous system simply wasn't equipped to handle dimensional transition without some kind of weird sensation.

"Thirty seconds to transit."

The stargate rushed toward them, growing until it filled their entire field of vision.

"Ten seconds."

Energy moved across the *Gallipoli*'s hull as they approached the portal's threshold.

"Transit commencing now."

They plunged into the stargate.

Reality exploded. Love's consciousness stretched across long distances while time stopped and accelerated simultaneously. Colors with no names blazed through her vision as the *Gallipoli* was torn apart and rebuilt at the quantum level. Behind her, soldiers groaned and retched as the transit effect overwhelmed… everything.

The transition lasted forever and ended in an instant. Ten million years, and a minute. It didn't make sense, and yet, it all made sense.

They burst through and into normal space, emerging in the Rass system where Admiral McKee's fleet was heading toward Rass's orbital defenses. Before the *Gallipoli*, debris fields marked destroyed enemy ships, and most likely some allied vessels as well.

"Transit complete," announced the radio officer. "All hands, prepare for combat operations. Launch bays, ready aircraft for planetary assault."

Through Love's cockpit window, Rass hung in space. It was beautiful. But in a way, so were most planets. Far up ahead, orbiting Rass, Zodark and Orbot fleets waited. Somewhere down there, Zodark ground forces were getting ready.

But the Republic fleet had arrived, and the real war was about to begin.

Chapter 5:
Gunner's Eye

Late 2098
RNS *Gallipoli*
Stargate 352-NHW

Chief Brian Ford gripped his starboard gunner station as the *Gallipoli*'s hull still vibrated from stargate transit. The gate passage always left his teeth feeling weird, like chomping down on a piece of ice with an exposed root. He was nervy as hell. Today felt worse than usual, and the feeling was taking longer to wear off.

Through his targeting monitor, the massive fleet of the second wave of the Rass invasion spread across the star-filled void. Hundreds of ships bore down on the planet. His hands moved automatically through post-transit equipment checks.

He paused, shook his head like a dog shaking off water to gather his bearings from the transit, then went back to work.

Across the narrow gunner bay, Petty Officer Second Class Torres checked his weapon systems. Nothing was wasted; the guy did everything well, but this time without the crappy attitude that had gnawed under Ford's skin when they'd first met. Ford watched him work through the precombat checklist. Every step was by the book, but efficient now instead of showing off.

Torres checked the .50-cal five-barrel magrail gun mount, tested the ammunition feed, and verified the targeting computer's link to his helmet display. The weapon could punch tungsten penetrators through four hundred millimeters of steel plate at eight thousand meters— enough firepower to shred enemy fighters and ground targets alike.

"Systems green," Torres reported, cycling through traverse and elevation one final time. "Ready for hot drop."

Ford nodded. Torres had come a long way since that disaster in the maintenance bay. He still wasn't Williams, but he'd earned his place on the crew. "Good. Keep it tight down there."

The gun station hummed along well at the moment. Torres had learned to trust his equipment instead of constantly second-guessing the settings. No more unauthorized modifications. No more complaints about outdated gear. Just a gunner who knew his weapon and his job.

Ford punched commands into the controls. Through his helmet comm, he could hear Torres breathing steadily as he powered up his targeting system. He'd learned their rhythm well.

Behind them, the troop bay was packed with Alpha Company's Second Platoon. Sixty-four soldiers in full combat gear, running through final equipment inspections. Ford was grateful they weren't hauling C100s today. Those things still gave him the creeps.

"Chief," Torres said through the comm, "I've got clear fields of fire on both sectors. Ammunition feed shows good."

Ford checked his own systems. Torres had learned to anticipate what needed reporting instead of asking basic questions. Good progress from the guy who used to quote manual procedures at them.

"Copy that. Remember… smooth is fast. No point proving anything down there."

"Roger, Chief."

Ford's targeting monitor flickered, showing the fleet engagement. The RNS *Midway* flew less than five hundred thousand kilometers from a Zodark starbase, and was closing in fast. Enemy contacts populated the sensor display. "Torres, get a load of this. Two dozen Zodark cruisers, at least one star carrier, three battleships. Plus Orbot ships mixed in."

The Republic and Primord fleets moved in perfect formation while Zodark vessels scrambled to defensive positions.

Sensor feeds showed the battle raging across Ford's screen. The *George Washington* opened fire with its massive plasma cannon, the energy beam lancing across the void to slam into an Orbot battleship. "That's what real firepower looks like. When Admiral McKee decides you're going to die, you die."

The precombat adrenaline surged through Ford, his hands steadying on the controls. This was what he lived for.

Love's voice crackled through their helmets, coordinating with flight control. Her. Green. Him. Torres. A crew again. Different from before, but functional. Trust built through shared experience instead of shared history.

"Weapons hot," Ford announced. "Stay sharp, Torres."

"Always am, Chief."

The tactical display updated as Primord battleships engaged. "See that? That's what happens when everyone knows their job."

"Contact," Torres reported. "Multiple fighters rising from atmosphere."

"I see them," Ford replied. "Let's get to work."

Ford's system chimed as it locked multiple simulated targets. The *George Washington*'s massive magrail turrets were systematically destroying Zodark cruisers, sending tungsten slugs through enemy hulls.

"Holy Lord," Torres muttered, eyes on the tactical holo. "Those cruisers are getting blasted."

"Navy knows what they're doing," Ford replied. "Clearing us a path through the heavy stuff."

"How long until we hit atmosphere?"

"Twenty-five minutes. Maybe less if they clear a lane sooner."

"Good. I'm tired of watching from up here," Torres replied.

Ford snorted. "We're just gettin' started and you're already bored?"

Torres shrugged. "Yeah, my mom always said I couldn't sit still for ten minutes."

Ford glanced over. Torres had his game face on. "Patience. Don't get too antsy on me, eh? Remember, we're deploying, not assaulting. Get in, let our people jump, get out."

"Can't wait, Chief."

The tactical display updated again. More enemy contacts rising from the planet's surface. It was going to be a busy day.

Ford wrinkled his brow. "Can you wait now?"

Torres grinned. "Yeah, spoke too soon. I'll let our drone pilots handle those."

"Good answer."

Ford secured his station as the space battle raged. Ships on both sides were taking brutal damage. Wounded vessels, wounded crews, and all so they could put boots on former Primord soil and kick the Zodarks off another world.

Primord ships finally reached the enemy starbase and the floating weapons towers, dismantling defensive platforms in cascading explosions. Soon it would be their turn. Ford looked at Torres one more time, seeing Williams's face superimposed over the young man's features.

The tactical display flashed red. New contacts were emerging from Rass's atmosphere. There were hundreds of them—enemy starfighters, moving fast toward the fleet.

"Here we go," Ford said. "You ready for this, Torres?"

"Been ready since we lifted off, Chief."

Ford nodded. Williams would have given some smart-ass comment about the odds. Torres just checked his ammunition count one more time.

Different styles. Same job. And both were damn good.

Chapter 6:
Against the Algo

Late 2098
RNS *Poseidon*
Nearing Planet Rass

The Republic fleet reached Rass with overwhelming force, spreading across orbital space. Forty-seven defense platforms hung in formation around the planet, massive fortresses bristling with weapon emplacements. Each platform surface was covered in laser cannon arrays and plasma torpedo launchers that could shred approaching vessels. These platforms could cause a lot of problems, and they most assuredly would. Hence, it was time to take them out.

Lee studied the tactical display as Admiral McKee's voice crackled through the fleet communications. "Battle group Four, switching your assignment to grid sectors 12-Alpha through 15-Charlie. Medium-tier installations. Too heavily armed for frigates alone but not requiring battleship-level firepower."

Lee's force consisted of the heavy cruiser RNS *Poseidon*, frigates *Polaris*, *Bolt*, and *Ranger*, plus cruisers *Duncan* and *Oceanus*. They were a perfectly balanced hammer for precisely this kind of work, so he felt that this should go well.

The strategic briefing echoed in Lee's mind as he watched Rass grow larger on the main viewer; the Zodark ships they were chasing now fell back to planetary defense patterns. Originally a rugged mining colony, Rass had evolved into a key mineral-exporting hub before the Zodark invasion three centuries ago. New intelligence updates revealed how brutal it had all become, something the Primords had of course known but was new to the Earthers: sixty million Primords had called it home before the conquest, with six million killed during the Zodark invasion itself. Now, after three hundred years of occupation, ninety-four million Primords lived under Zodark control, mostly enslaved, their high birth rates and long lifespans ensuring a constant supply of labor.

But Rass represented far more than liberation for its people. Its mineral wealth, central location near the Intus system, and position as a known hyperspace node made it invaluable. Capturing Rass would position the Republic at the very edges of Zodark-controlled space; it was the perfect launching pad for deeper invasions into enemy territory. Today's battle would determine whether humanity's allies gained a strategic foothold or suffered a devastating defeat.

Lee's characteristically thorough attack plan unfolded across the tactical display as Lieutenant Commander Sato coordinated fleet movements. "*Duncan* and *Oceanus* will engage platforms seven and nine simultaneously," Lee ordered, watching Sato relay targeting data through the fleet network. "Frigates will provide missile saturation while the cruisers close for magrail engagement." Sato's efficiency impressed him. She anticipated his orders, already preparing firing solutions and coordinating with each ship's tactical officers.

The first target loomed ahead on Platform Twelve. It was a monstrosity with radiating arms, each chock-full of laser cannons. Its central core housed plasma torpedo batteries, which were massive weapons capable of crippling a frigate. Sato's damage control teams stood ready while she monitored power distribution across all ship systems.

"All stations report ready, Captain," she announced.

"Rhom, target Platform Twelve's central torpedo battery," Lee commanded. "All magrail turrets, concentrated fire on the core structure. *Polaris*, *Bolt*, and *Ranger*, missile saturation on the outer laser arrays."

The *Poseidon*'s six twin-barreled twenty-four-inch magrail turrets swiveled toward their target, magnetic accelerators charging with a deep hum.

Chief MacGregor's voice came through the comm. "Power distribution optimal, sir. All weapon systems drawing full capacity."

"Range to target, ten thousand kilometers and closing fast," Reynolds reported from the navigation station. Around them, space was erupting into chaos as F-97 Orions tangled with Zodark Vultures. Bright flashes marked where missiles found their targets, and the occasional explosion bloomed where a fighter died.

"Taking light hits on the port quarter," Sato called out as Vulture laser fire raked across their armor. "Orions are keeping most of them off us, but some are breaking through."

Enemy fighters swarmed around Lee's battle group, and every Republic and Primord battle group out there. The Orions held their own, their superior missiles and maneuverability giving them an edge, but the Vultures fought with desperate fury.

"Reynolds, come to bearing one-six-zero mark fifteen, three-quarter thrust. Keep us clear of that fighter furball."

"Aye, sir. Bearing one-six-zero mark fifteen, three-quarter thrust," Reynolds acknowledged while he manipulated the helm controls. The *Poseidon* banked, its massive bulk responding smoothly.

"Sir, we're in optimal firing range," Rhom said from tactical. "Platform Twelve's hull integrity is at maximum, but I'm reading weak points in the central superstructure."

"Weapons free, Rhom. All magrail batteries, fire when ready."

The ship shuddered as all six turrets fired in sequence, tungsten rounds accelerating to devastating velocities. The projectiles slammed into Platform Twelve's defensive arrays, each impact destroying weapons emplacements and sensor nodes. Return fire came at once, laser beams lancing through space where the *Poseidon* had been moments before.

"Direct hit on their point-defense grid," Rhom reported. "Defensive capability down to sixty percent."

A Vulture fighter screamed past the bridge viewports, an Orion close behind. The Republic fighter's missiles caught the Zodark craft amidships, turning it into expanding debris. But three more Vultures dove toward the *Poseidon*'s starboard side.

"Reynolds, emergency turn to starboard, full thrust. Get us out of their attack vector."

"Aye, sir. Emergency turn starboard, full thrust." The inertial dampeners strained as the heavy cruiser pivoted, avoiding the worst of the laser barrage. Several energy bolts burned past the hull, close enough to make the bridge crew flinch. The ones that hit did very little damage.

"Frigate missiles away," Sato said. "*Polaris* reports good lock on target's arms three and five."

The *Poseidon*'s magrail batteries spoke again, six turrets hurling toward Platform Twelve. The frigates added their weapons to the attack, missiles streaking through the vacuum toward the fortress's weapon arrays.

At the moment, they weren't unleashing everything they had—ammunition conservation would matter in the long fight ahead.

Platform Twelve's defensive laser grid sparked and died under the assault. Secondary explosions rippled across its hull as power conduits overloaded. The massive structure listed to port, its artificial gravity no doubt failing.

"Platform Twelve destroyed," Rhom said. "*Duncan* reports Platform Seven is crippled and bleeding plasma from multiple hull breaches. *Oceanus* has eliminated Platform Nine's primary weapons."

Sato punched commands into her interface, coordinating the battle with five ships simultaneously while her eyes tracked ammunition expenditure and power allocation across the battle group.

Rodriguez leaned over her communications console, her voice blasting through the static as she relayed targeting data between ships. "All vessels report successful engagement. Ammunition status holding at eighty-three percent fleet average."

The next wave of targets appeared on the tactical display—three more defensive platforms in a defensive triangle around a critical flight corridor toward the planet. Lee examined the formation while Sato anticipated his next move, already preparing firing solutions.

"XO, coordinate with *Duncan* and *Oceanus* for simultaneous engagement," Lee ordered. "I want those platforms neutralized before they can establish better fields of fire."

"Aye, sir. Relaying attack vectors to Captain Burns and Captain Church," Sato replied. "Estimated time to optimal firing position, four minutes thirty seconds."

"Battle group Four, advance to grid 13-Bravo," Lee commanded over the fleet channel. "Maintain formation integrity and watch for coordinated counterfire."

Around them, and around the defensive platforms, Republic and Primord ships fought valiantly against Zodark and Orbot vessels while other allied battle groups took out orbital weapon fortresses over Rass. Flashes illuminated and crumpled within themselves, and starships and starfighters shot a myriad of weapons. Red tracers and beams crossed the spaces between.

The engagement with Platform Fifteen proved more challenging as concentrated laser fire finally found its mark. The *Poseidon* shuddered under multiple impacts, armor plating overheating under the sustained barrage.

"Direct hit to our forward sensor array," Rhom reported. "I'm reading cascade failures in the targeting grid. Secondary sensors are compensating, but resolution is degraded by thirty percent."

Lee grimaced. The damage wasn't catastrophic, but it created a critical vulnerability. Their point-defense systems relied heavily on those sensors to track incoming projectiles.

"Sir, it's worse than the initial assessment," Rhom continued, sweat beading on his forehead as he worked his console. "The primary targeting computer is completely fried. Synth repair teams are responding, but they're reporting extensive damage to the optical relay network."

No shortcuts in space, Lee thought.

"Rhom, switch to manual targeting for point defense," Lee ordered, weighing their tactical position. "How long until we have full sensor capability restored?"

"Synths estimate twenty-two minutes for primary repairs, sir," Sato interjected while coordinating damage control teams. "Emergency protocols are maintaining basic functionality."

"Manual tracking online, sir," Rhom confirmed. "Response time will be slower, but I can compensate with predictive algorithms."

Lee nodded. They'd continue the mission, but with reduced defensive efficiency. In space combat, that kind of handicap could turn fatal in seconds.

Lee's tactical instincts warred between aggressive momentum and ship preservation as they approached a small cluster of orbital platforms designated Platform Fifteen. The defensive installation sprawled across five hundred meters of space. Essentially, it was a central weapons hub connected to four satellite fortresses by reinforced support arms, each one covered with laser cannon arrays and torpedo batteries. The complex tracked their approach vector, its automated targeting systems locking onto *Poseidon* and the battle group. Platform Fifteen opened fire, plasma torpedoes streaking from its launch tubes while laser beams lanced across the void.

MacGregor's teams managed power flawlessly, cycling energy between sensors, weapons, and engines as the *Poseidon* moved through the defensive fire. The ship's hull groaned under the stress of rapid course corrections, inertial dampeners working overtime.

"All platforms in this sector show directed targeting," Sato observed, analyzing the enemy fire patterns on her tactical display. "They're sharing tactical data and concentrating fire on our formation's weak points."

Lee's battle group pressed the attack in spite of the intensifying resistance. The *Duncan* took several hits to her forward sections, her captain reporting minor hull breaches but maintaining combat effectiveness. The frigates maneuvered frantically to avoid concentrated fire, their smaller profiles making them harder targets but also more vulnerable when direct hits occurred.

"Incoming plasma torpedoes! Six contacts, bearing two-seven mark fifteen, impact in forty-three seconds!" The projectiles raced toward the *Poseidon*, their guidance systems locked onto the cruiser's electromagnetic signature.

Rhom's eyes focused on his manual targeting controls, the damaged sensor array forcing him to rely on visual confirmation and instinct. Bridge lighting dimmed momentarily as emergency power rerouted to the point-defense grid. "Point-defense guns tracking… I need fifteen more seconds to achieve firing solution."

Perspiration formed on his already sweat-soaked forehead as he tried frantically to compensate for their sensor damage, calculating intercept vectors in his head while the torpedoes closed the distance. Lee clenched his jaw. The projectiles streaked nearer as Rhom fought to lock weapons on targets—targets that were becoming harder to track with each passing second.

Chapter 7:
The Price of Fire and Blood

Late 2098
RNS *Poseidon*
Planet Rass

Rhom worked the manual targeting controls as six plasma torpedoes flew toward *Poseidon*. The tactical display colored their approach in red vectors. "Acquiring targets…got lock on lead torpedo…firing!"

The sixty quad-barreled point-defense turrets erupted across *Poseidon*'s hull. Each 30mm round carried its programmable proximity fuse, a technological marvel that could adapt its detonation range even after leaving the barrel. The first torpedo met its end in an incredible display of shrapnel as the high-explosive charges detonated, creating a cloud of metal fragments that absolutely shredded the incoming threat.

"Five remaining, impact in twenty-three seconds!" Rhom said.

The bridge lighting dimmed as emergency power continued to reroute to the point-defense grid, casting an amber glow over everything that made the tactical displays seem to burn with their own internal fire. The second torpedo died in another explosion, its hot-as-hell plasma core venting harmlessly into space. The third began breaking apart under the relentless barrage, its guidance systems failing as proximity fuses detonated around its hull.

"Two more!" Rhom called out, but these final torpedoes had learned. Their guidance systems adapted to his fire pattern, weaving through the defensive screen. The tactical computer recalculated firing solutions, adjusting the proximity fuse sensitivity to compensate for the torpedoes' evasive maneuvers.

The countdown timer burned through the seconds. "Fifteen…twelve…ten."

Rhom's targeting system locked onto the penultimate torpedo, the point-defense guns swiveling to track its erratic course. The proximity fuses detonated around the projectile, the overlapping shrapnel clouds tearing it apart in a shower of molten metal. The final torpedo screamed toward *Poseidon*, its plasma core glowing like an erupting volcano.

"Got them! All torpedoes neutralized!" The last threat vanished in an expanding fireball that was quickly extinguished, its destruction so close to the ship that the hull plating registered the thermal bloom.

Rodriguez's pitch cut through the aftermath as damage reports came across the communications array. Controlled mayhem hit across the battle group. "Sir, receiving battle damage assessments from the battle group. *Duncan* reports minor sensor damage to their starboard array, four casualties. *Oceanus* took hull scoring on sections two through six, though superficial damage, all sections sealed."

She paused, scanning the incoming data streams that cascaded across her interface. "*Polaris* has minor structural damage to her forward missile bay, but Captain Bayes reports full combat effectiveness maintained."

Lee grimaced. It wasn't the first time Bayes had pushed his ship beyond recommended limits. The *Polaris*'s captain had a habit of closing to danger-close range to maximize hit probability, often maintaining position under concentrated fire when doctrine called for evasive maneuvers. Aggressive tactics that got results but also accumulated damage faster than his ship could sustain over extended operations. Lee would address it with Bayes after the engagement. The captain's willingness to absorb punishment was admirable, but eventually *Polaris* would take a hit she couldn't recover from.

Sato coordinated response efforts at once. No wasted motion. No hesitation. "Dispatching repair priorities to all vessels. *Duncan*'s sensor damage should be repairable within thirty minutes using their backup arrays along with the few Synths they have. I'm also authorizing emergency ammunition redistribution protocols. *Polaris* can shift to close-range magrail support while *Ranger* handles long-range missile deployment. We'll redistribute tactical roles based on current capabilities."

Lee nodded approvingly. His XO was so good, he was getting tired of constantly thinking that very fact. She turned minor setbacks into manageable tactical adjustments. The battle group remained a coherent fighting force, bloodied slightly but unbroken.

Witkowsky monitored his electronic warfare console as the next wave of defensive platforms opened fire. "Sir, deploying sand-water countermeasures now. I'm reading incoming laser targeting from multiple sources."

Clouds of metallic chaff and sand-water particles erupted from *Poseidon*'s defensive launchers, creating an interference field around his small armada. The other ships followed suit, their own countermeasure systems adding to the protective screen. The enemy fire struck the barrier like rain against a window, ninety percent of the energy weapons dissipating harmlessly against the protective haze.

The sand and water particles scattered the coherent laser beams, breaking them into harmless fragments that blazed space in brief, beautiful auroras. The Zodark targeting computers struggled to maintain lock through the interference, their fire control solutions degrading by the second.

"Excellent work, Witkowsky," Sato called from her position. "Countermeasure effectiveness is holding at optimal levels. All ships are reporting similar success rates with the interference field."

She turned to Lee. "The enemy's targeting solutions are being disrupted across our entire formation. Their hit probability has dropped to less than ten percent while we maintain full offensive capability."

The universe has rules, and sometimes you can bend them in your favor, Lee thought.

Platform after platform fell to the battle group's assault, each fortress crumbling under magrail and laser fire and missile barrages. The magnetic railguns spoke volumes, turning metal into plasma on impact. Laser turrets added their own tune, melting armor plating.

"Platform Nineteen destroyed," Rhom reported. "Twenty-One is showing power failures across sixty percent of its grid."

The systematic destruction continued as Lee's ships moved through their assigned sector like reapers through wheat. Ammunition expenditure remained well within acceptable parameters. The Zodark platforms had been built to withstand assault, but not this kind of coordinated firepower delivered with Lee's sharpshooting perfection.

That's punching the ten-ring, Lee mused. *Precise shot placement.*

Sato tracked their progress on her chair's personal holo, managing each ship's tactical officer through the communications network binding the battle group together. Her console showed the steady degradation of enemy defensive capability, every destroyed platform opening new avenues of approach for the assault forces.

"Captain Church reports Platform Twenty-Two is structurally compromised. They're requesting permission to finish it with a missile salvo rather than continued magrail fire."

Lee nodded, watching as the *Oceanus* delivered the killing blow. The missile salvo struck the crippled platform, each warhead detonating in a ripple effect, reducing the structure to atoms.

By another half hour, the defensive grid was being torn to shreds. Platform after platform died, each fortress turned into debris. The tactical display updated as Lee's ships sliced through their assigned sector.

"Final count shows seventeen platforms destroyed in our grid area," Rhom reported, his targeting systems scanning for remaining threats. "Three installations remain active in adjacent coordinates."

Lee examined the holographic starfield. The remaining towers floated like defiant dragons, their weapons still tracking Republic formations.

Continue to divide and conquer, Lee thought.

"Rodriguez, open channels to all battle group vessels."

"Channels open, sir."

"*Bolt, Ranger, Duncan*—you're taking coordinates Eight-Six-Alpha and Nine-Two-Charlie," Lee said. "Two platforms, clean kills. We need that corridor swept for the transports. *Oceanus* and *Polaris*," he continued, "you're with us. We've got something special waiting. Coming on screen now."

The massive central tower dominated their sensor displays like a technological mountain. Weapons and defense systems clustered across its surface, constantly reshaping their arrangement. Three times larger than anything they'd encountered, the fortress represented a different class of hell entirely.

Finding himself nodding at the structure, Lee said to himself, *Big fish in a small pond. Time to throw some dynamite in the water.*

Baldry's sensors revealed layers of adaptive systems. "Sir, that platform's AI is analyzing our attack vectors. It's already adapted to counter the tactics we used on the smaller installations." The young ensign's voice carried concern. "The learning algorithm is processing our engagement patterns fast. It's running predictive models on our weapon systems, calculating optimal countermeasures for each ship class in our formation."

Lee crossed his arms. *An enemy that learns from every shot fired.*

Rodriguez's communications console erupted with priority transmissions from across the battle zone. "Captain, I'm receiving distress calls from Primord cruiser formations in adjacent sectors. The Primord cruisers, *Vortkah* and *Nesyth*, have both taken heavy damage from similar adaptive platforms. Admiral McKee is requesting expedited clearance of our sector so additional firepower can be redirected to support the Primord vessels."

The strategic picture crystallized. These massive platforms were the backbone of the entire grid. Lee figured if you took these down, then the smaller towers would fall like dominoes.

Kill the brain, the body dies.

Sato coordinated their approach as the fortress began targeting their formation. "Sir, the platform's learning curve is accelerating. Its hit probability has increased from twelve percent to twenty-eight percent in the last four minutes."

Enemy fire started finding gaps in their countermeasures, each shot more accurate than the last. The *Poseidon* shuddered under a near miss, overwhelming their port-side thermal buffers, emergency alarms echoing through the corridors.

"Damage control teams to sections three, decks four and five," Sato ordered, punching in commands on her control interface. "Engineering teams are responding, but we need to limit exposure to concentrated fire from that bearing."

"All ships will approach from multiple vectors," Lee commanded. "Stagger your attack runs by thirty-second intervals. Force that AI to split its attention between targets. Rhom, prepare concentrated fire on their primary sensor array. If we can blind it, we can kill it."

The *Oceanus* and *Polaris* moved into flanking positions as the adaptive platform's weapons found their mark. The *Duncan* took a direct hit to her forward sections, the cruiser's hull buckling under the impact. Strips of armor spun into the void.

The other ships in his battle group reported successful engagements across their assigned coordinates. The *Bolt* and *Ranger* had eliminated their targets, while the *Duncan*—despite her damage—

had managed to destroy the second platform before limping back toward the formation.

Today, Lee mused, *luck favors the bold.*

"*Duncan* reports fourteen casualties, sir," Rodriguez announced. "Seven dead, seven wounded. Their forward magrail turret is completely destroyed, and they're showing atmosphere leaks in three compartments."

Lee gnashed his teeth at the deterioration of the tactical situation. Fourteen casualties. Rodriguez's tone suggested relief. It could have been much worse. Lee understood what this meant immediately: "acceptable losses," the phrase that haunted every commanding officer in fleet combat. Meanwhile, two more Primord cruisers in distant sectors were taking devastating punishment from similar adaptive platforms.

"Sato, signal the fleet. We need authorization to concentrate our entire battle group against this single platform. Standard tactics aren't going to work against adaptive AI systems."

Admiral McKee's tone burst through the fleet communications. "Battle Group Four, you're authorized to concentrate full firepower against your primary target. Intelligence indicates these adaptive platforms are the keys to the entire defensive network. Neutralizing them will cause failure throughout the remaining installations."

The massive fortress continued its methodical targeting, its AI systems growing more dangerous with each passing minute. Lee could practically feel the enemy computer analyzing their every move, cataloging weaknesses, preparing countermeasures.

Lee began coordinating the concentrated attack approach, bringing all six ships of the battle group into optimal firing positions despite the increasing danger.

"Sir," Sato said, "if we commit our entire force against that platform, we'll be exposing ourselves to maximum retaliation. The AI will have six targets to analyze simultaneously, but it'll also have six targets to destroy."

The enemy was learning, adapting, evolving, and it was time to roll the dice.

"Incoming plasma torpedoes!" Rhom shouted from his station. "Four torpedoes, impact in eighteen seconds! It's targeting us, and us only."

Somehow, Lee marveled, *it must suspect my ship's the leader of the group.*

The point-defense guns erupted in controlled bursts, rounds streaking toward the incoming threats. "First torpedo destroyed!" Rhom said. "Second one's breaking apart… got the third! One torpedo remaining," he called out. "I can't get a lock. It's too close!"

The klaxons screamed their five-second warning, the piercing wail echoing through every corridor of the ship. "Brace for impact!" Lee commanded.

A plasma torpedo struck *Poseidon*'s starboard hull like the fist of Poseidon himself. The impact point was less than twenty meters from the bridge. The proximity sent shock waves through the superstructure that pressed Lee against his command chair as emergency lighting bathed the bridge in hellish red. Sparks erupted from Lieutenant Jacob Witkowski's station as the blast's energy feedback surged through conduits running directly beneath his console. The young officer's scream was cut short as he fell to the deck, his hair and face covered in flames.

Chapter 8:
Victory is Never Cheap

Late 2098
RNS *Poseidon*
Planet Rass

Sato leaped from her station and grabbed the emergency suppression unit mounted beside the science console. The molecular flame-retardant engulfed Lieutenant Witkowski in a cloud, instantly neutralizing the blaze consuming his uniform and hair. The horrible smell of charred flesh filled the bridge as the flames died.

A memory flashed in Lee's mind for the briefest of milliseconds. The smell of burnt flesh had filled the bridge when Captain James Oldendorf and several others, including his old captain's XO, had died on the RNS *Kentucky* all those years ago. That scent never left the brain. The moment one caught a whiff, it was unmistakable.

"Medical team to the bridge, emergency!" Lee yelled into his comm while scanning the damage control reports flooding his chair's holos. Sato knelt beside Witkowski, checking his vitals. The young officer was unconscious but breathing. His burns were severe, but they didn't look fatal thanks to her quick response.

The massive platform's weapons swiveled toward their formation again. Enemy targeting systems locked on to *Poseidon* as another salvo of plasma torpedoes launched from the fortress.

"Incoming fire!" Rhom shouted. "Multiple torpedoes, bearing two-six-nine!"

Admiral McKee's voice crackled through the fleet communications. "All battle group commanders, this is Fleet Command. Republic troop transports are through the stargate and on their way. ETA seventeen minutes. We need those orbital platforms neutralized for the ground assault to commence."

Point-defense turrets opened up immediately. The torpedoes streaked toward them.

"Sir," Baldry called out, studying his sensors, "that platform just adjusted its firing pattern. First salvo came in at standard trajectory, but this one's compensating for our evasive maneuvers from thirty seconds ago."

The emergency medics arrived faster than expected. They quickly stabilized Witkowski and prepped him for transport. Lee nodded to the lead medic as they hauled the unconscious officer toward the med bay. When he turned back, Sato had already made it back to her seat.

"Got two of them!" Rhom said. "One more incoming!"

The final torpedo detonated against their forward armor. Sparks flew from unmanned consoles as the bridge shook.

Hopefully Witkowski would be fine, but Lee couldn't think any more about that right now. They were under major attack.

In seventeen minutes, Republic troop transports would arrive. Lee exchanged a look with his XO that said everything neither of them wanted to voice. They needed to crack the most heavily defended planet they'd ever encountered and secure orbital space, and fast. Every second of delay increased the probability of facing fresh Zodark reinforcements with the Republic and Primord already battered forces.

"Rodriguez, acknowledge receipt and confirm Battle group Four is proceeding with final assault phase immediately," Lee ordered.

"Aye, sir. Transmitting confirmation to the *George Washington*," Rodriguez replied.

"Sir," Baldry called from his sensor station, "we're at the coordinates to engage this final platform in our sector."

Lee gave him a nod. *The fortress. The biggest of the lot. The bastard that just harmed my EWO. It has to go...*

He studied his tactical holo, which hovered above his chair. The massive adaptive platform loomed before Lee—before them all—like a damn mountain. It had already fired on them and a few others in his battle group, its AI systems having learned from every previous engagement. Weapon arrays shifted continuously across its surface, its focus seeming to be more on the *Poseidon* than the rest of the group. It knew, somehow, *Poseidon* was the lead.

"The fortress is repositioning its weapons arrays," Rhom reported. "It's moving guns away from sectors we've already targeted. The damn thing remembers where we hit the smaller platforms."

The bridge's main viewscreen showed all six ships of Battle Group Four moving into attack formation. Time to test whether human ingenuity could outthink this artificial intelligence.

"*Duncan* and *Oceanus*, approach from bearing two-eight-zero, staggered thirty-second intervals," Lee commanded. "*Bolt*, *Polaris* and *Ranger*, missile saturation from bearing zero-nine-zero. We'll take the primary assault vector straight down their throat."

"Sir," Sato interjected, studying her tactical readouts, "the platform's fire control is predicting our movement patterns with unprecedented accuracy, despite evasive maneuvers. It's not reacting to where we are… it's shooting where we're going to be. Without Witkowski, we can't disrupt their targeting computers. We need to—"

"Understood. Baldry, take over electronic warfare functions. Slave the EWO console to your station," Lee commanded. *Jacob Witkowski, we could really use your electronic warfare magic right about now!*

The coordination required split-second timing, with each ship's role designed to overwhelm the AI's ability to adapt to multiple simultaneous threats. Lee's ships maneuvered into position. He knew his captains trusted his plan.

The adaptive platform's surface looked a little like rolling ocean waves, at least for a second, as it simply rippled its weapons in a new alignment. Gun ports sealed themselves and reopened in new configurations. Laser arrays swiveled toward the approaching ships. Then, lasers belched from the Zodark structure, along with plasma torpedoes.

"Incoming," Rhom said while monitoring ammunition reserves and damage reports. He was already activating, then using, *Poseidon*'s point-defense system.

"All vessels report ready for synchronized assault," Rodriguez announced.

Sato studied her tactical analysis. "The AI can adapt to sequential attacks, but simultaneous strikes from six different vectors should confuse it a bit." She looked up at Lee. "The plan's sound, sir. Hit it with more variables than its computer brain can handle at once. Sounds too simple, but sometimes simple works the best."

"Agreed." Lee nodded.

The *Bolt* took heavy fire from the floating platform. Its captain's voice crackled through the comm. "Taking multiple hits to our forward sections. Port magrail turret is gone. We're still in the fight."

The enemy weapon platform's AI was switching strategies. Going after the smaller vessels.

"*Bolt*, adjust to bearing three-zero mark six," Lee ordered. "Keep that platform guessing."

"All ships, continue attack," Lee ordered. "Let's see how smart this thing really is."

"Captain," Baldry said, "the platform just reconfigured its entire defensive grid. It's clustering point-defense systems at the exact approach vectors we used against Platform Nineteen."

Lee nodded. "Understood. We'll overwhelm it the old-fashioned way. With a crap-ton of weapons fire."

The six ships of Battle Group Four accelerated toward their target, each captain knowing that they only had minutes standing between success and watching Republic troops die in an orbital shooting gallery.

Baldry called out range and bearing updates while he worked the electronic warfare operations. Around Lee, his bridge crew worked like mad, each officer focused on their role in what might be their most important engagement in all the years they've been together.

"Range to target, four thousand kilometers," Reynolds announced. "All ships are maintaining formation integrity."

"Sir"—Baldry's tone held a note of alarm—"the platform's targeting systems are cycling through our ship signatures. It's prioritizing targets based on our weapon loadouts."

Lee figured it would. It was an AI after all, and it'd no doubt figure out which ships in Lee's small armada were the biggest threats.

The adaptive platform came alive like a cornered badger. Its weapon arrays shifted as the six ships closed the distance. The fortress's surface moved, more gun ports opening.

"Optimal weapons range in thirty seconds," Rhom announced. "All magrail batteries charged and ready."

"*Duncan* reports ready," Rodriguez said. "*Oceanus* confirms targeting locks established."

The platform struck hard, and with malice. Lasers lanced out, finding the exact gaps in their defensive formation that shouldn't have existed. Lee's stomach dropped as he realized the AI had calculated their attack pattern three moves ahead.

"Evasive maneuvers, all ships!" Lee said into the comm.

It was too late.

The barrage hit *Poseidon*'s port side. The impact sent Lee slamming against his command chair as the ship bucked, the seat's restraints pulling Lee in tightly. Hull plating screamed under the assault. Metal shrieked as reinforced bulkheads buckled. Sparks erupted from overhead conduits, raining down on the bridge crew. The superstructure groaned worse than a pained whale as energy tore through reinforced bulkheads. Emergency klaxons screamed warnings while the bridge lighting blinked between normal and emergency red.

The main viewer flickered and died, then snapped back to life, showing static before clearing. The deck plates vibrated under Lee's feet as secondary explosions rippled through the ship's interior.

Lee gathered himself, tasting blood from where he'd bitten his cheek. Around him, his crew fought to maintain control as their ship shuddered under the damage. The main viewscreen showed a horrifying sight: atmosphere bleeding from three breached compartments in silvery streams, the air escaping extremely fast.

"Cap! Direct hit to engineering section four!" MacGregor's voice crackled through the comm. "We've lost the port fusion manifold and secondary power grid. I'm rerouting through backup conduits, but we're down to sixty-four percent power capacity."

"Structural integrity holding at eighty-two percent," Sato reported. "Emergency compartment seals are containing the atmosphere leaks."

The ship's acceleration faltered. Engines struggled. A dread washed over Lee, a familiar one, the one a captain feels when he must watch his vessel, his baby, bleed in space. The *Poseidon* was hurt, badly, but at least she was still breathing.

"All ships, maintain attack formation," Lee commanded. "We finish this now or we don't finish it at all."

"Sir," Rodriguez said, "*Duncan* reports her forward sensors are damaged. Captain Burns is requesting targeting assistance."

"*Oceanus*, slave your targeting computer to *Duncan*," Lee ordered. "Give them your sensor data."

Each captain knew the mathematics: either they overwhelmed the AI's adaptive capabilities in the next sixty seconds, or they'd face a fortress that had learned to counter every tactic in their playbook.

"Synchronized strike in ten seconds," Rhom announced, his targeting systems locked despite the ship's damage. "All vessels confirm ready status."

"*Duncan* confirms ready despite damage," Rodriguez reported.

"*Oceanus* ready," came Captain Church's voice.

"*Bolt*, *Polaris*, and *Ranger* all report target locks established," Rodriguez continued.

"Five seconds," Rhom called out. "Three… two… one…"

"All ships, fire!"

The space around the adaptive platform erupted. *Poseidon*'s magrail turrets spoke first, six twin-barreled guns hurling tungsten projectiles at incredible speed. The *Duncan* and *Oceanus* added their voices a split second later, their heavy guns and missiles sending streams of destruction toward the fortress.

From their flanking positions, the *Bolt*, *Polaris*, and *Ranger* unleashed their missile salvos. Dozens flew toward the platform from three different vectors, their guidance systems locked onto predetermined target points.

The platform's AI faltered for the first time. Its weapon arrays swiveled frantically, trying to track six simultaneous attack vectors. Point-defense systems engaged, but they couldn't stop everything.

The joint salvo made its case. Magrail rounds, plasma torpedoes, and energy beams converged on the fortress's central core. The first impacts struck the platform's outer ring, sending chunks of armor spinning into space. Secondary explosions flurried across the surface.

"Direct hits across all target zones," Rhom reported. "The AI's defensive pattern is breaking down."

"Core structure is compromised," Baldry added. "I'm reading massive power fluctuations."

The adaptive floating weapons platform blew to shreds in an explosion that lit up Rass's orbital space, only to be quickly extinguished by the void's vacuum. The central core went first, a white flash briefly outshining the planet below. Then the outer rings followed, each detonation feeding into the next. Debris scattered in all directions as the massive structure's core overloaded, taking its learning algorithms and weapon arrays into the eternal darkness, though some spun into Rass's atmosphere only to burn into nothing.

Victory tasted good. Damn good.

"Platform destroyed!" Rhom reported. "All targets in our sector are neutralized."

"Sir," Rodriguez announced, "Admiral McKee is signaling all clear. The orbital grid is down."

The celebration died quickly as damage reports flooded the communication channels. Rodriguez's face went pale as she compiled the numbers, her fingers hesitating over the transmission controls.

"Casualty reports coming in, sir," she announced, her voice heavy as hell. "Battle group total: twenty-three dead, forty-one wounded. *Poseidon*'s losses… seven dead, twelve wounded, three critical."

Lee closed his eyes briefly. A sigh escaped, just like all of those souls on his ship who'd died. Seven good people who wouldn't be going home to families, friends, lives that would now remain forever unfinished. The price of victory always came due in blood—always, and he hated it. Yet he loved everyone's sacrifice for the betterment of the galaxy, for the betterment of humanity.

"Acknowledge all casualty reports," Lee said. "Begin recovery operations and damage assessment."

"Sir," Sato said softly, "repair teams are requesting four hours for critical systems restoration. We can manage emergency repairs in two."

"Do what you can, XO. We may not have four hours."

Lee's personal comm unit chimed with a priority medical alert. He tapped the control, and Chief Medical Officer Dr. Aisha Flynn's voice came through, heavy with exhaustion and something worse.

"Captain," Dr. Flynn said. "I need to speak with you about Lieutenant Witkowski."

Lee's stomach dropped. The tone said everything. "How bad?"

"Sir… we lost him. The burns were too extensive, and the smoke inhalation damaged his lungs beyond our ability to repair. He fought for twelve minutes, but…" Her voice trailed off.

Witkowski…Jacob. Years together, through impossible battles and hopeless odds. The electronic warfare officer who'd saved their asses more times than Lee could count. The kid from Detroit who'd joined the Navy to fight for humanity's future, who'd perfected jamming techniques that had become fleet standard.

Gone.

"Thank you, Doctor," Lee managed. "Take care of the wounded."

Lee closed the comm and sat back in his chair.

The bridge felt quieter now. Empty. Witkowski's station would need a replacement, but there was no replacing the man himself. The young lieutenant had stayed at his post during the worst firefights.

Sato noticed his silence. "Sir?"

"Witkowski didn't make it," Lee said in a low hush.

The bridge crew went silent. Witkowski had been with them for a long time, through battles that should have killed them all. His electronic warfare expertise had been their edge against superior enemy technology.

"He was one of the best," Sato said under her breath. "His jamming systems probably saved half the fleet during this engagement."

Lee nodded. *And now we face whatever comes next without him.*

The priority transmission arrived shortly after as *Poseidon*'s repair teams started working frantically to restore critical systems. Admiral McKee's image appeared on the main screen, her expression mixing satisfaction with something that looked like concern.

"Outstanding work, Commander Lee. The orbital platforms are down, and ground forces will proceed with the liberation of Rass. However, I have new orders for you and *Poseidon*."

Lee straightened in his command chair, noting the formal tone that meant significant developments were brewing in Space Command's decisions.

"Effective immediately, you're to detach from the Rass operation and proceed to New Eden. Fleet Intelligence has a priority assignment that requires your specific expertise and *Poseidon*'s capabilities." The admiral's pause told Lee this might be a classified operation.

Lee nodded. "Understood, Admiral. We'll be ready."

McKee's image flickered out. It left Lee staring at the tactical display showing Rass and every destroyed ship, every ruptured satellite, and every downed weapons platform in the area. Seven dead crew members, including Jacob Witkowski, a damaged ship, and now mysterious new orders.

War was never predictable. But one thing was certain. Whatever information waited at New Eden would test them all over again. And they'd face it without one of their best.

Chapter 9:
Riding the Express

Late 2098
RNS *Gallipoli*
Stargate 352-NHW

Inside *Jack*'s cramped belly, just over sixty soldiers sat shoulder to shoulder. Each trooper wore the latest Republic HALO jump suits, formfitting armor designed for orbital insertion, complete with integrated helmets providing full environmental protection and heads-up displays. Their gear weighed a ton against Republic-issue harnesses. Coop shifted in his seat. There, he observed his TASC team prepare for what could be their last mission together, or their best, but one never knew.

As part of the 1st Battalion, 504th Infantry Regiment—the "Red Devils" of the 3rd Brigade, Republic Army's 82nd Orbital Assault Division—Coop had trained for this. Alpha Company had a reputation to uphold, and their commander, Captain Saho Nobunaga, had drilled into them that the Red Devils never left a job half finished.

Corporal Weber sat near the bulkhead, running comm checks with Alpha Company's other squads scattered across different birds in *Gallipoli*'s launch bay at the moment. "Charlie Four-One, radio check. Over." The responses crackled back through his helmet.

Staff Sergeant Crawford leaned over, eyeing a tactical tablet. He punched in commands across holographic terrain maps of their landing zone. Red dots marked known Zodark positions. Blue triangles showed where friendly forces would land, if everything went as planned. Coop almost laughed at the idea. The saying went that the only thing certain about battle plans was they would be wrong before the first shots were fired.

Man plans, God laughs, Coop thought.

Crawford's face stayed impassive as he memorized every ridge, every potential ambush point, every escape route they might need. Coop had seen that look before. Crawford was building a mental fortress of contingencies, which was why the man had done so well, and why he had been a lifeline—a savior in many ways—during their last campaign.

Technical Sergeant Li worked the sensor array, manipulating the interface like a concert pianist. She was the best at her job, as far as Coop could tell. Data streams flowed down her screen as she monitored Zodark movement patterns from the Republic and Primord probes that had managed to sneak on or near planet Rass, all flashing back data in real time. She'd prepped their targeting systems twice already. The woman never settled for good enough. Ever.

Sergeant Jade Vega sat across from Coop, her sniper rifle secured between her knees. She cleaned her scope, making sure she didn't miss any nook and cranny on her weapon. With Vega, there was never any nervous fidgeting. "Calm," they should name her. Or call her "The Best of the Best." Hell, she was ice in human form, and Coop drew strength from watching her work. Even Bear, his old buddy, had admitted Vega was the most dangerous person he'd ever met, though that meeting had been brief. That's how Vega was. One look at her, and you just knew.

The thought of Bear hit like an elbow to the throat, a knee to the groin, and a sucker punch to the solar plexus all at once. Coop's hand found the challenge coin in his pocket. It was Bear's coin. They'd joined TASC training together, two cocky pilots who'd thought they could advance their careers by selecting one of the most dangerous career fields in the service. Bear would've loved cracking jokes about the odds at the moment, making everyone laugh despite the circumstances.

Now Bear was gone, and Coop was here, trying not to throw up from nerves.

Lieutenant Spike Gill moved through the cramped space like he owned the place, checking on his soldiers. He stopped beside each man, offering a word, adjusting equipment, reading faces for signs of breakdown. Gill had that rare gift of knowing exactly when someone needed encouragement and when they needed space. His presence steadied the entire platoon without him saying much at all.

"Intel's reporting increased Orbot presence planetside," Crawford announced, looking up from his tablet. "First time most of you will see cyborgs in action."

Weber snorted. "Sci-fi movies pretty much nailed how those freaks look. Half machine, half ugly."

"You've never actually seen one," Li pointed out, not looking up from her sensors.

"Amazing thing called cameras," Weber shot back. "They record stuff."

The laughter that followed felt forced, but it served its purpose. Coop managed a weak smile, though his stomach kept doing barrel rolls. *Will I live through this? Will any of us?* The questions circled like Zodark Vultures in his mind. He couldn't shake the feeling that some of these people in this Osprey wouldn't be coming home, maybe even him.

His father would never be proud of him anyway. He might as well try to make himself proud instead.

Vega's tone burst through the chatter. "Quit worrying about what you can't control. Focus on what you can."

Vega always had simple wisdom that seemed to put everything in perspective.

She didn't look at anyone in particular when she said it, but Coop felt the words land square in his chest. Vega had a way of reading people that bordered on the supernatural. He straightened in his harness, forcing his breathing to steady.

The intercom crackled to life with Captain Love's voice from the cockpit. "Gear up, people. Corridor's opening and we have clearance for launch. Sixty seconds to departure."

Coop's heart picked up speed. This was it. He gripped Bear's challenge coin tighter, feeling its edges bite into his palm.

The Osprey's engines roared to life, vibrations traveling through the deck plates. Launch clamps released with metallic thuds reverberating through the hull. Suddenly they were moving, accelerating out of *Gallipoli*'s launch bay and into the black void of space.

Through the viewport, Coop caught glimpses of the Republic fleet spread across the darkness like a constellation of war. Ahead lay Rass, a blue-green marble streaked with clouds, hiding an army of Zodarks who wanted them all dead.

Most of the enemy's defensive platforms that had ringed Rass were gone, broken to pieces, with others clearly out of commission, especially where Alpha Company's Ospreys were heading. Twisted metal drifted, glowing cherry-red from recent explosions. The Republic and Primords were still battling a handful of remaining platforms, but not near them. Through the debris field that their Osprey and several others were heading toward, an almost empty corridor stretched toward the planet. Republic and Primord ships had created this path with blood and with fire.

The RNS *Poseidon* floated like a Goliath in the distance, her hull battered and bruised but intact. Cruisers and frigates flanked her. They'd built a highway to hell, and the Osprey was about to drive it.

"Defensive perimeter's holding," Crawford announced, studying his tactical display. "Looks like Captain Lee and his battle group along with the Primords made us a damn beautiful lane."

Weber keyed his radio. "Charlie Four-One, corridor status green. We're riding the express."

Explosions bloomed in the void ahead. Zodark Vultures tangled with Republic Orions, their energy weapons and missiles creating streaks of light. Coop watched an Orion take a plasma torpedo and tumble into the dark, its hull breaking apart. Somewhere out there, another drone pilot had just lost his bird.

The Jolly Rogers are out there. The thought hit Coop. His old squadron was flying some of those Orions, keeping the Vultures off their backs. His chest tightened.

"Five minutes to drop zone!" Love announced through the intercom.

Alert tones filled the cabin. The low rumble of engines shifted to a higher pitch as the Osprey began its descent. Coop forced himself to focus. Despite everything he hated about Strike, the man had taught him something important during his Jolly Rogers days, back when Coop had thought he knew everything about flying.

"Picture success before you arrive," Strike had said after a particularly brutal sim session. "Olympic athletes don't visualize failure. They see themselves crossing the finish line. See yourself completing the mission, Cooper."

Coop closed his eyes and ran the mental movie. Boots hitting Rass soil. TASC team establishing comms with the fleet. Alpha Company securing the landing zone. Everyone walking back to the extraction point in one piece. He'd done this visualization ritual on their last campaign, and it had worked for the most part. Most of them had made it home. Maybe if he'd done it more, Bear would have too.

He opened his eyes and looked around the cabin. Li was running final diagnostics on her sensor suite. Crawford studied approach vectors on his tablet, memorizing every detail of their insertion route. Weber coordinated with other squads across the comm net.

Vega sat motionless. She wasn't cleaning her scope anymore. She was in the zone, that place where elite operators went before stepping into hell. Her dark eyes met his. There was something there, somehow screaming confidence, and that any Zodark who crossed her path wouldn't live long.

Coop opened a private channel to his TASC team. "We're the bridge between air and ground," Coop said. "The moment we hit dirt, we link Alpha Company to the fleet. No delays."

Weber nodded once. Li gave him a thumbs-up without looking away from her screens. Crawford tapped his tablet and said, "Roger that, TASC lead."

The title still felt strange. Leadership seemed wrong somehow and right all at the same time. It was probably because Bear wasn't here; he felt half of him had left with his best bud.

"Three minutes out!" Gill called, checking his chronometer.

Around the cabin, Alpha Company's Second Platoon performed final gear checks. Soldiers tested their weapon systems, verified ammo counts, and secured loose equipment. Banter had died away, replaced by the focused silence of professionals preparing for war.

Lieutenant Gill moved through the cramped space one last time. He adjusted a soldier's harness here, checked a comm unit there. His calm presence steadied everyone around him. It always did, and probably always would.

Coop glanced out the viewport again just as Gill paused beside him, reading the tension in the younger man's shoulders. "You've got good instincts, Cooper," he said, adjusting a strap on Coop's harness that didn't need adjusting. "I've watched you make the right calls under pressure. Trust those instincts down there. They'll keep us all and your team alive." Gill nodded once and moved on before Coop could respond, leaving him with exactly what he needed to hear. Or, at least, it felt that way.

Out the holoport, Rass filled the view now, no longer a distant blue-green marble. From this distance, it looked peaceful. Beautiful, even. Hard to believe that beneath those clouds, Zodark forces were digging in for a fight. The planet's serene appearance was a damn lie wrapped in atmosphere.

Pretty poison, he thought. *The deadliest traps always look harmless.*

"Thirty seconds to jump!" Love announced.

Coop touched Bear's challenge coin one more time. Whatever happened down there, he'd make his old friend proud.

The soldiers around him stood and moved toward the rear of the cabin. Harnesses clicked. Weapons were shouldered. Just over sixty pairs of boots shuffled into formation, ready to leap into the unknown.

The Osprey's rear ramp began to lower. Below them, Rass stretched to the horizon.

"Ten seconds!" Gill shouted, his voice booming through everyone's helmet comms.

Coop stepped toward the ramp. Through the opening, he could see Vultures diving through the atmosphere, their cannons lighting up the sky. Energy weapons crisscrossed the darkness.

They were about to jump into that maelstrom.

Bear would have said something about the odds. Coop smiled grimly and stepped into the void.

Chapter 10:
First Blood on Rass

Late 2098
Planet Rass

The moment Coop's boots left the Osprey's ramp, hell opened up beneath him. Zodark anti-aircraft fire lit the sky. His heads-up display showed threat vectors in crimson as flak explosions bloomed around the descending troopers. Several bursts were close enough to rattle his ears.

The rush of wind through his helmet's audio pickups created a constant roar, along with the hiss of energy weapons and the distant thunder of explosions. His environmental suit's climate control struggled to regulate his body temperature as adrenaline surged through his system. The world spun beneath him. Green forest. Brown earth. Red blooms of anti-aircraft fire.

Through his visor's HUD, altitude readings scrolled past in amber numerals while his suit's systems monitored everything from heart rate to oxygen levels.

Coop fought to maintain formation as his chute deployed. The sudden jerk nearly pulled his shoulders off despite the harness. Around him, hundreds of other parachutes blossomed against Rass's clouded sky. Alpha Company, Bravo Company, Delta, Gamma, and more—all dropped from Ospreys.

Through the hellfire, the planet's surface revealed itself in glimpses between the drifting clouds. Below, massive industrial complexes spread far and wide across the terrain. Zodark military installations dotted the landscape, connected by supply roads running through what had once most likely been pristine wilderness.

Between the bases, patches of forest clung to life, the woodlands bearing the scars of three centuries of Zodark occupation. Enormous craters pocked the earth where strip-mining operations had exhausted the soil, leaving behind what looked like empty wounds. The forest canopy rushed up to meet them, a green carpet promising either salvation or death, depending on what waited beneath those trees.

A Zodark Vulture screamed past, its laser cannons spitting hate at the descending troopers. The alien fighter flew through the sky and banked just as magrail rounds stitched across the Vulture's hull, punching through its armor in a storm of debris. A Republic Orion fighter flashed past, its engines howling as it pursued the damaged enemy craft. The Vulture exploded in a giant fireball lighting up the sky.

"Thanks for the save, whoever you are," Coop whispered, wondering if one of his old Jolly Rogers squadmates had just saved his life.

"TASC Leader, my chute's not—" Weber's voice cut off as his main canopy streamed uselessly above him, his tangled lines preventing proper deployment. The communications specialist clawed desperately at his reserve chute. Coop's HUD showed Weber's altitude dropping fast. Two thousand meters, eighteen hundred, fifteen hundred. The altimeter numbers blurred past as precious seconds ticked away.

Weber's reserve deployed partially and slowed his descent but not nearly enough. Coop tracked Weber's fall through his HUD. Twelve hundred meters, nine hundred thousand, six hundred. Twenty seconds of free fall that felt like forever. The partially deployed reserve chute only cut his velocity by half.

Coop reached for him helplessly. "Weber, get—"

Too late.

His teammate slammed into the forest canopy at terminal velocity, branches snapping one after another before the horrible thud of impact echoed through the comm channel.

"Weber's down!" Coop shouted into his radio, knowing even as he said it, there wouldn't be any response from Corporal Weber ever again.

The loss slammed into Coop like a Zodark shoving him hard against a boulder. Weber had been a good soldier, always steady. They hadn't shared years of friendship and stupid jokes like Bear, but Weber had been part of his team and a good guy. As a drone pilot, death had been clinical for Coop. More distant. Just pixels on a screen. Now as a TASC officer, it was personal, immediate, and right in front of him. The high pressure of command felt heavier with each loss. These weren't just soldiers anymore; they were his responsibility. His family.

Coop's stomach lurched as his own altimeter ticked down toward the treeline. The branches rushed up faster than seemed possible. Suddenly, he was crashing through the canopy, small limbs slapping against his visor.

Coop hit the forest floor hard, dropping into the tactical landing position he'd drilled countless times. His knees buckled as he absorbed the impact and immediately rolled to avoid the incoming blaster fire sizzling past his helmet. The landing zone erupted in mayhem as Alpha Company's platoons touched down under heavy enemy fire across a dispersed area spanning nearly four hundred meters. Energy bolts blasted into tree trunks with wet hissing sounds, heating the wood so hot, steam rose from the smoking impact points. A Zodark blaster bolt struck a nearby tree, and the entire trunk exploded into splinters and boiling sap. The whir of Orbot servos announced the arrival of the biomechanical horrors. The cyborg wannabes were here.

Captain Nobunaga's voice burst through the comm net from his position two hundred meters to the northeast: "Contact front! Zodarks in the tree line with Orbot support! Second Platoon, establish fire base at grid four-seven-two. First Platoon, advance by bounds to objective rally point."

Twenty or so ten-foot-tall blue-skinned giants with three eyes were positioned among the thick trees one hundred and fifty meters northeast of their landing zone, each wielding energy blasters in two hands and blades in the other two. Behind them came the Orbots, their spiderlike mechanical legs carrying humanlike torsos. The cyborgs moved fast, their rifles tracking targets and expelling rounds.

An Orbot's kinetic projectile streaked past Coop's body, the sound similar to a miniature thunderclap. Near him, a private stumbled backward as an Orbot's round found his shoulder. The kid stayed on his feet, but his left arm hung useless. Moments after, the young man dropped into the undergrowth and out of view.

"TASC team, on me!" Coop bellowed as he cut away his parachute harness and dove behind a fallen log which provided minimal cover from the incoming fire. Technical Sergeant Li rolled in beside him from her landing position thirty meters away, her sensor array powering up in spite of the energy bolts hissing overhead. Staff Sergeant Crawford appeared through the smoke, dragging his tactical tablet and breathing hard, his face grim as he processed everything happening around him, including Weber's absence.

Crawford's datapad flickered, static lines running across the display. "Damn interference," he muttered, tapping the screen. "Zodarks are jamming our comms."

"Switching to magrails!" someone shouted from the perimeter. The crack of magnetic railgun rounds split the air, followed by the wet explosion of an Orbot's head disintegrating.

"That's how you do it!" Li yelled, adjusting her own weapon's firing mode.

An Orbot bounded through the underbrush toward their position. Coop's HUD helped line up his shot as he switched his M91 to railgun mode. His hands trembled slightly, not from fear, but from the overwhelming responsibility of coordinating fire support while men died around him.

Thing was, he'd done this before and successfully, and he'd do it again.

Calm yourself, Coop, he told himself.

Coop squeezed the trigger. The magrail round punched through the cyborg's torso. Biological matter sprayed across the forest floor. The Orbot collapsed, its spider legs twitching as its systems shut down.

From his position with Second Platoon's command element, Lieutenant Gill coordinated the overall defensive perimeter while Coop focused on his TASC mission. A Zodark energy blast burned a smoking crater in the earth just inches from Coop.

"This position's too hot," Coop shouted over the gunfire. "We need better cover to set up the TASC post."

Li spotted a cluster of boulders fifty meters back. Natural cover. "There!" She pointed.

The three-person team moved fast, bounding forward fifteen meters at a time. Crawford went first, diving behind the rocks as energy bolts sizzled overhead. Li followed, her sensor array bouncing against her back. Coop came last, providing covering fire.

The new position offered protection from three sides, better sightlines, and room to work.

"Crawford, get the TASC post operational," Coop ordered. "We need fire support coordination up and running now."

Crawford dropped his pack and pulled out the portable command array, unfolding the communication dish and tactical display unit. "Setting up the uplink to fleet assets," he said, punching in commands on the control interface. "I'm establishing encrypted channels to the *Duncan* and to the *George Washington*, to Admiral McKee's fire support coordination center."

Li positioned her enhanced sensor array on a stable outcropping, adjusting the array to maximize battlefield coverage. "Sensor grid is online," she reported. "I'm getting clear reads on enemy positions out to eighteen hundred meters. Uploading targeting data to the tactical network now."

The portable command post took shape within minutes. It was a compact but sophisticated setup, serving as their link between ground forces and the naval assets in orbit. Crawford's communication array whirred softly as it synchronized with fleet frequencies, while Li's sensors showed a detailed picture of the battlefield on their shared tactical display.

"TASC post is operational," Crawford announced. "We've got direct comms to fire support assets and real-time targeting capability." He worked frantically over his tablet, occasionally shaking it when static interference disrupted the connection.

"Li, I need targeting coordinates for the main concentration," Coop said while manipulating his laser designator's interface. His heads-up display showed a holographic overlay of the battlefield, with red enemy contacts clustered among the trees. The display wavered intermittently as Zodark jammers interfered with their electronics.

He selected the largest concentration of Zodarks and Orbots. Sixty-one contacts bearing northeast. He targeted them with his laser, all clustered behind fallen trees approximately one hundred and twenty-five meters from Alpha Company's scattered Second Platoon. Cyborg rifles tracked toward Alpha Company's position while their torsos swiveled in that direction. Behind them, more contacts appeared on Li's sensor display. A group of Zodarks moved to flank their position.

"Coop keyed his comm. "Any air assets, any air assets, this is TASC One-Six requesting immediate close-air support.""

Static crackled before clearing. "TASC One-Six, this is Reaper Two-One, flight of two Republic fighters on station. Ready to copy target coordinates."

Thank God, Coop thought. At least something was going right.

"Reaper Two-One, TASC One-Six. Stand by for nine-line brief," Coop transmitted. "Line one: Grid four-seven-three-five-eight-two. Line two: Heading zero-four-five, offset two hundred meters. Line three: Elevation one hundred and fifty meters. Line four: Enemy squad in treeline, mixed Zodark and Orbot forces. Line five: Magrail cannons, request gun runs. Line six: Marked by infrared laser. Line seven: Friendlies one hundred meters south of target. Line eight: No obstacles. Line nine: Egress south."

Crawford's datapad went completely dark for three seconds before rebooting. "Come on, come on," he whispered. As soon as it came back online, he started uploading targeting coordinates. Just then, a blaster bolt threw chunks of bark into the air around them.

"TASC One-Six, Reaper Two-One copies nine-line. Tally target area, request final attack clearance."

"Reaper Two-One cleared hot, danger-close one hundred meters."

An Orbot's rifle discharged with a crack, sending a projectile that punched completely through a tree trunk before embedding in the earth beyond. Thirty meters away, Corporal Jamison dove behind a boulder as splinters rained down on his position. The man popped up, returned fire, and watched his round spark harmlessly off an Orbot's leg.

"Damn things are tough!" Jamison said over the comm.

The Zodark formation pressed their attack, armed beasts moving through the forest with incredible speed. Their blades hummed as they slashed through branches, while their blasters laid down suppressing fire forcing Alpha Company deeper into their shrinking perimeter. An Orbot leaped over a fallen log in a single bound. Those things were quick.

Holy hell, Coop thought as the cyborg moved with unbelievable quickness. The Orbot's four mechanical legs carried it over obstacles like some kind of mutant spider, while its humanlike torso swiveled independently to track targets. This was everything like the sterile combat footage he'd seen in briefings and worse.

The shriek of incoming aircraft sliced through the battle's din. "Reaper flight inbound!" Coop shouted as a Republic fighter screamed through the forest canopy. The first strafing run walked tungsten rounds through a Zodark and Orbot position, each impact throwing dirt and alien body parts into the air. The AS-90 Reaper drone operator's voice crackled through the comm: "Good effects on target. Making second pass." The fighter pulled up, banked hard, and dove for another pass. Its second run placed deep divots into three Orbots while scattering the blue warriors.

"Reaper Two-One off target, good hits. RTB for rearm."

"Copy Reaper Two-One. Thanks for the assist."

Coop allowed himself a moment of satisfaction. The air strike had worked exactly as planned. Maybe he could do this job again after all. First time might not have been luck.

When the smoke cleared, the alien advance had been disrupted but not eliminated. Several blue-skinned corpses lay scattered among twisted metal fragments. But Li's sensors still picked up contacts moving through the forest. More enemies were approaching from multiple directions.

"Multiple groups converging on our position," Li reported as she fought to filter signal from noise through the electronic interference. "Estimate two companies, mixed Zodark and Orbot forces."

Lieutenant Gill's tone crackled over the comm: "All Alpha elements, we've got movement on three sides. Second Platoon, hold current positions."

Coop evaluated the tactical situation and raced through options. The air strike had reduced immediate pressure, but they were still outnumbered and in a precarious position. For heavier targets, he needed naval gunfire support, but that required different protocols and much greater minimum safe distances. The stress of making the right call pressed down on him. One mistake could kill his entire team.

Static filled Coop's earpiece, then cleared with an electronic squeal. "RNS *Duncan*, this is TASC One-Six requesting naval gunfire support. Stand by for call for fire."

More static, then: "TASC One-Six, RNS *Duncan* copies. Send your call for fire."

Coop took a breath, double-checking his coordinates. Getting this wrong wasn't an option. "*Duncan*, method of engagement: adjust fire. Target description: enemy in assembly area. Grid four-seven-four-two-one-five. Direction two thousand, four hundred mils. Distance four hundred meters from friendly positions. Request single round, HE, immediate suppression."

"TASC One-Six, *Duncan* copies call for fire. Shot out."

Forty seconds later, the first tungsten round from the RNS *Duncan* struck three hundred meters northeast of Alpha Company's position, sending a geyser of earth skyward. The impact was precise but needed adjustment.

"*Duncan*, TASC One-Six. Add one hundred, left fifty. Fire for effect."

"TASC One-Six, add one hundred, left fifty. Shot out."

Through the trees, Zodarks repositioned, but they were now caught in the adjusted impact zone.

"All Alpha elements, take cover!" Coop shouted over the comm link. "Naval gunfire impact, four hundred meters northeast!"

The adjusted tungsten rounds from the RNS *Duncan* arrived in sequence. Three projectiles, fired from orbit, struck the earth hard, and on point. The forest erupted in soil, shattered trees, and alien body parts. The bombardment targeted the enemy formation at a safe distance, each round creating a crater fifteen meters wide. When the dust settled, the immediate assault threat had been neutralized.

"RNS *Duncan*, TASC One-Six. Target neutralized, end of mission. Outstanding shooting."

"Copy that, TASC One-Six. *Duncan* standing by for additional fire missions."

Crawford's datapad finally stabilized, and the interference cleared as enemy jamming equipment was destroyed in the bombardment. He looked up from his display, sweat streaming down his face. "That bought us some breathing room, but Li's picking up more contacts moving through the sector."

Li's sensors showed enemy contacts still active in the surrounding forest, though significantly reduced after the bombardment. "Looks like scattered elements regrouping to the east," she reported. "But we've broken their main assault."

Alpha Company's defensive perimeter had stabilized across all platoons, but they remained deep in hostile territory with limited ammunition and unclear extraction timelines.

Coop grabbed his gear and prepared to move. They'd bought Alpha Company precious time with the coordinated air strike and naval bombardment, but he knew this was just the beginning. The reprieve wouldn't last long, and his next decisions could mean the difference between life and death for everyone under his care.

Through the trees, muzzle flashes marked where Republic soldiers fought desperately to hold their positions against continuing but reduced enemy pressure. The forest had fallen into an uneasy quiet, broken only by the occasional crack of Vega's sniper rifle or the distant rumble of explosions from other landing zones across the planet.

Chapter 11:
Arboretum Conversations

Late 2098
FTL En Route to New Eden
RNS *Poseidon*

Four hours ago, the *Poseidon* had slipped into faster-than-light travel with that odd sensation of reality bending around them. Through the bridge's main viewscreen, the swirling deep purples and electric blues of FTL travel bathed the deck. Stars stretched into bright lines while space itself expanded into forever.

At the moment, Lee sat across from Sato in the ship's arboretum, attacking his reconstituted beef stew with his metal fork. He hadn't realized how hungry he was until he'd started eating, but the food might as well have been sawdust. His mind wasn't on the meal.

We should be at Rass right now, he thought.

The thought gnawed at him worse than the tasteless protein substitute. While he sat here stabbing processed nutrients, Republic and Primord forces were fighting for every meter of contested space around planet Rass. His fellow captains were taking fire, making split-second decisions that determined whether officers and soldiers lived or died.

The arboretum's artificial sunlight streamed from overhead panels, warming his face as three Synths moved quietly between the hydroponic beds. Their footsteps were muffled by soft soil pathways winding between tomato vines and lettuce beds supplementing the crew's rations. Recycling water systems gave the area an air of peace.

Sato reviewed damage reports on her Qpad, her eyes moving left and right, scanning the data. "MacGregor's assessment came in," she said without looking up. "Port fusion manifold needs complete replacement. Along with sixty-eight hull plates, three bulkhead sections, and an entirely new forward sensor array."

Lee nodded, imagining exactly what Mac would tell him in private. Probably something blunt but brief. "She's hurt, Cap, but she's still in fighting shape," or something similar. Or—who knew?—maybe: "Backup systems are holding steady, but I wouldn't recommend another major engagement without proper yard time. We're operating on duct tape at this point."

MacGregor had a way with words.

Lee forced another bite down, tasting nothing. The recall orders had been confusing at first. Pulling them out of an active combat zone with damaged ships seemed counterintuitive. But then the follow-up transmission had clarified everything: the *Poseidon* was to escort a handful of severely damaged warships back to the New Eden shipyards.

"Still seems odd," Sato said, reaching for an apple from her tray. She tested its ripeness with her fingers. "Our damage isn't extensive enough to require shipyard time. Kita Station could handle our repairs easily, and it's much closer. All in all, faster too."

Lee set down his fork. "You're right. Which suggests Fleet HQ has something else in mind for us."

"Another assignment?"

"Probably." Lee leaned back. "They wouldn't pull an experienced heavy cruiser away from the front lines just to play shepherd unless they had plans for us once we arrived. My guess? Whatever they need us for requires the shipyard facilities at New Eden, or they want us close to HQ for quick deployment on something new."

Sato frowned slightly. "The timing still feels off."

"It does," Lee admitted. "But, actually, let's think about this. The fight for Rass is largely transitioning to ground operations soon. The space battle is mainly about maintaining orbital control. We already won most of the battle to seize it. Meanwhile, these ships we're escorting, well, they're in bad shape and need serious yard time, and we're the only functional heavy cruiser available to make sure they get there safely."

"And once we get there?"

"That's the question, isn't it?" Lee met her eyes directly. "My gut tells me Space Command has something waiting for us. Something that requires our specific capabilities."

Sato nodded slowly. "Ships like ours don't get pulled from major offensives without good reason. The *Poseidon*'s been their test bed for human-Altairian tactical coordination since we launched. If they're forming specialized units for operations requiring that kind of expertise..."

"Then they either want us to train others, or they want us running something bigger than a single ship." Lee picked up his fork again, pushing the tasteless stew around his plate. "Either way, I have a feeling we won't be her crew much longer."

The words hit him harder than he'd expected. These people were his responsibility, his family. The thought of being separated from them, of perchance leaving Sato to face unknown challenges without her support, felt like abandoning his post in the middle of a firefight.

Lee exhaled slightly. "But that's a big maybe."

They both ate in silence for a while, other unspoken possibilities hanging between them like a grenade about to detonate. Lee understood the subtext. Heavy cruisers with hybrid technology weren't recalled for routine assignments.

"What's the word from the department heads about crew readiness?" Lee asked, shifting to more immediate concerns.

Sato consulted her Qpad, scrolling through reports. "Engineering is proud of keeping us operational despite the damage. Tactical is riding high from the successful platform destructions. MacGregor says we're at about eighty-eight percent effectiveness."

"And the crew's state of mind?"

She paused. "Mixed, sir. Losing Witkowski from the bridge team hit hard. Dr. Flynn reports some increased requests for sleep aids, though nothing outside normal post-battle parameters. The crew performed exceptionally during the platform assault, and they know it."

Lee nodded. Witkowski's death still ate at them. Lee had felt the shift in bridge dynamics immediately. Good officers were irreplaceable, and losing them left holes that went beyond simple personnel charts.

"His replacement won't have his instincts," Lee said, watching a Synth adjust nutrient levels in the hydroponic systems. "Jacob could read enemy signal patterns like… he was brilliant. Absolutely fantastic, to say the least. A genius at what he did."

Sato set down her tablet. "The Academy's pushing officers through accelerated programs. We might get someone with technical knowledge, but not his intuitive grasp of electronic warfare."

"That gap could cost lives."

"Yes, sir. It could."

The heavy admission settled between them. Lee stood, motioning for Sato to accompany him. They walked deeper into the arboretum, past sections where apple trees bloomed. Beauty in a steel box, traveling through the void toward an unknown mission.

"What's your assessment of the damaged ships we're escorting?" he asked.

"The *Conquest* and *Trident* are in rough shape, but stable. The *Seattle* lost her entire sensor suite and is running on backups."

Lee picked a ripe tomato from the vine, testing its weight. Real food, grown in real soil, tended by artificial beings. Interesting combo. "How long until we reach New Eden?"

"Two days at current velocity."

"Good. That gives us time to prepare for whatever's coming next." He bit into the tomato, tasting real sweetness for the first time in days. "Start reviewing our personnel files. If this mission requires specialized skills or security clearances, I want to know our capabilities before we get briefed."

"Aye, sir. I'll have a complete assessment by tomorrow."

"And schedule a shipwide address for tomorrow morning. The crew deserves to know what we know. That we're escorting damaged ships home and likely getting new orders once we arrive. No point in letting rumors fill the gaps."

"What will you tell them?"

"That we're Republic Navy. We go where we're needed, fight what needs fighting, and trust our training to see us through." He wiped juice from his chin. "That we fought hard at Rass, accomplished our mission, and now we're making sure our wounded ships get home safely. And that whatever's waiting at New Eden, we'll handle it the same way we handled those orbital platforms. That we fight for humanity, for our families, for those we love, to keep them out of harm's way. We fight to free the galaxy from the subjugation it's under from evil slave owners hell-bent on ordering us around someday. Ultimately, that we fight for our freedom. For everyone's freedom."

Sato smiled. "That should work well."

"It had better. Because my instincts are telling me that whatever's coming is going to test everything we've learned about working together." Lee looked around the arboretum one more time, memorizing the peaceful scene. "Make sure all department heads understand we're maintaining full readiness protocols despite the escort duty. Whatever intelligence has planned, I want this crew ready for anything."

"Understood, sir."

Lee headed toward the exit, then paused. "One more thing, Noriko. Pull together a list of our most adaptable personnel. People who've shown they can handle unconventional operations and rapid mission changes. If they're splitting up this crew or forming new units, I want to know who I'd recommend for specialized assignments."

"Aye, sir. I'll have it by tomorrow as well."

As Lee walked back toward the exit, the artificial sunlight faded behind him. The peaceful arboretum represented everything worth fighting for, but his instincts remained on high alert.

Whatever waited at New Eden was significant enough to recall one of their most experienced ships from the largest offensive in Republic history. And deep in his core, Lee knew that by the time they left New Eden again, nothing would be the same.

Late 2098
Planet Rass

Love keyed her comm as Wolfpack Squadron held formation at seven thousand, six hundred meters, the four Ospreys flying through Rass's atmosphere. The air was getting thinner up here, but still thick enough for proper aerodynamics. Below them, the planet's surface spread out in browns and greens.

"Wolfpack Two, adjust bearing to two-six-three. You're drifting starboard," she transmitted, watching Lieutenant Manzel's transport correct course on her tactical display.

Green's voice crackled through her helmet from the copilot seat. "Wolfpack Three's running hot on their port engine. Temperature's climbing past redline."

"Copy that." Love switched to squadron frequency. "Wolfpack Three, monitor your port engine temps."

"Roger, Actual. We're seeing it too. Still within operational parameters."

High above them, barely visible as pinpricks of light against the star field, the space battle raged between Republic and Zodark fleets. Occasional flashes lit the upper atmosphere as ships died in the void. Love's long-range sensors tracked a Zodark satellite disintegrate under fire from a Primord cruiser, metal parts spinning away.

"Holy hell," Green muttered, pointing through the cockpit canopy. "Look at that."

A massive flash erupted far above them as a weapons platform burned against the blackness. Its structure cracked apart as explosions rippled through its hull. The thing had been gigantic, bristling with laser cannons. Now it was just another debris field.

A squadron of F-97 Orions streaked past their formation, chasing a flight of Zodark Vultures toward the planet's terminator line. The Vultures executed hard defensive breaks, trying to break contact, but the Orions stayed locked on their tails. Love watched the engagement unfold on her tactical display for the briefest of moments.

Eight Republic fighters against six enemy interceptors, the range closing fast.

"Orions are in the merge," Green observed. "Those Vultures are about to have a bad day."

The first Vulture exploded in a ball of plasma, its pilot's evasive maneuvers coming too late. The remaining five scattered, but the Orions pressed their advantage. Another enemy fighter died, then a third. The surviving Vultures dove for the atmosphere, seeking cover in the planet's defensive grid.

"Wolfpack Actual to all elements," Love transmitted, checking her chronometer. "Commence drop sequence in thirty seconds. Bravo Company, prepare for HALO insertion."

Through her rear camera feed, she could see the troops in *Jack*'s troop bay. Four platoons spread across four transports, ready to drop into hellfire. The soldiers she transported looked calm, though she doubted any of them felt that way. One guy's leg moved up and down, his comrade tapping it once to settle the man down. Nonetheless, all of these soldiers had done this before, but combat jumps always carried risk. Equipment failures, enemy fire, navigation errors. Any number of things could go wrong in the next few minutes.

Keep it simple. Execute the mission. Get everyone to the drop zone safely.

Green ran through the pre-drop checklist. "Cabin pressure equalized. Jump doors armed. Troop bay shows green across the board."

"Copy. Wolfpack Two, confirm your status."

"Two is green for drop. Bravo Company, Second Platoon ready."

"Wolfpack Three?"

"Three shows green. Third Platoon standing by." Lieutenant Hawthorne's voice carried a slight strain. His bird was still running hot but holding together.

"Wolfpack Four?"

"Four is green. Fourth Platoon ready for deployment."

Love watched her altimeter hold steady as the squadron maintained tight formation discipline. One-point-five kilometers below, the drop zone appeared clear on sensors. No enemy air activity, minimal ground signatures. Intelligence had been right about this sector. The Zodarks were concentrating their forces around the primary objectives, leaving the flanking approaches lightly defended.

"Ten seconds," she announced. "All elements, prepare for simultaneous drop."

Green monitored the troop bay cameras. "Soldiers are moving to jump positions. Chief Ford's got the doors ready."

"Thirty seconds to green light," Ford said over the internal comm.

And, finally, "Five seconds. Four. Three. Two. Mark."

Jack shuddered slightly as sixty-four Republic soldiers poured through the open bay doors, their black chutes invisible against the planet's surface. Love watched her tactical display track the deployment. Clean exits from all four transports, no equipment malfunctions, no missed jump windows.

"Clean drop, all personnel away," Ford reported over the comm link.

"All elements, drop complete," she said to all Wolfpack elements. "Form up for egress, heading zero-nine-zero back to fleet coordinates."

The mission's primary objective had been accomplished ahead of schedule, and damn it felt good.

One down. Now get everyone home.

Then Wolfpack Three began falling behind during the climb-out.

"Wolfpack Actual, Three experiencing hydraulic pressure loss and engine irregularities," Lieutenant Hawthorne reported. His voice carried more stress now, the kind that came with systems failing right before his eyes. "Request permission to reduce formation speed."

Love checked her tactical display. Three's airspeed was dropping, altitude variance increasing. The transport's icon showed multiple amber warnings across her screen. The transport was still flyable, but something was failing fast.

"Copy, Three. Reduce to best sustainable speed. We'll match your pace."

Green frowned at his instruments. "That bird's in trouble. Port engine's redlining, hydraulics showing amber across multiple systems."

Love calculated distances in her head. Seventeen kilometers to the fleet rendezvous point. Three's current rate of deterioration meant they might not make it without help.

"Wolfpack elements, reduce speed to match Three's capabilities. We're not leaving anyone behind."

Three's engine temperature spiked past critical as the formation climbed through eight thousand meters. Hawthorne's bird was bleeding hydraulic fluid, leaving a faint vapor trail.

"Wolfpack Three, maintain current heading while we assess your situation." Love throttled back to match Three's reduced airspeed. She pulled up Hawthorne's diagnostics on her tactical display. Yellow indicators rippled across the readout like cracks spreading through ice. "Command, Wolfpack Actual requesting immediate Orion fighter escort for damaged element. Grid coordinates four-three-alpha-niner-two-four-six."

"Affirmative, Wolfpack Actual. Jolly Rogers responding with four birds. Be advised ETA four-five seconds."

Love adjusted the formation's protective envelope around Three, positioning her remaining transports to shield the damaged bird from potential threats. She moved *Jack* into a covering position on Three's starboard side, with Two and Four taking port and high cover respectively. Green monitored the tactical display from his copilot seat, tracking incoming friendly contacts.

"Four Orions coming up fast from our six," he reported. "Bearing three-seven-nine, climbing at angels three-eight."

The Republic starfighters materialized out of the planet's glare. Love keyed the fighter frequency as they closed formation.

"Jolly Lead, Wolfpack Actual. We have a damaged transport requiring escort to fleet coordinates. Recommend high cover pattern at angels four-zero."

"Copy, Wolfpack. Jolly Lead has your formation. This is Raven. Moving to escort positions now."

The four F-97s spread into a protective diamond around the Ospreys, their pilots maintaining space while scanning for threats. Love's shoulder tension eased as the fighters took station. Each Orion carried enough firepower to handle a full squadron of enemy interceptors.

Professional backup. That's what we needed.

Three's hydraulic pressure dropped another ten percent.

"Wolfpack Actual," Hawthorne said. "Three showing multiple system failures. Port engine running rough, hydraulics failing, flight controls getting sluggish."

"Copy, Three. Maintain current heading. We're staying with you."

Love checked her fuel reserves. They had enough to reach the fleet, but not much margin for extended maneuvering. The damaged transport was slowing their egress, keeping them in contested airspace longer than planned.

The threat receiver in Love's helmet began chirping. It was a low, insistent tone meaning someone was painting them with targeting radar.

The threat display erupted in red contacts.

Six Zodark Vultures climbed out of the planet's shadow, their hulls black against the terminator line. They'd been waiting in the radar shadow, using the planet's bulk to mask their approach until the Republic formation was committed to its course and couldn't maneuver effectively.

Damn. They were hunting us.

"Raven, multiple bandits bearing zero-nine-zero, angels three-five and climbing fast," Love said, her pulse racing.

"Tally six Vultures. Jolly Flight engaging. Break left, break left!"

The Orions broke formation and dove toward the climbing Zodarks, their pilots calling out targets and weapon status. Energy weapons lanced across the sky as the fighters closed to engagement range. The Vultures spread into combat formation to avoid concentrated fire.

"All Wolfpack elements, evasive maneuvers. Maintain protective formation around Three."

Love threw *Jack* into a defensive barrel roll, keeping the damaged transport within her formation's defensive screen. The Osprey's engines whined as she pushed them past normal parameters, g-forces pressing her into her seat. The other Ospreys followed her lead, their pilots maintaining discipline regardless of the fighter engagement developing around them.

"Missile lock warning!" Green called out as his threat display lit up. "Vulture Three has tone on us!"

"Jolly Two, splash the bandit on the transports!" Love transmitted, pulling *Jack* into a hard defensive spiral.

The first Vulture died in a burst of orange flame as an Orion's missiles found their mark. The explosion lit up Love's cockpit for a brief moment before the debris scattered into the atmosphere. But the remaining five Zodarks pressed their attack, diving toward the slower transports.

"Jolly Three is hit! Jolly Three is hit!" The pilot's voice cracked over the frequency as his Orion took a laser bolt through its port engine and began trailing smoke. The damaged starfighter fell behind its wingman, leaving a gap in the defensive screen.

"Jolly Lead, we've got leakers," Green called out as two Vultures slipped through the fighter engagement.

On Love's tactical display, the enemy fighters committed to attack runs on the vulnerable transports. *Three can't maneuver. They're sitting ducks.*

The enemy fighters came in fast and low. Love pushed *Jack* into a split-S maneuver, trying to spoil the Zodarks' targeting solutions while keeping Three protected.

Hawthorne's transport couldn't match the maneuver. Three wallowed through the sky, its damaged systems preventing effective evasive action. Just then, the lead Vulture achieved weapon lock.

"Three, break right! Break right now!" she radioed to Hawthorne, knowing it was useless.

The lead Vulture fired.

A torpedo streaked across the gap between the fighters, its plasma warhead leaving a contrail. Seconds later, it struck Three's damaged port engine.

A bright flash consumed Wolfpack Three. The torpedo detonated the transport's fuel cells in a chain reaction, tearing the aircraft apart from the inside out. Debris tumbled through the sky where Hawthorne and his crew had been flying seconds before.

Love stared at the empty space on her tactical display where Three's icon had been. Lieutenant Hawthorne. Lieutenant Moore. Corporal Aquilar. Corporal Rose. Four crew members she'd flown with on several missions. Gone. Just like that.

Love swallowed, and swallowed again, deeply. Her heart hammered against her chest, but she forced her voice to remain steady. She couldn't think on it now, or feel a damn thing, not because she didn't want to but because she couldn't afford to put the rest of her squadron at risk.

"Command, Wolfpack Three is down. Continuing egress with remaining elements."

Two more Vultures broke through the Orion screen, diving toward the surviving transports. The dogfight scattered across ten kilometers of sky as Republic and Zodark fighters twisted through attack runs and defensive breaks.

"All Jolly elements," Love said, "priority protection on remaining transports. Do not let them through."

This battle had just shown its fangs, and Love knew they weren't out of hell yet.

Chapter 13:
Eight Minutes Out

Late 2098
Planet Rass

Ford operated the targeting console, tracking a Vulture that had broken through their defensive screen. The enemy fighter banked hard left, trying to line up another attack run on the formation. Ford squeezed the trigger, sending a stream of magrail rounds toward the Zodark craft.

The shots went wide, but close enough to force the pilot into a defensive spiral. *Good enough.* Sometimes making the enemy jink was better than hitting them clean.

On the tactical holo, Jolly Rogers Three had a bandit on his six. Another Vulture was closing in on one of their escort fighters.

The Orion drone operator pulled into a vertical climb that would have crushed a human pilot. The F-97's advantage showed in moments like this. No meat in the cockpit meant extreme g-force tolerances. The Vulture followed, trying to maintain weapons lock, but the Orion suddenly reversed direction in a maneuver defying normal flight parameters.

The Zodark fighter couldn't match the turn. 20mm magrail rounds from the Orion's guns tore through the Vulture's port wing, sending it tumbling toward the planet in a death spiral.

Three down.

Jack veered sharply as Love threw them into evasive maneuvers. Another Vulture had achieved a lock on their transport. Its targeting system tracked their hull signature. Ford swiveled his gun mount, trying to acquire the threat, but the enemy fighter stayed in their blind spot.

"Where is he?" Torres shouted over the comm.

"High and behind," Ford replied, adjusting his targeting display. "Can't get a clean shot. No worries. Stay calm, man," he added. "Let Love do her thing."

Love rolled the Osprey hard to starboard, using a cloud bank for concealment. The Vulture overshot, giving Ford a brief window. He opened fire, walking his shots across the enemy's flight path. The

Zodark pilot broke off, diving toward the planet's defensive grid rather than press the attack.

The remaining Vultures followed suit, their formation scattered and bloodied. They'd lost half their number to the Orion escort, and the survivors weren't eager to continue the engagement.

"All clear on sensors, Chief," Torres reported, his voice carrying a bit of a tremor, perhaps from watching Wolfpack Three die in front of them.

Ford nodded, running his eyes across the threat display. It was empty of red contacts, but the damage was done. Four good people had been reduced to ash and vapor in the space of a heartbeat.

That's the job, Ford thought. He hated it with every ounce of his being, but he had to deal with it to save humanity, and whatever else they were saving out there.

"How far to the *Gallipoli*?" Torres asked, tapping his navigation console. "My display's showing garbage data."

"Probably interference from all that weapons fire," Ford said, checking his own instruments, cross-referencing their position with the fleet coordinates Love had programmed into their flight computer. "Eight minutes at current speed," he added, noting how the formation had tightened up after the engagement.

Torres was asking the right questions, too, staying focused on his duties instead of replaying the Osprey's explosion in his head. Ford had seen plenty of gunners freeze up after real combat. Torres was made of sterner stuff.

"You did good back there," Ford told him. "Kept your head when it mattered."

"Thanks, Chief."

The Orion fighters maintained escort formation as they climbed through the upper atmosphere. Down below, Ford hoped the Republic ground forces were establishing their beachheads according to plan. Bravo Company and the other units were probably knee-deep in their own fights by now.

But individual losses like Wolfpack Three reminded everyone, especially Ford, that war collected its debts. Always had, always would.

"Chief," Love's voice came through the comm. "Run a full systems check. I want to know if we took any damage during those maneuvers."

Ford was already halfway through the diagnostic. Stress indicators showed minor fluctuations in the port engine housing, probably from the sharp banking they'd done to avoid that last Vulture. Fuel levels were lower than he'd like, but still within acceptable parameters for their return flight.

"Minor stress on the port engine mount," he reported. "Nothing critical. Fuel's at sixty-three percent."

"Copy that."

Love's tone held that particular pitch Ford had heard before. The sound of a pilot building walls around the emotional impact of losing people under her command. She'd compartmentalize everything until the mission was complete, much like she'd done with the loss of her husband, Jack, burying grief so deep it might never surface again. Smart move for staying operational, but he always worried it would come at a price.

On the other hand, Ford had seen pilots crack weeks after seemingly handling combat losses just fine, even years after they'd seemed like the Tin Man—emotionally armored, heartless by necessity. The human mind had its own timeline for processing trauma, and it didn't always align with operational schedules.

Something to watch for, he mused.

"*Gallipoli* coming up on comms," Torres reported. "Signal's getting stronger."

Ford glanced at the tactical holo one more time. Clear skies in the immediate area, but the real gauntlet waited above them. The space battle still raged in orbit, with Republic and Zodark fleets trading fire in combat between capital ships and starfighters. They'd have to thread their way through that mess of debris fields and weapons fire before reaching the *Gallipoli*.

Almost home. Still got to survive the ride up.

Chapter 14:
Danger Close

Late 2098
Planet Rass

Forty-five hours had passed since boots had hit dirt. By this time, Coop's voice might as well have been gravel. His throat was raw from shouting coordinates over gunfire that never stopped. The first twelve hours had consisted of learning to stay alive under constant fire. Hour twenty-four had brought rhythm. Hour thirty-six had nearly broken them when three Zodark companies hit simultaneously before orbital strikes turned aliens into smoking craters and steaming piles of blue beasts.

Now the war ground on. Fire missions came in steady streams. Close-air support. Naval gunfire. Artillery from the orbital platforms. Li's sensor array showed enemy contacts that multiplied faster than they could kill them, and Crawford's tablet showed target data that refreshed every few seconds with new threats.

Their defensive perimeter looked like the moon. Craters. Shattered trees. Burned earth where energy weapons had charred soil so hot it turned into glass. Zodark assault waves kept coming and Alpha Company kept killing them with well-placed fire support.

Crawford called Coop "Maestro" between missions. The nickname had stuck. But forty-five hours of continuous combat was breaking everyone down. Ammunition reserves dropped, soldiers collapsed from exhaustion, and the enemy showed no signs of stopping.

Weber would've handled the comm load better, Coop thought as another fire mission request crackled through his headset. *Now we're doing his job and ours. But we're still here. Still alive.*

Forty-six hours after insertion, there was still no letup.

"TASC One-Six, complex target. Need simultaneous engagement," Lieutenant Gill transmitted.

Coop studied his display. Three enemy formations moving to flank Alpha Company from different directions. It was a hell of a pincer attack. This required time-on-target coordination, multiple platforms striking within seconds of each other to prevent the enemy from taking cover between impacts.

"Copy, Alpha Six. I see all three formations. Setting up time-on-target."

Coop opened channels to three fire support assets: the RNS *Duncan* in high orbit, Republic artillery battery twelve klicks northeast, and an AS-90 Reaper flight circling overhead. Coordinating three different platforms with varying flight times pushed his skills to the breaking point.

"*Duncan*, TASC One-Six. Time-on-target mission. Grid three-five-seven-four-one-nine, enemy armor formation, fifteen-second delay from my mark."

"TASC One-Six, *Duncan* copies. Grid three-five-seven-four-one-nine, fifteen-second delay. Standing by."

Crawford worked his tablet despite hands that shook from stimulant overdose. "Artillery needs twenty-two seconds flight time. Reapers need eight."

"Copy." Coop keyed his radio. "Steel Rain Six, TASC One-Six. Grid three-five-seven-four-two-one, enemy infantry in the open, twenty-two-second delay from my mark."

"Steel Rain Six copies. Twenty-two-second delay. Ready to fire."

"Reaper One-Four, TASC One-Six. Grid three-five-seven-four-one-five, enemy command post, eight-second delay from my mark."

"Reaper One-Four copies. Eight-second delay. Weapons hot."

Coop checked his chronometer. This needed to work and his math, his team's math, needed to be on point. There were three different weapon systems, three different flight times, and one devastating impact window.

"All stations, TASC One-Six. Time-on-target in five… four… three… two… mark!"

Naval railgun rounds screamed down from orbit. Artillery shells arced through atmosphere. Reaper missiles streaked toward targets. The strikes hit within a four-second window, and the forest erupted, the ground shaking hard enough to rattle every damn rock from here to planet Intus.

"Outstanding work, Maestro," Crawford said.

The Zodarks had been tracking their transmissions. They had to be, because counterbattery fire started thirty seconds later. Enemy artillery rounds moved steadily toward Alpha Company's positions, each salvo closer than the last.

Li's sensor array lit up with incoming trajectory warnings, red tracks arcing toward their position. "Counterbattery fire! Multiple rounds inbound!"

Coop's display showed the artillery rounds' calculated impact points. Walking straight toward their foxholes. Thirty seconds out.

"Incoming!" he screamed into his comm.

Coop grabbed his radio gear and ran. Exploding trees threw burning fragments in every direction. The rapid displacement shattered their communication links. His TASC team scattered across the forest floor.

Li's sensor array sparked and died. Near misses showered them with dirt and metal fragments hot enough to melt skin. Crawford worked frantically to reestablish data links while Coop set up behind a cluster of boulders offering minimal protection.

"RNS *Duncan*, TASC One-Six. Repositioning due to counterbattery fire. Stand by for new coordinates."

This is why losing Weber hurts so much, Coop thought as another artillery round impacted nearby. *Good soldiers are irreplaceable.*

Forty-seven hours in, and a Zodark artillery round hit thirty meters away. The shock wave punched through Coop's chest armor. When the smoke cleared, Crawford was down, his right shoulder and upper chest peppered with burning debris.

Crawford gritted his teeth and tried to keep working his tablet left-handed. "I'm fine. I'm fine." His face had gone pale and perspiration beaded on his forehead.

"You're not fine." Coop crawled to Crawford's position even as another fire mission request came through his earpiece. "Li, get over here!"

"Can't move the array! Still trying to bring it online!"

Crawford grabbed Coop's wrist with his good hand. Blood seeped between his fingers, but his grip stayed firm. "Listen to me, Maestro. You're thinking like a TASC officer now, not a drone pilot. Trust your instincts."

Coop applied pressure to the worst wounds while simultaneously calling in danger-close artillery against the enemy battery. His hands worked the radio while his eyes assessed Crawford's injuries.

"Steel Rain Six, TASC One-Six. Fire mission. Grid four-eight-two-three-four-seven, enemy artillery position, fire for effect."

"TASC One-Six, Steel Rain Six. That grid is within four hundred meters of your position. Confirm danger-close."

"Confirmed danger-close. We're taking effective fire from that position. Request immediate suppression."

Crawford's voice dropped to a whisper as Coop wrapped field dressings around his shoulder, a grin spreading across his face. "Weber would be proud. You're a machine out here."

"Steel Rain Six, shot over."

"Shot out," Coop replied while continuing to check Crawford's wounds.

Artillery rounds shrieked overhead. Coop pressed his face into the dirt as the barrage hammered through the enemy position. Each impact sent tremors through the ground, and when the firing stopped, silence felt wrong.

"Steel Rain Six, TASC One-Six. Assess."

"TASC One-Six, target destroyed. Good shooting."

Crawford managed a weak thumbs-up. Blood had soaked through field dressings but his breathing stayed steady. Li finally got her sensor array functioning again, the damaged screen flickering with intermittent contacts.

"Multiple contacts," Li reported. "Two klicks northeast. They're regrouping."

Hour forty-eight and Coop's hands wouldn't stop shaking. Stimulant pills weren't helping anymore. They just made his heart race while his body begged him for sleep he couldn't give it. Two days without rest, two days of calling death from above while watching good people die.

Zodark assault troops broke through Third Platoon's perimeter at 0347 hours.

Private Fitz saw them first. Blue-skinned aliens moving through the tree line. He squeezed his trigger and watched rounds tear through alien armor. More kept coming.

"Contact left! Contact left!" Fitz screamed into his comm before a Zodark plasma rifle vaporized his head.

The breach widened. Zodark shock troops poured through the gap. Coop watched his tactical display light up with red contacts inside their defensive perimeter. For the first time in forty-eight hours, the enemy really was among them.

Sergeant Vega appeared beside his position without sound. Her sniper rifle hung across her back, her face streaked with camouflage paint and blood that wasn't hers. She pressed a ration pack into his trembling hands.

"Eat something."

How does she stay so calm? Coop stared at the ration pack, not able to remember his last meal, and couldn't remember anything except coordinates and fire commands and the endless cycle of explosions.

"Vega." Coop's voice cracked. "They're inside the wire."

She looked at his tactical display and studied the red contacts moving through Alpha Company's positions. "Yeah. They are." She unslung her rifle and checked the scope. "Time to blow some heads apart. Don't stare at me. Do what I say. Take a bite to eat."

"OK."

Vega studied his face. "You're running on fumes."

"We all are."

She nodded once. "In combat, pace yourself. Including your nerves." She tapped the side of his helmet like a coach encouraging a player. The casual gesture felt surreal in a place where death waited around every corner.

She almost smiled. "Your great-grandfather's journal. Remember, when you get back on your ship, and we succeed in this mission, you can go back and open it up and read it. Keep that in mind. A goal of sorts to stay alive, all right?"

Coop's ears had been ringing for hours. He just noticed it now. "What do you know about the journal?"

"We talked about it on the Osprey."

"Right." He didn't remember. Combat did strange things to memory.

Li's voice cut through the position. "Contact! Multiple vehicles heading our way!"

Coop reached for his backup radio to call Weber for communication support. His hand closed on empty air. The sick feeling hit again. That moment of forgetting followed by brutal reminder that

Corporal Weber was gone. The communications specialist's death felt both like yesterday and a lifetime past.

Weber should have been monitoring backup frequencies—he should have been making dumb remarks about their survival odds. Instead, Li was handling sensor operations and communications, all the while Crawford worked his tablet one-handed with blood seeping through bandages.

Li's patched sensor array sparked and went dark. She slammed her fist against the side of the unit. The screen stayed black. "Lost everything. Flying blind."

The enemy assault hit at the forty-eight-hour mark. Two companies of Zodarks closed in, supported by Orbot shock troops and mobile artillery. Coop's fire support network reached its breaking point. Multiple platoons called for simultaneous fire missions. He sent nearly their entire ammunition allocation downrange in concentrated barrages.

His voice gave out completely during the final fire mission. Words came out as croaks. His throat was so damaged that speaking became torture. Just then, Li's sensor array finally died with a shower of sparks. They were now truly blind just as the enemy assault peaked.

Lieutenant Gill's voice burst through the comm line. "All stations, prepare final protective fires. Danger-close. Real danger-close."

They were calling artillery almost on their own positions. It was a last desperate measure. Fire support was so close that survival was a coin flip. As Coop transmitted coordinates for the danger-close barrage, he thought about Bear's challenge coin in his pocket and Weber's empty radio position.

The incoming artillery would either save Alpha Company or kill them all. There was no middle ground left.

The first rounds hit two hundred meters out—close enough to scramble his inner ear and blur his vision. Broken metal whined overhead while the barrage destroyed the Zodark assault force. Coop hugged the bottom of his fighting position and let the earth absorb each impact.

When the explosions stopped, the silence felt unnatural. No more plasma fire. No more Zodark war cries. Just ringing ears and the smell of cordite.

"Alpha Six, TASC One-Six. Assess," Coop croaked into his radio.

"TASC One-Six, assault has been repelled. Enemy forces withdrawing. Good shooting."

They'd survived. Barely.

At hour forty-nine, there was a brief lull in combat as enemy forces pulled back to regroup. Alpha Company finally had a moment to breathe. Coop found himself alone in a foxhole, surrounded by debris from two days of continuous combat. Empty ammunition containers. Torn equipment. The lingering smell of explosives.

Twenty-seven Republic soldiers in Alpha Company had died in the last four hours. Coop knew because he'd watched the red Xs denoting their life signs disappear from his tactical display one by one.

His hands still trembled as he imagined pulling out Presley Paul Cooper's journal the way he usually did after a stressful day. The old pilot had flown P-51 Mustangs in World War II. Had kept detailed entries about aerial combat over Europe, and Coop had grown up reading those faded pages, learning about the strange mixture of terror and exhilaration that defined combat.

Coop also imagined uncapping a pen and staring at a blank page still left in the journal. The old pilot had sometimes ended his journal entries with reflections on fallen comrades, and he wanted to do the same. He couldn't at the moment, but he could pretend so that when he got back to the ship, he could remember to write: "Weber made terrible coffee but perfect radio calls. His voice was the last thing dying men heard before their salvation arrived. Some wars never change. Different weapons, same grief. Good soldiers still die first."

He looked up at the alien stars. The war would continue tomorrow. Tonight, for just a moment, he could remember why he fought.

Chapter 15:
Task Force 27

Late 2098
Victory Base Complex
Emerald City, New Eden

The shuttle's engines wound down as Lee stepped onto the tarmac at Victory Base Complex. New Eden's gravity settled into his body. It was just a fraction stronger than Earth's. Sato emerged behind him, surveying the sprawling military installation.

"Bigger than last time," she observed, shielding her eyes against the sun's rays. "They've been busy."

Lee nodded, watching construction vehicles move across the distant ridgeline. The base had doubled in size since his last visit a few years ago.

"The Republic builds some things to last, and this is one of them," he said. "We're not planning to leave or planning to lose any invasion here. We're here for the long haul. And I'm glad for it."

This planet was gorgeous. New Eden reminded him of Earth, abundant in the same vital resources, though even to his untrained eye, it seemed to possess a slightly richer concentration of valuable materials.

They walked past open hangar bays. Inside, maintenance crews worked on F-97 Orions and heavy bomber drones, Bobcats and other military ground vehicles. The whir of hydraulic lifts, the sharp crack of tools at work, and the shouted orders of crew chiefs directing their teams filled the air. Technicians in grease-stained coveralls walked between aircraft, performing whatever orders they'd been given. It was good to breathe planetside again, even on a tarmac smelling of propellant fluids.

Lee had been here before. He liked this place. New Eden was humanity's first ever conquered planet. Not given to them, per se, but something they'd earned the hard way, through the grit of war. They'd rid this world of slave drivers and killers, bringing a much better civilization here—one that would take much better care of this world, and hopefully, the people on it.

"Sir," Sato said as they approached the main complex, "any idea what this is about yet? If so, would love even something little coming my way. A clue…"

They'd discussed possibilities before, but Sato was fishing for any information he might have received during the handful of hours they'd been apart on *Poseidon*. Anything that came his way before they boarded the shuttle to New Eden.

"None." Lee studied the towering structure ahead of them. "But pulling *Poseidon* out of active combat for a meeting on New Eden? That's not standard procedure."

Yes, they'd also spoken on this, too, but it still crowded Lee's head. Sato's as well. He shook off the thought and continued walking onward.

The most striking feature of Victory Base Complex rose before them, a massive command center dominating the landscape. Unlike the temporary prefab structures scattered across most forward operating bases, this was a permanent installation. Republic engineers had built it to last, with reinforced walls and integrated defense systems that could withstand sustained bombardment.

Lee studied the imposing structure as they approached. The command center represented the Republic's commitment to holding New Eden, a statement in steel and stone that they weren't going anywhere.

"Impressive every time," Sato observed.

"It is," Lee agreed. "But whoever we're meeting chose to do it in there instead of the standard admin building. That tells us something."

As they walked on toward the structure, squads of soldiers marched in formation across the compound. The drone of idling engines filled the air as transport craft lined the parking ramps, ready for deployment when needed. On the ridge overlooking the base, construction crews worked alongside artillery pieces providing overwatch protection.

During his shuttle descent, through the viewports, several cities rose in the distance. Steel towers were everywhere. The speed of human expansion never ceased to amaze him. Give them a habitable world and they'd have a functioning civilization within four years, maybe less.

When they approached the main entrance, two Marine guards flanked the doorway, their rifles held at port arms.

"Commander Lee and Lieutenant Commander Sato," Lee announced, producing his credentials.

The senior guard, a staff sergeant with campaign ribbons from two different theaters, examined their identification. "Yes, sir. You're expected." He handed back their IDs and gestured to a corporal waiting inside. "Corporal O'Toole will escort you."

Inside, the corridors curved subtly. Their escort led them through a maze of passages that had been retrofitted with Republic communication lines and security systems.

"Commander Lee," Corporal O'Toole said as they approached a junction, "Admiral Costello asked that Lieutenant Commander Sato wait in the briefing room while you proceed to his office first."

Sato caught Lee's eye. "I'll be fine, sir. Go see what the brass wants."

Lee continued down the corridor alone. He found himself before another office, star charts of the New Eden star system lining one of the walls. Rear Admiral Scott Costello rose from behind his desk as Lee entered, twin stars on his collar.

"Commander Lee, good to see you," Costello said. "Congratulations on what you did at the Rass operation. Outstanding work."

"How's it going there, sir?"

"The Rass invasion? Very well. You are one of the reasons." And that was all the information he gave to Lee on one of the biggest operations humanity had ever conducted. To say the least, it didn't quench Lee's thirst for more info. But he wouldn't press.

"Thank you, sir." Lee noticed that the man looked tired. "And congratulations on your second star. Well deserved."

Costello's smile tightened around the edges. "Thank you, but I hope I'm not being set up to fail either."

The comment floated like smoke from a damaged console. "What do you mean by that, sir?"

Costello gestured for Lee to sit, then settled behind his desk. "Sometimes, you get promoted not because you did a good job but because no one else wants to do the job you're being promoted into."

Lee studied the admiral's face. Career officers learned to read between the lines of official statements, and Costello was speaking in code. "Are you by chance referring to the Republic's new naval shipyard?"

Costello nodded, his fingers tapping once against the desk. "Between the Moon and Mars. Closer to the asteroid belts and the minerals we need. It's a necessary move, and I fully agree with it. I'm just unsure if I'm the right person to lead it. But this is why they gave me the second star. More responsibility for a huge and daunting task."

The scope of the project came into focus. "How big are we talking?"

"Around one hundred shipyard slips, with another thirty closed dry-dock facilities. Pressurized environments where ship components get built and finished, then moved to open slips in vacuum for final assembly." Costello pulled up a holographic display showing the construction plans. "Take a look at this, if you don't mind. As you can see, we've made good progress on the refineries and factories needed to support it. The Altairians have been instrumental in that effort."

Lee leaned forward, studying the schematics. The scale was staggering. A facility that could triple Republic shipbuilding capacity within two years. "Sounds like they picked the right person for the job."

"You think so?" Costello's tone carried genuine uncertainty.

"I felt the same way when they promoted me to commander and gave me *Poseidon*. Thought they'd made a mistake." He paused, remembering those first weeks of doubt. "Then I read something in Viceroy Hunt's book—*Burden of Command*. He wrote that sometimes we get placed in positions of great importance not because we feel ready, but because those in command see something within us that maybe we don't."

Costello's attention sharpened.

"Hunt said that's part of being a commander," Lee continued. "The burden of seeing in people what they sometimes fail to see in themselves, then giving them the opportunity to grow into the officer you always knew they could become. Being a commander is about mentoring junior officers, identifying your own replacement, having the self-awareness to know you're not an island but an archipelago."

The admiral's eyebrows rose slightly.

"Hunt wrote there are no bad leaders, just bad mentors who failed to lead and be the change they wanted to see. You accept responsibility not just for your actions, but for the actions of those you lead."

Costello looked at Lee quietly for a long moment. Slowly, he nodded. "Lee, you're a very astute observer—that's why I'm recommending you for this promotion and new assignment." He leaned back in his chair. "Between us, I think this is going to be a long war, and we're going to need officers like you if we're going to see it through to victory."

"I appreciate that, sir. You're probably right about the long haul. The Zodarks haven't shown any interest in backing down. But keep the yards producing, and we'll send them all to hell."

Costello gave a nod. "I'll hold you to that, Commander." His expression shifted to business. "Which brings me to why you're really here. We're forming a new task force... Task Force 27, 'Frontier.' Eight ships initially, with the possibility of expansion based on mission requirements."

He activated a holographic display materializing above his desk. Ship profiles rotated in blue light. Frigates. Cruisers. Heavy cruisers. And a carrier. Lee studied the configurations, noting the mix of vessel types. This wasn't a standard patrol formation. The heavy cruiser presence meant serious firepower, but the frigate complement showed speed and flexibility.

"Your experience with hybrid human-Altairian technology and unconventional operations makes you an ideal candidate for command," Costello said.

Command. Not assignment. Not participation. Command.

Lee kept his expression impassive while his mind processed as fast as it could. Eight ships. Potentially more. Thousands of crew members across multiple vessels. Synths. Ospreys. Fighters, both ground and air. Maybe even Delta operatives inside that carrier. What the heck mission would this be for?

"What's the mission scope, Admiral?"

"Deep special operations beyond the current front lines. Missions that require both tactical flexibility and absolute operational security. The kind of work that can't be accomplished through standard fleet actions."

Lee leaned forward a little. That was a lot of words that didn't mean much if one didn't know what the heck the admiral was talking about, and Lee didn't know what the heck the admiral was talking about. Still, Lee tried to quickly decipher it.

The Zodark front stretched across dozens of star systems, but "beyond the current front lines" implied penetration into enemy-held space, perhaps. Deep reconnaissance. No. There was a carrier with his task force. Sabotage. Maybe. A clandestine mission? Or, perhaps, strategic strikes against high-value targets, but with the carrier, they could be supporting an ally to help defend or invade a moon or a planet. And who knew how many more ships, let alone carriers, would be added to his task force when the time came to fly into the great dark expanse.

"Command of a task force requires different thinking than single-ship operations, as you know, and as you've done on a few occasions and successfully, I might add," Costello said. "Your Academy records show exceptional leadership scores, and your recent performance coordinating multiple vessels during the Rass operation and throughout a handful of other operations surely demonstrates captain-level tactical thinking."

Lee swallowed down his surprise. Was he getting a promotion from commander to captain? Lee had commanded battle group elements before, but always as a temporary assignment. This sounded permanent. Career-defining. But in war, how permanent was anything, really?

"I appreciate the confidence, Admiral, but I should point out that much of our recent success stems from exceptional crew performance. My XO, Lieutenant Commander Sato, has been instrumental in our tactical coordination."

Costello nodded, making notes on his tablet. "That brings us to personnel assignments. Task force command typically requires specialized staff officers and expanded communications capabilities. Your current crew has performed admirably, but deep space operations may necessitate different skill sets."

The carefully neutral phrasing didn't hide the changes that flashed in Lee's mind. It simply meant that Lee's people might not be coming with him. Or some of them. Or most of them.

Stop assuming, Lee, he barked at himself.

Still, the thought hit like a plasma torpedo to his solar plexus. Sato, who could read his tactical intentions before he voiced them. MacGregor, who could coax performance from damaged systems that should have failed hours ago. Rodriguez, whose damage control teams had saved the ship at Rass. These weren't just subordinates. No—they were the team that had kept him alive through impossible situations.

"Sir, with respect, my crew's adaptability and experience with unconventional operations might be exactly what a deep space mission requires. They've proven capable of handling hybrid technology and multispecies coordination under combat conditions."

Lee knew he was advocating for his people, but couldn't bring himself to care about protocol. Command meant nothing if it came at the cost of abandoning the officers who'd earned his trust through shared combat.

Costello looked him over. Outside the office windows, construction teams continued their work on the expanding base. The sound of welding torches filtered through the walls.

"Your points about crew cohesion are noted, Commander. However, the final task force composition will depend on mission parameters that are still being classified at the highest levels." He stood, signaling the meeting's conclusion. "You'll receive detailed briefings over the next forty-eight hours as other commanders arrive."

Other commanders. Lee wondered who else had been recalled from active duty for this assignment. How important was this? The obvious answer: highly. He just wished he knew exactly what they were throwing him into. This vagueness was part of the job.

As Lee prepared to leave, Costello added one final comment. "This mission carries significant risk, Commander, but also significant opportunity. Lee, there are maybe a dozen officers in the fleet getting opportunities like this. What you do with it determines whether you join the ranks of senior command or remain where you are. Don't waste it." For a moment, he stared into Lee's eyes. "That will be all. Go get some rest, Commander."

So, not a promotion, but maybe after this, they'll raise me to captain, Lee thought.

He stood and saluted. "Understood, Admiral."

Leadership always extracted its toll, and Lee suspected he'd soon discover what currency it would demand from him.

Chapter 16:
Running on Empty

Late 2098
Planet Rass

Hour sixty-four of the conflict had brought the news Coop had been dreading. "TASC One-Six, Steel Rain Six. We're at twenty percent on precision rounds. Request ammunition conservation protocols." The artillery battery's report confirmed what Crawford's tablet had been showing for the last four hours—red indicators across every munitions category, naval gunfire down to basic kinetic rounds, and close-air support limited to gun runs only. The guided munitions that had kept Alpha Company alive were running out faster than supply drops could replenish them.

Coop stared at his tactical display showing enemy formations massing two kilometers northeast. Without smart rounds, they'd have to rely on area bombardment and pray the blast radius estimations were perfect. No more surgical strikes. No more danger-close missions with confidence intervals measured in meters.

Lieutenant Gill's voice crackled through the comm: "All stations, ammunition status critical. Make every shot count."

How the hell did we burn through so much ordnance? Three days of constant contact, and we're back to throwing rocks.

The reality hit like a Zodark blaster round shot through his eye and out the back of the head. The stress gave him a pounding headache and made his brain feel like it was cooking inside his skull. They were about to fight the biggest battle yet with the least firepower.

Alpha Company held a defensive position along Ridge 248, a natural chokepoint overlooking the Zex'ler Valley approach. The ridge gave commanding views of three separate avenues the enemy could use to advance on the Republic landing zones twelve kilometers south. Gill had positioned his squads to create cross-fire coverage, with heavy weapons teams covering the most likely attack routes. Dense forest stretched for kilometers in every direction with a handful of winding valley floors where Zodark forces had been probing their defenses for the last two days.

"*Duncan*, what's your status on orbital kinetics?" Coop transmitted while Crawford worked his backup tablet with growing frustration. The naval fire control officer's response was discouraging: "TASC One-Six, we've got tungsten rods and basic HE. No guidance packages."

Basic high explosives. It was worse than he thought. They needed resupply immediately.

Coop studied the terrain display, estimating impact zones for unguided projectiles. Dumb rounds meant bigger safety margins and lower accuracy. What used to require one carefully placed shot now needed three or four general area impacts.

Li's rebuilt sensor array crackled with intermittent contacts as she fought to maintain target acquisition through increasing electronic interference. "Multiple formations converging from the north. I count at least sixty vehicles." She'd been operating damaged equipment for three straight days, and the strain in her voice showed it.

Coop grabbed his radio and started coordinating what assets remained: artillery with basic shells, naval kinetics without terminal guidance, and close-air support limited to strafing runs.

Crawford nodded grimly from his position. "Work with what you've got. Make the enemy come to you through the kill zones."

The forest canopy above them rustled as another flight of Reapers passed overhead, their engines barely audible. Coop counted four fighters—half the number they'd had yesterday. Attrition was eating away at every asset in the theater. Even the ships in orbit were rationing their tungsten rod ammunition.

Crawford's tablet chimed with an incoming update. "Steel Rain reports barrel wear exceeding safety margins. They're requesting a firing pause for maintenance." Another piece of the fire support puzzle was falling apart. Coop marked the artillery battery as temporarily unavailable and reconfigured his coverage zones.

The breakthrough came at 0445 hours on the northern perimeter. Third Platoon's desperate transmission cut through the comm net: "Alpha Six, Third Platoon. We've got multiple breaches. Zodarks are through the wire in company strength. Request immediate support."

Coop's display illuminated with red contacts pouring through gaps in their defensive line. What had been a controlled engagement suddenly became a rout as enemy forces exploited the ammunition shortage. The careful defensive positions Gill had established were collapsing under sustained assault.

"All available fires, immediate suppression, grid four-two-three-seven-one-eight!" Coop shouted into his radio while watching the tactical situation deteriorate. But even as tungsten rounds hammered the breach point, more enemy formations were moving to exploit the success. Li's sensors showed the true scope of the disaster: two full Zodark battalions supported by Orbot troops, all converging on the gap Third Platoon couldn't hold.

The Orbots were the worst part. Their biomechanical forms could absorb damage that would drop a human soldier instantly. Coop had watched them shrug off direct hits from rifle rounds and keep advancing. Head shots were the best option on those cyborgs.

Lieutenant Gill's voice burst through the comm link: "TASC, we need everything you've got right now, or we're going to lose the entire ridge."

Coop opened channels to every fire support asset in the grid square. "All stations, all stations, this is TASC One-Six. Coordinated time-on-target, danger-close. Multiple grids, simultaneous impact." He rattled off six different target areas, each one requiring different assets and exact timing despite equipment failures and ammunition shortages.

Crawford manipulated his backup systems, sweat dripping from his chin as he worked firing solutions with damaged computers. Without connections to their destroyed fire control network, he had to calculate trajectory and timing manually. It was work their primary systems had done automatically in milliseconds.

The coordination took everything they had learned in three days of continuous combat. Naval kinetics from high orbit. Artillery firing at maximum rate despite overheated barrels. Every available *Reaper* in the air space converging on the breakthrough. "All stations, time-on-target in ten seconds. Mark when ready."

Coop held his breath as the different platforms reported ready. This had to work perfectly, or Alpha Company would be overrun within the hour. Li's sensors showed enemy forces less than two hundred meters from Third Platoon's fallback positions. Crawford's tablet displayed firing solutions that pushed every safety margin to the breaking point.

"Five... four... three... two... mark!"

The forest erupted in the largest bombardment of the campaign as every available weapon system fired simultaneously.

The forest disappeared.

Coop watched through his tactical display as many different weapon systems converged on grid square 4-2-3-7-1-8 at nearly the same time. Naval tungsten rods screamed down from orbit like silver lightning, each one carrying the kinetic energy of a freight train. Artillery shells arced through the morning sky in perfect curves while four Reapers dove from different vectors, their guns already spitting streams of magnetic hellfire.

The impact lasted four seconds.

Trees that had stood for centuries vaporized in the tungsten strikes. Artillery rounds walked across enemy formations in explosion after explosion. The Reapers' strafing runs burned lines through Zodark vehicles that attempted to retreat. Coop counted eighteen separate eruptions blooming across the breakthrough zone.

Through his binoculars, he watched a Zodark heavy vehicle turn into flames as rounds punched through its armored hull. The machine toppled into a burning grove, crushing the infantry squad that had been using it for cover. Orbot troops scattered from the bombardment, but even they couldn't outrun coordinated fires from multiple Republic platforms.

The forest floor erupted in fountains of dirt. Zodark war cries died in the killing ground those bastards thought to exploit. Coop's display showed red contacts winking out one by one as the bombardment found its targets.

When the guns fell silent, smoke rose from what had been dense woodland thirty seconds earlier. Twisted metal marked where Zodark vehicles had burned. Craters pocked the earth where tungsten rods had struck. The breakthrough zone looked like the surface of a dead moon. But Li's sensors were already noting new contacts.

"Multiple formations, northeast quadrant. They're coming through the Veth'var Pass." Her voice held the exhaustion they all felt, but the situation demanded immediate attention. More enemy forces were moving to exploit different approaches, learning from the destruction of their advance elements.

Coop studied the sensor data flowing across his holodisplay. Six new formations, each one probing a different avenue of approach. The

Zodarks were adapting. "Crawford, what's our ammunition status after that strike?"

Crawford's backup tablet flickered as he pulled up the latest reports. "Artillery's down to basic rounds only. Naval kinetics are at fifteen percent. The Reapers are Winchester on missiles." Winchester meant empty. No guided munitions left. Not until resupply arrived.

The forest that remained stood in patches between smoking craters. Steam rose from shattered trees where sap boiled from weapon impacts. Alien blood mixed with human ordnance residue, creating chemical reactions staining the ground in colors that didn't exist in nature.

Li's array displayed enemy forces flowing around the destroyed breakthrough zone. They'd learned that direct assault invited coordinated fires, so now they were testing multiple approaches simultaneously.

"TASC One-Six, Steel Rain Six." The voice of the artilleryman betrayed that he was about to share bad news. "We're experiencing barrel stress fractures on tubes two and four. Requesting maintenance stand-down."

Coop marked two more artillery pieces as unavailable. The sustained firing rate was destroying their equipment and fast. "Copy, Steel Rain. What's your operational status?"

"Four tubes available, basic rounds only. Estimated barrel life thirty rounds per tube."

One hundred twenty shells against formations that Crawford's tablet showed numbering in the hundreds. It all seemed so bleak, but such was war.

Crawford's main tactical computer chose that moment to die. Sparks erupted from the display housing, followed by the terrible scent of burning electronics. Blue smoke poured from ventilation ports as the system's cooling fans spun down with death rattles.

"Primary systems are down," Crawford reported, his wounded shoulder making the transition to backup equipment even more awkward. The backup tablet's screen was a quarter the size of his main display, forcing him to scroll through data that had been instantly accessible moments before. Critical information that should have been visible at a glance now required multiple menu selections.

Li's sensor array blinked off and on between contacts and static interference. "I'm getting partial reads only. Can't maintain continuous track on enemy formations." The degraded equipment forced them to operate half blind.

Every shot matters now. Miss once and people die. No pressure.

Coop found himself coordinating fires based on estimated positions and outdated intelligence. What had been precision strikes were becoming educated guesses with consequences measured in friendly casualties.

His thirty-seventh fire mission of the day came through the radio as enemy forces probed Third Platoon's eastern flank. Exhausted and operating on instinct, Coop read the grid coordinates from Crawford's backup display. "Steel Rain Six, fire mission. Grid four-two-eight-seven-one-three, infantry in the open."

The artillery battery confirmed the mission. "TASC One-Six, Steel Rain Six. Shot over."

Coop's blood turned to ice water. He'd transposed two digits. The rounds were flying toward grid 4-2-8-7-3-1—Bravo Company's position.

"Steel Rain Six, check fire, check fire! Abort mission!" His voice cracked as he grabbed the radio with both hands. "All stations, all stations, incoming friendly fire, grid four-two-eight-seven-three-one. Take cover immediately!"

Crawford caught the error on his backup display, but his reaction time was slower due to pain medication and the smaller interface. "Coop! That's danger-close to Bravo!"

Lieutenant Gill's voice boomed the comm net. "All Bravo elements, incoming artillery, take cover!" Friendly fire was every ground commander's nightmare.

The artillery rounds impacted two hundred meters from Bravo Company's positions. Close enough to shower them with dirt and debris, but far enough to avoid casualties. Gill's immediate response had saved lives that Coop's mistake had endangered.

"Steel Rain Six, TASC One-Six. Confirm check fire and abort."

"TASC One-Six, Steel Rain Six. Mission aborted. No further rounds in flight."

Crawford looked at him with concern. "That was close. Maybe too close." Li glanced up from her failing sensors, worry evident in her expression.

One wrong coordinate could kill his own people.

Coop, you idiot! Get your head in the game!

Hour sixty-eight brought the realization that his body was shutting down. Coop couldn't remember eating, though empty ration containers suggested he had. His hands trembled constantly now, requiring conscious effort to hold the radio steady. The stimulant pills Crawford had given him weren't helping anymore. They just made his heart race while his muscles ached from exhaustion.

Lieutenant Gill radioed with another fire mission request, but the words seemed to come from underwater. Grid coordinates blurred like heat mirages. For a moment, Coop couldn't process the tactical situation as had been second nature hours earlier.

"Fire mission, grid four-three-two-one-seven-eight, enemy armor." The words came out slurred despite his efforts to speak clearly.

"TASC One-Six, say again your last transmission," came the confused response from Steel Rain Six.

Crawford watched him with growing alarm. "You need rest," his wounded staff sergeant said quietly. But the radio was already crackling with another emergency fire mission from Second Platoon. Enemy forces were testing their lines again, and there was no one else qualified to coordinate the response.

Li was running both sensors and communications with failing equipment. Crawford was wounded and working with backup systems that barely functioned. The burden of keeping Alpha Company alive rested on Coop's shoulders, even as his body approached complete breakdown, his mind melting down as well.

The strike had worked. But barely. Enemy forces pulled back from the breakthrough, leaving scattered equipment and bodies across the killing field. Coop's display showed a stabilized line, though gaps remained where Third Platoon had lost positions. The immediate crisis was over, but the ammunition shortage meant the next assault would be much more difficult to repel.

Dawn broke over planet Rass, revealing the true cost of three days' continuous combat. Empty ammunition containers surrounded their fighting position. Damaged equipment sparked intermittently.

Crawford's backup systems showed new enemy formations massing in the distance. Then Li's sensor array sparked once more and went completely dark, leaving them blind as the war entered its fourth day.

Chapter 17:
Ancient Aliens and Coffee

Late 2098
RNS *Gallipoli*
Planet Rass Orbit

Love slumped in the crew lounge chair, her flight suit still damp with sweat from their last run. Two days…two days of nonstop insertions and extractions. Her hands shook slightly as she lifted the coffee mug to her lips.

Bitter. Like always, the stuff tasted like mud mixed with charred bread, but it kept her eyes open. Around the small table, her crew looked as wrecked as she felt. Green rubbed his temples while Torres stared blankly at the bulkhead. Ford nursed his own cup of the toxic brew.

"You know what I was thinking about?" Ford said, breaking the silence. "The Mayans."

Green groaned. "Not the ancient alien stuff again, Chief."

"Hear me out." Ford leaned forward. "Or, at least, let me get our brains onto something less daunting than memories of what we saw out there, and down planetside…"

Love waved a dismissive hand. "All right. Do your worst, Ford."

"So, these stargates we just came through? Well, the Mayans had this complex mythology about different worlds and cycles of creation. I think they might have known about interdimensional travel. Their calendar system tracked galactic alignments with perfection we can barely match today."

Love yawned. "Ford, the Mayans didn't have spaceships."

"I think they might have, or maybe seen them close up. But, still, if they didn't, that makes it very interesting. How'd they know about interdimensional travel? The precision of their astronomical observations is undeniable."

"You went from 'thinking' they knew about interdimensional travel to 'knowing' about interdimensional travel." Green rolled his eyes. "Anyway, regarding the calendar system, maybe they were just good at math."

"Math doesn't explain the crystal skulls found in their temples, carved with the precision of laser technology. The symmetry is out of this galaxy. Or the hieroglyphs showing figures in what look suspiciously like spacesuits."

"Spacesuits?" Green snorted. "Come on."

Ford pulled out his tablet, swiping through images. "Look at this. Mayan artwork from Palenque. Tell me that doesn't look like someone operating control panels inside a spacecraft."

Love glanced at the screen. Actually, it was quite true. That did look like control panels inside a craft. The carved stone indeed showed figures surrounded by what could be interpreted as technological interfaces. But exhaustion made everything look like something else. It didn't matter, though, because although Ford was smart, he was full of crap when it came to this sort of stuff. It was good to get her mind off the war, however, and banter a little.

"Could be anything," she muttered.

"The Popol Vuh mentions beings who came from the stars to teach humanity. Sound familiar? Every ancient civilization has similar stories. Sumerians called them the Anunnaki. Egyptians had their star gods. Indians wrote about the Vimanas—you know, flying vehicles that could travel between worlds."

Torres took a gulp of coffee. "So, you think aliens visited Earth thousands of years ago?"

"I think someone did. Someone with technology we're only beginning to understand." Ford gestured toward the bulkhead. "We're using stargates we can't build, can't replicate, barely comprehend. But the ancients somehow knew this stuff existed."

Green shook his head. "Correlation isn't causation, Chief. Plus, you're making a big leap there thinking what you read means they knew about stargates."

Ford shrugged. "The Mayan Long Count calendar ended in 2012. Know what started happening around then? The Pentagon confirmed alien contact and spoke about UAPs and the like."

"That came a bit later, but yes," Love said flatly. "Plus, who knows if you're interpreting these tidbits correctly in the first place? If you want something to be true, your mind can rationalize it."

Ford grinned. "Look, the Mayans wrote about cycles of destruction and renewal. What if they were describing cosmic conflicts? I think we're living through one of their predicted cycles right now."

"Every culture predicts some kind of apocalypse," Green pointed out.

"But they all describe it the same way. Fire in the sky. Battles between gods. The destruction of the old world and the birth of the new." Ford's eyes lit up. "What if we're living in one of those cycles they described?"

Torres leaned back. "You really believe this stuff?"

"I believe the universe is stranger than we think. And older. These stargates weren't built by any species we've encountered. Someone else made them. Someone who understood physics we're still discovering."

Love stared into her coffee. The conversation was helping keep her awake, but Ford's theories always made her head hurt. "Even if you're right, what difference does it make? We're still stuck fighting the Zodarks."

"Because understanding the past might help us understand what's coming next. What if the ancients knew about cycles like this? What comes after the destruction?"

"Which is?"

"Maybe humanity's supposed to join something bigger, like we're doing now, you know, by joining this galactic community. And if we prove ourselves worthy, then—"

Green gave a tired laugh, cutting Ford off. "By shooting aliens?"

"By showing we can work with other species. Like the Primords. Altairians. Tully. Maybe that's what the cycle of renewal means."

Love blinked to get the blur out of her eyes. "You're really stretching here, Chief."

The comm buzzed. Love activated it. "This is Love."

"Lieutenant, report to Briefing Room A-2 immediately. Bring your crew."

Love closed the channel. "Well, looks like the ancient aliens will have to wait. We're up again."

Ford drained his coffee. "The Mayans would say this is all part of the pattern."

"The Mayans are dead," Green said, standing up.

"Are they? Maybe they just moved on to whatever comes next. Ascended, en masse."

"Sure, that's what they did. Until we ascend en masse, let's go." Love stood, her legs fighting every bit of it. Everything ached. Her lower back felt like someone had been hitting it with a wooden bat. "Come on, people. Commander Granger wants us."

They made their way through *Gallipoli*'s corridors, where damage control teams worked on scorched bulkheads. Medical personnel moved stretchers through the passages. People were moving around fast, despite the tired looks in their eyes.

Through the observation ports floated the aftermath of the space battle. Debris fields glittered in Rass's reflected light. Broken ships drifted in twisted pieces. But the major threats were gone. Admiral McKee's fleet had systematically destroyed every orbital weapons platform around the planet. The starbase now flew Republic colors. Enemy ships were either destroyed or fleeing toward the outer system. And the Primord fleet held formation alongside Republic vessels.

Impressive.

Briefing Room A-2 was packed with transport crews. Love recognized pilots from Wolfpack Squadron and the medical evacuation units. Commander Granger stood at the holographic display.

"Ladies and gentlemen," Granger began, "orbital phase is complete. Enemy space assets have been neutralized. All orbital weapons platforms are destroyed or captured. The starbase is under our control."

The tactical display showed Rass rotating slowly. Green-and-blue continents were marked by red indicators where ground fighting continued.

"Ground operations are proceeding according to plan. However, we have multiple units requesting immediate medical evacuation. Priority Alpha casualties scattered across seventeen landing zones."

Love's stomach tightened. Priority Alpha meant soldiers who would die without immediate treatment.

"Transport Twelve," Granger said, looking directly at Love. "Alpha Company is requesting emergency extraction. Multiple casualties."

Cooper. Love's chest constricted slightly.

"They're essentially trapped on Ridge 248. Heavy enemy contact. They need immediate dustoff."

Ford straightened beside her. "Medical configuration, sir?"

"Full trauma setup. We're loading two flight surgeons, three trauma nurses, and a full critical care team. Your bird will be equipped with surgical suite capabilities."

Love nodded. That meant gurneys, surgical equipment, blood products, and enough life support gear to keep severely wounded soldiers alive during transport. It also meant extra weight and reduced maneuverability.

"Time frame?" Green asked.

"Immediate. Enemy forces are closing on their position. Weather conditions are fine, but this may be their only extraction window."

Granger manipulated the display. Ridge 248 appeared as a jagged highland surrounded by enemy positions. The tactical situation looked grim. No—worse than grim.

"Intelligence indicates heavy Zodark presence in the area. Expect significant anti-aircraft fire during approach and extraction. Orbot units confirmed in the operational zone."

Torres shifted uncomfortably. No doubt first time facing Orbots in a ground support role.

"Questions?" Granger asked.

Love raised her hand. "Medical team configuration?"

"Dr. Conway will lead the surgical team. Lieutenant Commander Patts handles trauma assessment. Three nurses with combat medical experience. Now, when you get down planetside, rules of engagement are as follows: cleared hot on all confirmed enemy positions. Suppressive fire authorized to protect medical operations. Fleet assets are standing by for close-air support if needed."

Love's mind turned the mission parameters over and over in her head. HALO insertion had been dangerous enough. Medical evacuation under fire was exponentially worse. But Cooper and his people were counting on them.

Coop. God, I hope he's all right.

The kid had always been decent to her, respectful when he'd had that obvious crush. Never pushed it when she wasn't interested. There was something about him that reminded her of one of her cousins back home, who was like a brother to her in many ways. She'd never had strong romantic feelings for Cooper, but there was definitely a protective instinct there. Like family.

"Osprey *Jack*, acknowledge mission assignment," Granger said.

"*Jack* copies," Love replied. "Emergency medical evacuation, Ridge 248. Priority Alpha casualties."

"Medical team is moving to your aircraft now. Launch in ten minutes."

The briefing dissolved as crews hurried toward their assigned bays. Love's team moved quickly through the corridors, the exhaustion temporarily forgotten.

When they entered their bay, she headed toward *Jack*, where medical personnel loaded equipment into her ship's troop compartment. Gurneys. Surgical instruments. Blood bags. Plasma units. Cardiac monitors. Everything needed to keep dying soldiers alive.

Dr. Conway supervised the loading. A compact woman with graying hair. Love figured the lady had been saving lives longer than Love had been flying.

"How many casualties?" Conway called over the noise.

"Unknown," Ford replied. "Alpha Company took heavy damage. That's what we know."

"We're prepared for fifteen critical patients," Conway said. "More than that, we'll have to make choices."

Love passed Conway and Ford on the ramp, hurried through the cabin and climbed into the cockpit, settling into the pilot's seat. There they were—the controls—welcoming her back from a short stint away. Green slid into the copilot position and started running preflight diagnostics.

Through the cockpit window, planet Rass hung in space. Beautiful from a distance. Hell when viewed up too close.

She found the worn photograph on the instrument panel. Jack's face smiled back at her, unchanged by time or war. Her husband. Jack. The love of her life.

Keep us safe, as always, and in all ways.

She pressed her finger to her lips, then touched his picture gently.

"I'll bring them home," she whispered.

Jack's engines rumbled to life as Love began the start-up sequence. Navigation systems online. Life support green. Weapons systems armed.

Time to go to work.

"Engine start-up complete," Green reported from the copilot seat. "All systems nominal."

Through the cockpit, the hangar bay launch tubes started to cycle open. Rass waited, its atmospheric curve almost at an arm's reach. Down there, Alpha Company bled. She needed to get down planetside sooner rather than later.

Love patched into the comm frequency. "Tower, this is *Jack*. Ready for immediate departure."

"*Jack*, you are cleared for launch. Bring our people home."

"Copy that." Love's grip tightened on the controls. "Ford, Torres, medical team, we're going hot. Strap in."

She touched Jack's photograph one more time, then focused on the mission.

It was time to bring them home.

Chapter 18:
Fire on Our Heads

Late 2098
Planet Rass

The damaged systems came back to life under Crawford's hands. The guy was like a field mechanic wizard who'd learned to make miracles from discarded parts. He'd stripped wire insulation with his combat knife. Bypassed burned circuits with spare cable. Somehow coaxed Li's sensor array back to partial functionality. Still, the holos staticked off and on, much of the time the resolution grainier than sand, but they could see enemy formations nonetheless.

The tactical computer remained dead weight, its screen just as black as space. Crawford had jury-rigged his backup tablet to interface with the sensor feeds, running cables through gaps in their fighting position's sandbag walls. "It's an ugly duck, that's for sure, but it'll do," he muttered. The makeshift repairs could easily crumble under the next artillery barrage, but they'd buy precious time.

Li worked over her patched-together display, squinting at the fuzzy readouts. She mashed holographic buttons across controls that responded only half the time. "Sweet mother of…" she whispered, then caught herself. "I count over two hundred vehicles, multiple formations converging from three vectors. My Lord…"

The forest below Ridge 248 burst with movement. Through Coop's binoculars, he saw Zodark infantry advancing in waves. Behind them, tracked vehicles churned through the underbrush, leaving broken trees behind. Crawford's tablet showed enemy icons heading like a deluge toward their position.

The odds weren't adding up in the Republic's favor. Four Republic companies against a regiment.

"All Alpha elements, hold current positions at all costs. Repeat, hold at all costs," Lieutenant Gill said on the command net. "No withdrawal authorized."

Coop cleared his throat. The command was heavy as hell and burned like acid behind his Adam's apple. Why? Because somewhere up the chain of command, someone had decided Ridge 248 was worth dying for.

Coop keyed his radio. "TASC One-Six copies. Hold at all costs." Orders were orders. Alpha Company would hold until they were all dead. But Coop intended to make the enemy bleed for every meter and keep as many of his men and women alive as possible.

Crawford's tablet crackled with incoming fire mission requests. The radio chatter told the story. That Third Platoon was falling back. That Second Platoon was taking casualties. There was an enemy breakthrough in sector four. The defensive line was breaking under pressure.

Bear would have laughed at this mess, Coop thought as enemy formations began to converge on their position. He would've called it a "target-rich environment" and asked for more ammunition.

Bear's sacrifice put us here. Helped make this invasion work. Now it's my turn to make it count.

Bear's death gave meaning to Coop. Gave him that extra punch, that extra jolt of adrenaline needed to keep going no matter what. And if they had to hold this ridge, he'd do it.

Zodark infantry reached the ridge's base, climbing through openings blown in First Platoon's abandoned wire barriers. They moved in small groups, using cover. These were veterans who knew their business.

Crawford's tablet beeped. "Multiple contacts, close range. They're inside our minimum safe distance."

Coop grabbed his radio and made the call no TASC ever wanted to make. "Fire Direction Center, fire mission, danger-close to friendly positions. Grid four-two-four-eight-one-five, troops in the open, immediate suppression."

After an uncomfortable pause, Battery Six-Two came back, saying, "TASC One-Six, confirm danger-close to your position."

Coop looked at Crawford, who nodded grimly. They both knew what danger-close meant when called on your own position. Chances of survival weren't great. "Confirmed. Bring it down on our heads. We'll take cover."

"Roger. Shot over."

The artillery arrived. Blast after blast, violent tremor after violent tremor. Forest turned into a crater in four seconds of destruction.

When the first shells screamed overhead, Coop pressed his chest into the dirt, covering his face in his arms. Li did the same while Crawford curled into a ball beside the sandbags.

The world exploded.

Orange fireballs erupted across the ridge. The ground bucked. Shrapnel whined. Trees disintegrated. Rocks flew in every direction.

WHAM. WHAM. WHAM.

Each impact drove them harder against the earth. Coop's skull throbbed. His spine compressed. The concussions crushed him like falling mountains.

More shells. More fire. More soil and rocks flying skyward.

Thirty seconds might as well have been thirty minutes.

Then ugly, ugly silence. Ugly. The worst. The type where, when Coop moved, he didn't know which parts of his body were still intact and which weren't. The type where he hoped the small particles of dirt now covering him weren't actually bits of human flesh.

Coop lifted his head. Smoke drifted across what used to be forest. New crater holes steamed where trees had once stood. He moved his legs. They worked. Then his arms. He blinked a few times, seeing if his eyes were still there and if his eyelids still moved left to right, and up and down.

The good news was they were alive. Somehow, impossibly, still breathing. The bad news—he didn't know for how much longer.

He surveyed the destruction below. The artillery had done its work, and damn well.

Forty to fifty Zodark infantry lay scattered across the field, maybe even more. Some in pieces. Others twisted. Blood started to swamp the charred earth. Body parts hung from shattered tree stumps.

Fourteen Orbot chassis scattered the hillside, torn apart by direct hits. Alien limbs jutted from crater walls. One Orbot's torso hung upside down from a burned tree.

Six Zodark vehicles had been caught in the barrage. Two armored personnel carriers split open like rotten fruit. Purple fluid dripped from their ruptured hulls. A tracked blaster gun lay on its side, turret blown clean off. The remaining vehicles were burning wrecks, their crews dead.

Crawford's tablet sparked and died. Smoke curled from the processor vents as he slapped the device. "Processor's busted," he said, reaching for his secondary backup. The screen flickered twice before stabilizing on a screen full of static.

Li pulled her hands back from her sensor console, steam rising from the metal housing. Even through her gloves, it looked like the heat was burning her palms by the way she was touching the console, then quickly taking her fingers away. She tapped it, only to wince. "This thing's running hot," she said, blowing on her fingers. The continuous operation had pushed their jury-rigged equipment past every safety margin Crawford had built in.

Coop's radio might as well had been a branding iron against his ear. He had to pause between transmissions, letting the overheated circuits cool while enemy forces kept coming. As Zodark infantry moved closer to their position, he knew he couldn't call in the fires that would stop them.

Equipment was failing faster than Crawford could patch it.

The counterbattery fire arrived twelve minutes later. The shell impacted ten meters from their fighting position, close enough to lift Coop off the ground and slam him back into the sandbags. The world turned white, then red, then tilted to the side. Dirt rained down in chunks.

Li was screaming.

Coop rolled over, blinking blood from his eyes. Li sat against the back wall of their position, her left leg twisted at a god-awful angle, making Coop want to puke. To add to it, shrapnel had torn through her shoulder and thigh, coating the remains of her sensor station in crimson. Blood was everywhere, and Crawford was on top of the issue, doing his best to field dress Li's wounds.

Crawford pressed gauze against the worst wounds while Li fought against screaming more. "She needs a casevac," he said over his shoulder. "Now."

Coop grimaced. "Negative on the dustoff. Continue mission." His left arm hung wrong, numb from the shoulder down, but his right still worked. That was enough to call fires.

Crawford stared at him like he'd suggested surrender—then held his tongue while his hands kept working, wrapping Li's leg.

Li spoke through gritted teeth: "He's right. Patch... me up. We've got... work to do."

Blood soaked through the first layer of gauze immediately. Crawford added another layer, then another.

The radio came alive with transmissions from across the ridge. Enemy formations were breaking through everywhere, and Alpha Company needed fire support. Gill's voice boomed through next, "TASC One-Six, where are my fires? We're being overrun down here."

Coop grabbed the radio with his good hand, reading coordinates from Crawford's damaged tablet. His vision kept blurring, doubling the enemy icons until he couldn't tell which ones were real. Concussion symptoms were getting worse, but the radio kept demanding answers.

Battery Six-Two responded immediately: "Shot over." The artillery was still functioning, still ready to deliver death on target. As long as Coop could give them coordinates, the guns would keep firing.

High above, Reaper engines whined through the chaos. "Reaper Two-One, station for close-air support," came the transmission. The cavalry had arrived.

Coop keyed his radio. "Reaper Two-One, TASC One-Six. Multiple armored vehicles, grid four-two-seven-eight-two-three. Request immediate attack."

"Copy, TASC. Reaper Two-One inbound hot. Thirty seconds."

The Reapers screamed overhead. Laser bolts and magrail rounds lanced down from the sky. It all turned Zodark armor into molten slag. Secondary explosions rippled across the valley as ammunition cooked off.

Below, Coop's fighting position looked like a bomb had gone off inside it. Which it pretty much had, give or take a handful of meters.

The sandbag walls sagged where shrapnel had torn through the fabric. Sand leaked from dozens of holes, creating small piles. But the natural rock walls they'd built against, which were part of the ridge's granite face, had held firm. Scorch marks blackened the stone where fragments had ricocheted off. Crawford's run of cables hung in tangles. Half of them had been severed by flying metal.

Li's blood covered almost everything within arm's reach. The sensor console. The radio mount. Red pools soaked into the dirt floor, mixing with hydraulic fluid from their damaged gear. Their overhead cover had partially collapsed, and the camouflage netting fluttered in shreds.

Li fashioned a makeshift sling for her own wounded arm and crawled back to her sensor console, all the while cringing in pain. "Multiple formations converging on our position," Li reported. "They'll be on top of us in five minutes."

At the moment, Alpha Company's defensive line was collapsing section by section, falling back toward the ridge's peak. Soon there would be nowhere left to retreat.

The radio crackled with a new voice. Deep. Iron-steady. And veteran-calm. "*Duncan* to all ground units. Naval fire support available on request."

Duncan. The Republic heavy cruiser. Guns that could level city blocks.

Coop's radio crackled. "TASC One-Six, be advised, enemy forces have breached the outer perimeter. Zodark assault troops are inside the wire." The words hit like another artillery round. Alpha Company's outer ring had fallen. Hostile forces were now climbing the ridge from so many different directions, it was hard to tell which to shoot first, which to run from first. Or maybe it didn't matter, because without a doubt in Coop's mind, they'd all soon converge on the remaining Republic positions.

They were about to be overrun.

Coop punched in commands on his radio. "*Duncan*, TASC One-Six. Request immediate naval gunfire support. Grid four-two-five-eight-one-seven. Massed enemy formations. Danger-close."

"TASC One-Six, *Duncan* copies. Shot over."

They're going to glass this whole ridge, Coop thought as he lay on the ground, wishing he could just burrow through it, knowing this might be the last time he breathed. *Better than letting the Zodarks have it.*

The space above them split open with thunder. *Duncan*'s tungsten rounds reached down from orbit. The sudden impact turned half the valley into a lake of molten lava.

Chapter 19:
The Extraction

Late 2098
Planet Rass

The tungsten rounds from *Duncan* had turned half the valley into Armageddon. Fires and smoking rock stood where Zodark formations used to advance. But despite the destruction, the surviving blue beasts kept coming.

"Multiple breaches on the north slope," Li said, her makeshift sling dark with fresh blood.

Coop blinked hard, trying to clear his vision. The concussion made everything black around the edges. Numbers on Crawford's backup tablet blurred together. "How many?"

"Too many to count."

Through the haze, Zodark infantry swarmed up the ridge. Behind them, more tracked vehicles. More Orbots. More destruction moving toward their position, heading their way.

Fewer than four hundred Republic soldiers held a hilltop against what now looked like a full brigade. Somehow Coop knew this information, but couldn't remember who gave it to him, and when. It had to be recent. Just under four hundred troops occupied Ridge 248, a bluff controlling the approaches to three major landing zones. Losing it would compromise the entire planetary operation.

They would hold or die trying.

Gill came over the radio. "All Alpha elements, pull back to final defensive positions. Repeat, fall back to the peak."

Coop keyed his radio. His words slurred a little. "TASC One-Six… withdrawing to… to secondary position."

Something's wrong with my speech. The thought drifted through his head like the tenth shot of whiskey down the gullet. *Concussion's getting worse.*

Crawford grabbed essential gear while Li tried to stand. Her wounded leg buckled immediately. "Can't put weight on it," she gasped.

"I got you." Crawford slung Li's good arm over his shoulder, supporting most of her weight.

Coop tried to help but stumbled. The world went sideways for a moment. Blood ran down his face from where his head wound had reopened. Again.

Where's my helmet and how long has it been off my head?

Coop's hand went instinctively to his head, where he found matted hair and dried blood. His throat mic still functioned, pressed against his neck by the tactical collar, but without the helmet, everything felt disconnected. *Again, why did I take it off, and when?* There—beside the smoking sensor array, what used to be his helmet now looked like a charred piece of abstract art, its faceplate shattered and internal systems melted.

No more time to worry, or care.

He dashed out of his TASC post, following Li and Crawford. Together, they scrambled up the slope toward the ridge's peak. Behind them, their original fighting position disappeared under Zodark small arms fire. Blaster bolts scorched the granite walls they'd called home for the past eight hours.

The new position was just a shallow depression behind some boulders. Natural cover, but barely enough space for three people and their gear. Crawford set up his smoking tablet while Li tried to make her damaged sensors work… again.

"Grid coordinates are… are…" Coop stared at the display. The numbers weren't making sense. "Crawford, what's our position?"

Crawford looked at him sharply. "You just asked me that ten seconds ago."

Did I? Coop touched his forehead. His fingers came away with fresh blood. *Focus. Alpha Company needs fires.*

Battery Six-Two came over the radio. "TASC One-Six, multiple fire missions waiting. Send coordinates."

Coop tried to read the tablet. The numbers kept doubling. "Crawford, help me out here."

"Grid four-two-five-nine-one-two," Crawford said clearly. "Troops in the open, immediate suppression."

"Roger. Shot over."

The artillery came down on target. Explosions rippled across the northern slope, tearing into advancing Zodark formations. But more kept coming. Always more.

Li's rebuilt sensor array sparked and went dark. "Lost primary sensors," she reported. A thin stream of smoke curled from the housing. "This thing's gone."

Crawford's tablet was literally smoking now, too. The processor vents glowed red in the dim light. Warning indicators flashed across the holo. "Everything's malfunctioning," he muttered, trying to reroute power to keep it functional.

Coop grabbed his radio, but the metal housing burned his palm through his gloves. He had to hold it with several extra pieces of torn fabric. "Multiple contacts, advancing on all sectors," he spoke, his words coming out slower than normal. "Request immediate… immediate…"

What was the word? His brain felt beyond warped. Drunk, even.

"Immediate fires," Crawford prompted quietly.

"Immediate fires."

Li's sensor array was lit up cherry-red now. The power coupling looked like a miniature star about to go supernova. "Crawford, this thing's dying."

The Zodark artillery round impacted ten meters away at the exact moment Li's equipment gave up entirely.

The screen went black. The equipment's whir stopped.

"Medic! Medic!" shouted a soldier somewhere down the line. The sound of Zodark weapons closed in. Someone yelled grid coordinates. The wet crunch of another artillery impact, then another soldier shrieked as shrapnel found flesh.

"Frag out!"

The grenade detonated thirty meters away. Then another. Closer.

Through it all, that sound, that Zodark war cry, a rising shriek that made his skin crawl. It was getting louder.

Crawford's tablet screen flickered once, then died. No sparks. No drama. Just… gone. Every piece of equipment in their fighting position was dead or dying. The air filled with smoke and the copper-sweet smell of blood.

They were blind. Deaf. Cut off from all fire support coordination just as enemy formations reached the ridge's base.

Coop tried to sit up. His right arm was on fire. A chunk of burning debris from the artillery blast had landed on his sleeve and melted into the fabric.

Then something hit him, and hard. Right in the chest. He could smell burnt skin. When he looked down, he realized the smell came from him.

The Zodark blaster bolt had punched straight through his tactical vest. The energy weapon had burned a hole the size of a fist into his chest plate and the flesh beneath. The edges of the impact site glowed ember-red, the surrounding tissue already blistering and peeling.

"He's hit!" Li yelled. To Coop, it sounded like she was far away and in a tunnel.

Crawford jumped into action, ripping open Coop's vest to assess the damage. "Stay still," he said, cutting away melted fabric and charred gear.

Coop tried to speak but could only make garbled sounds. His whole body felt wrong. His muscles spasmed and his nerves were misfiring. His vision cut out in segments.

The burn extended across his entire chest, third-degree at the center where the bolt had struck, second-degree radiating outward. His heart beat irregularly. Every breath felt like inhaling fiery daggers. At least, that much he could tell. Everything went into slow motion. A blink seemed to take decades before he'd open his eyes again to see Crawford asking questions, his comrade's expression tight, and Coop shaking his head before shutting his eyes. This happened over and over. One time he opened his eyes, seeing Crawford injecting something—medical nanites, probably—directly into the wound. Then closing them once more.

Can't think straight. Can't see right. Can't talk. Everything hurts.

Crawford worked frantically with their remaining medical supplies. Li dragged herself over despite her wounded leg, trying to help stabilize Coop's injuries.

Enemy rifle fire cracked overhead. Zodark infantry were coming closer, their final approaches to the ridge's peak. Without coordination, the remaining Republic positions would fall within minutes.

Coop drifted in and out of awareness. Explosions seemed to come from a great distance. When he tried to focus on Crawford's face, it blurred and doubled and paused.

How can he pause?

It didn't make sense. Shock. He was going into shock.

Sometimes he thought he was back in training. Sometimes he was calling fire missions that had already happened. Sometimes he was looking up at Li's concerned expression as she checked his pupils.

Body's shutting down, he thought. *Trauma response. But Alpha Company's still fighting.*

Somewhere in the functional parts of his mind, he understood they still needed him.

"Dustoff Control, this is Alpha Six-Three," Crawford shouted into his radio. "We need immediate medevac. Blaster wound to the chest. Critical."

Chief Ford's voice came back steady. "Alpha Six-Three, Dustoff Control copies. LZ is hot. Ten minutes minimum."

Ten minutes. Alpha Company didn't have ten minutes. Or maybe that wasn't a long time. He couldn't concentrate, couldn't figure anything out.

Gill's voice burst over the radio. "All stations, enemy assault troops on the ridge. We're being overrun."

Li grabbed Coop under his arms while Crawford took his legs. They started dragging him toward the improvised landing zone on the ridge's eastern slope, Li limping big-time. Coop's burned arm left a trail of blood. His chest screamed with every movement.

Blaster fire streaked overhead, those distinctive bolts that had nearly killed him, or hell, might end up killing him after all.

Zodark small arms fire intensified as they stumbled down the slope, using crater lips and fallen trees for cover. Li grunted and cried out a few times, the pain in her leg most likely unbearable. Coop tried to protest the evacuation, mumbling about unfinished fire missions and his responsibility to Alpha Company. But his words came out as unintelligible sounds, and even he had no idea what he was trying to say.

The Osprey dropped through the smoke, its engines screaming as the pilot pushed through a wall of ground fire. The bird touched down hard as the side door slid open.

Jack. *That's the bird's name.* Jack. *But who's flying it? Why can't I remember?* Coop thought.

Chief Ford jumped out before the skids settled, someone Coop easily recognized. Behind him came a doctor, the flight surgeon, medical bag already open.

"Well, look what the Zodarks dragged in," Ford said with a grin, kneeling beside Coop's stretcher. His voice was calm, like this was just another day on the prairie. "Don't worry, Coop. We'll have you patched up and chasing nurses in no time."

Why does everything feel like a dream?

"Doc, severe blaster burn to the chest, second- and third-degree burns on the right arm, head wound with embedded fragments, possible concussion," Crawford reported as they lifted the gurney.

"Got it." The doctor checked Coop's pupils while they moved toward the Osprey. "He's responsive. We can work with this."

"Easy does it, Cooper," Ford said. "You're all good. I've seen worse, and they walked out of the med bay just fine."

Coop couldn't reply. His mouth wouldn't work. His thoughts swam way under the ocean, and they were trying to swim to the surface.

As they loaded him into the bird, Coop's fragmented vision caught one last image of Ridge 248.

Smoke rose from dozens of impact craters across the hilltop. The sky was dark with particulates and chemical residue, turning midday into artificial twilight. Enemy formations still advanced up the slopes while Alpha Company's remaining positions burned.

We held. For as long as we could.

Inside the Osprey, the doctor worked over him. IV lines. Stem cell injectors. Medical nanites flooding his system. Something for the pain. The medical equipment beeped and hummed around them.

The pain's fading. Everything's getting soft around the edges. The doctor's face keeps moving in and out of focus. Where's Ford? My chest feels like it's on fire and freezing at the same time.

"Vitals are stabilizing," The doctor called over the engine noise. She was talking to someone else now. A nurse? Another doctor? Were they in the air, flying out of here?

They're talking about me like I'm not here. But I am here, aren't I? Everything feels so far away.

The doctor adjusted the IV drip while the other person checked his bandages one more time. "You're going to be fine, soldier. Just let the medicine do its work."

Fine. Will I be fine? What about Alpha Company? What about the ridge? Why does my chest hurt so much even through the meds?

The medical cocktail pulled him deeper into darkness. The last thing he saw was the doctor watching over him, then taking notes on his tablet.

Coop wanted to ask if they were in the air yet. For some reason he wanted to tell the doctor he was a pilot, but not really. A drone operator. No, he was a TASC member but used to be a pilot. Same with his dad, his grandfather, his great-grandfather, and on and on and on…

Sleep. Just for a minute. Just…

Then the darkness took him completely.

Chapter 20:
Strategic Logistics

Late 2098
Rear Admiral Scott Costello's Office
New Eden

Rear Admiral Scott Costello stared at the intelligence report on his desk. Five days had passed since he'd first read these words, but it all still unsettled him.

Several monitoring stations had been destroyed. Outposts near the gas planets and moons were destroyed. Hit-and-run attacks had taken place against the Tully mining vessels in their asteroid and ice belts, as well as hitting civilian shipping between Tully, Primord, and Altairian territories.

That morning five days ago, the attacks had seemed like border skirmishes. Now they looked like calculated preparations for something larger. Costello had hoped the conflict would remain between the Pharaonis and Tully, something both the Galactic Empire and Dominion could avoid. But the report had changed everything. The enemy left the five outposts near the stargates alone, which was good. But why? And how long would it be until they moved against them as well?

Soon, he thought. *Something about Zodarks and Orbots seen operating in that area doesn't feel right. Something more is happening. Something big is being staged.*

The Altairians had delivered the report personally. Handolly and Pandolly waiting while Costello had processed what he'd read. The urgency in Handolly's voice haunted Costello's analysis.

"Admiral, you must act. This could get worse than just a territorial dispute between the Tully and the Pharaonis."

Costello understood the implications immediately. The Tully weren't numerous. Their four star systems and fourteen colonies held only hundreds of millions of citizens spread across vast territories. Long-lived species rarely reproduced quickly, and the Tully were no exception. They lived into their mid three hundreds, but their population grew at a glacial pace. Low fertility, long lives, careful expansion.

Which made them naturally cautious about military commitments. They maintained a warrior class. Costello had read the cultural assessments comparing them to ancient Sparta, but that caste remained small by necessity. The Tully simply couldn't afford the population losses that aggressive warfare demanded.

What they could do, and did brilliantly, was mine and trade.

And that was what made these attacks so dangerous.

Costello's thoughts drifted to his planning sessions with Admiral Halsey over the past five days. The mining disruptions they'd been analyzing threatened more than Tully prosperity. They threatened the Republic's entire shipbuilding program.

And now, the Tully mining operations were going dark.

The armor plating came from Tully refineries. The heavy-steel alloys that formed capital ship superstructures came from Tully foundries. Without steady Tully deliveries, several production schedules would collapse.

Costello had realized that four days ago, during his second meeting with Handolly. The Altairian diplomat had been characteristically blunt about the timeline. Continued disrupted operations, and shipyards would start missing delivery dates. Heck, eventually, new construction would halt entirely.

The task force concept had emerged from necessity rather than preference—a Republic force created to stabilize the sectors while the Altairians provided logistics, and if necessary, a quick reaction force if the Republic needed help.

It was a lot to coordinate and think about in one day, but it'd been five days since, and things were starting to fall in place.

Costello's door chimed.

"Enter."

The Altairians stepped through. Handolly carried himself well, as usual. The typical diplomat, and although a typical diplomat, Costello had grown to like the alien quite a bit. Pandolly, on the other hand, moved like a seasoned fleet commander, a veteran with more battles under him than Costello cared to count.

The two Altairians barely reached Costello's shoulder, their small bodies quite typical of their species. They had six-fingered hands and leathery white skin that never seemed to age. Their short-cropped white hair shined under the office's lighting system while their unblinking cobalt eyes did just that—didn't blink. Costello had grown accustomed to their appearance over the years, but visitors often found that stare a little disconcerting.

"Gentlemen." Costello gestured to the conference table. "Thank you for coming."

They settled into chairs. Costello opened his datapad while the Altairians waited patiently.

"Let's review where we stand," Costello began. "Lee's task force is assembling ahead of schedule. Twelve ships. Republic integration protocols are proceeding smoothly. We should have everything coordinated within nine months."

"Nine months?" Handolly's tone carried concern. "The mining operations—"

"Are critical, I understand." Costello pulled up logistics timelines. "But we're assembling ships from different squadrons, different commands. They need integration training, coordinated exercises, unified communications protocols. Rush deployment gets people killed."

Pandolly nodded slowly. The warrior caste among the Tully might be small, but they'd held their territories for centuries through preparation and patience. The Republic could learn something from that approach. "The timeline is acceptable if it means the task force functions properly."

"Lee's promotion to captain is in the works," Costello continued. "And I'm recommending his executive officer, Lieutenant Commander Sato, for promotion to commander and her own ship."

"Which ship?" Handolly asked.

"The RNS *Invincible*. Heavy cruiser. Captain Loggins requested transfer to the shipyard project for medical reasons. Sato has the experience we need. Admiral McKee's fitness reports single her out as exceptionally capable with hybrid operations."

McKee. Costello made a mental note to check on her fleet's status. Last report had them engaged in heavy fighting in the Rass system, but holding their own. McKee wouldn't be available for consultation on personnel matters, but her evaluations carried weight. If she recommended Sato for command, that was good enough.

"Lee doesn't know he's losing his XO yet," Costello said.

"I am guessing he will not like it," Pandolly observed. "Losing a trusted officer during a critical transition must be difficult."

"No, he won't like it, but he recommended her for command himself in his last three fitness reports. He'll understand."

Pandolly leaned forward. "Admiral, forgive the interruption, but the Serpentis situation has deteriorated. We detected movement near the closest Zodark sector."

Costello's attention sharpened. "How large?"

"We are still gathering intelligence," Handolly said. "But the monitor stations are gone. We have no early-warning network around the Pharaonis stargate."

Costello activated the system display. Serpentis rotated slowly, its three stargates marking critical chokepoints. Twelve million Tully civilians lived in that system, most of them in the mining colonies and refineries that kept many Alliance shipyards running. Twelve million people who reproduced slowly, lived long lives, and represented a significant portion of their species' total population.

Lose them, and the Tully would never recover. Not in Costello's lifetime, probably not in several lifetimes.

"Current defenses?" Costello asked.

"Orbital platforms. A patrol squadron. Ground forces sufficient for internal security." Pandolly's assessment was clinical. "Inadequate for serious invasion."

"And the Tully won't coordinate defense with the Ry'lians," Costello said. Centuries of border conflicts and cultural animosity didn't disappear just because both species joined an alliance. They'd fight the Dominion together, but asking them to defend each other's territory was a bridge too far.

"No, Admiral. Which is why Alliance intervention is necessary."

Costello studied the display. The stargate network made Serpentis irreplaceable. Control those gates, and you controlled access to both Tully and Ry'lian heartland territories. The Dominion knew it. The Pharaonis knew it. And now the Zodarks and Orbots were probing the defenses.

"This operation just became more than border stabilization," Costello said quietly. "We're talking about protecting Alliance strategic logistics and a significant civilian population."

"Indeed," Handolly replied. "That changes force composition and mission parameters."

Costello leaned back in his chair. He needed to brief Admiral Halsey on the situation. She'd want to know about the Zodark movements and the threat to the mining operations. Admiral Bailey would need to be informed as well. But the actual task force assembly, personnel assignments, and operational planning? That was his responsibility.

"I'm moving forward with the task force deployment," Costello said. "I'll coordinate with you, the Altairians, on logistics support and combined operations. Lee gets everything he needs to succeed."

"And Commander Lee?" Pandolly asked. "You are confident in this selection?"

"Absolutely. Admiral McKee's fitness reports identify him as exceptional at independent operations. He handles complex situations well and takes good initiative. For extended deployment in contested territory with Altairian coordination and diplomatic considerations, he's the right choice."

"We trust your judgment, Admiral," Handolly said.

Costello turned back to the tactical display. "Gentlemen, here's how we'll structure this. Twelve Republic ships, twelve Altairian ships for logistics and support. Enough firepower to secure the system and protect the mining operations."

"And if the Zodark force is larger than anticipated?" Pandolly asked.

"Then we adjust," Costello said. "But Lee's task force will have nine months of integration training. They'll be ready."

Handolly's cobalt eyes remained fixed on Costello. "The Tully are grateful for Alliance support, Admiral. This intervention will not be forgotten."

"We protect our own," Costello said simply. "The Tully are Alliance members. That means something."

After they departed, Costello stood alone with the rotating display of Serpentis. Three stargates. Fourteen mining colonies. Twelve million civilians. Strategic resources that kept Alliance shipyards running.

And somewhere out there, enemy forces were moving into position.

Nine months until Lee's task force deployed. Nine months to hope the situation didn't deteriorate beyond repair.

Costello pulled up the production schedules one more time, studying the delivery timelines for armor plating and heavy-steel alloys. The numbers were already slipping.

He closed the file and began drafting his briefing for Halsey. The task force operation was his responsibility, but the strategic implications needed to be communicated up the chain of command.

And if Lee succeeded in stabilizing the system, if the mining operations resumed normal production, if the Alliance shipyards stayed on schedule, then the Republic's shipbuilding program would survive.

Chapter 21:
Blind Corridors

Late 2098
Victory Base Complex
Emerald City, New Eden

The secure conference room quieted as Admiral Costello activated the holographic display. Stars and shipping lanes materialized above the table. Purple and red indicators marked Pharaonis and Zodark incursions along the Serpentis border as Lee absorbed the scope of their new mission. The star map rotated slowly. Each crimson dot represented another dead monitoring station.

Lee didn't know much about the Pharaonis. They were allied with the Dominion, which represented evil incarnate to Lee. Demons— like the Orbots and Zodarks. All of them could just die like mosquitoes in a flame for all Lee cared.

The Pharaonis were nothing less than nightmares given form. To see a mutant ant-like monster bigger than yourself, well, it didn't sit well the first time, and Lee wished never to see one in person.

"Intelligence reports suggest coordinated strikes," the briefing officer said, highlighting patrol routes. "Twelve stations destroyed in the past two weeks. Multiple species working in concert. Pharaonis raiders supported by Zodark frigates and cruisers. Occasional Orbot signatures detected, though their role remains unclear."

Lee leaned forward and studied the pattern. The attacks weren't random raids. Someone had mapped their surveillance network and systematically eliminated their eyes and ears. "What's the timeline between strikes?" he asked.

"Forty-eight to seventy-two hours. Never the same interval twice."

Smart. Varied timing prevented Republic forces from anticipating the next target. Lee studied the destruction path and noted how it created a blind corridor straight toward the Serpentis system. "They're clearing a route."

Costello nodded. "That's our assessment. Question is, for what?"

The briefing lasted three hours. Pharaonis raiders had destroyed monitoring stations while Zodark forces had hit mining operations and shipping lanes. Tully ore haulers. Civilian transports between Primord and Altairian territories. Ice mining facilities in the outer belts. This had created blind spots in the early-warning network. Orbot forces appeared in sensor logs occasionally, but intelligence couldn't determine their purpose. Technical support? Reconnaissance? The signatures vanished before anyone could get close enough to confirm.

Everything pointed to coordinated preparation. Several Pharaonis ships had been spotted shortly after the last stations had gone up in flames. Then they'd bugged out via FTL. Zodark raiders followed similar patterns, striking civilian targets and withdrawing before allied forces could respond.

Lee absorbed the tactical data. The enemy moved well. Each strike built toward something larger. The alliance had been reacting instead of anticipating. Today, that would change.

When the briefing ended, Captain Eamus Roberts led Lee through the tactical overview of Task Force 27.

"Twelve ships under your command," Roberts said. His gruff manner couldn't hide his approval of Lee's assignment. "Four Type-001A *Decatur*-class frigates for picket duty and rapid response. Three Type-002A *Kraken*-class heavy cruisers for main battle line. Three more cruisers for escort and patrol work. Two support vessels for logistics. More might be added."

Lee studied the ship roster. There was a good mix of firepower and flexibility.

Roberts acted like he didn't like anyone, but Lee had learned to read the man's subtle approval. And for a moment, there was that glint in Roberts's eye, perhaps with a sense of paternal pride. There was something there, and it gave Lee confidence.

"I personally recommended you, Lee. So did Costello. You're well liked, so don't let us down, OK?"

Lee nodded. "Understood, sir."

"Good."

Task force operations meant coordinating multiple captains, each with their own crews and capabilities. Lee had studied the theory at the Academy and had commanded joint operations with the Primords. Now he'd lead Republic forces again, but this time with Altairian support if needed. The Altairians would provide logistics and potentially quick reaction forces if things went sideways, but this was a

Republic operation. This would be a test. Would the support structure work when needed? He'd find out soon enough.

"Command protocols follow standard Republic doctrine," Roberts continued. "You'll have tactical autonomy within mission parameters. Altairian forces will maintain separate operations unless circumstances require their intervention. They'll provide logistics support and respond if you request assistance, but this is your show."

That distinction mattered. Support meant backup, not oversight. Lee would coordinate Republic forces without worrying about joint command structures or competing objectives.

"What's the Altairian force composition?"

"Twelve ships maintaining standby positions. Similar capabilities to our task force, different technology base. They'll remain ready to assist if the situation escalates beyond your force's capabilities." Roberts pulled up technical specifications. "So, if you need them, combined firepower should handle anything the Pharaonis or Zodarks can field."

Should. Lee had learned to distrust that word when it came to military planning.

The afternoon session focused on the Serpentis system's geography. Three stargates created natural chokepoints. Controlled access to Tully and Ry'lian territories. The system's position made it strategically vital, a crossroads connecting multiple alliance territories. They'd patrol that area, but the sector was vast. There were huge amounts of space to cover.

"Lose Serpentis, and the Dominion gains staging areas for attacks into alliance heartland," Roberts explained. "Twelve million civilians on the primary world. Orbital infrastructure worth billions. Don't let us down."

"I won't, sir. Current defensive posture?"

"Minimal. Orbital platforms around each stargate, patrol squadrons, ground-based missile batteries. Adequate for border raids. Insufficient for sustained assault."

That was the problem. The Tully had built defenses for the last battle, not the next one. Static positions worked against conventional attacks. Coordinated strikes by multiple species required different thinking.

Lee questioned Roberts about enemy intentions. "Border raids serve multiple purposes. Testing defenses. Gathering intelligence. Probing response times. What makes this different?"

"Scale and coordination," came the reply. "Previous Pharaonis operations involved single ships, maybe squadron strength. These strikes use multiple attack groups with Zodark support hitting economic targets: destroying mining operations, interdicting shipping lanes, and attacking and boarding civilian vessels. The Zodarks seem focused on disrupting commerce while the Pharaonis eliminate our surveillance network."

Movement detected near Zodark sectors suggested preparation for something larger. Whether that meant full invasion or coordinated harassment remained unclear. The alliance couldn't afford to find out through enemy action.

After the strategic briefing, Costello pulled Lee aside. His expression didn't look good.

"Promotion recommendations have created complications for task force staffing," Costello said. "Sato deserves advancement to commander and her own ship. Word is she'll get the RNS *Invincible*."

The words hit Lee hard. Losing Sato meant losing his executive officer. The person who understood his command style better than anyone. His sounding board, too. The woman he'd spent hours talking to almost daily, and heck, his lunch buddy.

He did everything he could to maintain a straight face. Career advancement couldn't be delayed for personal preferences.

"She's earned it," Lee said. He meant every word, though he couldn't withhold his sigh.

"That's what makes this difficult," Costello replied. "Her familiarity with hybrid operations makes her perfect for independent command. But it leaves you without your most experienced officer."

Lee understood the logic while hating the necessity. Sato had proven herself under fire and demonstrated the tactical thinking and leadership skills that marked successful commanders. Her promotion served the larger mission even if it complicated his immediate situation.

"When does she transfer?"

"In three days. The *Invincible* is already here at New Eden for final preparations. The ship will deploy as part of the task force."

Costello's expression softened slightly. "You'll still work together within the task force, just not on the same bridge."

Small comfort. Command partnerships developed over time, built through shared experience and mutual trust. Starting over with a new executive officer meant rebuilding that relationship from scratch.

Lee spent the next morning reviewing *Poseidon*'s upgraded systems with Chief MacGregor. The engineering bay was busy as usual, with technicians completing several final modifications. New communication arrays would coordinate task force operations across all ship classes. Enhanced sensor packages provided fleet-level tactical awareness. The modifications transformed his ship into a better command platform without changing her fundamental character. It meant, in simple terms, they'd just taken an already badass ship and made it that much better.

"Captain, these new processing cores can handle data streams from eleven other vessels," MacGregor said, wiping grease from his hands. "Maybe more if they add ships later. Redundant communication systems mean we'll stay connected even under heavy jamming."

Lee studied the tactical displays. "What about power consumption?"

"Within acceptable parameters. The fusion manifolds can handle the load." MacGregor pulled up power distribution charts. "We've rerouted some systems to balance the draw. No impact on weapons or propulsion."

"Good. How long for full integration testing?"

"Six hours for basic functionality. Full tactical simulation tomorrow morning. Can't wait."

Lee winked. "I bet you can't."

Lee understood his flagship's enhanced role would determine task force effectiveness when the shooting started. If the shooting started. Something deep down told him he was hoping too high for a peaceful mission.

That afternoon, Sato reviewed personnel files in Lee's quarters. Her upcoming promotion to the *Invincible* required selecting officers and understanding her new command responsibilities.

"That young man, Lieutenant Marsh, would work well as your new tactical officer," Lee said, studying her notes. "Looks like he's got good instincts and knows the ship's systems. From what I'm reading."

"What about Lieutenant Rhom for your executive officer?"

Lee considered the recommendation. "Solid choice. Good under pressure." He paused. "Not you, though."

Sato looked up from the files, a sly grin on her face. "Is anyone as good as me?"

"Negative. No one is."

She lost her smile. "Listen, Ripley. I know you're losing me, but there's plenty as good as me if not better. Don't put me on that pedestal no one can reach."

It was good advice and went deeper than just those mere words. Lee knew exactly what she meant, and he'd take it to heart. "Rhom would be a fitting XO."

She nodded. "Yes, he would. Now, let's get back to my ship, shall we?"

"With pleasure."

After they discussed several officers perfect for Sato's bridge, they talked tactical coordination between *Invincible* and *Poseidon* during fleet operations. Sato's familiarity with Lee's command style would prove valuable when managing independent operations within the task force structure.

"You'll maintain standard fleet protocols," Lee said. "But if things go sideways, trust your instincts. Don't wait for orders if the situation demands immediate action."

"Understood. What about communication procedures if we need Altairian support?"

"Standard alliance protocols. They'll be monitoring our operations and ready to assist if requested. But this is our operation. We call for help only if we need it."

Her advancement represented recognition of exceptional ability. Lee struggled with losing the partnership that had defined his command experience. The promotion served both officers while dissolving the team that had made their success possible.

"Sir, I need to say something," Sato said, setting down her datapad.

"Go ahead."

"Working with you these past years has been the best assignment of my career. You gave me opportunities to grow. Trusted me with responsibilities beyond my rank. I won't forget that."

Lee's throat tightened. He wouldn't cry, but this was as close as he'd get. "You earned every opportunity, Noriko. The *Invincible* is lucky to get you."

"Thank you, sir."

The silence stretched between them. Years of shared crisis and victory reduced to military courtesy. Lee checked his watch. "I've got a meeting with MacGregor. We'll finish this later."

He walked out into the corridors, leaving Sato with her files and her future.

Lee walked *Poseidon*'s corridors thinking about command without Sato. The heavy cruiser would remain his home and flagship, but losing his executive officer felt like losing part of the ship's soul. Her competence had allowed him to focus on tactical decisions while trusting her to handle everything else. Finding a replacement who could match her capabilities during task force operations seemed impossible.

She would be nearby on another ship. It would eventually feel normal. This was just how it was in the military.

He entered the arboretum and checked his watch. *On time.* The artificial sunlight filtered through the leaves, creating shaded patterns on the deck plating. MacGregor waited near the small fountain, studying a tablet.

"Chief."

"Cap. Thought you might want to discuss the crew situation."

They sat on the bench facing the miniature garden.

"Losing Sato's going to hurt," MacGregor said. "She knows this ship better than most officers know their own quarters."

"I've been looking at potential replacements," Lee said, pulling up his datapad. "I've got three names on the short list. What have you heard about them?"

"Let me see who you're considering."

Lee turned the screen toward him. "Lieutenant Connor Rhom, Lieutenant Jennifer Abel from the *Carthage*, and Lieutenant Marcus Gomez from the *Bolt*."

MacGregor scrolled through the files. "Rhom's solid. You already know that from working with him as TAO. Smart, follows orders, knows the ship inside and out. The crew respects him, and he's got good instincts in high-pressure situations. I've seen him handle some hairy tactical scenarios without breaking a sweat."

"What about Abel?"

"I worked with her briefly… way back. Sharp tactical mind, good with coordinating multiship operations. She's got a reputation for being a bit of a perfectionist. Some say she micromanages her department heads, but I think that's just inexperience. She's probably already grown out of it." MacGregor paused. "The challenge would be the fact that she doesn't know the *Poseidon* or our crew. There'd be a learning curve."

"And Gomez?"

For about five minutes, MacGregor read the profile. He looked up. "He reads damn good, Cap. Tactical background that trumps even Sato's, it appears. Looks like he's excellent with damage control scenarios and keeping systems running under combat conditions. Crew on the *Bolt* seems to speak highly of him. Seems fair, decisive, doesn't play favorites, according to this report." MacGregor handed the datapad back. "All three are qualified. But if you're asking me who'd be ready fastest while maintaining operational readiness, it's Rhom. He already knows you, knows the ship, knows the crew dynamics. You could slot him in tomorrow and he'd hit the ground running."

Lee nodded slowly. "That's what I'm thinking too."

"How long to train a new XO while maintaining operational readiness?"

"Depends on the officer. Rhom would need maybe a few months, six at most, as he knows me, and he knows the ship better than most, especially the bridge and those at the consoles. Longer to anticipate my thinking like Sato does, I'm thinking, but shouldn't take too long. And… it's a rhetorical question, Mac."

"Sorry, Cap. I mean, you could always choose me if you're desperate enough." MacGregor's grin made it clear he'd rather wrestle a plasma conduit than handle command duties.

They discussed crew development and the challenge of maintaining effectiveness during personnel transitions. Lee knew that duty required accepting changes that regulations demanded but experience regretted.

"The crew's going to feel this too," MacGregor said. "Sato's popular. Respected. Losing her affects morale."

"Captain Oldendorf once told me that good officers leave because they're good officers. The crew understands that. We celebrate her promotion because it means we trained her right. Then we show them that *Poseidon*'s strength comes from everyone, not just one person."

"Damn right. Besides, they all know you'll work twice as hard to make sure the new XO doesn't get them killed."

Lee appreciated MacGregor's perspective. The chief engineer had seen enough personnel changes to understand their impact on ship operations.

"What about the new systems integration?"

"That's the easy part," MacGregor said. "Technology's predictable. People aren't."

The next day, the briefing covered task force departure schedules and initial deployment orders. Lee would retain command of *Poseidon* while coordinating eleven other vessels through border stabilization operations. Intelligence suggested they might add eight additional ships, though the Altairians would maintain their twelve-ship support force on standby.

His and Sato's promotion ceremony was scheduled soon. Sato's assignment to *Invincible* is confirmed, but departure timeline remained classified. However, rumor said it was months and months out, probably nine.

Lee watched Sato prepare for her transition with the competence he had observed throughout their partnership. Her advancement from executive officer to independent command represented the natural progression of proven ability. The separation was both an ending and a beginning. The cost of success in a service that demanded excellence.

Oldendorf had been right about command: you lose the people who make it possible. The price of building good officers was watching them leave to build their own commands.

Chapter 22:
The Sulfur Skies

Late 2098
Planet Rass

Love kept the Osprey low against Rass's surface. She flew the *Jack* between massive stone spires rising from the planet's gouged terrain. Although darkness pervaded everything during this night run, the moon's light showed glimpses of death below: bomb impact craters, kilometers of scorched trees, and a destroyed Zodark base.

And although the night sky offered concealment, *Jack*'s engines glowed against her thermal sensors like damn flares. Eight tons of ammunition and medical supplies shifted in the cargo bay with each course correction. They needed to get these items to Republic ground units surrounded and cut off from main forces, and now.

It'd been several days into this battle, and to say it bluntly, it sucked. Like always. But you did what you needed to do in order to save the galaxy—one person, one sacrifice, one hero at a time. At the moment, the Republic and the Primords had taken orbital superiority, and they were in the middle of killing Orbots and Zodarks planetside and stealing this world back for the Prims.

"Combustion efficiency's down twelve percent," Green reported from the copilot seat. He scanned the engine readouts. "This atmosphere's got too much sulfur dioxide. Engines are running rich."

"Can you compensate?" Love asked, adjusting as they banked around another formation.

"Already am. Fuel consumption's up twenty percent, but we'll make it." Green manipulated controls across the fuel management panel. "Just don't ask for any miracles if we need more push."

"Copy that." Love checked their bearing. Twenty kilometers to the surrounded Republic forces…might as well be twenty thousand.

Green's sensor display blinked with contacts. "Two Vultures, bearing zero-nine-five, range three thousand meters. They're pacing us."

The enemy fighters held position on her tactical display. Too far for an immediate threat, too close for comfort. "They're herding us into something. Ford, you got eyes on anything?"

"Negative. But I don't like how quiet it's been."

Rock walls pressed close as they descended into a massive canyon.

Laser fire erupted from concealed positions along the canyon walls. Beams blasted through the darkness. Love threw the *Jack* into a nosedive, the Osprey groaning as g-forces spiked past the yellow line. The cargo shifted hard against its restraints. She leveled out only meters from hitting the ground, her adrenaline rushing. She pulled back on the yoke, rising her craft slightly in what could have been the deepest canyon she'd ever flown through.

Torres opened up immediately with his .50-cal magrail gun. The weapon's whine cut through the engine noise as he tracked muzzle flashes along the canyon rim. "Contact left, contact left! Multiple positions!"

The Vultures dove from above, adding their fire to the ambush. Green activated chaff dispensers and flare pods. "Deploying chaff! Flares away!"

A laser bolt punched through *Jack*'s starboard armor. Ford's voice crackled over the intercom. "Hull breach starboard side, frame twenty-six! Fire suppression activated! It's like a molten crater glowing orange back here."

Her damage control board erupted in warning lights. "How bad, Chief?"

"Bad enough. Lost some secondary power routing, but the main bus is intact. We're still flying, and that's always a good thing."

She pushed the engines harder. The canyon walls blurred past as *Jack* accelerated through the kill zone. Torres shifted fire to the diving Vultures, forcing them to break off their attack run.

"ECM active," Green announced, his electronic warfare suite flooding the area with false signals. "That should mess with their targeting."

The canyon opened into a vast plain scarred by bombardment. Love used the terrain, diving the *Jack* into the larger craters and popping up at unexpected angles. More Zodark forces emerged from hidden positions, turning their supply run into a running battle stretching across five kilometers of a battle storm.

Torres burned through ammunition belts. His door gun chattered without pause. "Target right, two o'clock! Got him!" A Vulture spun away, trailing smoke and fire.

Jack responded differently, the controls mushy where they should be crisp. "Green, get me artillery support. Let's even the odds. This is getting nuts."

Green switched to the artillery frequency. "Thunder One-Four, Thunder One-Four, this is Wolfpack Actual. Fire mission, over."

"Wolfpack Lead, Thunder One-Four. Send it."

"Grid two-six-five-three-nine-two, enemy armor in the open. Danger-close, say again, danger-close. We are three hundred meters south of target area."

"Roger, danger-close. Shot over."

"Shot out." Green monitored his targeting holo. "Rounds complete. Time of flight, forty-five seconds."

The artillery struck quick and heavy. Geysers of earth and flame erupted across the plain. Ammunition stores and fuel dumps exploded in mighty blasts as the barrage found its targets.

Ford transmitted through the intercom, "Hydraulic pressure dropping in the cargo bay. Ramp actuators are bleeding fluid. I'm rigging manual backup."

"How long?" Love asked.

"Give me two minutes. We'll get one shot at this drop, so make it count."

The approach to the surrounded Republic forces became rather difficult, to put it mildly. Every damn Zodark unit in the area converged on their position. Love abandoned evasion, pointing *Jack* straight at their objective and pushing for maximum speed. The engines screamed, shouted, and found every other noise known to man as she accelerated past redline limits.

Green dumped chaff and flares in a constant stream, the countermeasures creating a light show against the night.

Ford's voice came over the comm again. "Manual backup online. Cargo bay ready for emergency drop."

Her navigation display showed five kilometers to the landing zone. Five kilometers through the apocalypse.

Love keyed her comm. "RNS *Oceanus*, Wolfpack Actual. Request immediate fire support, danger-close."

"Wolfpack Actual, *Oceanus* copies. Tungsten rods inbound."

Tungsten rounds began falling around them like silver lightning. Each impact brightened the dark, turning Zodark positions blood, guts, charred dirt, trees, and m metal. The Republic heavy cruiser cleared a path through the enemy formations.

The pocket of Republic forces appeared ahead, marked by smoke grenades and the muzzle flashes of friendly weapons. She brought the Osprey into a hover over the designated drop zone, a cleared patch between shattered buildings where Alpha Company of the 504th Infantry Regiment—the "Red Devils"—had scraped together what passed for a landing area.

"Covering fire, covering fire!" Lieutenant Gill's voice crackled through the radio. Republic positions erupted with suppressing fire, trying to keep Zodark heads down while the *Jack* hung exposed above the zone.

Ford worked the manual release system. "First pallet away!" A supply bundle dropped into the smoke. "Second pallet away!"

Republic soldiers rushed the supplies through the tactical holodisplay. They dragged ammunition crates and medical boxes toward cover.

Good, thought Love. *Damn good.* They needed every round down there, every medical supply they could get.

Mortar rounds walked across the landing zone. Love shifted position, the Osprey sliding sideways through the air as explosions erupted below them. The aircraft shuddered with each blast wave.

"Heavy weapon team, rooftop, eight o'clock!" Green called out coordinates on his targeting display.

Torres swiveled his door gun toward the building. The .50-cal magrail spoke, sending rounds through the Zodark position. Bodies tumbled from the roof.

"Last pallet away!" Ford announced. "All supplies delivered!"

Love pulled the *Jack* into a climbing turn, gaining altitude for the return journey. The port engine ran rough, contaminated by debris from multiple hits, no doubt. Hydraulic fluid leaked from punctures in the lines, leaving a thin trail in their wake. But the aircraft responded. She'd flown worse.

Green rerouted power through damaged circuits. "Primary hydraulics down to sixty percent. Secondary's holding steady."

The Osprey shuddered with each course correction. Controls responded with half-second delays. Nothing she couldn't handle. Love had been flying damaged aircraft since her first combat tour. This was nothing—less than a flesh wound for the bird.

Zodark reinforcements appeared on the horizon. Fresh Vultures rushed to intercept before the *Jack* could escape the combat zone. Six contacts appeared on her threat monitor…too many for a straight fight.

She pushed the aircraft toward a debris field from an earlier battle, hoping to use the wreckage for cover. The area stretched for kilometers. Twisted alien architecture looked like a massive cathedral hit by orbital bombardment. Multiple levels of gnarled metal and what appeared to be concrete structures provided perfect concealment.

"Taking us into the debris field," Love said, maneuvering the *Jack* between collapsed support beams and shattered platforms.

She flew the Osprey through gaps barely wider than their wingspan, using damaged alien transports as cover. The aircraft settled into shadows between two destroyed vehicles. She throttled engines back to minimum power, dropping their heat signature.

The Vultures circled overhead, searching—six bastards looking for something to kill. Their engine signatures burned across her passive sensors. Ford and Torres kept their weapons trained on the nearest approach vector, ready to fire if they were spotted.

Minutes crawled past. The enemy fighters expanded their search, probing deeper into the debris field. One Vulture passed directly overhead, close enough to rattle loose debris from the wreckage above.

"Come on," Green whispered. "Keep moving."

The fighter banked away, its engine wash stirring dust from the building.

Laser fire erupted around their position without warning. Energy bolts burst through the debris field, trying to flush them out. The Vultures had found them.

"Time to go," Love said, bringing the engines to full power.

Jack burst from cover, accelerating through the wreckage. Love used every piece of debris for concealment, forcing the Vultures to approach through predictable vectors where Green could target them with the chin turret.

Torres and Ford opened fire with their magrail weapons.
Tungsten rounds slammed enemy armor as the fighters closed distance.
The lead Vulture rolled left, trying to avoid the defensive fire, but
Torres tracked its movement. His rounds stitched across the fighter's
port side.

A trailing Vulture misjudged its approach, clipping a collapsed
communications tower. The fighter cartwheeled into the ground,
exploding in a fireball.

Love used the distraction to break for it, pushing toward
Republic-controlled airspace. Green emptied their last chaff dispensers,
creating false targets for enemy torpedoes.

The remaining five Vultures pressed their attack. Laser fire
bracketed the fleeing Osprey, burning past the cockpit canopy. Love
threw the *Jack* into a barrel roll, g-forces pressing her into her seat. The
damaged port engine coughed, losing power for three seconds before
catching again.

A torpedo streaked past their starboard wing, missing by meters.
It erupted in greens and purples off in the distance, trees burning, soil
finding fire.

Love pulled into a climbing spiral, forcing the Vultures to
follow her into a vertical engagement. Torres and Ford kept firing, their
magrail rounds forcing two fighters to break off their attack runs.

Republic airspace opened ahead. Eight F-97 Orions streaked
past the *Jack*, engaging the pursuing Vultures. The lead Orion locked
onto the nearest enemy fighter, missiles away. The Vulture exploded
into an orange blaze. A second fighter tried to evade, pulling into a
steep climb, but an Orion's cannon fire cut it in half.

"Wolfpack Actual, Jolly Rogers Lead," came the transmission.
"You're clear to proceed. We'll handle cleanup."

"Copy, Jolly Rogers. Thanks for the assist."

The Jolly Rogers. *Cooper's old squadron*, Love thought.
Wonder how he's doing?

Love pointed *Jack* toward the upper atmosphere, climbing
toward the *Gallipoli*. The port engine coughed and wheezed, but it kept
running. Green monitored the hydraulic leaks, calculating whether
they'd make it back without losing flight controls.

Her tactical display still showed the ongoing battle around
Ridge 248. Alpha Company's beacon still transmitted, which meant

they were still fighting. War meant you never knew who'd make it through the next hour.

But Cooper was tough. She'd flown him back to medical. He'd survived this long, and she would punch him in the face if he died. But he wouldn't, because she knew he'd survive longer, just like Love and her crew would. She'd made it this long, and she'd throw one hell of a tantrum if God, or whoever ran things in the afterlife, took her sooner rather than later.

Chapter 23:
Thirteen Days Gone

Late 2098
RNS *Mercy*

The synthetic's blue optical band moved across Coop's face as he pressed his back against the bulkhead. His chest throbbed with deep, burning pain. His right arm hung useless, the burns sending random signals that felt like electrical storms under his skin.

What the hell's going on with me?

The Synth moved closer with that perfect robotic gait he'd seen too many times. It was as if the synthetic was trying to mimic a human. It was getting close, but failing.

"Patient Cooper, you need to return to your bed." The voice carried no emotion.

Why am I in a med bay? Coop blinked several times. *Am I on a ship? Why am I on a ship? What happened?*

Coop's vision split the world into fragments. The medical bay became a battlefield. White walls turned into ridge lines. The gentle whir of life support systems morphed into the whine of incoming artillery. Was this reality or a nightmare? What was happening to him?

"Stay back." The words came out thick and all sideways and wrong, his tongue refusing to cooperate, working on its own. "I know what you are."

A doctor appeared in his peripheral vision, moving slowly with hands visible. "Cooper, you're safe. That is a C200, a medical synthetic. It's here to help."

Help? What was here to help? Coop wondered.

Help.

The word bounced around his skull without meaning. Synths didn't help. They killed. They'd tried to eliminate humans in the Great War. Coop tried to push himself further into the corner, but his legs wouldn't support his weight properly.

The synthetic stopped three meters away. "Patient displays elevated stress indicators. Recommend sedation protocol."

"Negative." The doctor stepped between them. "Cooper, look at me. You're aboard the RNS *Mercy*. It's a medical ship. You're no longer in combat. There are no enemies here."

Coop's chest burned, each breath sending fresh waves of pain through the blaster wound. The tremors spread through his body, each one making the injury scream. He tried to remember how he'd gotten here, but the memories scattered when he reached for them.

"Where's my team?" The question came out almost as thin as a whisper.

"Look, you've been out a while—thirteen days, actually, but I'm here to help you. We all are, Cooper. Regarding your team, I don't have information on them, but you did well. Just cooperate with us, and we'll help you get better, all right?"

Everything felt wrong, disconnected. The synthetic's optical sensors tracked his every movement. It made Coop's skin crawl.

"Almost two weeks," he said, the number penetrating the fog. "I've been out that long?"

"Affirmative. You had a severe concussion, burns, major trauma to your chest from a blaster weapon." The doc kept his voice steady. "Your body is still healing. What you're experiencing is normal."

Normal. Nothing about this felt normal. Coop tried to stand, using the wall for support, but his legs betrayed him. He slid back down, his chest yelling at him as the movement pulled at damaged tissue. Across from him sat a medical bed, the sheets all screwed up. Was that his? Had he crawled out of that just now, or had that Synth thrown him and that was why he was on the ground?

The damn Synth!

The synthetic moved forward again. "Patient requires immediate medical attention."

"I said stay back!" Coop's voice cracked.

The synthetic stopped.

The doctor knelt down, staying just outside arm's reach. "Cooper, I need you to listen. The C200 has been monitoring your vitals for just about two weeks, just like you said. It's the only reason you're alive. You took a direct hit from an enemy's weapon. The medical nanites and stem cells are repairing the damage, but it takes time. The tremors will fade. The confusion will clear."

"How long will it take for the confusion to clear?" The question came out before Coop could stop it.

"Weeks. Maybe a month, and on rare occasions, two months. Trauma and pain medication can mess with your head, but you're improving."

Months. The word smacked him across the face. Months of being useless, disconnected from his body, his mind. Months of not knowing if his hands would work when he needed them. Why weren't his hands working? Why were his fingers still curled? He tried to straighten them, only to realize his toes were curling as well. They hurt. Were they spasming? Toe cramps?

The synthetic's sensors whirred. "Patient's stress levels remain elevated. Recommend—"

"Shut it down, or shut it up!" Coop slurred his words, and the world started to tip upside down around him. He was dizzy. The meds, or something, maybe his concussion, really had control of him and wouldn't let go, and now this Synth wanted to try to mess with him. "Get that thing away from me."

The doctor hesitated, then nodded to the Synth. "Station yourself outside."

The C200 pivoted and walked toward the hatch. As it passed through the doorway, Coop's heartbeat eased slightly. The immediate threat was gone, but the wrongness remained.

"Better?" the doctor asked.

Coop tried to nod, but the movement sent fresh waves of nausea through his system. His chest continued its deep, burning ache, the pain pulsing with every heartbeat.

"The blaster burns caused severe trauma," the doctor explained. "The nanites are rebuilding tissue layer by layer. It takes time."

Time. Another word that meant nothing. Coop closed his eyes, trying to find something solid in the bedlam of his thoughts. Bear's face flickered through his memory, then Weber's, then others he couldn't quite name.

"Did we win?" The question surprised him.

"Rass? Republic and Primord forces are doing well, controlling several sectors of the planet. Your fire missions were crucial."

Fire missions. Coop remembered bits. Coordinates. Timing. The satisfaction of watching tungsten rods turn Zodark armor into molten slag. But the memories felt like they belonged to someone else, viewed through broken fiberglass.

His whole body jerked suddenly. He grunted as the movement pulled at his chest wound, sending fresh agony radiating outward. The spasm lasted ten seconds before subsiding, leaving him gasping, his face coiled in pain.

The doctor made notes on his datapad. "The spasms will decrease as your body heals. Eventually, the confusion will waver too as we reduce your pain medication. Physical therapy will help rebuild your strength."

The doctor's face moved closer. The man crouched down to Coop's level. Something flickered behind the man's eyes. Professional concern, maybe.

"Where are we going?"

The doctor's face softened a bit. "Mars. Why? Because—"

"Mars? Why the hell—"

They weren't going to Mars. The doc was tricking him. But why?

"Cooper, I need you to focus on my voice. Your injuries are severe, but they can heal with proper treatment."

Coop studied the doctor's face, noting the perfect symmetry, the way his pupils dilated at exactly the same rate. Too perfect. Too controlled. He was a fake. Had to be.

"Why won't you tell me about my team?" Coop asked.

"I've explained that I don't have current information on your unit's status. My concern is your recovery."

The deflection came too smooth, too quick. Coop's foggy brain started connecting fragments that might not belong together. The Synth outside the door. The evasive answers. He didn't know how the Zodarks had done it, but they had. This doctor was a Zodark in disguise.

Coop moved suddenly, swinging wildly at the doctor's face, his coordination so poor the blow barely grazed the man's cheek. The doctor jerked back, standing quickly.

"I need assistance in here," he called.

The doors hissed open. Medical staff flooded through the doorway. Coop kicked out with both legs, missing everything but air, his body refusing to obey basic commands. They surrounded him anyway, hands grabbing his arms and shoulders.

"Get off me!" Coop yelled. "You're not Republic!"

He thrashed. They gripped harder. His chest hurt. Blood seeped through his bandages, streaks looking too red, too bright under the medical bay's lights, that they too couldn't be real. All of this was fake. Then the pain shot through his body like he was sitting in an electric chair and someone had just activated it… but he kept fighting.

The Synth appeared in the doorway again, moving toward him with that perfect gait, those overly precise humanlike strides. In its hand, a medical scanner hummed.

Coop's panic reached critical mass.

"Orbot!" The scream tore from his throat. "It's an Orbot!"

The synthetic continued its approach with the calm of a robot. Why couldn't these people see what it was? Because they too were in disguise. They too were Zodarks. They too had worked with the Orbots to snatch him.

"Patient exhibits severe paranoid ideation," the Synth said. "Recommend immediate chemical restraint."

A nurse appeared beside him, sedative injector in her grasp. The needle found Coop's neck before he could twist away. Relaxation flooded through his system, turning his muscles into jelly against his will.

The terror still burned in his mind even as his body refused to respond. The synthetic's face hovered over him, and Coop tried to scream a warning, yet it came out as an incomprehensible whisper.

"Vitals stabilizing," the Synth reported. "Trauma response remains elevated."

The medical staff stepped back. Coop's vision blurred at the edges, but he could still see their faces.

"Where's Alpha Company?" The words slurred together. "Where's Gill? Vega? Crawford? Li?"

"We'll check on that information for you," the doctor said.

The lies came too easy. The deflections too smooth. Why couldn't they give him straight answers about his people? Why did every question get buried under medical jargon and promises to investigate? Because this was the enemy, not the Republic.

Coop tried to grab the nurse's arm as she adjusted his IV drip, but his coordination had dissolved into nothing. His fingers barely made contact before his hand fell back to the bed. The simple movement exhausted him completely.

How did I get on the bed?

The nurse smiled and increased the drip rate. Fresh sedative hit his bloodstream.

"Sleep now, Cooper. Everything will be clearer when you wake up."

But nothing would be clearer. He could feel it in the way they moved, the way they looked at each other when they thought he wasn't watching. The medical bay became a prison of white walls and concerned faces that might not be human at all. They couldn't be. No human would do this to him. What did they do to his chest? Why was he burned? Who'd put someone in a white prison of white, white, white everywhere?

An enemy. That's who...

As consciousness faded, one terrible certainty remained: he was completely alone, surrounded by Zodarks and Orbots wearing the faces of allies.

The drugs pulled him into a horrible dream where the explosion on Ridge 248 bled into Bear's memories. His grandfather's P-51 Mustang dove through flak over Germany while Zodark artillery pounded the forest around him. Bear's voice resounded through the cockpit, calling out target coordinates that became his own fire missions.

The nightmare looped through generations of Coopers at war. His great-grandfather's trench warfare. His grandfather's aerial combat. His dad's sacrifice during the Great War. His own broken body in this medical jail. Each explosion blended into the next until he couldn't tell which war he was fighting or which Cooper he was supposed to be.

In the dream, Bear turned toward him with holes where his eyes should have been. "You left your comrades behind, Coop. Every single one."

Chapter 24:
Diesel and the Long Road

Late 2098
Mattis Military Complex
Mars

Coop's eyes cracked open to red dust swirling outside reinforced windows. Mars. The realization hit through the haze of medication. His throat felt like sandpaper. His chest ached with every breath, the blaster wound still healing deep in his tissue. His right arm burned constantly, the damaged nerves firing pain signals that wouldn't stop.

Mattis Military Complex sprawled across the Martian highlands. Its interconnected domes and structures were built into russet cliffs. DARPA facilities squatted in the distance, their black towers rising high. The sight should have comforted him, or wowed him, to say the least. Instead, fragments of paranoia whispered at the edges of his consciousness. Were those really Republic facilities? His pain-fogged mind couldn't tell the difference between reality and the nightmares that had consumed him aboard the *Mercy*.

The shuttle transporting him here landed, its engines winding down. Medical personnel moved around his gurney, their voices distant. Coop tried to speak. To tell them he remembered going insane on the ship, remembered the paranoia eating his thoughts. Wanted to say he was sorry. Thank God they'd pumped him full of chemicals to calm him down. Without the sedatives, he would've convinced himself these people were Zodarks wearing human faces. Even now, medicated and rational, part of him wondered if the Synths here were really medical units or something worse. His chest throbbed. The burns still fired random pain signals through his body.

A doctor's voice cut through the haze as she reviewed his chart. "Severe blaster trauma to the chest, third-degree burns on the right arm extending to the shoulder, moderate traumatic brain injury with residual inflammation." Her words were clinical, detached, but Coop caught something else underneath. Concern? Pity? The blaster hit and concussion had scrambled his body's responses worse than a computer hit by an EMP.

She looked at him directly for the first time, studying his face. "You're going to be here a while, Lieutenant. But you're alive, and that's more than we expected when they dragged you off the battlefield. I know this isn't what you want, but trust me, I'm not the only one that will be glad you survived. You're a hero."

She continued speaking, but his mind couldn't register much. TASC officer. Multiple commendations. The phrases drifted through his consciousness, but they felt like they belonged to someone else. Some other Cooper who could coordinate fire missions without his hands shaking, who could speak without his tongue feeling thick and uncooperative.

He lost consciousness as they transported him through the hangar.

****

The next day brought unwelcome clarity. Coop sat in his hospital bed, fingers of his left hand tracing the edges of the bandages covering his right arm. Every movement of his chest sent shooting pains through the wound. There, he couldn't do much but stare at the red horizon through his private room window. The pain medication kept the worst agony at bay, but it couldn't touch the deeper ache of not knowing who he was anymore. The headache still lingered, a dull throb behind his eyes.

The medical staff had been brutally honest about his condition. His TASC unit had been hit hard by Zodark artillery. They still couldn't tell him who'd survived and who hadn't. Nonetheless, multiple burns covered his body and he'd sustained a serious concussion. Major head trauma, which was probably why, even after medication, his head still ached. Nausea accompanied him constantly, made worse every time he tried to sit up and his chest wound protested. At least he could hold down liquids. He'd lost fourteen pounds according to his chart. His reflection in the dark window showed a stranger's gaunt face staring back.

To distract himself from the medical reports, he'd researched the facility housing him. Coop's mind drifted to yesterday's reading about James Mattis on a datapad the med facility loaned him. The name had been familiar, but the details surprised him. The "warrior monk" had commanded Marines through three wars, always reading, always learning. Mattis led from the front in Iraq, pushed innovative tactics in Afghanistan, built the pre–Great War Marine Corps into something unstoppable. What struck Coop most was the seven thousand books Mattis had collected on strategy and history. A general who believed knowledge was another weapon in the arsenal.

Coop wondered if Mattis had ever felt his body betray him, had ever fought battles against pain where victory seemed impossible.

The casualty reports from Rass made his personal suffering feel insignificant and overwhelming at the same time. Numbers cascaded across Coop's consciousness. The data kept changing as reports filtered in, but the most current report had been clear enough. Almost one hundred thousand Republic casualties on Rass. Almost one hundred thousand Primord losses. The numbers climbed higher each day as search and rescue teams found more bodies. The Rass campaign had devoured entire divisions. Turned the star system into a damn graveyard.

Cooper tried to process the mathematics of mass death, but his aching head couldn't hold the figures. Had Alpha Company survived? Had Gill made it off the ridge? Vega? The questions circled his mind on endless repeat, each cycle bringing fresh spikes of pain behind his eyes. He kept trying to figure out who Li was, that name floating in his brain like an itch he couldn't scratch. Weber had died. He remembered that, and then there was Crawford. That name meant something too. He couldn't bring up anyone's face, no matter how hard he tried.

By afternoon, the intelligence updates drew an even grimmer picture. The data streams continued their brutal accounting. Four hundred thousand Zodark dead and the campaign was still going on. Orbital bombardments had glassed entire continents. Cities reduced to craters. Coop's fire missions had helped create this devastation, dropping tungsten rods and naval gunfire on coordinates he'd called in. His head pounded as he tried to remember details. Each attempt to remember his team sent fresh waves of agony through his skull. The scale overwhelmed him.

A knock at the door interrupted his spiral into darkness.

The physical therapist filled the doorway. Chief Petty Officer Tucker "Diesel" Webb stood six foot eight and weighed three hundred pounds of solid muscle. His laugh boomed through the medical ward, reminding Coop of Bear's infectious humor. Diesel made Bear look small, which Coop hadn't thought possible. The man's massive hands could probably crush a Zodark head, but they moved with surprising gentleness as he checked Cooper's chart.

"Ready to get this party started, flyboy?" Diesel's grin stretched across his face. Combat ribbons decorated his uniform. A Purple Heart caught Coop's attention. Clearly the man's specialty was now rebuilding broken soldiers. Turning damaged warriors back into functional humans.

Coop attempted to respond, but his tongue felt thick and uncooperative. The words tangled in his throat. His chest ached with the effort of trying to speak. His right hand spasmed against the bedsheets, the burned nerves misfiring. The simple act of trying to speak exhausted him, left him feeling like he'd run a marathon.

Diesel nodded with understanding. He'd no doubt seen plenty of trauma patients. "We'll take it slow, Coop. One step at a time. No pressure, no timelines. Your body's doing repair work right now, and healing takes time. Even with the stem cells and nanites. They're doing their job as well, so don't worry, we'll have you back to new, all right?"

Ten minutes later, Diesel wheeled Cooper through corridors stretching toward infinity. Reinforced windows lined the walls, offering glimpses of Mars. The alien landscape made Earth, New Eden, and Intus seem like half-remembered dreams from another life.

Outside, red plains rolled toward mountain ranges scraping the thin atmosphere. Olympus Mons dominated the horizon, its peak lost in perpetual dust clouds. The sight should have been magnificent, but Coop felt nothing. His emotional responses had flattened into a gray emptiness that worried him more than the physical damage. This military base clung to cliff faces with the stubbornness of engineers who'd built for war, not comfort. Kinda like his body's struggle to heal itself—or so he imagined.

"This place houses twelve thousand personnel," Diesel said, navigating past security checkpoints. "Medical, research, training. DARPA runs half the complex." Marines nodded as they passed, their respect for any wounded warrior automatic, or so Coop thought. He tried to nod back, but his chest protested, leaving him frozen in place. The bandages under his robes felt too tight, too uncomfortable. He just wanted to take them off—also to see how the healing was progressing from just yesterday. Maybe it would be too minor to tell.

The DARPA sections fascinated and unsettled him. Blast doors marked with classification warnings blocked entire sections. Coop's tired vision doubled the security text, turning warnings into meaningless blurs. Scientists in lab coats hurried between restricted areas, carrying projects that might end the war or start new ones. Coop wondered if they were developing better ways to treat gunshot wounds, or new weapons that would create more casualties like him.

The therapy room sprawled across two levels, looking more like a high-tech workshop than a medical facility. It was filled with equipment looking more like torture devices than medical tools. Neural stimulation pods whirred with electricity. Robotic limbs hung from ceiling mounts, waiting for new owners. Balance beams, coordination ladders, and fine motor control stations filled the space. The sheer variety of rehabilitation equipment told him they dealt with every kind of damage war could inflict. Diesel positioned Coop's wheelchair beside a padded table.

"Time to see what we're working with." Diesel helped Coop stand, supporting most of his weight. "Let's start simple. Just try to squeeze my hand."

Diesel extended his massive palm. Coop focused all his concentration on his right hand, willing his fingers to respond. Pain shot up his arm. The burned tissue didn't like that, not one bit. His arm twitched once, jerked sideways, then collapsed. Tremors rippled through his body. Damaged nerves firing every which way. Diesel caught him before he hit the floor.

"OK, OK, OK. Well, that's actually not bad for day one," Diesel explained, lowering Cooper back into the wheelchair. "I saw your fingers try to move. That means the nerve damage isn't complete. The burns scrambled your peripheral nerves and you took a hell of a hit to the head. Your body's trying to heal, but it takes time."

Exactly what the docs on RNS *Mercy* had told him on so many occasions.

Yet today's failure to squeeze his hand into a fist hit Coop harder than he expected. He wanted to scream. Over and over again, because after more failures on top of failures, no matter what Diesel asked him to perform, his body wouldn't obey. His body had become an enemy, a stranger wearing his skin and refusing to follow orders that hurt too much to execute. Easy movements that once came automatically now required enormous effort and kept failing. What if this was permanent? What if he never regained control? The thoughts spiraled downward before he could stop them.

"Hey." Diesel's voice blasted through the panic. "Seen worse cases walk out of here, Coop." Diesel's voice carried conviction, and Coop couldn't help but believe the guy. "You will too. Just not today. And not tomorrow. But eventually. I've got a soldier who came in here with worse burns than yours, and shot up to hell. Now he's back to full duty. Your body's tougher than you think."

Hours later, he was in the rehabilitation ward, and it was busy. And in here, Coop's failures felt small among so many others fighting their own battles. A sergeant practiced walking on prosthetic legs, each step guided by neural impulses translating into mechanical movement. The man's face showed fierce concentration as he navigated an obstacle course, his mechanical limbs responding faster than organic ones ever could. Advanced processors read his brain patterns, turning thoughts into motion, so said Diesel when he noticed Coop staring. An Army lieutenant wrote her name with a robotic arm, synthetic muscles responding to commands her severed nerves could no longer carry. Her handwriting looked better than Coop's had even before the injury.

Cooper watched a pilot coordinate movements with both replacement arms. The man's new limbs could crush steel or handle delicate electronics. The man noticed Coop watching and offered a casual salute with his prosthetic hand.

"That's Captain Hicks," Diesel said. "Lost both arms to Zodark blasters. Been here eight months. Now he benches five hundred pounds. Technology's caught up to what we need it to do."

Coop felt a flicker of something that might have been hope. If Hicks could come back from losing both arms, maybe recovering from burns, a blaster shot, and trauma wasn't the end of everything.

An hour later, after failed attempts at basic coordination exercises, Diesel wheeled Cooper back toward his room. They passed a mirror mounted on the wall. Coop's reflection caught his peripheral vision. He turned away immediately, unable to face what war had etched into his features. Scar tissue covered the right side of his face where burns had left their mark. The damage extended down his neck, disappearing under his medical gown.

Diesel slowed the wheelchair. "Mirror work comes later, when you're ready. Scars tell stories, Coop. Yours says you stood your ground when hell came calling. You lived through the ridge when a lot of good people didn't. That's got to count for something." He paused the wheelchair completely. "And don't worry about the cosmetics. We've got regenerative treatments that'll have you looking like a recruiting poster again. Takes time, but it works."

Coop's hand moved unconsciously to his damaged face, feeling ridged flesh where smooth skin once was. The scars were just surface damage. The real question was whether they could fix the nerve damage in his arm, whether the pain would ever stop, whether his body would ever feel like his own again.

Military regulations prohibited family travel to combat medical facilities during active operations. His mother couldn't visit even if she wanted to. That brought relief rather than sadness. She'd already lost Dad to divorce. Seeing her son broken and burned might finish what grief had started. Better she remember him as he was than see what the ridge had made him. At least until the regenerative treatments worked their magic.

As they reached his room, Coop found his voice again. "Diesel. The…" He cleared his throat. His chest spasmed for a second, his face contorting, until the discomfort eased and receded. "The people who don't make it back… what happens to them?"

Diesel jerked his head back in surprise. "What? You can talk? All this time and you just kept quiet?"

Coop didn't want to keep quiet—and, heck, he didn't know how or why his voice had suddenly decided to work—but he didn't correct Diesel.

The physical therapist's expression grew serious. "Well, Cooper, some find different ways to serve. Some go home and find new purposes. Some…" He shrugged. "Some don't make it back in here"— he tapped his temple—"even if their bodies heal. But that's not going to be you, Coop. I can tell the difference."

Coop wanted to ask how he could tell, but exhaustion was pulling him under again. His body could only handle so much before shutting down. The pain, the effort, the constant struggle against damaged tissue.

Still, he managed a thought that surprised him with its clarity. The war had taken his body, his coordination, his face. But it wouldn't take his dignity. That was the one thing he'd keep, no matter how long the road back took.

Chapter 25:
Captain's Insignia

Late 2098
Victory Base Complex
Emerald City, New Eden

The dress uniform felt different this time. Heavier somehow. Lee had earned this, but with it came even higher expectations beyond fabric and insignia. At least, to him it did. More responsibility, like always. A way toward admiral. A means to help humanity from a higher position. And numerous other reasons he'd thought about for years.

Lee adjusted the collar, studying his reflection in the mirror of his temporary quarters at Victory Base Complex. The formal change of command ceremony would take place in six hours. This marked the end of his tenure as commander and the beginning of his new role as captain. His service record lay open on the desk behind him, documenting years of successful operations earning him a below-the-zone promotion. An advancement arriving earlier than the standard timeline, and all because of his exceptional performance in the field, or better yet, in the stars.

Task Force 27 required experienced leadership, and his hybrid technology expertise made him the logical choice for expanded command responsibilities. At least, that was how he saw it, and damn if he wasn't proud at the moment. He wished his mom and dad could see him now. Though they'd shunned him when he'd left their religious community, a small part of him still hoped they might understand what he'd accomplished, especially this. He knew better, though. Military service was exactly what they'd condemned, but the thought persisted anyway. He hadn't spoken to them in years, but he'd kept tabs through government officials who checked on his family from time to time. They were alive and well, thriving in their religious community, and all he could do was smile at that knowledge, bittersweet as it was. His promotion would be announced alongside Sato's advancement to commander and her assumption of command aboard the RNS *Invincible*. A transition testing both officers as they moved to new roles without each other, but within the same task force structure.

Lee stepped out of his quarters and strode down the hall. He checked his watch. He'd be on time.

When he made it to the briefing room, he sat down. Other captains, including Sato, sat amongst each other. All forming Task Force 27, and all Earthers. The Altairians joining this task force as logistics and support were no doubt being briefed now, though exactly where, Lee didn't know.

Admiral Costello stood before holographic displays, his hands clasped behind his back. The screens showed recent Pharaonis activities in what Lee learned was called the Trrahan system, a system that neighbored Serpentis. The data meant new developments might shift their entire operational timeline.

The intelligence represented new data collected over the past seventy-two hours, indicating coordinated strikes. Like Lee thought, and like many of the higher-ups believed, it suggested preparation for larger operations. An invasion, perhaps.

Recently, systematic attacks had eliminated monitoring stations, satellites, early-warning buoys, and defensive outposts along established trade routes. Each destroyed facility created blind spots in the alliance's early-warning network. What did that mean, specifically? Approach vectors that once provided advance warning could now conceal entire fleets. Multiple alliance territories sat exposed. The intelligence blackout meant they were operating without crucial reconnaissance data.

They didn't know what they didn't know.

Task Force 27 needed to reach the system immediately. But protocol demanded otherwise. New captains like Sato had to complete crew integration and basic operational drills before deploying to combat zones. Standard procedure required a minimum of one week for commanding officers to establish operational readiness with their crews. The good news? Sato would have longer, and the military would rather deploy a prepared force than rush unprepared units into combat. So they waited. Like usual, the military waiting game was in process.

"The pattern's too clean for random raids," Costello said, highlighting destruction sites across the sector map. "They're avoiding certain installations while targeting others. This implies external technical support."

Lee studied the tactical displays, noting how the attacks formed a pattern across the sector. "What's their primary objective? Territory or resources?"

"Both. Mining colony seizures have been their most concerning development." Costello switched to a new display showing asteroid mining facilities. "Attacks on extraction operations have resulted in the capture of three major facilities that produce titanium and rare elements essential for alliance shipbuilding. Pharaonis forces have fortified a few of these positions and begun extracting resources for their own military production. They'll continue if we don't stop them."

"They're turning our infrastructure into Dominion supply sources," Sato observed.

Costello nodded. "Correct. The seized facilities were producing approximately forty percent of a two dozen sectors' strategic metals. Without those resources, some alliance shipyard production schedules will face significant delays."

Costello's expression grew more serious. "Your task force will be our primary response to this escalation. The assessment concludes that early intervention represents the most effective method for containing Pharaonis aggression before it can threaten core alliance territories.

"The updated intelligence paints a concerning picture of Pharaonis expansion," Costello continued. "These mutant termite creatures have demonstrated tactical coordination that exceeds previous assessments of their military capabilities. It means they're being helped, and by how many races in the Dominion, well, we're meaning to find out. That's why I've chosen the best of the best for this operation." He looked at everyone in the room. "Beyond the mining seizures, they've established forward operating bases near critical junction points. Success in the Trrahan system would provide Pharaonis forces with staging areas for expansion toward more strategically valuable targets, including the Serpentis system with its critical stargate network."

Costello eyed Lee. "Captain, your task force will operate under Tully oversight, naturally. But the tactical decisions will be yours."

The briefing ended with another ten minutes of discussion. Lee filed out with the other officers, his mind turning to the enemy, because the Pharaonis weren't just raiding anymore. They were building something along with the Zodarks and Orbots.

Two hours later, Lee stood in Victory Base's Fleet Observation Center, watching the RNS *Invincible* through the massive holographic display near the room's far wall. The battlecruiser hung in space, her hull plating practically shining. No battle scars. No laser burns marked close calls with death. They'd cleaned her up well, and she was a true beauty.

The ship squatted in space. Three turrets crowned her forward section, each mounting twin twenty-four-inch magnetic railguns. The other killers were the phased-array laser banks positioned near her bottom forward section. Lee noted dozens of other weapons before footsteps echoed toward him and took his mind from his examinations. He turned, his arms crossed, and couldn't help but smile.

"Commander Sato."

"She's gorgeous," Sato said, joining him at the observation deck.

Lee nodded, studying the antiship missile pods clustered along *Invincible*'s hull. "Fast, heavily armed, and built for independent operations. Everything a task force commander needs in a subordinate vessel."

"Independent operations," Sato repeated, her voice carrying a note he couldn't quite read. "Strange how that sounds both exciting and terrifying."

He slightly jerked back with her reply. "I've never heard you say *terrifying* before…"

"You've never seen me command my own ship before. And neither have I." She grinned. "*Terrifying* in a good way, Captain. I'm nervous, but nerves help. It means I'm going to be fully aware, and ready. I'll make sure I'm more than just prepared."

"A bit of advice?"

She bit her lower lip. "I was waiting for that."

"Trust the instincts that got you here. You've been making command decisions for years. Now you just won't have me second-guessing them." He paused, his expression softening slightly. "The crew will test you early. Not maliciously, but they need to know their captain's backbone. Show them the same resolve you've shown me when I was wrong about something. And, Noriko?" He used her first name deliberately. "Don't try to be me. Be the commander you already are."

"Resolve, huh?" Her expression hardened. "I've watched you command for years, Ripley. Studied every decision, every crisis response. Not to copy them, but to understand the thinking behind them." She turned back to the *Invincible*, her hands clasped behind her back, mirroring his posture. "The hardest part won't be proving myself to the crew. It'll be not reaching for the comm to ask what you think when the first real crisis hits." She paused, then looked at him directly. "But I suppose that's when I'll know I'm actually ready for this."

"Indeed."

Before them, the holographic display shifted, showing *Invincible*'s bridge layout. Enhanced communication arrays designed for fleet coordination dominated the tactical stations. Improved displays would provide real-time data sharing between vessels during joint operations. The Republic's engineers had built this ship for the kind of complex multispecies operations that Task Force 27 would conduct.

"Your crew assignments finalized?" Lee asked.

"Most of them. Lieutenant Marsh accepted the TAO position. Lieutenant Commander Black accepted the executive officer position. He's good, Ripley. Damn good. Almost as good as me." She winked.

Lee smiled. "High praise."

"Thomas Rose of the RNS *Maine* requested transfer to serve as my chief engineer. Says he wants to work with the new fusion manifold systems."

Lee stared at Sato. Years of shared successes, near deaths, and the kind of trust that only developed under heavy fire. Command partnerships like theirs were rare. Breaking them up was necessary for career advancement, but that didn't make it easier.

"It's the beginning of something important," he said. "You've earned this command. *Invincible* needs a captain who understands both tactical innovation and crew management. That's you."

The observation center's doors opened. A Republic Navy aide approached with a datapad.

"Captain Lee, Admiral Costello requests your presence in Auditorium One. The ceremony begins in thirty minutes."

Lee checked his chronometer. Time moved differently when you were contemplating major life changes. "Thank you, Petty Officer."

The aide departed. Sato straightened her dress uniform jacket.

"Ready to make this official?" she asked.

"Been ready for years."

She grinned. "Same."

Fifteen minutes later, Lee and Sato stood just beyond the threshold of Victory Base's main auditorium, taking it all in. The air was electric in a controlled sort of way. Maybe electric because that's what Lee was feeling, but the atmosphere buzzed with something more than a normal, formal military ceremony.

Republic personnel filled the front sections while Altairian diplomats occupied designated areas, their pale forms and cobalt-black eyes observing human traditions with apparent interest. Alliance representatives from various member species dotted the audience, no doubt understanding that promotions based on demonstrated competence under fire strengthened the coalition, keeping them all alive.

Lee and Sato made their way down the aisle and stood at attention on the elevated platform. They faced Admiral Costello and his command staff. The symbolic transfer of authority would mark his transition from ship commander to task force commander yet again, while establishing Sato's advancement to independent command within the same operational structure. It was more complicated than it sounded, but Lee figured it would work better than expected.

After everyone sat and the auditorium quieted, Costello stepped forward, his voice carrying across the large chamber.

"We gather today to recognize exceptional service and to invest new authority in officers who've proven themselves worthy of expanded responsibility."

Lee felt the eyes of every person in the auditorium, knowing that his performance in the coming months would either validate this promotion or demonstrate that competence at one level didn't guarantee success at the next.

"Lieutenant Commander Noriko Sato," Costello continued, "you are hereby promoted to the rank of commander and will assume command of the Republic Navy Ship *Invincible*, effective immediately.”

Costello stepped forward with the commander’s insignia. Sato removed her lieutenant commander’s bars, handing them to Lee in a gesture speaking to their partnership. He pinned the new rank on her collar, their eyes meeting briefly. The mixture of pride and loss in her expression probably matched his own.

“Commander Sato, do you accept command of RNS *Invincible* and all responsibilities therein?”

“I accept command, sir.”

“Commander Lee,” Costello said, turning to him. “You are hereby promoted to the rank of captain and will assume command of Task Force 27, effective immediately.”

Costello pinned the rank to Lee’s uniform. He couldn’t help it, but a soft sigh escaped his mouth. It just happened, and Costello noticed it, and his eyes understood the exhale, one high ranking officer to another. It took one hell of a beating to get here, and Lee, like many other captains in the Republic, deserved every ounce of the new insignia.

“Captain Lee, do you accept command of Task Force 27 and all responsibilities therein?”

“I accept command, sir.”

Costello’s expression shifted slightly, seeming more personal than ceremonial. The admiral had a reputation for caring about his officers, making you feel valued rather than like just another name on a roster.

“Both of you have demonstrated the leadership, tactical acumen, and moral courage that the Republic requires in its senior officers,” Costello said. “Your new commands will test those qualities in ways that your previous assignments could not prepare you for.”

The admiral paused, his gaze moving between Lee and Sato. “Task Force 27 represents our commitment to alliance cooperation and border security. Your success will determine whether the Pharaonis threat remains contained or expands toward our core territories.”

Lee exchanged a look with Sato. The sadness of separation mixed with excitement for new challenges passed between them. And boy was Lee proud of her achievement.

"Commander Sato," Costello said, "your independent command of *Invincible* will require adapting to Altairian operational methods while maintaining Republic tactical doctrine. Captain Lee, your task force coordination responsibilities extend beyond fleet command to alliance diplomacy."

The ceremony concluded with the traditional reading of orders. Lee and Sato saluted Costello and his staff, then turned to face the audience. Applause filled the auditorium, but Lee's attention focused on the Altairian diplomats whose cooperation would determine mission success. He'd make sure to work well with them, even if they were just in support roles—he'd be the best damn Republic officer they'd ever met.

Command ceremonies marked endings as much as beginnings. His partnership with Sato was over, but his new responsibilities were just starting, and she'd still be there with him, just in a different ship. The knowledge that they would still fight, and bleed, together gave him a second of calm, a feeling that everything would work out just fine.

Chapter 26:
First Day of Command

Late 2098
RNS *Invincible*
Planet New Eden

Two days had passed since the ceremony that had transformed Noriko from Lieutenant commander to commander, and from executive officer to ship's captain. The orbital docking station above New Eden spread out across her viewport, its berths housing the vessels that would soon carry the Republic's fight to distant stars. Slip fourteen held the RNS *Invincible*, which was her ship now, surrounded by the skeletal framework of the station's maintenance gantries.

Sato stepped through the airlock. Her boots struck the deck plating. *Clink. Clink.* For some reason, it made her feel powerful, made her feel right for the job. It was the sound of a commander walking.

The shuttle bay was busy. Reactor technicians fine-tuned power distribution, environmental systems crews tested life support redundancies, and engineers calibrated the enhanced sensor arrays that would make *Invincible* into the task force's eyes and ears.

The official assumption of command had occurred during the ceremony, but this moment carried more for her than any formal proceedings. Standing in her ship's shuttle bay, watching her crew work, Sato understood that leadership meant more than rank insignia or ceremonial transfers. These people would follow her orders into combat, trust her judgment when death waited beyond the next stargate, and depend on her competence to bring them home. Command wrapped around her like a cloak, but unlike an item of clothing, she'd never be able to take it off. It was there for life now.

Chief Petty Officer Jerome Knight approached from the maintenance bay. Sato had handpicked him from a dozen qualified candidates, drawn by his reputation for keeping ships operational under impossible conditions. His service record read like a catalog of Republic victories, with too many to name.

"Captain," Knight said, offering a hearty salute. "Welcome aboard the *Invincible*. She's a fine ship, ma'am. The crew's eager to show you what she can do."

"Thank you, Chief. I've read your service record. Impressive work on the *Constellation* during the Intus engagement."

Knight's eyes sharpened with approval. "You did your homework, Captain. That's good. The crew needs to know their captain understands what they're capable of."

"I intend to find out firsthand. How soon can we complete predeployment checks?"

"Eighteen hours, ma'am. We're installing the new communication arrays and running final calibrations on the tactical systems. She'll be ready when you are."

The tour of the *Invincible* introduced Sato to new faces. Chief Petty Officer Mendoza showed her the enhanced communication arrays, tapping in commands across control panels as he explained the expanded range and encryption capabilities. Lieutenant Zhau showed the improved tactical displays that would coordinate fleet operations, the holographic projections painting holos of battle space, making previous systems look primitive.

Her quarters reflected the transition from executive officer to commander, from following orders to giving them. Sato arranged her few personal items on the desk: a photo of her mother taken after their escape from occupied Japan, and a small calligraphy set reminding her of peaceful moments between battles. The captain's chair behind her desk felt a bit too large, built for someone who would make decisions that rippled across star systems. Sitting there made Sato feel like a queen on her throne—it felt unfamiliar but good, and she knew get more used to it with each passing day.

The communication panel chimed. "Captain, this is Commander Black. Task Force briefing in Conference Room Alpha in ten minutes."

"Acknowledged. I'll be right there."

Sato walked through corridors that belonged to her now, past crew members who straightened when she approached.

Conference Room Alpha resounded with conversation as senior staff reviewed tactical displays and intelligence reports. Commander Patricia Black, her new executive officer, stood beside the main holographic projector, her auburn hair pulled back in regulation style, her green eyes sharp as a tack. Black had commanded a frigate squadron during the Intus campaign, earning a reputation for aggressive tactics, but executed to near perfection.

"Captain on deck," Black announced.

"As you were," Sato said, taking her position at the head of the table. "Let's begin." Nerves tingled through her veins. She tried to blink them away, and when that didn't work, she steadied her breathing and focused.

Black activated the holographic display, showing Task Force 27's expanded composition. "Task Force 27 now includes twenty ships under Captain Lee's overall command. Our entire fleet is presently integrating a new frigate squadron—RNS *Temper*, *Deluge*, *Onslaught*, and *Dignity*. Along with the battlecruiser RNS *Sovereign* for an added heavy fire support, while the cruisers *Joseph Stilwell*, *Patch*, *Wingate*, and *Kenney* give us more balanced offensive and defensive capabilities for our coming extended operations."

Sato studied the ship roster. The naming conventions honored World War II generals who'd changed how wars were fought. Alexander Patch had led the Seventh Army when they'd hit southern France. His amphibious tactics still showed up in how the Republic took planets. George Kenney had reinvented air power in the Pacific, and his coordinated strikes had become the blueprint for fleet combat in space. Orde Wingate's crazy long-range raids behind enemy lines? That was basically what Republic recon teams did now. And Joseph Stilwell had somehow kept the allies working together across China, Burma, and India. All lessons keeping the current alliance from falling apart.

"What's our operational timeline?" Sato asked.

"Seven days until departure," Black replied. "Captain Lee wants all vessels ready for extended deployment. We're looking at minimum six months in the Serpentis sector."

Lieutenant Commander Kenji Yamamoto, the ship's intelligence officer, stepped forward. "Captain, I have updates on recent developments in Tully space. Alliance negotiations have established operational parameters for Republic support operations."

Sato nodded. "Proceed."

Yamamoto activated a sector map showing a group of territories surrounding the Serpentis system. "The Tully have been fighting the Zodarks for a long, long time. How do you fight an adversary that long without defeating them? The answer lies in their nature. The Tully are primarily traders. They have extensive cargo hauler fleets but limited military infrastructure compared to their economic reach.

"The Pharaonis attacks have devastated Tully commercial operations. Their cargo hauler fleets normally transport nearly forty percent of the rare minerals and strategic metals used in Republic and Alliance shipbuilding. With trade routes compromised and mining facilities seized, our supply capabilities have been cut by nearly half. Our shipyards are already experiencing production delays. If the Pharaonis consolidate their hold on Tully space, we'll lose access to resources essential for maintaining fleet strength. That's why this mission matters beyond border security. We'll preserve the industrial capacity that keeps our ships operational."

The display shifted to show political boundaries and alliance relationships. "The situation is complicated by historical animosities. The Primords and the Ry'lians despise each other. They will not work together. The same applies to the Tully and Ry'lians. They were mortal enemies who fought multiple wars. Now they find themselves in the same alliance, forced to attend council sessions together. It took seventy-five years to get them to speak civilly during meetings."

"And they're both requesting our assistance," Sato observed.

"Correct, Captain. Both the Tully and Ry'lians have been raising alarms about border incursions for months. Outside of Altairian-controlled space, the Serpentis system holds the only stargates linking Tully and Ry'lian territories. Unfortunately, it also connects their space to Pharaonis and Orbot systems two jumps away."

Lieutenant Sean Marsh, the Tactical Action Officer, highlighted threat assessments on the display. "The Pharaonis threat has escalated beyond mining facility seizures and communication disruption. Intelligence confirms deployment of a small fleet concentration in the Trrahan system. Twelve vessels operating in coordinated formations. This suggests Dominion technical support and strategic planning that exceeds previous assessments of Pharaonis military capabilities."

This, Sato knew. She'd been briefed. Extensively. The tactical situation, the political mess, the threat assessments. They all knew she knew it.

But this wasn't about the intelligence. This was about something else entirely.

This was about watching—watching how her senior staff operated, how they presented information, and how they responded to questions. It was about them watching her back, seeing how she processed briefings, what details she focused on, and how she made decisions.

A new ship meant new crew dynamics. Officers who'd served together for years had established rhythms. Shorthand communications. Unspoken understandings. Now they had to learn *her* command style while she learned their capabilities.

Did Yamamoto always provide this level of detail? Or was he testing her patience? Was Black's crisp presentation her normal style, or was she being extra formal with a new captain? How would Marsh react under pressure? When lives depended on split-second tactical decisions?

These briefings would become their foundation, the way they worked through problems here would determine how effectively they functioned when the shooting started. Trust had to be built. Competence demonstrated. Leadership established. Not through ceremony or rank insignia. Through the daily work of turning a collection of skilled individuals into a cohesive command team.

Sato leaned forward, studying the tactical projections. "Coordinated formations indicate external training and possibly shared technology. What's our assessment of their combat effectiveness?"

"Unknown, Captain," Marsh replied.

Lieutenant Sofia Delacroix, the communications officer, added her report. "Subspace relay destruction has created communication blackouts affecting three star systems. Alliance colonies are isolated from central command, preventing coordinated defensive responses. The pattern suggests systematic preparation for major offensive operations."

Again, Sato already understood this information, and it was a joy, a true joy, for her to watch her staff present this information to her. Her nerves, though charred when she entered the briefing, was now bubbling with electric excitement and intense focus. This, as a commander, was where she belonged.

Twenty more minutes ticked by, and the briefing room emptied around Sato as officers gathered their tablets and headed for their duty stations. She remained at the holographic projector. There, she studied the displays showing their operational area. The Serpentis system floated in blue light, three stargates marking the crossroads where three civilizations met. Where Republic, Tully, and Altairians decisions would ripple across star systems. Other sectors materialized on the screen, the Trrahan system being one of them, their first planned recon sector.

"Captain?" Commander Black waited by the door. "Anything else you need?"

"I'm good. Thank you, Commander."

Black nodded and left. The room quieted. Sato touched the holographic controls, rotating the display to examine approach vectors and defensive positions. Each angle revealed new complexities, new variables that could turn routine patrol into a death trap. She jotted them down on her pad. She'd spend the evening memorizing them, figuring out which threats were real and which ones were just her nerves talking. Because when they hit Tully space and everything went sideways, she wouldn't have time to check her notes. Just her, her crew, the task force, and whatever decisions came out of her mouth in those split seconds.

The corridor stretched ahead as she walked toward her quarters. Crew members stepped aside, giving salutes. As executive officer, she'd been part of the crew. As commander, she stood apart from it. Lee had warned her about this isolation, the way leadership created a vast distance of space between you and everyone else.

Her mother's face surfaced in her memory. Sitting in their cramped apartment in San Francisco, teaching her daughter the breathing techniques that had kept them alive during the escape from Fukuoka, Japan. Mama had been twenty-eight then, younger than Sato was now, carrying responsibility for two lives while Asian Alliance intelligence had once hunted them through the ruins of Kyushu, one of the lower islands of Japan.

The memory shifted to that final dinner in their house outside Fukuoka: Papa laughing at something Sato said, chopsticks halfway to his mouth when the door exploded inward. Men in dark suits. The lead police officer's pistol already drawn. Papa rising from his chair, Mama reaching for Sato, her father trying to shield them when the first shot punched through his chest.

Blood on the tatami mats. Mama grabbing her hand, pulling her toward the back door while more shots shattered dishes and splintered wood. Running through narrow streets while sirens wailed in the distance. Hiding in drainage tunnels that reeked of sewage and fear.

That strength lived in her blood now. The ability to function when everything fell apart. To make decisions when death waited around every corner. But command demanded she find her own version of that courage, her own way of carrying others through the darkness.

Hundreds of crew members, including the C100 synthetic units assigned to security details, were now under her leadership. Each one trusted her to bring them home.

She reached her quarters and paused outside the door. The corridor was empty. Through the viewport, New Eden's surface spread below, green continents and blue oceans looking peaceful from orbit. Down there, Republic citizens lived their lives, raised families, built futures. They depended on the fleet to keep them safe.

Sato placed her hand over her heart and began the breathing exercise her mother had taught her during those terrifying nights in the refugee camps. Four counts in, feeling her lungs expand, her rib cage lift. Six counts out, releasing tension from shoulders and jaw. The rhythm slowed her racing thoughts, centered her focus on the present moment instead of the thousand variables that could go wrong in the Tully systems.

The technique had served her through Academy stress tests, through her first combat engagement when Zodark fighters swarmed their formation, through the long hours on *Poseidon*'s bridge when Lee trusted her to make tactical decisions that kept them alive. Now it would carry her through the transition to command, connecting her to family wisdom when circumstances threatened to overwhelm her judgment.

Four counts in. The responsibility was real. Six counts out. But she'd trained for this moment since the Academy, learned from the best officers in the fleet, proven herself under fire.

Four counts in. Lee believed in her abilities, or he wouldn't have recommended her for promotion. Six counts out. Admiral Costello had approved her command based on performance, not politics.

The breathing steadied her pulse, cleared her mind of doubt and anxiety. She was ready for this. Ready to lead. Ready to make the hard decisions that command demanded.

Sato touched the door control and stepped into her quarters. The captain's chair behind her desk no longer felt too large. Command wasn't something you grew into gradually. You either carried it or you didn't, and she did.

Chapter 27:
Delta Drop

Late 2098
Planet Rass

Ford's hands rested on his starboard gun controls while *Jack* descended through Rass's night sky. The troop bay behind him carried twelve armored giants—Delta operators in battlesuits.

Cold LZ my ass, Ford thought. *Intel's been wrong more than right lately.*

Hours ago, Commander Granger's holographic display had shown the insertion zone as a somewhat peaceful landing zone. No enemy activity was detected within five kilometers. Intelligence confirmed Zodark forces had pulled back from the sector two days ago, consolidating around their primary defensive positions near the capital. The Delta team's mission required stealth, and lots of it. They were to infiltrate twenty kilometers behind enemy lines, gather intelligence on Zodark command infrastructure, and exfiltrate before dawn.

Simple. Clean. And doable, especially for a Delta team.

Ford had studied the terrain map from his position at the back of the briefing room, noting the approach vector Love would fly. Three weeks into the Rass invasion and years of constant combat operations had taught him to distrust intelligence assessments that looked too clean.

The Delta team leader, Master Chief Zaines, had stood near the holographic display. Like the rest of the genetically modified spec ops personnel, this guy was huge. At that moment, twelve operators surrounded him. Their powered armor made them look like walking tanks, each capable of ripping Orbots apart with bare hands.

Ford had worked with Delta before. These weren't soldiers. They were weapons wrapped in human skin and high-tech armor, plus smarter and braver than all the rest.

Zaines nodded once at the mission parameters, his face expressionless. "Wheels up in twenty minutes. We'll handle our end. You just get us there and get yourselves out."

The finality in his voice said everything about how Delta operated. They'd disappear into the night. The Osprey crew's job ended the moment boots hit dirt. After that, the special operators would either complete their mission or die trying.

No middle ground existed in their world.

Now, in the present, Ford glanced at those same twelve giants sitting motionless in the troop bay. Master Chief Zaines sat nearest the ramp. The man hadn't moved in twenty minutes. Just sat there with the patience of someone who'd done this a thousand times before.

Different breed. Drop them into hell and they'll ask for the temperature to be turned up.

Green's voice cracked through Ford and Torres's helmet. "Torres, I'm getting thermal blooms on my display. Multiple contacts, bearing one-three-five, range eight hundred meters from the LZ."

Ford's stomach dropped as his own sensors confirmed the reading. Enemy forces. Right where intelligence had sworn the area was clear.

His targeting display showed the contacts in red. Zodark infantry signatures mixed with the distinctive heat patterns of Orbot cyborgs. Twenty hostiles, maybe more, moving directly toward the insertion point as if they knew exactly where the *Jack* was heading.

"How many?" Love's voice stayed calm over the intercom, but Ford heard the tension underneath.

"Fifteen confirmed," Green replied. "Looks like a Zodark patrol with Orbot support. They're closing on the LZ fast."

The mission parameters had just gone from stealth insertion to potential disaster. If they aborted, the Delta mission died before it started. If they committed, the *Jack* would be flying into a hot LZ that could light them up the moment they descended.

Love's decision came fast. "We're going in. Mission's too important to scrub."

Ford's hands tightened on his gun controls. *Of course we are. Because when has anything gone according to plan in three weeks?*

He keyed his intercom to the troop bay. "Deltas, LZ is compromised. Twenty hostiles approximately seven hundred meters from your insertion point, and closing. We'll suppress during your exit, but you're hitting dirt hot."

Master Chief Zaines's voice came back flat. Hell, he even seemed unbothered. "Copy. We're good."

No questions. No concerns. Just acknowledgment that they'd be fighting the moment they left the aircraft.

Ford heard movement through the internal feed. Twelve battlesuits standing, weapons coming online. The subtle hum of powered armor activating filled the troop bay.

These guys are either crazy or they've got balls made of titanium. Probably both.

He checked his ammunition count one more time. Twenty-four hundred rounds of .50-cal magrail.

Torres spoke up: "Chief, I've got the western approach covered. Anything coming from that direction gets shredded."

"Good. I'll take the northern sector. Stay sharp."

Jack descended into the LZ, Love pushing the Osprey through a steep approach, making Ford's gut climb into his throat. His gun mount swiveled automatically, tracking thermal signatures highlighted on his targeting screen.

Zodark infantry. Now five hundred meters northeast, sprinting toward the clearing where *Jack*'s skids would touch down.

The enemy had detected their approach. Whether it was through sound, thermal signature, or just bad luck, it didn't matter now. The Zodarks were coming, and they'd arrive seconds after the Deltas exited the craft.

"Weapons free," Love said. "Light them up."

Ford squeezed the trigger before she finished speaking.

His .50-cal magrail erupted, the weapon's roar filling his gun compartment as tungsten rounds streaked toward the treeline. His targeting computer tracked individual Zodarks, coloring them in red on his display. Three, four, five contacts dropped as his fire found them.

He gritted his teeth. *Come on, you blue bastards. Keep coming.*

The *Jack*'s landing lights stayed dark. There was no point advertising their position when the enemy already knew they were there. The Osprey's skids hit earth with a thud, and the *Jack* trembled.

"Ramp down!" Ford shouted into the intercom, his left hand hitting the hydraulic control while his right stayed on the gun.

The ramp began lowering. Ford watched the twelve Deltas move as one toward the opening, their armored boots shaking the deck.

Master Chief Zaines led them out, his battlesuit's weapon systems already tracking targets. The moment his boots hit Rass soil, the night exploded.

Deltas poured off the ramp. Ford's external cameras caught flashes of combat. A Delta's armored fist caved in a Zodark skull, another operator's magrail rifle punching through an Orbot's torso. Master Chief Zaines moved through enemy contacts like they were made of sand from a beach, and he was the first tsunami wave.

Four seconds—that was how long it took all twelve operators to clear the ramp and engage.

Ford kept firing, his gun slamming rounds into the northern approach where more Zodarks emerged from cover. Torres's weapon chattered from the port side.

"Two more Orbots down!" Torres yelled.

The last Delta cleared the ramp.

"Ramp up!" Ford called, hitting the hydraulic control. "We're clear!"

The hydraulics pulled the ramp closed while Love lifted *Jack* off the ground. Ford's gun stayed hot, tracking movement in the trees. A Zodark broke cover, weapon raised toward the ascending Osprey.

Ford's rounds caught the alien in its chest, dropping it before it could fire.

"Gaining altitude," Love said. "Torres, watch our six."

"Already on it, ma'am."

Ford scanned his displays, watching the thermal signatures of the Delta team spread out below them, moving with terrifying speed through the Zodark patrol. The special operators didn't need extraction. They needed the enemy to keep coming.

Jack ascended higher into the night sky, engines transitioning to full power. The landing zone fell away beneath them, lit by muzzle flashes and the glow of Orbot power cores rupturing under Delta weapons fire.

Ford's hands relaxed on his gun controls, but his eyes stayed on the sensors. The insertion was complete. The Deltas were on their own now.

Intel had been wrong about the cold LZ, but the mission continued anyway, because that's what happened when you flew for people who didn't know how to quit, and lived to keep their people free from tyranny and subjugation.

"Contact, five o'clock high!" Green's warning came with new threat tones screaming in Ford's helmet.

Two Zodark Vulture fighters dove from above, their engine signatures burning hot on his thermal display. Had they been waiting, lurking in the darkness above the LZ?

Ford swiveled his gun toward the diving fighters, but they were too fast, too high. His firing angle couldn't reach them.

"Torres, can you get a lock?"

"Negative, Chief! They're in my dead zone!"

The Vultures came in high and steep, diving from *Jack*'s dorsal blind spot where neither gun could elevate enough to track them. Ford's mount maxed out at sixty degrees, and the fighters were coming in at seventy-five.

The Vultures opened fire, energy bolts slicing through the night. Love threw *Jack* into a defensive spiral, the Osprey corkscrewing through the air as enemy fire bracketed their position.

Ford gripped his gun mount, fighting the g-forces trying to tear him from his station. His display showed one Vulture overshooting, unable to match Love's tight turn radius.

The second Vulture adjusted, tracking *Jack*'s evasive maneuvers. The Vulture had a firing solution. Ford's radar warning receiver was screaming for attention, alerting him the enemy had a lock on him. The intercept angle tightened, the enemy pilot compensating for every evasive turn Love made. They were seconds away from taking what would no doubt be some direct hits.

Ford's threat warning screamed louder. Missile lock.

"Countermeasures!" Love said.

"ECM active! Trying to break the lock!" Green replied.

Jack's electronic countermeasure suite kicked in, flooding the Vulture's targeting radar with false returns and jamming signals. Ford watched his threat display flicker as the ECM fought against the enemy's fire control system.

For three seconds, it worked. The missile lock tone wavered, the Zodark targeting computer confused by the electronic noise Green was pumping out.

Then the tone steadied again. Solid lock.

"He's burning through!" Green shouted. "Too close! His radar's overpowering our ECM!"

The Vulture was less than eight hundred meters away now, well inside the effective range where raw signal power could punch through countermeasures. The enemy pilot knew it too, pressing the attack despite the jamming.

Come on, Love, Ford thought. *Do that thing you do.*

Love did.

She killed the *Jack*'s engines for two seconds—a maneuver that should've been impossible, that violated every safety protocol. The Osprey dropped like a stone. Ford's stomach launched into his throat as the *Jack* fell three hundred meters in two seconds. The Vulture's targeting computer tracked where they should have been, a spot in empty air that *Jack* no longer occupied.

The Vulture's targeting solution fell apart as its prey disappeared from where it should've been.

Love fired the engines again, pulling the *Jack* into a climbing turn that had Ford's vision graying at the edges. The maneuver flipped their geometry. What had been above was now level. What had been unreachable had entered Torres's firing cone. The Vulture screamed past, missing by meters.

Torres's gun found it, tungsten rounds slashing across the fighter's port wing. The Vulture rolled away trailing smoke, breaking off its attack run.

"Splash one!" Torres called out. "Damaged and running!"

Ford's display showed the second Vulture retreating, its wingman crippled. They'd lost their advantage and knew it.

That's right. Run away, you bastards.

Jack leveled out at four thousand meters. Ford's hands finally relaxed on his gun controls.

"*Gallipoli* is twenty minutes out," Love announced over the intercom.

Ford ran his post-combat checks automatically, scanning for damage they might've missed during the egress. His gun showed green across the board. Ammunition count: 1,847 rounds remaining.

He'd burned through over five hundred and fifty rounds in less than two minutes of sustained fire.

A month ago, that would've seemed like a lot. Now it was just another day. The good news was that the Republic and the Primords were winning, slowly but steadily taking this planet back from the Zodarks and those cyborg pricks.

And lately, the statistical accounting of combat had become routine. Rounds expended, targets engaged, threats neutralized. Each number represented violence, death, and mayhem mixed with a slow success in a way that meant the tortoise would win the race, and not the hare.

Torres's voice broke the silence. "Chief, you ever wonder what those Delta guys are doing down there right now?"

Ford glanced at Torres still at his gun station, scanning the darkness below for threats that weren't there anymore.

"Probably something we're better off not knowing about," Ford replied. "Spec ops live in a different world than us. We drop them off, pick them up if we're lucky. Everything in between stays classified until we're all dead and buried."

He meant it too. Delta missions involved the kind of work that kept Republic citizens sleeping peacefully in their beds, blissfully unaware of the lethality required to maintain that peace.

Ford had seen enough classified after-action reports to know that special operators did things regular forces couldn't stomach. That was their job.

His job was simpler: fly the missions, work the gun, bring the crew home, be a mechanic, and a handful of other jobs within his job description.

"You think they'll make it back?" Torres asked. "I do. I mean, those guys are badass."

Ford looked down through the darkness. Master Chief Zaines and his eleven operators were down there somewhere, moving through enemy territory, probably tearing things up wherever they could, and somehow being silent about it.

"They're Deltas," Ford said. "They don't take prisoners, they don't leave witnesses, and they don't miss. The enemy just doesn't know they're already dead."

Torres was quiet for a moment. "That's kind of dark, Chief."

"That's kind of honest."

Ford checked his chronometer. Ten minutes to *Gallipoli*. Then they'd refuel, rearm, and wait for the next mission.

The Rass campaign had settled into this grinding rhythm: constant operations, brief rest, and more operations. You stopped thinking about when it would end and focused on surviving the next flight.

That was war.

Chapter 28:
Gallentine Hope

Late 2098
Mattis Military Complex
Mars

The medical consultation room at Mattis Complex might as well have been a courtroom. It smelled like one…and felt like one. Heck, it probably would have tasted like one if that were possible. The only difference was it didn't look like one.

It had a metal desk, two chairs, and an examination table. Wall-mounted displays showed test results in blue light. Coop sat across from Colonel Laura Joff, chief medical officer, while a medical technician took notes in the corner.

Coop's hands shook in his lap. He could walk now, moving carefully, and he'd refused the wheelchair they'd offered yesterday. He was a man, not a cripple.

Weeks of evaluation aboard the RNS *Mercy* and two weeks here had produced the same conclusion. Severe peripheral nerve damage. Motor function assessments. Psychological evaluations. All pointing to the same verdict.

Colonel Joff manipulated the holographic medical scan floating between them. Red scarring showed along his right arm and chest like battle damage on a combat display. "The blaster burns caused significant damage to the peripheral nerves in your right arm," she said, pointing to the worst areas. "Your nerve tissue shows extensive scarring here, here, and here."

The scan rotated slowly. Coop watched his own damaged body displayed in clinical detail, almost like he was a lab rat. And it all looked like severed cables somehow. At least, that was how he was imagining it all.

"These nerves control fine motor coordination," Colonel Joff continued. "TASC systems require precise responses. Your hands need to operate multiple communication frequencies simultaneously while coordinating targeting data. You need steady fingers to input grid coordinates under fire. One wrong digit kills friendly forces. The laser designators require rock-steady aim to mark targets for naval gunfire.

Your damaged nerves, at this moment, aren't able to provide that level of function."

She pointed to specific areas on the scan. "TASC controllers manipulate communication arrays, targeting computers, and fire control systems while processing incoming data from multiple sources. The peripheral nerves controlling hand-eye coordination and fine motor skills show significant damage from the energy weapon. Yes, your chest is healing nicely, but this is what's giving your arm some issues repairing. It's going to take time. Now, even minor tremors would make precise equipment operation impossible. Artillery coordinates require exact input. Meaning, your current motor function couldn't handle that responsibility safely."

Coop cleared his throat. His chest ached dully, better than last week, but the pain was still present. "You said I can get better." For some reason, he didn't believe her, so he asked, "Have you ever seen or heard anyone improving with these kinds of injuries?"

She nodded. "Improving, yes. Total recovery? Many have demonstrated complete nerve regeneration. If not, the body develops alternative neural pathways to bypass damaged regions. Medical nanites can accelerate tissue repair. Stem cell therapy can regenerate nerve fibers. In some cases, patients with similar injuries have achieved full functional recovery through intensive rehabilitation protocols combined with advanced regenerative treatments."

Colonel Joff paused, consulting her notes. "Several cases show damaged nerves successfully regenerating with proper treatment. Nanite-assisted repair allows new nerve tissue to grow and assume functions previously controlled by damaged pathways. These patients regained complete operational capability."

It's like she looks at me... hell, her patients... as damn robots. I ain't a Synth, Coop thought before leaning forward. The movement pulled at his chest wound, which was still healing but manageable now. "Could they remain at their posts? Same jobs, same responsibilities?"

"I don't have specific data on career retention rates for recovered TASC personnel," Colonel Joff replied. "I know some remained in military service and built successful careers. Whether they returned to identical positions... well, I'm not certain. I could research that information if you'd like."

"No," Coop said quickly. "Don't look that up." If they hadn't gotten their old jobs back, Coop didn't want to know—he didn't want doubt in his head. He swore to himself, right then and there, that he'd fix himself one way or another. "So, exactly how did they get better? Surgery? More therapy?" His right hand spasmed as he spoke. He grimaced.

Colonel Joff pulled up another display. "The nanites are already working. Look here... nerve regeneration along the damaged pathways. Stem cells are differentiating into new nerve tissue. We're seeing millimeter-by-millimeter progress. Your chest wound is healing well ahead of schedule. The arm nerves are slower, but they're responding."

She zoomed in on the scan. "See these bright spots? New myelin sheaths are forming. The nanites are essentially rebuilding your peripheral nervous system. But it's not instant. Nerve tissue regenerates at roughly one millimeter per day under optimal conditions. You have extensive damage. We're talking months, possibly a year or more for complete recovery."

"A year?"

"Maybe less with your progress so far. The treatments are working, Lieutenant. Your body is healing. But nerve regeneration doesn't follow a schedule we can control."

The room went quiet. Coop stared at the scan, watching the regeneration markers blink.

Colonel Joff set down her tablet and leaned back in her chair. "Lieutenant, I want to show you something else." She pulled up a new file on the holographic display. "We've recently integrated some Gallentine medical technology into one of our rehabilitation wings. The results have been exceptional."

Coop looked up from the scan. "Gallentine technology?"

"Exactly. They've been sharing certain medical applications. We're understanding how it works, getting better at it as we use it more, but we're still learning in the process. What matters is that the results speak for themselves."

She pulled up multiple comparison scans. Five patients, all with various degrees of nerve damage. The progression timelines showed regeneration rates far beyond standard treatments.

"These patients"—Colonel Joff gestured to the display—"all received standard Republic treatment initially. These patients"—she highlighted a second set of data—"received Gallentine-enhanced therapy in addition to our nanite treatments. Look at the difference."

Coop leaned forward, studying the numbers. The recovery times were dramatically shorter across the board.

"This patient"—she pointed to one of the scans—"was given standard Republic treatment. Eight months to functional recovery. This one received Gallentine-enhanced therapy. Two months to the same level of recovery."

Coop's eyes widened. "Two months?"

"The Gallentine technology interfaces with our stem cell and nanite protocols. It accelerates the biological processes, makes your body heal faster and more completely. But, Lieutenant, you still have to do the work. The physical therapy, the rehabilitation exercises, all of it. The technology enhances what your body is already trying to do. It doesn't replace your effort."

She zoomed in on one of the patients' scans. "We've been using it for about two months now in Wing Two. The results have been consistently remarkable. Even patients who were looking at yearlong recoveries are healing in months."

Coop's right hand clenched involuntarily, then relaxed. For the first time since entering the office, he felt something other than despair. "Can I… can I get that treatment?"

Colonel Joff smiled slightly. "Lieutenant, I've been reviewing your case. Your injury profile, your service record, your physical condition… you're a good candidate. I think you'd do well with this protocol."

"When can I start?"

"In the next few days, after we complete your physical therapy baseline assessments. Diesel needs to understand more about your current limitations first before we begin the Gallentine treatment. We need accurate measurements to track your progress properly and ensure the treatment is calibrated correctly for your specific injuries."

She pulled up another display, this one showing a treatment schedule. "Here's what we're looking at. Once we begin, you'll have weekly sessions with the Gallentine equipment, and physical therapy three times a week, but Diesel will also adjust your regimen as needed. The technology accelerates healing, but you have to meet it halfway.

Your body has to be actively repairing itself for the Gallentine tech to amplify the process."

Coop studied the schedule. Sessions every week. Hours of physical therapy several times a week. Neural stimulation periods. Rest intervals. Nutrition protocols. It looked demanding.

And it looked like hope.

"How fast?" Coop asked. "Realistically, how fast could I recover?"

Colonel Joff consulted her notes. "Based on the response rates we're seeing with similar cases and your current progression… if the treatment goes well, I'd estimate three to four months for significant functional recovery. Maybe five months for full clearance to return to active duty."

"Five months." Coop tested the words. Not eight. Not a year. Five months.

"That's assuming good response to treatment," Colonel Joff cautioned. "Some patients respond faster, some slower, and some don't fully heal, but close enough to live a normal, wonderful life. But, Lieutenant, you're a solid candidate for this. I think you could do well."

She closed the displays and looked at him directly. "You want back in the fight. I can see it. The Gallentine technology gives you a real shot at making that happen, faster than we could have offered you even six months ago. But you need to understand, this isn't a miracle cure. It's advanced technology meeting your body's natural healing processes. We provide the technology and the expertise. You provide the effort."

Coop stood. "When exactly do I start the baseline assessments?"

"Diesel will contact you within the next day or two to schedule. Once he's completed his evaluation, we'll get you into Wing Two and begin the Gallentine protocols." She handed him a datapad. "This has information about the treatment, what to expect, and some preliminary guidelines. Read it. Understand what you're committing to."

Coop took the datapad with his left hand, his right hand twitching at his side. "I'll be ready."

Colonel Joff nodded. "I believe you will be, Lieutenant. Dismissed."

Coop moved toward the door, his gait steadier than when he'd entered. He paused at the threshold and looked back.

"Ma'am, thank you. For giving me a real shot at this."

"Don't thank me yet, Lieutenant. Thank me when you're back with your unit. Now go. You have reading to do."

Coop pushed through the door and into the corridor, immediately grabbing the handrail that ran along the medical wing's walls. His right arm hung awkwardly at his side, the fingers occasionally twitching. Each step was controlled, measured. Plant left foot. Shift weight. Right foot forward. Breathe through the chest discomfort.

A young soldier in a wheelchair rolled past, both legs missing below the knee. The guy nodded at Coop like they were members of the same club now. The broken club. Coop looked away.

I just need to get back to Rass, Coop thought. *To help my Company. To prevent more people from losing their legs. Hell, losing their lives.*

Coop's gait was careful as he moved from wall to handrail to door frame. A nurse carrying medical supplies rounded a corner at the same moment Coop reached out with his right hand out of reflex, forgetting it wouldn't respond properly. His uncoordinated movement clipped her arm, sending her supplies scattering across the floor and knocking her sideways into the wall.

"Sorry, sorry," Coop muttered, immediately bending to help gather the items on the floor. Except his right hand wouldn't cooperate again, and he nearly fell over trying to reach a dropped tablet with only his left hand. The nurse steadied him with one hand while collecting her things with the other. "It's fine, just watch yourself," she said, more concerned about his condition than the spilled supplies. Coop straightened awkwardly and continued down the hall without making eye contact.

He wanted to scream. The simple act of picking up a tablet became impossible when a quarter of his body wouldn't cooperate properly.

The nurse's kindness stung worse than her anger would have. Pity. He hated pity. Who wanted to be pitied?

If this Gallentine tech works… He smiled. His first smile in a long time.

After several wrong turns and pauses to rest and let his chest catch up, Coop finally reached his quarters in the patient housing wing.

He fumbled with the door controls, his right hand refusing to cooperate with the biometric scanner. After three attempts, the door slid open and he stumbled inside, immediately engaging the manual lock.

The small room contained a bed, desk, chair, and personal storage unit. Coop collapsed into the chair, exhausted from the short journey that should have taken five minutes but had stretched to twenty, maybe thirty. His breathing was labored. His hands shook.

The room felt like a cell. Medical personnel had removed anything that could be used for self-harm. No sharp edges. No cables. No glass. They'd sanitized his environment the same way they'd sanitized his future. Clean. Safe. Empty.

His reflection caught in the dark window. Healing scars across his face and neck. Trembling right hand. The face of a man who'd lost more than nerve function. He'd lost the thing that made him Cooper. And his face was badly scarred. When would that start healing, changing, getting back to normal? They might as well label him a monster too.

Coop pulled out his great-great-grandfather's WWII journal. He opened to a blank page and began writing with his left hand, his normally neat handwriting now shaky and childlike. "Working to get back. A few months, maybe more. The doc says it's possible, and that they have a new Gallentine technology that can enhance the healing process. For the first time in a long time, I'm enthused about something."

The pen was foreign in his left hand's grip. He tried switching to his right hand. His fingers cramped after three words, the pen slipping from his grasp. He switched back to his left hand, the letters forming like a kid's first attempts at cursive.

"They want me try this new tech." He stopped, his hand cramping from the unfamiliar writing motion. "Bear died believing in me. I won't let damaged nerves be the thing that ends the Cooper line. This will work. I'll get back in action sooner rather than later."

The words blurred on the page. His eyes were tired from concentration, another lingering effect from the head trauma, though that was nearly healed now.

He flipped through pages of his grandfather's entries. Presley Paul Cooper's handwriting remained steady even under fire. Even facing death over Germany. Even watching friends die in burning aircraft. The man's penmanship never wavered.

Coop's left-handed handwriting looked like a drunk toddler had grabbed the writing utensil.

What would Presley think of this? His great-great-grandson reduced to a medical curiosity. A case study in nerve damage. The Cooper who couldn't hold a pen steady in his dominant hand, much less fly a drone into combat. But he had hope now, and hope would get him healed.

He closed the journal and set it on the desk, staring at the red Martian landscape through his window. The planet's surface spread out forever, barren.

That night, Coop lay in bed staring at the Martian sky through his window. Sleep wouldn't come as Colonel Joff's words replayed in his mind. His left hand moved unconsciously, mimicking control inputs from his drone pilot days. The movements felt natural, automatic. His right hand lay still, fingers twitching occasionally as nanites rebuilt damaged pathways.

Thing was, there was a path. The doctor had shown him. Scans proved it. And Coop swore to himself he'd find it and take advantage.

Chapter 29:
Grounding Exercises

Late 2098
Mattis Military Complex
Mars

Coop arrived fifteen minutes late and made no apologies for it. He settled against the hallway wall outside Dr. Maya Drexler's office, watching other patients shuffle past with their own broken bodies. That man with prosthetic legs. A Navy pilot whose left eye tracked differently than her right. A soldier who kept checking corners that weren't there.

His right hand rested in his lap. The tremors had backed off some over the past two days, which he supposed was progress, thanks to Diesel pushing him during their daily physical therapy sessions. It still kicked up when stress hit, though. Still reminded him that his body wasn't yet his, but in time, he knew he'd take it back as his own. His chest barely bothered him anymore. Just a dull ache when he moved wrong. The blaster wound was healing well. But the arm… the arm was taking its sweet time.

Other patients came and went. Coop checked his watch. Maybe she'd give up and reschedule. Maybe he could buy himself another week of avoiding whatever conversation he was supposed to have with the woman.

The door opened.

"Lieutenant Cooper, please come in. We can start now."

Dr. Maya Drexler stood in the doorway. Midforties, graying hair pulled back, eyes that had clearly seen too many broken soldiers to be fooled by avoidance tactics. Coop had researched her. Twelve years treating combat trauma. Three deployments as a field psychologist. She knew the games, and his trick obviously didn't work on her.

Coop pushed himself up from the wall, using the door frame for balance. The office was small. Two chairs facing each other. A desk. No escape routes.

He took the chair closest to the door anyway.

"How are you feeling today?" Dr. Drexler settled across from him with a tablet.

"Fine."

"Your physical therapy reports show good progress."

"Good, good."

"Sleep patterns are improving."

"OK, good."

She made notes on her tablet. Coop watched her fingers move across the screen and wondered what she was writing. Probably that he was being difficult. Good. Maybe she'd recommend he skip these sessions.

"Tell me about your team," she said. "Crawford, Li, Weber. You've been asking about them constantly."

Coop stared at her. "How do you know that?"

"I do my job well, Lieutenant. Part of that job involves reading medical notes, talking to staff, understanding my patients' concerns. Your nurses mention it. Your physical therapist mentions it. Diesel, right? He's a good man. He says you ask about them every day." Dr. Drexler shifted in her seat, crossing one leg over the other. "Crawford and Li survived their injuries. Both recovered. Sergeant Vega and Captain Gill are also still alive, both in one piece."

Coop's shoulders sagged. Relief hit him. "They're alive. Thank God they're alive."

Dr. Drexler made more notes. "That relief… it's real. Hold on to it. You also mention someone named Bear frequently. Tell me about him."

Coop froze completely. His left hand clenched into a fist. He opened it and closed it, acting like he was exercising his fingers. "Bear died on Nightfall. Covert mission before Rass. That's not something I talk about."

Dr. Drexler nodded slowly, her voice steady. "I hear that. Losing someone close in combat… it sticks. If it's too raw today, we can circle back. No rush. But when memories like that surface, even fragmented, it's often a sign your mind's ready to process them. Safely. Here." She paused, watching him. When Coop stayed quiet, she leaned forward a little. "Notice your hand right now? The clenching. That's a common stress response. Let's try something quick. It's called grounding. Name three things you can see in this room."

Coop blinked, caught off guard. "Uh… the desk. Your tablet. The door."

"Good. Two things you can feel."

"The chair under me. Air on my skin."

"One thing you can hear."

"My breathing."

She nodded. "See? Back in the present. Simple tool. Use it when fragments hit hard."

Coop exhaled, unclenching his fist.

"The ridge," she continued gently. "Ridge 248. You coordinated fire missions for seventy-two hours under constant enemy assault."

Coop's breathing shallowed. Fragments surfaced like shrapnel from a grenade. "Equipment kept failing. Lost Weber on the drop. Crawford got wounded. Li got wounded. I got hit by a blaster and burned half to hell calling in danger-close artillery on our own position to stop the enemy breakthrough."

"You're remembering this clearly."

"Yeah. I remember that." His voice turned flat. "Wish I didn't."

His right hand trembled as he spoke. "We held until they pulled us out. Alpha Company did their job. I did mine until I took a direct hit."

Dr. Drexler glanced at her tablet. Stress indicators climbed, and Coop could see his heart rate spiking on the display. "You saved thousands of lives with those fire missions. Multiple commendations are being processed. But I'm guessing that doesn't land right for you."

Coop shook his head. "Doesn't feel like saving anyone."

"What does it feel like?"

Coop looked at his hands. The left one worked fine. The right one betrayed him every time stress hit. Both had punched in codes that ended lives. Both had operated equipment that called down death from orbit.

"Feels like I broke something that can't be fixed."

Dr. Drexler set down her tablet. "What broke, Lieutenant? Say more about that thought."

Coop met her eyes for the first time since entering the office. "Me. The team. Everything. If I'd called it different, maybe no one gets hit."

"That's a common stuck point. Self-blame. Hindsight makes us rewrite the story, but in the moment, under fire, with failing gear? You made calls based on what you had. Most vets I see carry that weight.

It's not fact, though. It's a belief we can challenge. Over time." She paused. "For now, notice how that thought fuels the tremors. Body and mind are linked in trauma recovery. We work both."

Coop's right hand twitched involuntarily, as if to prove her point. "What if it doesn't get better? The arm, I mean. The chest is fine now. I barely notice it. But this…" He lifted his right hand, watching the fingers spasm. "What if the nerves don't regenerate? What if I'm stuck like this?"

Dr. Drexler cleared her throat. "That fear is real. Let's name it: fear of permanent disability. Valid concern, given your injury. But, Lieutenant, you're, what, a little over a month into treatment? Nerve regeneration takes months and months, especially yours, because the damage was extensive. The medical team says you're responding well to the nanites and stem cells. Your chest healed faster than expected. Why assume the arm won't follow?"

"Because it feels… stuck. Like it's not improving."

"Feels stuck, or is stuck? There's a difference. Feeling is immediate. Actual healing someone with that much nerve damage happens slowly. Your brain catastrophizes because uncertainty is hard. Especially for someone who's used to being in control." She paused. "What does Diesel say about your progress?"

Coop sat straighter. "He says I'm doing better. Shows me the scans. Says the nerves are regenerating. There's a new tech they're going to put me on to speed up my recovery."

"But you don't believe them?"

"I want to believe them. But it hasn't started yet—however, I do have hope. Plus, I don't care what anyone says. I'm going to get better."

"Good. Now, we can't control the timeline of nerve growth. We can control showing up to PT, following treatment protocols, not giving up before the healing's done. Which one are you focused on?"

Coop shifted in his seat. His right hand trembled in his lap, a constant reminder of what he couldn't control. "So… pills? More PT? And the new tech? I'm focused on getting back to my old job."

"OK, then we build from here. Coping tools, like that grounding. Processing memories without avoidance. Cognitive work to shift those stuck points. And yes, continuing the physical rehabilitation and using the new technology from the Gallentines." She gestured to his hand. "That tremor? Partly nerve damage, partly stress response. We address both. Look, you're grinding through PT and doing a great job. That's strength, and not something that's broken."

"That's it?"

She nodded. "For today. We've covered ground."

"That was…"

"That was what, Lieutenant?"

Coop hesitated. "Uh…"

"Easy?"

He raised his brows. "Yeah. Kinda."

"First sessions often are as we build trust. Next time, we dig deeper. Arrive ten minutes early."

"Yes, ma'am. Will it be easy like this time?"

She lowered her chin, eyes on his. "Easy? No. Healing is about showing up. Doing the hard work so in time, the hard work is then easier. You've done hard things before, right? This is no different. Practice that mindset. Who you want to be starts with facing the fragments, not dodging them."

Coop frowned. "I don't understand."

"Then start asking yourself: What if I'm not as broken as I think? We'll explore that next time. You may go."

"Well, uh… thank you, ma'am." For the first time in a long time, and maybe it was her words, or just her gentle nature, but Coop felt… good. Felt calm. Felt life might actually stop kicking him in the butt if he started kicking himself in the butt, instead. And somehow that thought made sense to him, that kicking himself would push him into a higher gear.

"You're welcome," Dr. Drexler replied.

Coop pushed himself up from the chair and exited her office. Thirty minutes later, he found himself making his way slowly toward the cafeteria, using handrails and wall support. His gait was mostly steady now, the chest wound barely slowed him down anymore. But his right arm hung awkwardly at his side, the hand occasionally jerking without warning. He waved off passing medical staff who offered assistance.

Near the pilot training wing, voices drifted from an open doorway. Coop paused.

"Manned fighter program's expanding again," one pilot said. "They need experienced combat pilots who can handle atmospheric operations and electronic warfare environments."

The second pilot responded, "Yeah, saw the posting. You gonna put in for it?"

Coop pressed against the wall, listening as they walked past.

"Different skill set than drone operations. More about spatial awareness, manual dexterity, and tactical thinking under pressure. Manual flight controls for missions where drone systems get jammed or compromised. Deep space reconnaissance, hostile electronic environments, situations requiring human judgment and split-second adaptation."

Their voices faded down the corridor. Coop stood there, processing what he'd heard.

He continued toward his quarters, his mind turning over the conversation. "Probably just propaganda," he muttered to himself, dismissing it. "Some recruiting pitch to give broken pilots some hope or something."

His right hand trembled as he walked. Manual dexterity. The requirement mocked him. How could he fly anything when his dominant hand wouldn't even hold steady?

Halting for a second, he tapped the top of his head with his knuckles. *Stop taking the easy way out of things, Coop*, he told himself, realizing he sort of knew now what Dr. Drexler was talking about. *I'm going to heal myself. It's not a maybe. It's a must.*

He reached his room and slumped into the chair beside his desk. The idea of manned fighters felt like fantasy compared to his current reality, but maybe it could be done… someday. "They want pilots who can fly manually. I can barely hold a coffee cup steady right now."

He stared at his trembling right hand, watching the involuntary movements. The fingers twitched. The wrist rotated slightly without his command. Damaged nerves misfiring while nanites worked to fix them.

Like most days here, he sighed and stared off into the Martian terrain. *Manual flight controls. Human judgment. Electronic warfare environments.* Those words kept jumping into his mind.

He didn't know how long he stared out into nothingness, seeing everything Mars was holding out in front of him but not really seeing it.

Thoughts invaded. Thoughts kept him active but also turned into a pit of time lost down rabbit holes.

He stood and walked out of the room. Fifteen minutes of walking, and he landed at the medical center's holo console, researching everything he could find about the Republic's manned fighter program. His left hand operated the interface while his right hand rested on the desk, occasionally jerking and forcing him to pull it back so he wouldn't accidentally trigger commands.

The program details made his heartbeat quicken.

"Requirements: Combat flight experience, manual dexterity, psychological resilience, ability to operate under extreme stress."

He scrolled through mission profiles. Deep reconnaissance behind enemy lines. Electronic warfare environments where drone links failed. Atmospheric combat where split-second human decisions meant survival.

His eyes lit up as he read. It existed. It was real.

A path back to the cockpit.

Still, his medical files painted a different picture. Severe peripheral nerve damage. Motor function compromise in right arm. Recovery timeline: eight to twelve months minimum.

Eight to twelve months.

He shook his head, remembering the hope, the new Gallentine tech. *Get it into your head. You're not broken. You're healing, and you will heal quicker with the new technology.*

Coop stared at that timeline. The doctors had been clear that his prognosis was good. And now, it could, and most likely would, speed up than it would have had the Gallentines not created a new healing apparatus for humans. He needed to stop questioning it and just believe.

He was going to make it. The nanites were working. The stem cells were regenerating tissue, even without the Gallentine healing tech. The scans proved it. This would be his goal. His mission. And it started for real, and right this minute. He'd heal. He'd get better. No doubt in his mind.

"No matter what," he whispered to himself out loud so that the words would become ingrained in his brain, "I'm going to make myself better. Going to get over this injury."

He would heal. Not might. Would. He swore to himself he would one hundred percent heal from this. And that Diesel would sure as hell fix him up, along with the Gallentines' new gift to humanity.

The physical therapist had said it himself—other soldiers had come back from worse. Captain Hicks with no arms. Sergeants with prosthetic legs. Pilots with reconstructed faces.

Coop pulled up the manned fighter application requirements again and read them line by line. Combat experience. Check. Flight training. Check. Psychological resilience.

That one made him pause.

Dr. Drexler's voice echoed in his memory.

In truth, to him, it started not to matter because he was realizing that broken things could be repaired. Equipment failed and got fixed. Ships took damage and returned to service. Soldiers got wounded and came back stronger.

He opened a new file on the console and started typing with his left hand.

"Personal Recovery Plan. Blake Cooper. Objective: Return to flight status."

The cursor blinked after those words, waiting for him to fill in the details. Waiting for him to figure out how to put himself back together… not only physically, but mentally too.

Coop looked at his right hand. Still trembling. But trembling less than yesterday. And yesterday less than the day before.

Then he looked at his left hand. Steady. Strong. Ready to work.

One hand could fly a fighter if it had to. For now, it didn't matter. He'd find a way.

Chapter 30:
Simulation Twenty-Three

Late 2098
RNS *Invincible*
Planet New Eden

The tactical display showed a challenging picture. Captain Sato clenched her hands into fists for a moment before relaxing them. At this very second, she sat in her command chair as the twenty-third training simulation reached the most important point. RNS *Invincible*'s bridge was a ball of electric energy, her crew pushing through another brutal scenario designed to break their coordination when it mattered most.

Commander Patricia Black monitored crew performance from her position beside the captain's chair. Tactical Action Officer Lieutenant Sean Marsh worked the tactical display while Lieutenant Commander Kenji Yamamoto fed intelligence data from his station. Lieutenant Sofia Delacroix managed communications traffic.

The main holo displayed two Republic heavy cruisers facing impossible odds. *Invincible* and *Prince Edward* stood against a Zodark battleship and heavy cruiser materializing from simulated hyperspace. Chief Petty Officer Jerome Knight's damage control teams waited at battle stations throughout the ship. Lieutenant Zhau's enhanced sensor arrays quantified the threat bearing down on them.

Four weeks of constant drilling had brought the crew to basic competency. Sato felt every hesitation, every delayed response that would cost lives when the enemy stopped being pixels and started being plasma torpedoes.

"Contact bearing two-one-three mark sixteen," Marsh announced. "Zodark battleship and heavy cruiser, range thirty-two thousand kilometers and closing."

The simulated enemy vessels crept closer on the main display. Dark hulls full of enough firepower to reduce Republic ships to floating debris. Sato studied their formation and noted how the Zodark commander positioned the battleship forward, using its armor plating to protect the cruiser's vulnerable flanks.

"Signal *Prince Edward* to maintain formation," Sato ordered.

Delacroix worked her communications panel, coordinating with the other Republic vessel. The tactical situation was brutally simple: two Republic ships against superior firepower. Survival required perfect coordination. Sato's heart rate climbed despite knowing this was a simulation. Her crew needed to function as a single unit when combat started.

"Enemy vessels opening fire," Yamamoto reported.

Plasma torpedoes and energy beams streaked across space, forcing immediate decisions. Sato watched the incoming salvo and chose her poison.

"Hard to starboard, emergency acceleration. Signal *Prince Edward* to concentrate fire on the battleship's forward section. Deploy countermeasures."

"Countermeasures deployed," Marsh reported from his console. Sand canisters and water countermeasures erupted from *Invincible*'s hull. The ECM suite activated, jamming frequencies designed to confuse enemy targeting systems.

Three plasma torpedoes lost lock and spiraled off into empty space. The jamming worked. Sato watched enemy fire scatter as her ship's defensive systems did their job. Sand and water particles absorbed and dispersed the concentrated laser beams, turning ship-killing energy into manageable heat radiation.

Laser fire struck the dispersed countermeasures instead of armor plating. The concentrated beams lost coherence, spreading their energy across thousands of fragments. What should have been armor-penetrating strikes became diffused light, scattering beautiful colors across space.

Slight vibrations rippled through *Invincible*'s deck as unconcentrated laser energy found the ship. Tremors, nothing more. The kind of impacts that rattled coffee cups instead of breaching hulls. The countermeasures had saved them from serious damage.

"Minimal damage reported," Knight announced. "Hull temperature elevated but within acceptable parameters. Countermeasures effective against current enemy fire patterns."

"Fire missiles, all tubes," Sato ordered. "Target the battleship's forward section, range nine thousand kilometers."

"Missiles away," Marsh confirmed. "Time to target, eighteen seconds."

The Havoc-II missiles streaked through space, their armored tips glinting as they closed the distance. The tactical display tracked their progress. Eighteen warheads raced toward the Zodark battleship's forward armor. The missiles maintained formation for the first ten seconds, their targeting systems locked onto the enemy vessel's most vulnerable points.

Zodark point-defense systems came online. Bursts erupted from the battleship's hull, swatting missiles from space. Six Havoc-IIs died in bright flashes, their warheads detonating harmlessly against defensive fire. Eight more pushed through the killing field, weaving between energy bursts as their guidance systems adapted to enemy countermeasures.

"Prep magrails for firing," Sato ordered. "All six turrets, target the battleship's command section."

"Magrails charged and ready," Marsh reported. "Range seven thousand kilometers."

"Fire."

The twin-barreled twenty-four-inch turrets roared like a lion that shook the bridge. Twelve tungsten slugs accelerated to enormous velocity, crossing the distance in four seconds. The projectiles struck the Zodark battleship just as the surviving missiles found their target. Combined kinetic and explosive force overwhelmed the enemy's defenses.

"Direct hits on target," Marsh called out. "Enemy battleship showing armor degradation but maintaining course."

The Zodark ships kept coming. Their commanders never hesitated, never second-guessed, never showed mercy. This was training, simulation, but it mimicked exactly how Zodarks fought.

The enemy battleship's lasers found *Prince Edward*. The simulation registered catastrophic damage to the other Republic vessel, systems failing across a myriad of decks.

"Signal from *Prince Edward*," Delacroix announced. "They're reporting main engine failure and requesting immediate support."

Sato stared at the tactical display. Protocol demanded she protect the damaged vessel. Tactical reality suggested something else entirely.

"Negative on close support," Sato decided. "Signal *Prince Edward* to withdraw. We'll engage both enemy vessels to cover their retreat."

Black turned toward her, eyebrows raised. The look said everything about abandoning allies to face superior numbers alone. Sato ignored the silent question. Command meant making choices that saved lives even when they felt like betrayal.

Invincible shuddered under fire from both Zodark vessels as her gamble played out. Every gun in the enemy formation now targeted her ship exclusively.

"Multiple hits amidships," Knight reported from damage control. "Simulated hull breaches on decks two through four. Engineering reports reactor containment stress."

The training simulation registered critical damage. Sato watched her ship's status displays bloom red as the enemy pressed onward. Her crew was good, but good wasn't enough against these odds.

"Return fire, all batteries," Sato ordered.

Marsh coordinated the weapons response while Yamamoto tracked damage to the enemy formation. The Zodark heavy cruiser had taken punishment, armor plates peeling away under sustained fire. But the battleship remained largely intact, its massive bulk absorbing everything they threw at it.

Sato realized her tactical gamble was failing. The enemy had superior firepower, better positioning, and numerical advantage. Her decision to sacrifice *Prince Edward*'s support was about to cost her ship and crew. They were losing this engagement.

The tactical display showed the truth in cold numbers. Sato stared at the damage assessments, the casualty reports, the mission failure that painted her bridge displays red. Her crew had performed their duties. She had failed them.

"Captain, recommend immediate withdrawal," Black said quietly. "We've taken too much damage to continue the engagement."

The XO was right. Retreat meant accepting defeat in front of her entire crew. Sato studied the tactical display one more time, looking for any advantage she might have missed. The simulation offered no miracles.

Her father's voice echoed from childhood memories. *Pride comes before the fall, Noriko. The wise general knows when to bend rather than break.*

Sato had been thinking like a junior officer trying to prove herself. Not like a captain responsible for hundreds of lives. The distinction cut through her arrogance.

"Signal fleet withdrawal," Sato ordered. "Maximum acceleration, course one-eight-zero mark eleven."

Invincible turned away from the enemy formation, her simulated damage making the maneuver sluggish and painful. The Zodark vessels pursued for several minutes before breaking off, their mission accomplished. The training simulation ended with Republic forces in full retreat, leaving Sato to face the aftermath of her tactical decisions.

She sat in her command chair, reviewing the disaster. Twenty-three straight victories over the past month and a half had built her confidence into something dangerous. Arrogance disguised as competence. Her decisions had been textbook perfect in isolation, but warfare wasn't fought in isolation. It was fought against enemies who adapted, who exploited every weakness, who turned your strengths into vulnerabilities. At least she'd retreated when necessary. Kept her ship and crew breathing.

The tactical review showed her mistakes. She'd positioned her ships to maximize firepower while exposing them to concentrated enemy fire. She'd abandoned mutual support doctrine. She'd commanded like someone who believed her own press releases instead of someone who understood the responsibility of command.

"Simulation terminated," the computer announced as the bridge holos returned to normal operations.

Sato's crew remained at their stations, avoiding eye contact after the disastrous training session. They'd performed their duties with professionalism while she'd led them into a tactical woodchipper. Silence stretched across the bridge.

"Department heads, ready room in twenty minutes," Sato announced.

The officers filed off the bridge without the usual post-exercise chatter while Sato remained in her command chair, reviewing the simulation data on her personal display. Every decision she'd made seemed logical on its own, but the cumulative effect had been catastrophic. The loss came fast and ugly even though her crew had performed adequately.

Captain Lee entered the bridge as the last of Sato's crew departed for their debriefing sessions. He'd observed the entire training exercise from the task force command center, watching his former XO struggle with her first independent command decisions. His footsteps echoed across the empty bridge as he approached the command chair where Sato still sat.

"Interesting tactical choices," Lee said, settling into the chair beside hers.

Sato looked up from her displays. Lee's expression showed understanding rather than criticism. No judgment, no disappointment. Just the patient attention of someone who'd made his own share of command mistakes.

"I got cocky," Sato said. "Twenty-three successful exercises and I started believing I was unbeatable."

"What specifically went wrong?"

"I positioned us for maximum offensive capability instead of mutual support. Abandoned doctrine because I thought I could outfight superior numbers through aggressive tactics." The decision had blown up fast. Sato pulled up the tactical replay, highlighting her formation decisions. "Classic mistake. Individual ship optimization instead of fleet coordination."

Lee studied the display. "The enemy commander exploited that immediately."

"Split our formation, concentrated fire on isolated units, forced me to choose between supporting a damaged ship or maintaining offensive pressure." Sato traced the enemy's attack pattern. "I chose wrong."

"Command decisions under pressure reveal character. What did you learn about yourself today?"

Sato considered the question. The honest answer tasted disgusting. Like rancid meat.

"That I still think like an XO trying to impress my captain instead of a captain responsible for my crew's lives. That success can be more dangerous than failure if it builds the wrong kind of confidence."

"Good. What else?"

"That tactical brilliance means nothing if it gets people killed. That my job isn't to win simulations, it's to bring my people home alive."

Lee nodded. "The hardest lesson for any new captain. You can't command from the tactical manual. You have to command from here." He tapped his chest. "What will you do differently next time?"

"Focus on fleet coordination instead of individual ship performance. Maintain mutual support doctrine even when aggressive tactics look more appealing. Remember that my crew's survival matters more than my tactical reputation."

"The enemy won't give you time to think through every decision. How do you prepare for that?"

Sato met his eyes. "Drill until the right decisions become instinct. Until I stop thinking like Noriko Sato trying to prove herself and start thinking like Captain Sato keeping her people alive."

Lee nodded. "That's the difference between a good officer and a great captain. The willingness to learn from failure instead of being broken by it."

"My crew deserves better than what I gave them today."

"Then give it to them tomorrow. And the day after that. Command is about getting better every single day until your people trust you with their lives because you've earned it."

Sato straightened in her chair, feeling something shift inside her chest. The sting of defeat was still there, but it had transformed into something sharper. Something useful.

"Request permission to run additional training scenarios, sir. My crew and I have work to do."

Lee smiled as he stood. "Granted. And, Captain? Today wasn't your worst day in command. It was your first real day. Everything before this was just preparation."

Chapter 31:
Exponential Healing

Late 2098
Mattis Military Complex
Mars

Coop sank into the translucent sludge for the third time, and it still felt weird. Three weeks of this—once a week, ninety minutes each session—and his brain hadn't fully accepted that alien goo counted as medicine.

The medium enveloped him like warm honey. Translucent. Slimy. Apparently, it worked miracles beneath the surface. He settled back, letting the stuff do its job.

Week three. Getting used to this. Sort of.

The warmth shifted to that usual cool tingling within seconds. His right arm lit up with sensation. Not pain, really, and instead, more like awareness. As if his nerves were remembering that they existed. The damaged pathways from shoulder to fingertips suddenly felt active, connected in ways they hadn't been since the blaster hit.

The technician, who was the same young guy from week one, checked his tablet without looking up. "Neural activity's spiking faster than last week. The medium's really interfacing now."

Coop stared at the holographic display mounted above the tub. Tiny lights flickered along his arm, more of them than last session. More than the first time.

Three things were happening at once. The tech had explained it week one, but Coop understood it better now after feeling it do its thing.

First: enhanced nanites. Way beyond Republic standard models. These things targeted nerve damage with precision human technology couldn't match. Coop had watched the scans. Microscopic machines rebuilding myelin sheaths, reconnecting severed pathways, cleaning out scar tissue that might've stayed there forever with standard treatment.

Second: optimized stem cells. These were preprogrammed, designed specifically for peripheral nerve regeneration. They knew exactly what to become, where to go, what to fix.

Third: the part that still seemed like science fiction. The medium itself acted as a temporary neural bridge. Created electrical pathways around damaged tissue while the nanites and stem cells did their work—similar to building a detour around a collapsed road while simultaneously rebuilding the original route.

Gallentine science, Coop thought. *Making our best tech look primitive.*

The coolness intensified. Coop's fingers twitched, and it wasn't the random spasms he'd been fighting for weeks, but controlled movement. Small. Barely noticeable.

He flexed his right hand. The fingers curled. Not smoothly. But they responded to commands that would've been impossible three weeks ago.

His chest felt different too. The blaster scar, thick and angry after the initial healing, had softened noticeably. The deep ache that accompanied every breath had faded to almost nothing. Week one, the sludge had felt like it was pulling at the scar tissue. Week two, the pulling had become relief. Now, in week three, he barely noticed the old shot wound unless he thought about it.

"Nerve regeneration's ahead of schedule," the tech said, studying his readouts. "Your baseline from week one showed approximately eight percent functional recovery in fine motor control. Week two jumped to fifteen percent. Today's preliminary scan shows twenty-three percent."

Twenty-three percent. In three weeks.

"Colonel Joff estimated five months for significant recovery," the tech continued. "At this rate? You might cut that to four months. Maybe less. The Gallentine medium works exponentially. Each session builds on the previous one. Your body's learning to work with it."

Coop stared at the display. More lights appearing. More pathways reconnecting. His right hand lay beneath the translucent sludge, fingers moving in small circles. Controlled. Deliberate. Still shaky, but improving.

This might actually work, he mused. *Holy crap!*

"How's the sensation?" the tech asked. "Any numbness? Tingling outside normal parameters?"

"Feels good," Coop said. "Better than last week. The tingling's stronger, but not painful. My fingers feel… more there. Like they're mine again."

The tech nodded, making notes. "That's the neural bridging. Your brain's relearning how to communicate with those pathways. By next week, you should see even more improvement. The medium adapts to your specific injury pattern. Gets better at targeting what needs fixing."

Ninety minutes. Coop closed his eyes and let the sludge work. The coolness spread through his arm, his chest, everywhere the blaster and its aftermath had damaged him. He'd stopped fighting the weirdness of it and stopped questioning alien science that did things Republic medicine couldn't touch.

It worked. That was what mattered.

The session timer chimed. The medium began draining, the translucent goo flowing away through hidden vents. Coop stood, slimy and dripping, feeling simultaneously exhausted and energized.

"Shower's through there," the tech said like he did after every session, pointing to the adjacent room. "Take your time."

Coop stepped into the shower, hot water sluicing away the remaining sludge. He watched it circle the drain while flexing his right hand under the spray. The fingers moved. Curled into a fist. Opened. Still trembling slightly, but the improvement from three weeks ago was undeniable.

Colonel Joff said five months. Who knows, maybe three now?

He dried off, dressed in his PT gear, and headed for Diesel's therapy room.

Fifteen minutes later, Coop stood in the familiar space, surrounded by resistance equipment and balance beams and all the tools Diesel used to rebuild broken soldiers.

Coop's fingers trembled around the resistance ball, muscles fighting themselves. But they held. The ball stayed put.

"One." Diesel's voice rumbled beside him. "Two."

Coop's hand cramped. The tremors got worse.

"Three. Four."

His vision tunneled. Everything narrowed to five fingers wrapped around orange foam.

"Five. Six. Seven. Eight. Nine."

The ball dropped. His hand spasmed open, fingers jerking like they'd touched live wire. Nine seconds, though. Last week he'd managed six. Three weeks ago he couldn't manage one.

Diesel made a mark on his tablet. "Nine seconds, flyboy. That Gallentine sludge is doing work." He looked up, genuine surprise in his eyes. "I've seen a lot of recovery protocols. This? This is something else. Your nerve function's improving faster than anything I've tracked before."

Around them, Coop barely registered the Marine sergeant on parallel bars or the Army specialist relearning how to hold a spoon. His focus stayed locked on Diesel's countdown.

Nine seconds. Three more than last week. Measurable, undeniable progress.

Diesel pulled up comparison scans on his tablet. "Look at this. Week one baseline, your grip strength was eighteen percent of normal. Week two, twenty-six percent. Today? Thirty-four percent. You're exceeding expectations, Coop."

Cooper remembered the words of the other tech: *exponential healing*.

"How's it feel?" Diesel asked. "Besides the obvious shaking."

Coop flexed his right hand. "Connected. Like the signals are actually getting through instead of getting lost halfway. Still not right, but… better. A lot better."

"That's the Gallentine tech doing its job. The nanites are rebuilding pathways, but you're still working with damaged tissue. It takes time for your brain to relearn how to use the new routes." Diesel set down his tablet. "But, brother, I gotta say… I'm impressed. You're healing fast."

Better, but still a long way from what he needed.

"Balance beam," Diesel said. "Let's see if that coordination's keeping pace with the nerve recovery."

The beam stretched across the floor. Coop positioned himself at one end, arms out for balance. Heel to toe. Right foot forward. His leg barely dragged now. The coordination improved week by week. He made it three steps. Four. Five. Six. Seven. Eight.

Don't think about it. Just move. One foot. Then the other.

Halfway across, his right leg wobbled but didn't give out. Coop caught himself, adjusted, kept going. Nine steps. Ten. Eleven.

He made it to the end.

Diesel clapped his hands. "Last week you made it eight steps before I had to catch you. Week before that, five. This Gallentine healing tub is the real deal. I'm telling you."

Coop stepped off the beam, breathing hard from concentration. "How long before I'm cleared for duty?"

"Depends on the duty." Diesel consulted his notes. "TASC work? You'd need fine motor control at ninety percent or better for safe operation. You're at thirty-four percent. Even with this accelerated healing, you're looking at two, maybe three more months minimum."

Three months. Better than five. Better than a year.

"But," Diesel continued, studying Coop's face, "if you're thinking about something else… something that needs gross motor function more than fine motor precision… you might be closer than you think."

Coop tried to look innocent, but his face refused to cooperate.

Diesel shook his head. "You been researching that manned pilot program, haven't you? I can tell. You got that look. But, hey now, focus on today. Not tomorrow. And especially not yesterday, all right?" Diesel said. "You ain't flying nowhere if you can't pass the medical clearance. We clear?"

Coop nodded. But both of them knew the truth. *I'm already gone. Already thinking about cockpits and flight sticks and getting back out there.* Coop was already thinking about tomorrow. About next week. About getting back in the game. The opportunity might actually be real—not some fantasy for the next life. He might actually pull this off and get into the manned fighter program, and become a pilot instead of a broken TASC operator with fried nerves in his arm.

He might actually succeed.

****

Back in his quarters, Coop pulled up the manned fighter program requirements again before his butt hit the chair. His left hand navigated the datapad, years of drone operations making the interface second nature. His right hand rested in his lap, trembling less than a week back. Less than when he first got here. Progress. Small, but real.

The requirements list materialized:

Combat flight experience (required). Manual flight control proficiency (required). Tactical decision-making under pressure (required). Psychological resilience (required). Medical clearance (required).

That last one always made his stomach drop. But he kept reading.

The program overview laid it out plain. Deep space reconnaissance. Electronic warfare environments where drone links died. Atmospheric combat requiring split-second human judgment. Missions where jamming made remote operation impossible. Situations demanding a pilot in the cockpit, not controlling things from thousands of kilometers away.

Coop's pulse kicked up. This was about going where drones couldn't, fighting battles requiring human instinct and adaptation—everything he'd proved he could do on Ridge 248 when the equipment failed and he'd kept calling fires anyway.

He scrolled deeper, hunting for the medical requirements section for the umpteenth time, just in case they'd changed things. His finger hovered over the link, and finally, he pressed down with his thumb.

The page loaded. Coop scanned through general fitness standards, vision requirements, cardiovascular benchmarks. Standard stuff. Then he found it, buried in subsection three:

Fine motor skill assessment: Not required for initial qualification. Gross motor function must meet minimum operational standards. Candidates with documented fine motor limitations may qualify if gross motor function, cognitive ability, and tactical reasoning remain within acceptable parameters.

He read it three times. *Fine motor skills: not required.*

The finger work that TASC demanded, the microsecond accuracy with laser designators, the exact coordinate entry where one wrong digit meant friendly fire casualties—well, none of it applied here.

Coop pulled up Colonel Joff's notes, cross-referencing with his medical file. Her assessment jumped out at him:

"Patient demonstrates exceptional tactical cognition and spatial reasoning despite initial head trauma (now resolved). Peripheral nerve damage isolated to right arm, affecting fine motor pathways controlling finger precision and dexterity. Gross motor function shows accelerated recovery with Gallentine-enhanced treatment protocol. Arm movement, shoulder rotation, core stability, all improving ahead of projected timelines. Chest wound from blaster impact: healed to ninety-two percent baseline function."

Fine motor versus gross motor. Fingers versus arms. TASC equipment needed steady hands for delicate work. Fighter controls needed strong arms for stick and throttle. He could barely hold a pen steady, but he could grip Diesel's resistance ball for nine seconds and counting.

His brain raced through the requirements again, mapping each one against his current state. Flight stick control: gross motor, arm and shoulder movement. Improving weekly. Throttle management: left hand fully functional, right hand supporting. Spatial awareness: undamaged. Tactical thinking: proven under fire for seventy-two straight hours.

He wasn't disqualified. *Holy crap, I might actually not be disqualified. They haven't changed things on me.*

A notification blinked on his desk holo. The time stamp showed it had arrived three hours ago while he was in therapy: Message received—Cooper, R. (Senior).

Coop stared at those words. They'd popped up at just the wrong time. When he needed motivation the most, something happy in his life, his old man jumped on the interface to hack away any enjoyment.

Yes, his father. The man who'd barely spoken to him other than some terrible words about something Coop couldn't even remember. The man whose disappointment had been a constant buzzsaw by his ear ever since Coop had stopped being whatever his father needed him to be.

His finger hovered over the play button. Part of him wanted to delete the message unread, avoid whatever criticism awaited in it. Another part of him desperately needed to know what the old man had to say now that his son was injured and grounded.

He took a breath. Tapped play.

His father's face materialized. Older. Grayer. That rigid military bearing still there, his spine straight while even sitting down.

"Blake."

The name sounded strange after so long.

"Your commanding officer sent word about your injuries. About what happened on Rass."

A pause. The old man's jaw worked like he was chewing words.

"I've read the after-action reports. What you did on that ridge— you know, coordinating fires for three days straight while everything fell apart around you. I..."

His dad cleared his throat, then paused for a long while. Was he holding back tears?

"Your grandfather would've been proud. I am too, even if I've been... not so good at showing it."

Did he just... did Dad just say he's proud? The admission blasted like a nuclear bomb in Coop's mind. Coop's throat tightened.

"I know you're thinking about what's next. Cooper, men don't quit when things get hard. We adapt. We find new ways to fight."

His father's expression softened.

"Whatever you decide to do, whatever path you take back to service, you've got my support. Awkward as that probably sounds coming from me after all this time."

And just like that, his dad ended the message. Almost like he was too embarrassed to show any emotion, to say anything good about his son. Then the holo faded too and Coop sat in silence, staring at emptiness. Something tight unwound in his chest, something that had been knotted there since childhood, growing with every disappointed look, every comparison to grandfather, every time he'd failed to be the Cooper his father wanted.

His right hand trembled. His left reached for the datapad.

Coop opened the application. The form loaded in sections. Personal information. Service record. Medical history. All autopopulated. Then the cursor blinked in the "Personal Statement" section.

Required field. Minimum 200 words, maximum 1000.

He typed: "I'm applying for the manned fighter program because I want to continue serving the Republic in a combat capacity."

Generic. Sounds like everyone else. Delete. Delete. Delete.

"My experience coordinating fire missions on Ridge 248 demonstrates my ability to make tactical decisions under extreme duress."

Just facts. They can get facts from my file. Delete. Delete. Delete. *Reads like a stupid resume.*

"Despite my injuries, I believe I can contribute meaningfully to—"

Why start with "despite"? Like I'm apologizing for existing. Delete.

An hour burned away and the cursor kept blinking, kept mocking him.

How do you sell yourself when half of you doesn't work right? Am I just kidding myself with this? Can I really do it without being disqualified? I'm fooling myself, aren't I?

His father's voice hit him for the second time. "Cooper, men don't quit when things get hard."

He tried the professional approach: "My combat experience includes seventy-two continuous hours coordinating fire missions under hostile conditions. I demonstrated tactical decision-making and adaptability when standard equipment failed. I maintained operational effectiveness despite equipment degradation and personnel casualties."

He read it back. It sounded like an after-action report. Clinical. Distant. The kind of thing written about someone you'd never met.

Delete.

Delete.

Delete! he thought.

The problem wasn't what he was saying. It was what he *wasn't* saying. Like his drone piloting. Like the many years he'd spent serving the Republic in many aspects. His accomplishments, his…

That his nerves were damaged, that his right hand shook so badly some mornings he couldn't hold a spoon.

Yet, despite all of it, never flying again felt worse than the burns, worse than the blaster wound, worse than his body betraying him daily.

But you can't write that in an application. Can you?

He started typing again. This time he didn't think about what sounded professional or impressive or safe.

He wrote the truth.

"My name is Blake Cooper. My great-great-grandfather flew P-51 Mustangs over Germany in World War II. My grandfather flew combat missions in the Great War. My father served for thirty years.

I've flown drone missions in two major campaigns, and I've coordinated fire missions in two campaigns, one covert, the other on Rass. On my last combat engagement, I took a Zodark blaster round to the chest. The energy weapon damaged peripheral nerves in my right arm."

The words flowed now. Unfiltered.

"My right hand doesn't work right yet. But I'm healing. Gallentine-enhanced treatment is rebuilding the damaged pathways faster than standard protocols. I can't do the precision work TASC requires. But my left hand works fine, and soon so will my right hand and arm. My tactical thinking is intact. My ability to make decisions under pressure hasn't changed. My commitment to this fight hasn't changed."

He kept typing and the story poured out.

"I'm not asking you to ignore my limitations. I'm asking you to see what I can still do. Manned fighters need pilots who can think when systems fail, who can adapt when everything goes wrong, who won't quit when the mission gets hard. Look at my records. You'll see what I do under great stress, and how I succeed, because that's what Coopers do. We adapt. We fight. We don't quit."

His fingers paused over the keyboard.

"I know I'm still healing. But I'm not done. Not yet. And with the Gallentine treatment protocol, I'll be ready when you need me."

Coop read the statement three times.

Raw. Honest. Maybe too honest. Any sane personnel officer would see "my right hand doesn't work right" and stamp REJECTED across his file before reading further.

Should I soften it? Make it sound less desperate?

His cursor hovered over the edit button.

But that's the point. They'll see my medical file anyway. The blaster wound diagnosis. The peripheral nerve damage. The occupational therapy reports documenting every tremor, every failed coordination test, every reminder that his body didn't work the way it used to.

Better to own it than pretend he was something he wasn't.

Better to control the narrative than let them write it for him.

Still, once he pressed submit, there was no taking it back. No pretending he was OK with a desk job. No safe exit where he could tell himself he never really tried.

He thought about Bear, who'd looked at impossible odds and grinned like the universe was telling a joke only he understood.

About his grandfather's journal, filled with missions flown despite fear and loss.

About his father's message. Awkward, stilted, but there.

About Diesel's amazement at the Gallentine healing results. About Dr. Drexler asking "What if you're not as broken as you think?" About Colonel Joff's assessment: "three to four months for significant functional recovery."

Someone had to benefit from the Gallentine technology. Someone had to prove that damaged soldiers could come back stronger. So, why not him? Why not the person who'd coordinated fires for three days straight while his equipment was failing and people were dying?

If he could do that, he could do this.

Here goes everything.

He pressed the submit button.

The progress bar filled and a confirmation message appeared in the middle of the screen: "Application received. Review process: 1–2 weeks. You will be contacted regarding next steps."

He closed the datapad and sat in the Martian silence.

His future hung somewhere in a database, waiting for strangers to decide if he was worth the risk. But for the first time since the ridge, since the explosion, since waking up in medical with half his arm not working, he felt like maybe he had a fighting chance.

Chapter 32:
Recorded Voices

Late 2098
Mattis Military Complex
Mars

Coop stood on the balance beam, arms at his sides. One foot in front of the other. His right leg dragged just enough to notice. Not much. Two weeks ago, he'd been grabbing the rail every three steps. A month ago, he'd fallen off completely.

"Full walk, turn, walk back," Diesel said. "Three reps."

The beam stretched six meters ahead. Coop moved forward, feeling the signals travel from his eyes to his feet. The pathways worked now. Scrambled before, but clearer each day. He reached the end, executed the turn without touching anything, and walked back.

"Again."

Coop repeated the exercise. The leg drag lessened on the second rep. By the third, it barely registered.

Diesel marked something on his tablet. "I don't need a scan to tell me what I'm seeing. Your neural pathways are reorganizing. Damaged areas recruiting healthy tissue to compensate. That's textbook neuroplasticity, and you're showing accelerated recovery patterns." He looked up. "That Gallentine tech combined with your hard work? You're recovering faster than anyone I've worked with in twenty years. Whatever's happening in that thick skull of yours… well, my friend… it's working."

Coop stepped off the beam. His balance held.

"Take five," Diesel said. "I need to grab updated protocols from the office."

The big man left. Coop grabbed his water bottle and took a drink. His hand didn't shake as much anymore. They still trembled when he tried to hold small objects, but the gross motor function was coming back faster. Nine weeks had gone by since he'd been injured on Ridge 248. Six weeks had passed since he'd submitted his application to the manned fighter program. He hadn't received any response yet.

Military bureaucracy doesn't work like this, he thought.

They rejected you or accepted you. Standard processing took seven to ten business days, and on the actual form, it said one to two weeks. He'd passed that mark long ago. The silence meant something had gone wrong in the system, or someone up the chain was sitting on his paperwork.

But the physical recovery? That was undeniable. The Gallentine treatments were working. His grip strength had jumped from eighteen percent to thirty-four percent. His fine motor control was climbing steadily. The frustration wasn't about whether he'd recover, it was about the bureaucratic delay keeping him from the next step.

"Sometimes you're right here with me," Diesel had said yesterday. "Other times your mind wanders. What's going on, Cooper?"

"Nothing."

"Bull. You're thinking about something. Been doing it for days now."

Coop hadn't answered. Diesel had let it drop.

Across the room, a young man sat on a bench between parallel bars: Private First Class Rivera. Both legs were gone above the knee from an Orbot ambush on Rass. Sweat soaked through his PT shirt. Coop had seen him here every day for the past six weeks, performing upper body exercises while waiting for his prosthetics to arrive from the fabrication facility at Olympus Station.

Coop walked over. Something pulled him that direction. He'd been doing this lately: talking to other patients, and finding purpose in small ways. "How's it going?"

Rivera glanced up. "Fine."

"Yeah?"

Rivera wiped his face with a towel. Looked away and didn't answer.

"Waiting's the worst part," Coop said.

"Another week for the legs. Biointegrated neural interface models, full tactile feedback. Supposed to be better than the old mechanical rigs." Rivera met his eyes. "Doesn't make the waiting easier. I just want to walk again, you know?"

Coop knew. "They'll get you sorted."

"Yeah." Rivera gripped the parallel bars. "Docs say I'll be running in three months. I want to get back."

"Back? Where?" Coop asked.

"In combat."

"Yeah."

Rivera nodded, looking off. "I owe it to the guys who didn't make it off that rock." He pulled himself up, arms straining. "What about you? You going back?"

"Trying to."

"Heard you got pretty banged up."

"Blaster wound to the chest. Peripheral nerve damage in my right arm from the energy weapon." Coop held up his right hand. The tremor showed, though only a bit. "Fine motor control's still recovering. Gross motor function's coming back faster than expected, thanks to some new Gallentine medical technology."

Rivera lowered himself back down. "That why you're here every day? Trying to get back in the fight?"

"Something like that."

"You're that TASC guy, right? The one who held Ridge 248?"

Coop didn't answer. Somehow, what he did had spread, and he didn't know why. He was just doing what he was supposed to do—keeping everyone alive.

"You are. Blake Cooper. Call sign Coop." Rivera's expression changed and showed a kind of recognition. "My squad talked about that fight. Said you were lead TASC controller for Alpha Company, 3rd Brigade. The Red Devils of the 82nd Orbital Assault Division."

"Yeah."

"You called in fire missions for seventy-two hours straight while your position was getting shelled. Danger-close artillery on your own coordinates. Orbital strikes from *Duncan* while Zodark forces were breaching your perimeter." Rivera pulled himself up again. "You were the last one out. Bought the time that saved the whole theater that day."

The words didn't land right. Coop had called in fire because that was the job. Stayed because leaving meant Alpha Company died. Nothing inspirational about it. Stay and coordinate support or run and watch everyone get overrun.

A crutch clattered to the floor three meters away. A woman bent to retrieve it, her hand shaking from motor control issues. Coop moved without thinking, and picked up the crutch, and handed it to her.

"Thanks," she said.

He returned to Rivera, who'd finished another set on the bars.

"You'll get there," Coop said.

Rivera settled back onto the bench. "Yeah. Yeah, I will."

The woman with the crutch hadn't left. She settled onto a nearby bench, adjusting her position with careful movements. It was a fresh injury and Coop recognized the signs: the uncertainty in every motion, and the concentration required for actions that used to be automatic.

"You just arrive?" he asked.

"Two days ago. TBI from an artillery strike on Rass. Left temporal lobe damage affecting motor planning and speech processing." She touched the side of her head where regenerative nanites worked beneath the skin. "Docs say I'm lucky. Could talk when I woke up. Some of the others in my unit can't even remember their names."

"How's it going over there? On Rass?"

"Better than expected. Republic and Primord forces are pushing the Zodarks back sector by sector. Last I heard before I shipped out, we'd taken forty percent of the planetary surface. Enemy's consolidated around their primary installations, but they're losing ground every day." She met his eyes. "It's a grind, but we're winning."

Coop liked what he heard, and when he was about to reply, someone spoke his name. And it was a familiar voice.

"Cooper."

Coop turned. Diesel stood in the corridor entrance with someone in Army utilities. The uniform's cut and bearing registered before the face did. But when the face registered, Coop almost fell over.

Oh my... holy heck!

It was Crawford. Staff Sergeant Crawford from Alpha Company, one of the TASC controllers on his four-man team—the tech wizard who'd kept their equipment running when everything else was falling apart.

Crawford's right arm hung in a sling. Regenerative dermal patches covered his neck and disappeared under his collar.

Coop's stomach dropped. Crawford should be on Rass with the company. The Rass campaign was ongoing. Then he saw the medical bracelet marking him as a recovery patient.

His face split into a grin anyway. Relief mixed with concern.

"What the hell happened to you?" Coop asked when Crawford reached him.

"Took shrapnel and plasma burns. Zodark mortar strike while we were calling in fire on a fortified position." Crawford shifted his weight, favoring his right side. "Caught me across the shoulder and upper chest. Tried to hide it. Kept working. Figured it wasn't that bad." He grimaced. "Wasn't until I couldn't eventually lift my arm that I realized I'd torn the rotator cuff. The burns went deeper than I thought. Damaged the brachial plexus nerve bundle, they say. Whatever that is, but it really acts up at night. When you can't sleep because of pain, well, it sneaks up on you and you don't know who you are, or what the hell you're doing."

"That bad?"

"Bad enough they pulled me off Rass. Can't use the arm anymore. But they're going to put me on this Gallentine new healing tech. Should help." Crawford gripped Coop's good shoulder with his good hand. "Docs here say they can fix it, and that I'll get better with all the treatments they're going to do. Should have full function back in two months." He grinned again. "But, man… you're here. I can't believe I'm actually seeing you in person."

Coop wanted to give him a hug, but when was the last time he'd given anyone a hug? "I hate to say it, Crawford, but I'm glad to see you."

"Same."

Coop looked down. "How's the Company?"

"Still in it. Down to about sixty percent strength from the original drop. We picked up replacements, but they're green. Most of them haven't seen an Orbot up close yet." Crawford's jaw worked. "The old hands remember what you did on Ridge 248. Weber's gone, and… yeah, you knew that too. But, Li made it. Vega's still out there raising hell."

"Li?"

"Li took command of the TASC team after I had to jet off Rass. Doing good work, I hope. Vega's got twenty-nine confirmed kills now. Captain Gill's putting her up for a commendation, last I heard."

Coop's legs stopped working right. It wasn't the injury…it was something else. He sat down hard on the nearest bench. Crawford sat beside him, moving carefully, protecting his injured shoulder.

"I should be there," Coop said. "With the Company."

"You're where you need to be. Getting better so you can fight again. Simple as that."

The grief came then. Not the clean, simple kind. The complicated mess of surviving when others didn't. Coop had held it together so many times through the injury, through the surgery, through weeks of rehabilitation. He'd focused on recovery because focusing on anything else meant feeling like this. Nine weeks—Alpha Company had been fighting for nine weeks while he learned to walk a balance beam. Weber was dead. Crawford had gotten torn up. Li was running the TASC team that should've been Coop's.

"I've lost almost everyone," Coop said. The words came out rough. "From Ridge 248. Most of them are gone. From the Red Devils."

Crawford just sat there. "You're still here. That means something. To Weber's memory. To the soldiers still fighting. To everyone who needs you to get back up and keep going." He stood and pulled Coop up with his good arm. "You don't get to quit, remember? You said it so many times it practically burned my ears off. You're a Cooper, and they don't quit. They sacrifice, and you did that just as good as the other Coops, I reckon."

Coop merely sat there, nodding, and letting himself feel the full energy of being alive.

Crawford reached into his cargo pocket and pulled out a small storage chip. "Well, I did something."

"Yeah?"

"Before I left, I spoke with the team. They wanted me to bring you something. Recorded messages. Every soldier in Alpha Company who served with you on Ridge 248 contributed. Well, the ones who are still alive. Li. Vega. Even Captain Gill. I didn't know when I'd see you again, but thought if I did, I'd have something for you."

He handed Coop the chip. Coop looked it over. "Wow. I don't know what to say."

"They want you to know they haven't forgotten. What you did. What it cost. What it meant." Crawford raised his brows. "Some of these messages are from soldiers who didn't make it the next day, though. Remember Tony Gatto?"

"That little spry punk who had more energy than…" Coop's expression dropped. "Oh, no. Don't tell me…"

"Tony recorded his a day before he died."

Coop closed his fist around the chip. "I can't watch this now, but thank you."

"No prob. When you're ready, they're there." Crawford checked his chronometer. "I've got physical therapy in an hour, but after that I'm free. Let's get some chow. Real food, not the rehab center slop."

Coop pocketed the chip. The grief hadn't disappeared. It sat there, solid. But Crawford's presence made it bearable.

They walked toward the facility exit. Diesel watched from the corridor and gave Coop a subtle nod.

"You hear anything about the manned fighter program?" Crawford asked.

Coop stopped. "You know about that?"

"Li mentioned it before I shipped out. Said he bet you'd be thinking about applying, no matter what shape you were in."

"He was right. Applied six weeks ago. Standard processing is seven to ten days, maybe up to two weeks, but I'm past that with no word."

Crawford frowned. "That's not right. Military doesn't leave people hanging like that. Something's stuck in the system, or someone's sitting on it." He pulled out his datapad with his good hand, balancing it against his sling. "Give me the details. I'll make some calls. See what's blocking your application."

The offer caught Coop off guard. "You don't have to do that."

"Yeah, I do. You're still one of mine, even if you're not in Alpha Company anymore."

"What, you suddenly got the ear of an admiral or something?"

Crawford laughed, and winked. "Just got some connections. Plus, the Republic needs good pilots. If you've got the aptitude and you're recovering well enough to fly, someone needs to push that application through, and maybe I can give it a bigger nudge."

They stepped into the glass-enclosed walkway connecting the medical facility to the main complex. Mars stretched out below them in rust. The thin atmosphere created a sky that always looked too pale and too pink. Olympus Mons dominated the western horizon, a mountain so massive it defied human scale. The base disappeared into atmospheric haze while the summit reached into space itself.

Everywhere outside, red dust covered the landscape. The permanent stain of a planet humanity was slowly transforming into something livable. According to the scientists, Mars would have breathable air once they figured out terraforming, and someday, centuries from now, children would run across these plains without pressure suits.

Coop breathed against the glass and felt Crawford's presence beside him. Felt the grief and the purpose and the forward motion all mixed together into something he could carry into whatever stood in front of him next. And, by God, he hoped that was the manned fighter program.

Chapter 33:
Convoy Escort

Late 2098
RNS *Invincible*
Planet New Eden

The display populated with training contacts as Captain Noriko Sato absorbed everything on the bridge. On the tactical screen were seven civilian transports, three escort frigates, and her battlecruiser, *Invincible*.

Yes, her ship. Not Lee's. Not anyone else's. The command chair held her weight differently than the XO station ever had. For years, she'd stood beside Lee, sat beside him, and watched him make the calls. And from that, she'd really learned the rhythm of command. Now that rhythm was hers to set.

Two months in command: sixty days of simulations, crew evaluations, and proving she belonged in this chair. The drilling had been relentless, but necessary.

She'd earned this. Every late watch, every tactical brief, every simulation where she'd pushed herself harder than anyone else pushed her. The promotion ceremony felt like yesterday, but two months of constant drilling had transformed her crew into something sharp. Something ready.

Or so she thought.

XO Black reviewed the exercise parameters. Standard convoy escort through hostile space. The mission briefing had been straightforward: get seven civilian vessels through the threat zone without losing a single one. Basic formation work. Bread and butter for any Republic captain.

"All stations report ready, Captain," Black said.

Sato's heartbeat kicked against her ribs like a drumbeat. "Signal the convoy to form up. Escorts take positions alpha, beta, and gamma."

The civilian ships lumbered into formation, their bulk making even *Invincible* look modest. Lieutenant Commander Yamamoto confirmed sensor arrays tracked all friendly contacts while Lieutenant Delacroix established communication protocols with each transport.

Chief Knight reported damage control teams at ready stations throughout the ship.

Perfect. Everything running like clockwork.

"Formation established," Black reported. "All ships acknowledge."

Sato studied the main holo. The civilian transports created a rough diamond pattern with *Invincible* in the center and the three frigates spread at optimal defensive intervals. She'd calculated the spheres of protection, the response patterns, the firing solutions for every likely threat vector. Her crew had drilled these formations until they could execute them blind.

"Multiple hostiles inbound," Marsh announced from tactical. "Bearing zero-three-two mark twenty-one. Six frigates." He worked the display, highlighting threat vectors in red. "Range thirty-two thousand kilometers, closing fast."

The enemy formation split, two groups of three approaching from divergent vectors. Sato recognized the pattern from years of experience. Classic probe maneuver, testing defensive positioning before committing to full assault.

"Signal all ships, maintain escort formation." The words came out smooth. "Weapons free on my mark."

Black turned from her station. "Captain?"

"Marsh, prepare firing solutions on lead elements. We'll break their formation before they reach effective range."

She held in a grin, because from the look of things, this sim would end shortly after it began. Sometimes, they threw *easy* at you, and this simulation would prove to be one of those easy simulations.

"Aye, Captain," Marsh said. "Solutions locked."

The enemy frigates accelerated, their formation tightening as they closed the distance. Twenty-five thousand kilometers…twenty thousand…they'd reach effective weapons range in ninety seconds.

"All batteries, fire," Sato ordered.

Invincible's turbo lasers opened up, followed by the escorts. Magrail rounds and missiles streaked toward the enemy formation. Two enemy frigates took hits, their armor absorbing the impacts on the tactical display. But they kept coming.

The enemy returned fire before Sato's defensive umbrella could properly form. Plasma torpedoes streaked toward the convoy from multiple angles. Marsh coordinated point defense while Delacroix relayed targeting data to the escort frigates. Point-defense guns hammered at incoming torpedoes, destroying most.

Not all.

A civilian transport took a direct hit. Its hull breached in simulation mode, emergency alarms wailing through the communication channels. Red casualty markers flashed on the tactical display, until the ship broke up and debris spun into the dark expanse.

Sato's shoulders drooped a centimeter before she propped them back up. Overconfidence had consumed her like fire, and it was quickly extinguished. "Return fire, all batteries. Signal escorts to concentrate on Attack Group Baker."

She'd made the right call. Offensive pressure would scatter the enemy formation and protect the remaining transports. The mathematics supported her decision. Every tactical manual agreed.

Black sat at her station beside the captain's chair. Said nothing. Her silence felt heavier than words.

"Enemy frigates breaking formation," Marsh reported. "Attack Group Baker withdrawing to one-eight thousand kilometers, bearing three-four-zero mark one-five. Attack Group Able maintaining course, zero-four-five mark two-six."

"Pursue Attack Group Able," Sato ordered. "Keep pressure on them."

Invincible surged forward, her escorts following. The enemy frigates scattered, drawing them further from the convoy centerline. Another civilian transport died when a plasma torpedo slipped through the weakened defensive screen. Two down. Five remaining.

The mission had been keeping them all safe; yet two in a short time span had been eliminated. But she wouldn't fail them all. She could self-correct.

"Captain," Black said quietly, "we've lost two of seven civilian transports."

Sato gnashed her teeth. She knew exactly how many they'd lost. Hell, the red markers burned in her peripheral vision. Black was only doing her job, stating facts, but each word punched harder than the last because Sato knew the truth: she was doing a *bad* job.

The XO pulled up the damage assessment. Civilian casualties mounted while Sato's formation chased enemy frigates through empty space. The tactical display showed the truth. *Invincible* had moved three thousand kilometers from the convoy centerline, pursuing targets that kept drawing her further away.

The remaining five civilian ships sat exposed in the middle of hostile space, waiting for the killing blow that would end this exercise in complete failure.

Black's voice practically boomed. "Captain, the mission isn't killing enemies. It's saving civilians."

Sato stared at the five remaining transport icons, then at the enemy formations she'd been pursuing. Every instinct screamed to engage, to destroy, to prove *Invincible*'s combat superiority.

But she was wrong. Dead wrong. Heck, she'd been commanding like a warrior when the mission demanded a damn guardian.

"All ships, immediate recall to convoy position." Her throat tightened. "Form defensive sphere around remaining civilian vessels. Tight formation, interlocking defense coverage."

Marsh looked up from tactical. Confusion crossed his face before professional discipline took over, and Black nodded once, already coordinating the new defensive parameters.

The escort frigates turned hard, burning toward the convoy as enemy contacts closed from two vectors. The escorts had never pursued as aggressively as *Invincible*. While Sato chased Attack Group Able three thousand klicks from convoy center, her frigates maintained closer proximity, no more than fifteen hundred kilometers out. Now that gap mattered.

Invincible's engines roared at full thrust. The distance closed. Four thousand kilometers. Three thousand. Two thousand.

"Enemy formations converging on convoy center," Yamamoto reported. "Two attack vectors. They're going for the kill."

The tactical display recalculated firing solutions. The enemy had seen their opening. Five exposed civilian ships. No heavy cruiser protection. Standard tactical doctrine said press the advantage.

She'd handed them that advantage on a silver platter. *I gave them this opening. Chased their bait like a fresh ensign who couldn't tell the difference between a tactical feint and an actual threat. Lee would have seen this coming three moves ago. Hell, I should have seen it.*

"Time to defensive formation?" Sato asked.

"Fifteen seconds at current burn," Black said. "Enemy close quarters weapons range in ten."

They'd lose at least one more transport. Maybe two.

Unless…

"Helm, emergency deceleration burn at mark." Sato leaned forward. "Marsh, prepare full broadside. Target lead enemy frigate, Attack Group Baker."

"Captain?" Black turned from her station.

"We can't reach defensive formation before they fire. So, we hit them hard enough to break their attack run." Sato's hands steadied against the armrest. "Make them choose between pressing their attack or surviving ours."

"Aye, Captain," Marsh replied. "Solutions locked."

Invincible's main engines burned against her forward momentum. The maneuver killed their velocity while bringing all weapons to bear. Risky, exposed…the kind of move that got ships destroyed in real combat.

"Fire," Sato ordered.

Every weapon on *Invincible*'s starboard side opened up. Turbo lasers burned through the lead enemy frigate's armor. Magrail rounds punched through exterior plating. Missiles streaked toward the formation's center.

Two frigates broke formation entirely. Attack Group Baker lost cohesion as ships burned in different directions, trying to avoid *Invincible*'s withering fire. Their coordinated assault fell apart.

"Attack Group Able still closing on convoy," Yamamoto said. "Range five thousand kilometers."

Invincible completed her deceleration burn and surged back toward convoy centerline. The escort frigates reached defensive positions, their point-defense systems coming online around the civilian transports.

"Defensive sphere established," Black reported. "All civilian ships inside protective envelope."

Attack Group Able fired. Plasma torpedoes streaked toward the convoy from several angles. Point-defense guns hammered the incoming ordnance. Marsh coordinated fire with the escort frigates, creating overlapping fields that shredded torpedoes before they reached the civilian ships.

Most of them.

One torpedo slipped through. *Invincible* moved into its path, her forward armor taking the hit meant for a civilian transport. The bridge shuddered. Damage reports flooded in from forward sections.

"Hull breach, decks three and four," Knight reported. "Damage control teams responding."

Sato barely heard him. Her focus stayed locked on the tactical display. The enemy formations regrouped, testing the defensive sphere from different trajectories. Looking for gaps.

She wouldn't give them any.

"Maintain position," Sato ordered. "All ships hold the line."

An enemy frigate flew past *Invincible*'s starboard quarter at three hundred meters, close enough to see scorch marks on its hull plating. Lasers raked *Invincible*'s armor. Sparks flew across the tactical display as damage indicators lit up.

"Target acquired," Marsh said. "Firing."

Magrail rounds hammered the frigate's aft section. The first salvo punched through armor. The second hit something critical. The frigate's reactor containment failed. A massive explosion lit the holo. When it cleared, pieces of the enemy ship tumbled through space. Chunks of hull plating, a severed weapons pod, what looked like part of the bridge section.

"Splash one," Marsh reported.

Two more enemy frigates vectored in from port, weapons cycling. Another accelerated straight at the convoy from above the defensive sphere. Plasma torpedoes streaked from multiple angles. Point-defense batteries tracked and fired. Turbo lasers blasted through the dark. The enemy kept coming, kept probing, searching for any gap in the formation they could exploit.

Sato's ships held the line.

Delacroix reported critical damage to the escort frigate *Ranger*. Yamamoto tracked enemy movements, calling out attack vectors. The hostile force probed every angle, every gap, every weakness.

There were no gaps. Not anymore.

Minutes stretched into an eternity. *Invincible* absorbed punishment that would have crippled a lesser vessel. Her armor scored under sustained fire. The civilian transports cowered behind her bulk, protected by the shield wall Sato had finally learned to build.

Another enemy blew apart before them, direct hits from Sato's ship and the rest of her battle group.

But why didn't she do this from the beginning? What did she miss? *The mission parameters were right there in the briefing: escort and protect, not seek and destroy. I read them, acknowledged them, and then forgot them the moment the enemy appeared. Like the words didn't matter once the shooting started.*

"Enemy frigate breaking off," Marsh reported. "Remaining contacts withdrawing to maximum weapons range."

The hostile force had burned through its offensive capability against a defense that finally refused to crack. Sato's formation remained tight, creating a killing zone no sane commander would enter.

The enemy chose survival.

"Simulation complete," the computer announced.

The bridge fell silent. Sato stared at the tactical display. Five civilian transports intact. *Invincible* registered enough damage to put her in dock for weeks. The escort frigates had taken similar punishment.

Two ships lost before she'd figured it out.

She secured her station and headed for the ready room, each step heavier than the last.

Lee waited in the ready room. He'd watched the entire exercise from Task Force command.

Sato dropped into the chair across from him. Every muscle ached with tension she hadn't noticed during the fight.

"I lost two ships before I understood the mission," she said.

Lee said nothing. Just sat there, hands folded on the desk, studying her with that expression she'd seen him use on junior officers who needed to work through their own mistakes.

"I thought I was protecting them by engaging the enemy. Standard tactical doctrine."

"Standard for what kind of engagement?" Lee's tone was neutral.

"Fleet action. Ship-to-ship combat."

"And this was a convoy escort." Lee leaned forward. "Different mission. Different success metrics. You did what most commanders would do, what logic says to do. Engage threats. Destroy them before they reach your convoy. The mathematics support it, right?"

Sato's throat tightened. She wanted to agree, to justify her decisions.

"But experience trumps logic," Lee continued. "In most cases. That's what this exercise was designed to teach you. To recognize when your instincts are fighting the wrong battle. You reverted to warrior instinct. Attack the threat. Destroy the enemy." He paused. "Tell me what the enemy was doing when they split formation."

Sato watched the replay in her mind—the enemy formations splitting, her own ships pursuing, and the convoy sitting exposed.

"Drawing me away," she said quietly. "They weren't trying to win a ship-to-ship engagement. They were trying to isolate the civilian transports."

"And you let them. Because you saw enemy contacts and your training took over." Lee sat back a little. "Your training as XO was about destroying threats. Your job as captain is completing the mission. Before every engagement, ask yourself one question: what does success look like for this mission? Not victory. Success. Then build everything around that answer.

"We deploy in about seven months, so they tell us. Seven months to a potential combat zone where the enemy doesn't restart when you fail." He let that sink in. "Will you recognize the difference next time? Between the battle your instincts want and the battle the mission requires?"

Sato met his eyes. "I will, sir. From now on."

"Good." Lee's voice softened. "You did what logic dictated. Don't beat yourself up for that. But now you know. Experience teaches what logic can't. Some officers never learn that lesson. You learned it in a simulation instead of real combat, and you corrected yourself in real time. That's what I wanted to see. That's what Command wanted to see. That's what makes you ready."

He pulled up a different tactical scenario on the display.

"Run it again tomorrow. Show me a captain who knows her mission before the first shot is fired."

He headed for the hatch, then hesitated.

"You saved five ships today, Noriko. And you figured out why you lost two. That self-awareness, that's what makes a superb captain."

The door closed behind him.

Sato sat alone in the ready room, studying the tactical replay. Learning the lesson that would define her command because sometimes the hardest battle was knowing which fight to take.

Chapter 34:
Ninety-Eight Percent

Late 2098
Mattis Military Complex
Mars

Coop's right hand gripped the resistance ball while his left worked the coordination board. Diesel had him doing two things at once now. Squeeze the ball, touch the sequence of lights as they lit up. Repeat. His hand barely trembled today. Yesterday had been hell, spasms firing through his fingers every few seconds until he'd wanted to kick something, and it confused him. What about the Gallentine tech? What happened? It was working, and then his healing reversed. But, today felt different. Clean signals. His neural pathways were finally learning the new routes around the damage.

"Thirty seconds on the squeeze. You're getting much stronger." Diesel watched the readout. "How's the left hand feeling?"

"Good. Better than good." Coop hit the light sequence without missing a beat. Red, blue, green, yellow, back to red. His fingers moved where he told them to move.

"Take five. You've earned it."

Coop grabbed his datapad from the bench and moved to the corner where the water dispenser stood. His fingers fumbled the screen unlock once—still not perfect, but worlds better than three months ago. The message opened.

Lieutenant Blake Cooper. Manned Fighter Program. Application Status. He stared at the words without processing them. Read them again. Then a third time to make sure he wasn't misreading it.

Three months since Ridge 248. Three months of Gallentine treatments, physical therapy, watching his grip strength climb from eighteen percent to eighty-two percent. Diesel had actually whooped when he saw the latest scan.

Across the room, Crawford worked his shoulder with a pretty blonde therapist named Vicky. She had him doing resistance band pulls, his face all screwed up with pain as damaged nerves fired wrong signals. Everyone had a crush on Vicky. She was used to it. Crawford was no different, though he tried to hide it behind jokes about how much he hated physical therapy.

Coop came back to the present. The acceptance letter detailed reporting instructions to the manned fighter training squadron at Naval Space Force Station in Salon-de-Provence in France.

Wait... what? Coop thought.

He'd expected to wait weeks for a response. It had taken a hell of a lot longer, so the acceptance felt surreal.

"Lieutenant Blake Cooper, you are hereby accepted into the Republic Navy Manned Fighter Training Program based on your exceptional combat record, proven tactical abilities, and drone fighter ace status. Your experience coordinating fire missions under extreme combat conditions on Ridge 248, combined with your flight expertise, makes you an ideal candidate for this program.

"Report to Mattis Personnel Processing Center within fourteen days for comprehensive medical evaluation and clearance verification. Upon successful completion of medical screening, you will receive orders for immediate military transport to Naval Space Force Station Salon-de-Provence, France, Earth. Failure to report will result in automatic program dismissal."

Fourteen days.

Coop's hands shook—from adrenaline this time—as reality crashed through his skull. They wanted him. Not despite his injuries, but because of who he was. A drone ace. A combat-proven tactical controller. Someone who'd held a ridge for seventy-two hours while everything fell apart around him.

Fourteen days to push from eighty-two percent to ninety-five. Maybe higher. The Gallentine treatments were still working. He could feel the improvements each week. Fourteen days was enough time to show them he was ready.

Diesel caught the change in Coop's expression and moved closer. "What's going on?"

Coop showed him the screen.

The big man's face split into a grin so wide it looked painful. "Well damn. Fourteen days. That's definitely doable. We can push you hard this week and next, get that grip strength up several more percentage points. You're already at eighty-two percent. Let's shoot for over ninety or better before your eval."

They both knew what this meant. The therapy sessions had worked along with the Gallentine technology. The neural pathways had rerouted enough and would continue to do so. Someone up the chain believed Coop could fly again.

Coop laughed—a real laugh starting deep in his chest and exploding outward. Diesel stared at him like he'd grown a second head, then joined in. The sound echoed through the therapy room and drew looks from other patients. Crawford glanced over from his shoulder torture session. Coop gave him that look Crawford knew meant something big had happened. Crawford grinned and threw a thumbs-up with his good arm.

Diesel grabbed Coop's shoulder with one massive hand. "That's the sound I've been waiting to hear. You're going to kill it up there, Cooper."

Coop wiped his eyes and realized he was crying too. Laughing and crying at the same time.

He left the therapy area fast, though with a little unevenness to his gait as the chest wound still pulled sometimes when he moved too quickly. He moved through corridors he'd memorized during weeks and weeks of rehabilitation and reached his quarters. He initiated the communication link to Earth before his brain could talk him out of it.

The last message his dad sent had meant something. The words about pride and support had cut through years of silence. Coop didn't know why he was calling now. It felt weird. Wrong, even. But the acceptance letter burned in his pocket and his dad deserved to know.

The connection took longer than normal. Distance creating lag even with tech that bent physics into submission. Static filled the holo before his father's face materialized.

"Blake?" His father blinked like he didn't trust what he was seeing. "Yes. Yes, Blake. How are you, my son?"

The words came out formal. Awkward. Years of distance sat between them.

Coop's throat went tight. "I'm good. Better. I got accepted."

"Accepted?"

"The manned fighter program. They want me. I have a medical eval in fourteen days, then I ship to Earth for training."

His father's face went through emotions Coop couldn't name. Pride maybe. Fear definitely. Something else that looked like regret.

"Fourteen days." His father repeated the words. "You've earned this, Blake. They're lucky to have you."

"Yeah."

Silence stretched. Similar to the type that filled their house when Coop was a kid. When his father would watch him fail at something and say nothing because disappointment didn't need words.

"Your grandfather would be proud," his father finally said.

Coop waited. Knew there was more. Hoped there was more.

His father's lips flattened into a straight line. "I am too."

The connection flickered. Threatened to die.

"Your mother," his father said. "You should call her. Let her know you'll be back on Earth soon."

"Do you two ever talk?" The question came out before Coop could stop it.

His father's face went blank. "No. Haven't seen or talked to her in years."

"Oh."

"Do you? Talk to her, I mean."

"Sometimes." Coop shifted his weight. "Few and far between. I haven't talked to her in, I don't know, six months."

His father nodded like that made sense. Like they both understood how Cooper men pushed people away until the distance became permanent.

"Well." His father cleared his throat. "You should. She'd want to know."

"Yeah. I will."

More silence.

"Go make us proud, son." His father's voice cracked on the last word. "Go make yourself proud."

The holo cut out before Coop could respond.

He sat in the silence and felt something loosen in his chest. A first step toward potential understanding.

Coop stood and moved to his locker. Pulled out his duffel bag. His personal effects had arrived a while ago. Shipped from the forward operating base on Rass. He'd kept the items here in his quarters ever since, a connection to who he was before the ridge.

The journal went in first. Presley Paul Cooper's words and his own scrawled entries. The legacy fit alongside standard-issue flight suits and the personal effects that had survived the war.

Bear's challenge coin went in his chest pocket, right over his heart where it belonged—where it had always belonged since they'd pulled him off that godforsaken ridge in the Rass system.

He grabbed his toiletries from the small bathroom: razor, toothbrush, and the prescription bottles for pain management and nerve regeneration support meds. The doctors said he'd need the regeneration supplements for another few months while the Gallentine-enhanced healing finished its work. His arm was getting better every week, but the process wasn't complete yet.

The room looked bare without his stuff, just white walls and a narrow bed and a window showing Mars in all its red glory. He'd arrived here broken. Convinced his flying days were over. Hell, even convinced his military days were over, except behind a desk, which he'd never accept. Now he was preparing for Naval Space Force Station Salon-de-Provence and the manned fighter program.

New determination replaced the doubt that had eaten him alive for the first few weeks after his injury.

Over the next fourteen days, Diesel pushed him harder than ever. Double sessions. Triple reps. The Gallentine treatments continued on schedule. Grip strength jumped to ninety-four percent. Fine motor control improved noticeably. His right hand still trembled with delicate tasks, but the gross motor function was nearly back to baseline.

"Ninety-six percent," Diesel announced on day thirteen, reviewing the latest scans. "You hit your target early and went over. Hell, you might crack ninety-seven or, hell, ninety-nine, before you leave."

Coop flexed his right hand, watching the fingers respond well. "Feels good. Feels ready."

"You're ready. Go show them what a Cooper can do."

The medical evaluation on day fourteen took three hours. Medical ran him through coordination tests, peripheral nerve function scans, and reflex assessments. The doctor who signed his clearance looked impressed, happy for him even. "Ninety-eight percent recovery in this short time?" the doctor said, reviewing the scans. "Impressive. The Gallentine treatments have exceeded all projections. You're cleared for flight training, Lieutenant. Continue the regeneration supplements, and you should hit full recovery within another week or two. Remarkable work."

Personnel cut his orders. Official transfer to Naval Space Force Station Salon-de-Provence. Assignment to manned fighter training squadron. Pay grade verified. Medical records updated. Everything stamped and signed and loaded onto his personnel chip.

They issued him new uniforms—standard Navy flight gear. A Republic Navy duffel to replace his worn Army bag. Everything crisp and new and smelling like a supply warehouse.

Coop shouldered his bag and headed for the transport hub. He didn't look back at the medical facility where he'd spent three months rebuilding himself and didn't think about the therapy sessions or the doctors who'd initially estimated a potential five months for recovery. His feet carried him through corridors and down lifts until he reached the departure terminal.

The shuttle to Earth sat on the pad with engines already warming. Heat shimmer rose off the hull in waves. Coop climbed aboard with four other pilots, all heading to the same program. None of them looked at each other. They were too busy processing their own demons and second chances.

The cabin stretched narrow and cramped with acceleration couches lining both sides with cargo netting overhead. Viewports showed the rusty Martian landscape and distant mountains under a butterscotch sky too thin to breathe. Coop strapped into his seat near the front while the engines vibrated through the deck.

A crew chief moved through, doing final checks. "Buckle tight. We're burning hard to make the Earth transit window."

The engines spooled up, and acceleration pressed him back into the couch as the shuttle lifted. Mars fell away beneath them. The red landscape shrank as they climbed toward orbit and the long flight to Earth.

Coop pressed his forehead against the viewport. G-forces built as they punched through the thin atmosphere. His vision grayed at the edges. He gripped the armrests and held on as the pressure built. His right hand spasmed once, twice, then steadied as muscle memory from years of flight training kicked in. His body remembered what his damaged nerves had to relearn.

The shuttle broke atmosphere. Mars became just another rust-colored ball in the black. Ahead lay Earth and whatever came next, and what came next was a quick moment of panic. Why? The call to his mom. He'd forgotten. Said he'd do it and then packed his gear instead like some kind of moron in a hurry to leave a practically lifeless planet that couldn't even grow a potato without major help.

But maybe he'd just surprise his mom in person. Yeah, that's what he'd do. Show up at her door and give her the biggest surprise of her life, just like the surprise he'd just been given. It was a chance to show that he was worth something more than another statistic, and show he was the best damn pilot for the job.

Chapter 35:
Task Force Integration

Late 2098
Victory Base Complex
Emerald City, New Eden

Four months had passed since the start of the Rass invasion, and since Captain Lee and the crew of the Poseidon had departed that contested system.

Captain Lee stood beside Admiral Costello in a conference room at Victory Base Complex. The door opened. Two Altairians entered, their cobalt eyes taking in every detail of the room and the people within.

Pandolly moved first, followed by another Altairian who stood a shade taller, less gaunt through the shoulders. The newcomer was still thin by human standards but built different than Pandolly.

"Captain Lee," Pandolly said. "I bring Gandolly, Altairian Liaison Officer assigned to your operations."

Lee extended his hand. Gandolly studied it for a moment before clasping it. Six fingers and a thumb, grip firm but not crushing.

"Lieutenant Commander Gandolly," Lee said. "Appreciate you making the trip."

"We serve the alliance," Gandolly replied. "Your reputation precedes you, Captain."

They settled around the table. Twelve Altairian ships had been assigned for logistics and support operations. Twelve Republic vessels formed the primary combat element. The Altairians would provide resupply capabilities, technical assistance, and reinforcement if Republic forces became overwhelmed in the Tully systems.

Costello handled the formal briefing: strategic overview, mission parameters, and rules of engagement. Lee listened, watching how the Altairians processed information, their eyes never blinking, never shifting, and just simply absorbing everything.

"Captain Lee," Pandolly said, "Lieutenant Commander Gandolly will serve as your primary Altairian liaison for operational matters in the sectors you will be operating. He has authority to coordinate support elements and facilitate communication between Republic and Altairian forces.”

Lee nodded. “Understood. Commander Gandolly, I look forward to working with you.”

“And I with you, Captain,” Gandolly replied. “I have reviewed your combat record extensively. Your adaptability and tactical innovation will be valuable assets in our cooperation.”

“Likewise,” Lee said. “I’ve worked with Primord forces, but this will be my first extended operation with Altairian support elements. I’m looking forward to learning your capabilities.”

Pandolly stood. “Then I leave you in capable hands. Commander Gandolly will brief you on Altairian support protocols and coordination procedures.” He looked at Lee directly. “Captain, I trust you will make good use of our resources.”

“We will, sir. Thank you.”

Pandolly departed, leaving Gandolly as the sole Altairian in the briefing.

“Your combat experience,” Gandolly said to Lee after Pandolly left. “Tell me what you’ve learned.”

Lee recognized the question for what it was, an assessment of sorts.

“New Eden was my first real command,” Lee said. “Took over when Captain Oldendorf and the XO died on the bridge. I was TAO at the time. Suddenly, I’m running the ship with half the senior staff dead and Zodark cruisers closing in.”

“You survived.”

“We survived, but lost ten percent of the crew doing it.” Lee met those black eyes. “I learned that command means making calls that could get people killed, because there’s no perfect decision. Just the one you can live with.”

Gandolly leaned forward. “And Intus?”

“Joint operation with Primord forces. It was my first time coordinating with nonhuman tactical doctrine. They fight different, you know, more aggressive, but not… if that makes sense.”

“I am making sense of what you are saying,” Gandolly replied.

“Yes,” Lee said. “They’re fluid, precise aggression might be the word for it, actually. It’s kind of how Earthers fight planetside during ground combat. Like us, they’re concerned with preserving assets, but in doing so, they pack a huge punch." Lee paused. "So, I learned to adapt my thinking. Their way isn't wrong, just different. The campaign succeeded because we figured out how to complement each other instead of competing."

"We went over your engagements near Rass," Gandolly said. "Orbital platform suppression, nearly fifty defensive installations with adaptive AI targeting systems. You lost seven crew members including your electronic warfare officer."

Lee shifted, and Gandolly caught the change. "I am sorry if we brought up some sadness. Were you close?"

"With my EWC officer?" Without waiting for a response, Lee continued, "Yes, and no. He was the best at what he did, and he did mean a lot to me, but we didn't talk much besides our time on the bridge together."

Gandolly dipped his head. "I see. Now, back to the platforms. They were learning from every engagement. Waiting would have made them stronger, and you did not wait, Captain. You learned just as the AI learned, and you defeated an advanced, and enhanced, system. It was impressive."

"Many other captains in the fleet did the same," Lee said.

"Not like you," Gandolly replied. "You learned faster than the rest, and hit harder, and destroyed those platforms to get the first wave of troops onto Rass. Impressive, too, I might add."

Lee raised his brows. "I guess I did."

"You did." Gandolly nodded once. The gesture carried meaning Lee couldn't quite read, but felt in his gut. It was a respect between officers who'd sent people to die for the benefit of the galaxy and would do it again.

"Your hybrid technology integration," Gandolly said. "How do you approach it?"

"I let the tech do what it does best. Republic magrails for kinetic strikes. Altairian turbo lasers for sustained fire. I try not to make one system behave like the other. Use them in sequence, you know? Magrails to crack armor, lasers to exploit the breach. That kind of thing."

"Communication protocols for support operations?"

"Direct channels between flagships. Dedicated liaison officers. Prearranged tactical codes for common maneuvers. But most important?" Lee leaned toward Gandolly. "Trust your counterpart's judgment. If you're second-guessing every call, you've already lost coordination."

Gandolly's head tilted slightly. "You have worked with Altairian commanders before."

"Negative, sir," Lee responded. "I have experience with convoy escorts, reconnaissance missions, and smaller cooperative operations with the Primords, but not the Altairians. And, to add to that, I've never personally commanded a task force with integrated Altairian support elements this size."

"Neither have I," Gandolly said. "This is new ground for both of us."

"Then we figure it out together," Lee said. "I've got tactical innovations you might not have considered. You've got experience in areas where Republic doctrine is still developing. We share what we know and we learn from each other. We don't let pride get people killed. That's what I've learned, especially by dealing with the Prims."

Gandolly's expression didn't change, but something shifted in his posture. He seemed less formal and more engaged.

They talked for another hour. It was a real tactical exchange. Lee described the sand-water countermeasure system Poseidon had used against the Rass platforms. Gandolly explained Altairian sensor disruption techniques that could blind enemy targeting without triggering their defensive protocols. Gandolly outlined logistics coordination methods for supporting Republic combat operations engaging superior numbers.

For most people, the discussion would teeter on boring, then fall off the side to outright dislike. For Lee, elation, excitement, entertainment… well… all the *e* words still couldn't describe his enthusiasm during the conversation. They were talking his talk, and it felt better than great.

By the time Costello called the meeting to a close, something had formed between them. *Is it friendship?* Lee contemplated. Not really, because that took time, shared experience, and blood spilled together. Instead, and importantly…they had found respect for each other.

"You deploy in five months," Gandolly said, standing. "I will coordinate all Altairian support elements for your task force operations, Captain Lee. I look forward to working with you."

"Likewise, Commander."

They exchanged formal salutes before the Altairians filed out, closing the door behind them.

Costello poured himself another coffee. "That went better than expected."

"He's a good officer," Lee said. "We've got common ground between us that we can build on."

"Let's hope it's enough."

An hour later, Lee sat across from Rhom in a briefing room about ten doors down from the conference room he'd been in, reviewing after-action reports from the four months of training exercises. Numbers didn't lie, and it all told him Rhom had handled the simulations well while making solid tactical calls under pressure. The crew responded to his leadership without hesitation.

"You've earned their respect," Lee said, scanning the performance metrics. "The bridge operates smoothly under your command." He raised an eyebrow. "I can't tell you how much I like that."

Rhom nodded. "I'm not Commander Sato."

"No. You're not." Lee set down the datapad. "You're Connor Rhom. That's what the *Poseidon* needs now."

"The crew knows me as TAO. Different dynamic as XO. I'm a little—"

Lee interrupted him. "They've served with you for years. They know your capabilities, they've watched you make the calls that kept them alive even as TAO." Lee leaned back, crossing his arms and exhaling a little. "Trust takes time to build at the executive level. You're getting there. The data shows it."

Rhom's expression carried awareness of what wasn't said. The rhythm would be different. Sato had anticipated Lee's thinking through years of partnership. Rhom brought his own strengths, his tactical mind, his weapons expertise that was second-to-none, and calm under fire that steadied the bridge crew when everything went to hell. Yet Sato was there even during lunch with Lee, so they knew each other inside and out, more than anyone on the ship knew anyone else. But in time, Rhom and Lee would function similarly—but different, because Rhom would be his own person, a different XO. And that's what would matter.

"I won't try to be her," Rhom said. "Just need to know you're good with that."

"I'm good with it. You're ready. Crew's ready. We deploy in about five months, if everything goes as scheduled, if training keeps progressing, and everything else pans out. Any concerns before then, you bring them to me. Otherwise, we're set."

Rhom stood. He saluted, then left without any unnecessary words.

Lee pulled up the next file. Lieutenant Junior Grade Bjorn Phillips was a transfer from RNS Gladstone after that cruiser took catastrophic damage during Rass. The service record read clean. He had commendations for electronic warfare excellence and was combat tested against those same platforms that had killed Witkowski.

The door opened and Phillips entered, back straight, eyes forward. He was a young officer, trying not to look nervous and almost succeeding.

"Have a seat, Lieutenant."

Phillips sat with his hands flat on the table, waiting.

"Tell me about Chief Diaz," Lee said.

The young officer's jaw tightened, barely visible, but there. "Best ECW chief in the fleet, sir. Taught me everything worth knowing about electronic warfare. When that plasma torpedo hit our station, Chief Diaz shoved me toward the secondary systems and told me to keep the jamming active." Phillips's voice stayed level. "He stayed at primary to reroute emergency power. The bulkhead collapsed on him before damage control reached our section."

Lee nodded. He'd lost good people too and understood exactly what that felt like.

"You kept the systems running."

"Yes, sir. Switched to backup arrays and maintained jamming effectiveness while the station burned. Gladstone withdrew under degraded targeting from enemy forces, and we lost Chief Diaz. Didn't lose anyone else from my section."

"Forty-eight hours of sustained combat against those platforms. You were there for all of it."

"Yes, sir. Nine platforms were destroyed before Gladstone took critical damage and had to withdraw."

Lee had watched Phillips during the training exercises over the past four months. The young officer adapted fast, learning the hybrid systems without complaint. He integrated Republic and Altairian technology like he'd been doing it for years instead of months.

"You've been training with us for four months now," Lee said. "We had hybrid systems aboard Poseidon—Republic standard equipment interfaced with Altairian technology. How's it working for you?"

It'd been long overdue to talk with this man, as Lee liked to have at least one private conversation with every crew member during their time serving on the Poseidon.

"I've reviewed the technical specifications repeatedly, sir. During training, I believe I've demonstrated quick adaptation to new systems. I'm ready for deployment."

The confidence wasn't arrogance, it was competence. Lee recognized the difference. Phillips had earned his place through fire. He'd lost his mentor but kept fighting, just like Lee on the RNS *Kentucky* all those years ago. Phillips was exactly what Poseidon needed.

"Welcome aboard, Lieutenant. Officially." Lee stood. "You've got big shoes to fill. Witkowski was one of the best. But you've proven yourself already. Now let's see what you can do when it counts."
****

Four days after the joint conference and meeting with Phillips and Rhom in the briefing room, Lee walked the corridors of Victory Base Complex. Task Force 27 existed now, and not just on paper.

Twelve Republic combat vessels. Twelve Altairian support ships, if needed. One mission.

Recently, the shakedown exercises the task force underwent had revealed some problems. There were communication delays when Republic and Altairian systems tried to sync, and tactical protocols that didn't translate between species, plus formations that looked good in theory but fell apart under simulated combat stress.

Lee and Gandolly had worked through every issue. Together, they created coordination procedures that used each species' strengths, established support protocols both sides could execute without hesitation, and ran simulations until the integration became second nature.

The final assessment sat in Lee's datapad. All vessels were reporting ready status. The Republic captains understood Altairian logistics capabilities, and the Altairian commanders were adapting to Republic combat doctrine. Resupply procedures would prevent coordination failures. Communication arrays now functioned across species barriers.

The intense stress of commanding a Republic task force with twelve vessels settled across Lee's shoulders different than a small battle group command. Thousands and thousands of more crew members depended on his very decisions and multiple species trusted his judgment. More ships meant more variables. More variables meant more ways things could go wrong.

Lee turned down the corridor toward the conference center. The briefing started in two minutes; it was a strategic review.

The conference room filled with captains. Lee stood at the head of the table as intelligence displays populated with threat assessments. Admiral Costello occupied the position to his right. Gandolly sat opposite. The Republic and Altairian captains filled the remaining seats.

Sato entered last. She moved different now, carrying herself with the confidence of independent command. Lee caught her eye for half a second. She nodded once without expression, then took her seat among the other captains.

"The Pharaonis have escalated beyond border raids," Lee said, bringing up the tactical map. "Coordinated strikes. Mining facility seizures. Communication disruption across three star systems." He highlighted sectors in red. "Pattern suggests preparation for major offensive operations."

They'd gone over this many times, but the more, the better.

Gandolly added Altairian intelligence to the display. "Monitoring stations have detected increased fleet movements near Pharaonis space. Electronic signatures indicate Orbot technical support. They are fielding more advanced weapons than previous assessments indicated."

Costello pulled up the strategic overview. "The Serpentis system is their objective, we believe; it has three stargates connecting Tully and Ry'lian territories. As you can see here, they're moving two small fleets from different sectors to this way point at one of the stargates. It's marked on the star map." Costello pointed, highlighting a red icon on the holo. "If they take it, they can easily get all three, especially if or when they send in more, bigger fleets. They'd gain staging areas for dual-axis assault into alliance heartland. Twelve million civilians are at risk. And if they commit to this, and take over the stargates, that leaves billions more lives at risk. That's why we need to react now."

"Intelligence suggests they're also doing this to test our response patterns," Sato said. "Each raid gathers data on alliance coordination. They're measuring our response times and defensive capabilities."

"Agreed," Lee said. "They're preparing the battlefield. Our mission is disrupting their timeline, and eliminating their timeline altogether. To force engagement before they're ready, we will arrive unexpected."

The planning session extended through the morning. Gandolly identified probable enemy staging areas based on recent raid vectors. Republic and Altairian captains contributed tactical analysis from similar operations. Gandolly outlined Altairian resupply protocols and how they could support Republic rapid response operations.

Sato asked questions, showing her growth. How would Invincible coordinate with frigate screens during patrol sweeps? What communication protocols prevented friendly fire when multiple task force elements converged on the same contact? How did battlecruiser firepower support lighter vessels without creating targeting conflicts?

She was thinking about how her ship fit within the larger strategic picture, and how her vessel supported task force objectives.

Lee watched her engage with other captains as a peer. The transition was complete. She wasn't his XO anymore. She was Captain Sato, commander of her own ship, equal among equals.

The years of partnership had created an unspoken understanding between them. When she proposed formation adjustments, Lee knew her thinking without explanation. When he outlined engagement protocols, she anticipated the tactical reasoning. But the dynamic had fundamentally shifted.

By 0300 hours, operational orders crystallized to aggressive patrol patterns through the Trrahan Sector, a show of force to deter further raids. This allowed for rapid response capability if Pharaonis forces engaged. Lee reviewed the briefing materials with Costello and the Altairian commanders while captains dispersed.

After the briefing concluded, Lee found Sato in the observation deck at 0600. Like him, she didn't go to sleep. New Eden spread before them. Green, lush forest, a blue lake in the distance, and a vast city on the horizon with vehicles flying to and fro. It was a nice, beautiful space for retired Earthers, and even those wanting to raise families here, start school, and bring in their businesses. If he was a civilian, who knew? Maybe he'd have chosen New Eden over Earth to raise two and a half kids at a home with a white picket fence, and a lovely wife as his partner.

"Your questions during the briefing were good," Lee said. "You're thinking beyond *Invincible* now, seeing how your ship fits the larger mission."

Sato studied the terrain before them. Animals that looked like a cross between an antelope and a lion stood in front of the massive window, grazing on grass. "The training exercises teach me that," she replied. "I lost ships in simulations because I forgot the mission and chased. Rookie mistakes, but I got over them and learned."

"That's what training is for. But what did you take from that?"

"That experience and logic aren't the same thing. That my job is completing the mission, not proving I'm the best tactical officer in the room." She glanced at him. "You tried to tell me that for years."

"Some lessons can only be learned through command and through making the mistakes and correcting them. You're ready, Noriko."

"I hope so." She turned back to the window. "Twelve Republic ships. Twelve Altairian support vessels. Thousands of crew members. Multiple species. That is—"

"Exactly what command feels like." Lee finished her sentence for her and stood. "You handle it the same way you handled being XO. One decision at a time. Accept that you can't control everything, and when you accept that, you'll then understand that you can control a whole hell of a lot."

They stood in silence for a while, just watching nature. A bird
flew into the lake and pulled out a fish, the splash big even from this
distance.

"Six months until deployment," Sato said quietly.

"Negative. Five months."

She gave him a look.

"Remember," he replied with a smile, "we didn't sleep last
night, so our brains aren't working properly." He held up five fingers,
winking. "So, five months until we find out what the Pharaonis have
prepared." Lee checked his chronometer. "Until then, you'll make sure
Invincible is ready."

"She will be. We both will be."

Lee nodded once.

The observation deck's lighting shifted as New Eden's sun
began to rise. The planet's cities began to brighten against the dawn.
Billions of people who'd been sleeping peacefully were now yawning,
waking up, getting ready to eat their breakfast and go to work, all
because officers like Lee and Sato stood ready to fight tooth and nail
for their freedom, and for their very lives.

Chapter 36:
One Hundred Fifteen Days

Late 2098
Forward Operating Base Redemption
Planet Rass

Love flew the *Jack* through Rass's night sky at two hundred meters, low enough to taste the war. They were five months into the Rass campaign: one hundred fifteen days on this rock for her squadron specifically. She'd stopped counting missions, stopped counting faces. The numbness became her survival. You felt everything or you felt nothing, and nothing kept you flying when the mission board never stopped adding names.

War ran on bodies and metal. After five months of grinding combat across the planet, you stopped asking which gave out first.

The *Gallipoli* had departed for New Eden just five weeks after the initial invasion stages, her hull scarred from constant operations during the opening campaign. Critical repairs, they'd called it. Mandatory downtime. But Wolfpack Squadron got reassigned as Firebase Redemption needed transports. In fact, the entire northern continent needed air support. The Republic was winning, but winning meant flying until the birds broke or the pilots did. Staging from the FOB cut response time by forty percent. That meant more soldiers lived. That meant Love kept flying.

The firebase sat in a contested valley twenty klicks behind the current front lines. Five months of war had turned Rass into hell, but the Republic was pushing the Zodarks back sector by sector.

Still, the base was close enough to the fighting that mortar rounds sometimes dropped in the perimeter. They were also close enough that pilots could launch, execute, and return inside twenty minutes instead of the one-hour cycle from orbit.

Green sat beside her in the copilot seat. They'd flown together so long, his breathing matched hers during drops and pickups. Ford and Torres manned the guns in back, ready for whatever hell waited at the extraction point. The four of them had become something beyond crew these days, a machine built from repetition and shared survival and stories.

Master Chief Zaines's Delta team had gone deep and found a Zodark command bunker coordinating the entire northern continental defense. Zaines called in orbital strikes. turning the facility into a crater, and hence completed the mission. Now they needed out. But extraction from behind enemy lines meant fighting through every Zodark and Orbot unit in the sector, all of them racing toward the team that had just destroyed their command structure.

Love checked her navigation display. Twelve minutes to the LZ. The tactical feed showed red contacts everywhere—Zodark rapid response forces, and Orbot hunter teams, every enemy unit in the sector converging on the Delta team's position.

"Contacts multiplying," Green said. His voice stayed level. "We're flying into a hell in a handbasket."

What the hell does that even mean? Love thought. *Hell in a handbasket? Isn't that something they said over a hundred years ago?*

"Then we fly fast." Love pushed the throttles forward. *Jack* surged ahead, eating distance. The Osprey's engines whined as she pushed past recommended speed, the airframe shuddering from the strain. Below them, Rass's scarred landscape blurred into darkness: bomb craters and burned forests. It was the aftermath of five months of combat.

The LZ materialized through the darkness—a bomb crater fifty meters wide, still smoking from the orbital strikes Zaines had called down. The tactical display updated as they approached, Green's sensors showing a picture making Love's stomach perform flips. Red contacts appeared in a 360-degree ring around the LZ. The Deltas were surrounded.

Love brought *Jack* into a hover over the impact zone as blaster fire erupted from the treeline.

"Contact left!" Torres called from his gun position.

Ford and Torres opened up immediately, their guns blasting into the darkness. Tracer rounds colored fiery orange lines through the smoke. Green worked the countermeasures while calling out threat vectors. "Eight contacts, treeline northeast. Four more southeast. Enfilade positions, both flanks."

Love held *Jack* steady in the hover, the Osprey shuddering as fire from Orbot and Zodark positions stitched across the hull. Each impact sent vibrations through the stick. She'd learned to read the damage through her hands. Light hits felt like taps. Heavy rounds felt like hammer blows. These were somewhere in between.

Four Deltas broke from cover and sprinted toward the Osprey. Their battlesuit armor sparked where Zodark blasters found marks. One operator dragged another, the wounded Delta's leg trailing uselessly.

Ford crackled through the intercom. "Ramp down, twenty seconds!"

The Osprey bucked as a round detonated against the port-side armor. Warning lights flashed across her instrument panel, but Love ignored them.

When the Deltas reached the ramp, they pulled themselves aboard quickly. Love watched through the internal camera feed as Ford helped drag the wounded operator inside. She now saw that the man's leg was gone below the knee. His armor's medical systems had sealed the wound, but he'd need a trauma team within the hour or the damage would kill him.

Ford called the count. "Four aboard, eight still out there!"

Love keyed her comm. "Zaines, status on remaining personnel."

The master chief's response came between bursts of automatic fire. "Pinned down in the southern treeline, seventy meters from your position. Orbot heavy weapons team has us zeroed. We move, they cut us apart. Need suppression on my mark."

The remaining eight Deltas were trapped in a fighting position with cross fire established, keeping them pinned. Moving meant exposing themselves to gunners who didn't miss. It was a classic suppression tactic, meant to keep the enemy locked down while reinforcements closed the trap.

"Ford, Torres, I need concentrated fire on the southern treeline, grid reference." Love read the coordinates from her tactical display. "Green, mark the target."

"Marked," Green replied. "Orbot heavy weapons position, two emplacements."

"On it," Ford said. Both door guns swiveled toward the target coordinates. "Firing now."

Tungsten rounds hammered the treeline. Trees exploded into splinters. Ford and Torres walked their fire across the Orbot positions, suppressing the heavy weapons just long enough for the Deltas to move.

"Moving now!" Zaines transmitted.

But Zodark reinforcements arrived fast. A full platoon emerged from the western approach, their blasters lighting up the crater. The eight Deltas made it fifteen meters before concentrated fire forced them back to cover.

"Negative on extraction," Zaines called. "Too hot. We'll hold here. Get those four to medical. Come back when you've got fire support we can use."

Love pulled pitch and climbed out of the kill zone. Behind them, the forest erupted as Zodark forces closed on the LZ. Laser bursts chased them into the darkness as the *Jack* accelerated.

Yet the decision to leave burned in her gut. They were leaving eight operators behind—but staying meant losing everyone.

Come back. That's what he said. Not if. When.

"Torres, you good?" Love asked.

"Port gun's running hot but functional. We're good."

Green checked the damage readout. "Hull integrity at ninety-one percent. Starboard engine temperature elevated but within limits." He paused, studying the sensor data. "We took hits to the fuel system. Lost eight percent capacity from ruptured lines. Still enough for one more run, but it'll be tight."

Love tapped on the tactical frequency icon on her dash. "Firebase Redemption, Wolfpack Actual inbound with wounded. Need medical standing by."

"Copy, Wolfpack Actual. Pad Three is clear. Medics are ready."

She pushed the *Jack* harder. The wounded Delta might have minutes, not hours. Behind her, she heard Ford talking to the operators.

Four out. Eight still trapped. Love grimaced. *I don't like this game.*

Firebase Redemption squatted in a valley between two ridgelines, its defensive perimeter marked by automated gun towers and minefields. Love brought *Jack* down hard on the landing pad. The skids hit concrete with a metallic screech. Medics rushed the ramp before the engines spun down, and the wounded Delta was pulled onto a stretcher and disappeared into the medical tent. The other three operators followed, moving with exhaustion. Their battle armor was scored and dented from impacts that would have killed regular troops, but Deltas didn't go down easy.

Ground crews crowded the bird. Fuel lines connected. Ammunition belts loaded. The mechanics patched holes that should have grounded lesser aircraft. Every bird that landed got the same treatment. Patch, refuel, rearm. Send it back out. The tempo never slowed.

Love climbed out and surveyed the damage. A laser burn scored the starboard side, the metal blackened and bubbled. She ran her hand along the scar. The heat still radiated from the impact point. Fresh damage layered over older wounds. The *Jack* was practically held together with Band-Aids.

Ford appeared beside her, his fatigues already stained with hydraulic fluid. He walked the hull, assessing any and all damages.

"How bad?" Love asked.

"Laser burn's superficial. Hull integrity's solid." Ford tapped the scorched metal. "She took worse last week. The *Jack*'s tough." He moved toward the port side, checking the fuel system damage. His expression tightened. "Fuel lines are patched but we're running on reduced capacity. You've got one more flight in her, maybe two if we're lucky."

Chief Warrant Officer Walzi approached from the maintenance bay, wiping his hands on a new towel, marking it with black. His coveralls were permanently stained with hydraulic fluid and engine grease—there was a career's worth of repairs written in the fabric.

"Lieutenant." He nodded at the damage. "Your girl's holding up better than most. We'll have her patched in ten."

Love checked her chronometer. The second extraction window was closing. Zaines and eight operators were still on the ground, and every minute they waited, the enemy tightened the noose.

"Make it eight," she said.

Walzi grinned. "Yes, ma'am." His crew was already moving, pulling replacement parts from the supply Connex. They'd done this setup before. Every pilot knew Walzi could patch anything given enough time and spare parts. The question was always whether the bird would survive the next flight.

Ford was directing the ground crew, pointing out stress points and systems needing attention. Torres and Green climbed down, stretching muscles cramped from the flight. Torres favored his right side slightly. The young man had taken a piece of shrapnel during the first extraction but hadn't mentioned it. He probably wouldn't have until the mission was complete. That was how it worked after one hundred fifteen days. You flew hurt most of the time, in one way or another.

Love walked back inside the craft and into the cockpit. Alone for thirty seconds, she touched the picture of Jack taped to the instrument panel. His face smiled back at her.

Keep us safe. One more time.

"Thanks for the luck," she whispered. "Need a little more tonight."

The maintenance crews worked with speed. Walzi's team knew their business. Eight minutes later, he gave her the thumbs-up. The patches wouldn't pass a safety inspection, but they'd hold for one more flight. Maybe.

Green settled into his seat beside Love. He'd pulled the damage reports while they were on the ground. He didn't say anything, just pulled up the tactical display showing the LZ situation. It had gotten worse. Ford and Torres took their positions at the guns, and Ford's voice came through the intercom. "Guns loaded. Ready when you are."

Second run. Eight operators waiting, and the enemy knows we're coming back.

She spooled up the engines and lifted her bird into the air, then surged forward.

Time to save some Deltas.

Chapter 37:
Legacy and Limestone

Late 2098
Naval Space Force Station Salon-de-Provence
France, Earth

Coop stepped off the military transport at Naval Space Force Station Salon-de-Provence. He knew this place well, not from actual experience but from history books. He'd read about it—Base Aérienne 701, home of the legendary Patrouille de France since 1964, where French aviators had etched their names into two world wars. The base had hosted flight operations since 1909, when aircraft were still fabric and prayer. It had endured German occupation during World War II, its runways bombed and rebuilt three times. The installation had produced more aces than any other European facility, their names scored onto plaques lining the main hangar.

The Ecole de l'Air et de l'Espace occupied the northern section, its buildings defying time itself. Concrete structures from the 1920s stood unshaken, their walls thick enough to survive everything humanity had thrown at itself. In truth, they'd been restored a few times, but the legends said otherwise, that they'd been through hell and back without much of a scratch.

The Provençal landscape spread beyond the runway. Rolling hills were dotted with olive groves. Mediterranean light cut sharp shadows across limestone cliffs, worn smooth by millennia of frigid gale winds.

Coop adjusted his duffel bag, his right hand steady now. It was a small miracle he still couldn't quite believe. Three months ago, that hand had trembled constantly. The Gallentine treatments had exceeded every projection. His chest barely registered the old blaster wound anymore except as a faint pulling sensation when he twisted wrong. Ninety-eight percent recovery. Nearly full function. He felt better than he had in months, almost like the injury had never happened.

Presley Paul had trained with French pilots during World War II. His journal mentioned Salon-de-Provence specifically, called it the crucible where warriors learned to think three moves ahead before they learned to kill. Now Coop stood where his great-great-grandfather had once stood, carrying a legacy instead of limitations.

Up ahead, the processing center occupied a converted hangar from the 1950s. The steel framework was visible beneath the modern Republic modifications. After Coop made it inside, along with the few others he'd arrived with, he presented his orders to a master sergeant whose nameplate read Garnier. The man's accent was thick Marseille, requiring Coop's full concentration to parse the rapid-fire French mixed with military English.

The sergeant scanned his orders once, which was standard security protocol. Nothing flagged, nothing delayed.

Outside the processing windows, Coop watched other arrivals. A tall woman with pilot's wings. Two men carrying themselves like veterans, their uniforms showing campaign ribbons from New Eden and Intus. A younger guy, maybe twenty-two, fresh Academy shine still on him. Green as unripe olives, they'd say.

Garnier handed back Coop's chip and gestured toward the barracks. "*Batiment C, chambre deux cent quarante-sept.*" Room 247, Building C. His French pronunciation was automatic, then he switched to English. "Your roommate arrived yesterday. Seems quiet enough."

The walk took him past the flight line, where T-22 Phantoms sat in rows. Maintenance crews worked between them. Coop's feet carried him toward the distant buildings, while his eyes stayed locked on those trainers.

He'd read about them in the manned fighter pilot program briefings. They were transitional aircraft bridging the gap between basic flight and actual combat craft. Scramjet-assisted, Mach 4 capable, with enough AI to keep you alive but not enough to do the flying for you. They were built to teach pilots how to think at hypersonic speeds, how to manage energy in the thin air at twenty-five thousand meters, how to handle a machine that could outrun most missiles. Stealth coating kept them slim and dark with angles designed to scatter radar. The manned pilot program was new, and these were the aircraft that would either prove trainees could still fly or wash them out trying.

The barracks smelled like every military building ever constructed: floor wax, coffee, sweat, and bad breath. Building C had been constructed in 1967, its architecture distinctly French military, softened by shuttered windows and tile roofs. Room 247 held two bunks, two lockers, two desks. His roommate's gear already occupied the left side. An Italian flag patch sat on the desk. Combat boots, size eleven, stood at parade rest beside the locker.

He dropped his duffel on the right bunk and stared out the window at the flight line.

This is it. No going back now. Either I make it here or I'm done.

Two hours later, he sat in a classroom. It was filled with thirty-two pilots at 0945 sharp. Coop took a seat in the third row. The instructor, Commander Etienne Belmont, had flown combat missions during the Great War. His face carried scars that regenerative medicine hadn't completely erased, and wrinkles he may have wanted to keep so they could tell his story more accurately, whatever that was. Burn tissue ran from his left temple down his neck, disappearing under his collar.

The man wrote on the board in block letters: "Manned Fighter Tactical Theory."

First day, and they were already starting. This wouldn't be easy, but nothing ever was with Coop.

Belmont presented a scenario. "There are three Republic fighters against six Zodark Vultures in a contested asteroid field. Electronic warfare is preventing drone link operations. What tactical approaches would you suggest?" he asked.

Hands went up.

Coop listened to their answers. Aggressive pursuit. Defensive formations. Split the enemy force. Standard Academy responses. Textbook answers that would get you killed in real combat.

When Belmont pointed at him, Coop's mouth opened before his brain caught up.

"Use the asteroids for ambush positioning. Vultures rely on coordinated targeting. Break their sensor lock by forcing close-quarters maneuvering, where their numbers become a liability instead of an advantage. Make them afraid to fire because they'll hit each other. Force proximity kills where their wing coordination breaks down. Some will even take themselves out trying to track targets through debris fields."

The room went quiet.

Belmont stared at him for three seconds. Then nodded.

"Exactly. Force the enemy to fight your battle."

Several pilots turned to look at Coop, and he felt their eyes but didn't care. These people hadn't watched their equipment explode. Hadn't coordinated danger-close artillery while everything fell apart around them. Hadn't earned the right to judge him.

The Academy punk three seats over muttered something about veterans who couldn't let go of past glory.

Coop kept taking notes. The guy's opinion meant exactly nothing.

Coop wasn't a child anymore, wasn't here to make friends.

He was here to fly again.

****

The PT course started at 0530 the next morning. Twenty kilometers. Full combat load. Time standard: two hours.

Coop lined up with the others. His grandfather's journal sat in his locker, the last entry he'd read still burning in his mind: *The body follows where the mind leads, but only if the mind refuses to accept defeat.*

The first kilometer felt strong. His legs carried him well. His body responded like it used to—coordinated, steady, no lag between thought and movement. Breathing controlled. The morning air sliced cold across the Provençal hills, where lavender fields gave way to military proving grounds.

Kilometer three, and he was keeping pace with the lead group. His right arm swung naturally—no tremors, no compensation needed.

By kilometer seven, he'd settled into a rhythm. His feet hit the ground in steady cadence, left-right-left-right, no dragging, no coordination issues.

Other pilots ran beside him, matching his pace.

The young man from the Academy—the one who'd muttered about veterans—struggled to keep up at kilometer twelve. Coop passed him without comment.

By kilometer fifteen, Coop was in the top quarter of the formation. His breathing stayed controlled. His legs felt strong. The old injury was just a memory now, scar tissue and healed nerves that worked better each day.

The finish line appeared. He completed the run in one hour and fifty-two minutes. Well within standard. Top fifteen percent.

Coop crossed and slowed to a jog, then a walk, breathing hard but steady. No tremors. No vision problems. Just the clean burn of muscles pushed hard and responding exactly as they should. Thanks to the constant PT he'd received, he was in dang good shape. He needed to give Diesel a medal.

Several pilots nodded at him as they finished. Respect for someone who'd clearly put in the work.

The veteran with Intus ribbons jogged over. "Good run, Cooper. You've done this before."

"Yeah," Coop said. "Once or twice."

****

The next week brought the obstacle course.

Coop attacked it with controlled aggression. His right hand gripped the rope properly during the climb. Both hands worked together, alternating grips; he pulled himself up like someone whose nervous system responded to commands. The strength was there, and the coordination was perfect. He couldn't believe his luck.

At the top, he paused for two seconds to plan his descent, then went down fast and controlled.

The balance beam section came next. Each step landed where he intended. He walked it with arms out for show more than for balance.

One step. Two. Three.

Perfect.

He made it across without a wobble.

The young Academy pilot who'd mocked him watched with something that definitely looked like respect now.

The wall climb came next. Coop's hands found holds instinctively, left and right working well together. He pulled himself over the top and dropped down the other side.

His landing was textbook. Both legs absorbed the impact together, knees bent, ready to move.

Behind him, a voice called out. "That Cooper guy's legit. Drone ace and can run like he's twenty."

Another replied: "Yeah. Combat vet who still has it."

The words carried across the course. Coop kept moving, a small smile pulling at his mouth. *Let them talk. They're not wrong.*

****

By week's end, Coop was running with the lead group regularly. Other pilots timed their runs to match his pace, to push themselves harder.

A veteran ran beside him during the twenty-kilometer course, matching his breathing, his footfalls, his controlled pace.

Two others joined them by kilometer ten. They were a formation of pilots pushing each other to be better.

They crossed the finish line together.

Coop's time was one hour and forty-eight minutes—in the top ten percent.

Commander Belmont waited at the training facility exit. Coop straightened his posture, breathing hard.

"Lieutenant Cooper. One moment."

Belmont led him away from the other pilots. They walked toward the flight line where Phantoms sat in evening light turning their hulls into bronze sculptures. The instructor stopped beside a T-22 Phantom, his hand resting on the hull.

"I've seen your medical files. The blaster wound. The peripheral nerve damage. The Gallentine treatments." He turned to face Coop directly. "Most pilots with that kind of combat injury take a year to recover. You're at high function in three months. Remarkable."

Belmont's expression shifted slightly. The scar tissue pulled at the corner of his mouth.

"But I've also seen your tactical assessments. Read the after-action reports from Ridge 248. Watched you lead the PT runs when you could be taking it easy, coasting on your combat record. Read and watched everything I could on several missions with your Orion drones." He paused, studying Coop's face. "I've trained the first candidates through this program. Half washed out within the first month. Not from lack of skill. From lack of will. The thing that keeps you flying when every rational thought says land the bird."

The wind picked up, carrying scents of wild thyme from the hills.

"The manned fighter program's about making the right decisions when everything's going wrong. When your systems fail, your wing is gone, and the mission demands you press forward anyway." Belmont's hand tightened on the Phantom's hull. "You've already proven you can do that better than anyone I've seen."

He paused, letting the words sit for a short while.

"Your recovery has exceeded expectations. The pathways have adapted. But that's not what makes you valuable to this program."

Belmont tapped Coop's chest, right over his heart. Something rare in the military, if not straight up… never. So, it took Coop off guard, and he took a stumbling step backward.

"*This*. The part that doesn't quit. The part that led PT runs this week when you could be hanging back, taking it easy." He dropped his hand. "I flew sixty-two combat missions during the Great War. Lost my entire squadron. Weapons fire cooked half my face off before I made it to the ejection pod." He touched the scar tissue. "Medical board said I'd never fly again. Neural damage. Trauma. The same vocabulary they initially used on you."

He crossed his arms. His eyes held Coop's.

"Keep showing up, Lieutenant. Keep pushing yourself and the others around you. You've proven your body has caught up to your determination." Belmont gestured toward the Phantom with his scarred hand. "These machines need warriors who refuse to break. You've already proven which one you are."

The instructor turned toward the Phantom. "Report to Flight Operations at 0600 tomorrow. You're cleared for simulator training. Let's find out what you can actually do in a cockpit."

Coop stood there as Belmont walked away. His right hand hung steady at his side.

He looked at the fighters. Twenty meters of composite armor and weapons systems.

Beautiful.

He turned and walked back toward the barracks, his gait smooth and even. Tomorrow. Simulator training. The first real test of whether he could translate combat experience into manual flight.

Tomorrow would bring more obstacles. More chances to prove Belmont right. More opportunities to become the pilot his family legacy demanded.

Chapter 38:
The Third

Late 2098
FOB Redemption
Planet Rass

The second run started the same as the first. Love brought the *Jack* back over the extraction zone at two hundred meters. Night had turned the forest into a wall of shadows. The tactical display painted the truth in red and blue icons. Red everywhere. Blue trapped in the center.

"LZ's compromised," Green said. His hands worked the sensor controls. "Multiple contacts, all sides." The sensor data showed what Love already knew. The Zodark reinforcements had arrived, a full company surrounding the crater, perhaps more.

"Yeah, watch this," Love said.

She activated the missile pods. Two pods on each side of the fuselage, eight missiles per pod. The targeting computer showed threats across her HUD, red diamonds marking Zodark positions in the treeline.

"Assigning targets," she said. "Green, lock 'em up."

"Contacts designated," Green replied. "Fire control has solutions."

Love squeezed the trigger. The first volley screamed away. Four missiles tracked separate targets. The forest erupted in orange explosions. Secondary blasts rippled through Zodark positions as ammunition cooked off.

"Reacquiring," Green said. "Eight more contacts, northeast quadrant."

Another volley. Another four explosions. The treeline burned.

The comm crackled and Zaines's voice came through all calm despite the gunfire behind it. "Dustoff, LZ is compromised. Heavy contact on three sides." Background noise told the rest. Automatic weapons fire. Explosions. The whir of Zodark rifles. The Deltas were in a fight for survival.

Love studied the tactical display. The Deltas had fallen back to the crater's eastern edge. Zodark forces held the treeline. Orbot teams prowled the perimeter, their thermal signatures distinct from the organic troops. They'd fortified since the first extraction. Dug in and fired and fired and fired.

She dropped the *Jack* lower. One hundred meters… fifty.

"Chin gun hot," Green said, activating the weapon. The targeting reticle appeared on his HUD. He squeezed, and the gun talked and talked. Tracers burned through the darkness, jumping across Zodark positions. Bodies tumbled. Return fire eased off.

"Coming in from the north," she transmitted. "Using the wreckage for cover."

A destroyed Zodark vehicle smoldered at the crater's edge. Love brought the Osprey in behind it, the hull blocking direct fire from the eastern treeline. The advantage lasted exactly four seconds before Zodark forces adjusted their positions.

Blaster fire erupted immediately and Torres and Ford opened up, their guns cracking into the darkness. Green called threats like he was reading a grocery list. "Four contacts northeast, six southeast, two more moving west." His voice never changed pitch, steady as a metronome. Forty-nine days had taught him to separate emotion from information, apparently. It was the first time Love noticed it, and maybe she might tell him good job when they got back to the base. If they got back.

The display showed the Deltas moving. Five operators broke from the eastern position. One of them tossed smoke grenades. Three canisters spewing thick gray fog across the crater floor.

"Smoke's up," Zaines transmitted. "Ten seconds."

The fog built fast, obscuring the Deltas' movement and the *Jack*'s field of fire. Love's visual went white.

"Sensors only," Green said, switching displays. Thermal imaging cut through the smoke, coloring the Deltas as bright silhouettes against a cooler background. The Zodarks appeared too, moving to flank.

"Contact left," Green said, swinging the chin gun. He fired blind, trusting the sensors. The thermal signatures dropped.

The Deltas fought their way toward the Osprey through fire that should have shredded them. Their battlesuits flashed with impacts as the five operators used the crater's terrain for cover. They bounded in pairs, one element moving while the other provided covering fire.

Five operators reached the ramp and pulled themselves aboard. Their armor was scored, charred, and dented. One operator's faceplate was cracked. Another moved carefully, as if fighting through pain. Two of them were bleeding, their suits breached.

Zaines and two others stayed behind, their weapons never stopping. Covering fire that kept the Zodarks pinned long enough for their teammates to board.

"Five away," Zaines transmitted. "We've got Republic soldiers trapped in a wrecked Linebacker fifty meters west. Vehicle's mobility-killed, crew's pinned down. We're moving to extract them now, then we'll set charges on the LZ to deny it to the enemy."

Love's tactical display showed the disabled vehicle in amber—a Linebacker medium tactical armored unit, one of the updated air defense variants descended from the old M2 Bradley lineage. The crew compartment was intact, but the massive wheels and tires were torn to shreds.

Love checked her Osprey's gauges. Fuel at forty-two percent. Missiles depleted. The damage indicators showed yellow across multiple systems.

"Master Sergeant, I'm bingo on missiles and low on fuel," Love transmitted. "Need to RTB, get these wounded to medical, refuel and rearm. We'll be back for you."

Zaines hesitated. The comm stayed silent for a few moments. Background fire intensified.

"Copy that, Dustoff. We'll hold position and complete the mission. But hurry. This LZ's getting hotter by the minute."

"Five aboard," Ford called.

A Zodark blaster bolt punched through the port-side fuselage. The impact shook the entire airframe. Engine three—front left—shrieked as the energy weapon's heat burned through turbine housing. Warning klaxons screamed.

"Engine three's hit!" Green shouted. "Losing power!"

The engine temperature spiked red. Metal screamed as the turbine seized. The power output dropped to zero.

"Yep! Engine three's dead," Love said. "Shutting it down before it catches fire."

The Jack lurched left as asymmetric thrust tried to yaw them into a spin. Love corrected with right rudder, bringing the Osprey back to controlled flight. Three engines now. The remaining turbines screamed louder, taking the extra load.

The *Jack* climbed out of the crater as rounds turned the LZ into hell. The dash holo showed three blue icons surrounded by red, Zaines and two Deltas against a company. She hoped to the moon and back that they'd hold until Love returned.

She pushed the throttle forward. Behind her, the battle continued. Engine two's temperature gauge climbed into the yellow. The rear right engine, running rough from a damaged coolant pump, was overheating fast.

"Engine two's temp is climbing," Green said. "Coolant pressure dropping."

"How bad?"

"Bad. The pump's failing. Can't keep it cool much longer."

Love watched the gauge tick higher. The engine was cooking itself from the inside. The damaged coolant pump couldn't circulate fast enough to handle the increased load from engine three being offline.

The temperature hit red. Engine two coughed once, twice, then the power output dropped by half.

"Engine two's going!" Green's voice rose. "Losing thrust!"

"Shutting it down," Love said. She killed fuel flow to engine two before the turbine could seize and tear itself apart. "We're down to two engines."

Two engines remained: engine one—front right—and engine four—rear left. Both were on opposite sides. The *Jack* shuddered, flying on half power, barely maintaining altitude.

The sound of combat faded as distance grew, but the tactical feed still showed those three icons. They were still fighting, still breathing.

Third run's going to be worse, she thought. It had to be. By now, they knew someone was coming back, and the Zodarks would be more than ready.

Firebase Redemption's landing pad came up fast. Love brought the *Jack* down. The medics were already moving before the ramp dropped. They rushed forward with stretchers, carefully loading the two wounded Deltas. The other three operators walked off under their own power, their armor smoking.

Love killed the engines and climbed out. Torres was already shouting at the weapon techs. "We need those pods swapped now!"

The techs hurried forward, detaching the spent missile pods and fastening fresh ones in their place. Torres helped them, checking connections and arming circuits.

Ford barked orders at the maintenance crews while conducting his damage assessment. "I need that number three engine detached and replaced! Coolant line on engine two needs patching!"

A tech climbed up to inspect engine three. The turbine housing was blackened, warped from a near miss.

"Engine three took a direct hit," Ford said. "Totally destroyed. We don't have time for a replacement. That's a two-hour job. Detach it, secure the mount. We'll fly on three."

Another tech was working on engine two. "Coolant pump's failing, Chief. Proper replacement is an hour minimum."

Ford grimaced. "Bypass what you can, patch the lines, top off the reservoir. Make it last one more run. That's all we need."

The maintenance crews swarmed the *Jack*. One team wrestled with the burned-out engine, unbolting the mounting hardware. Another team patched the coolant line. A third team topped off hydraulic fluid reservoirs.

Love watched the mayhem for a moment, then headed for the operations center, her flight suit soaked with sweat.

Commander Granger stood at the tactical display, studying the northern sector. The map showed Zodark forces consolidating around the extraction zone, red contacts multiplying by the minute. The enemy was reinforcing and turning the LZ into a fortress.

Granger looked up when she entered.

Love straightened. "Sir, Master Sergeant Zaines and two operators stayed behind. They're extracting Republic soldiers trapped in a disabled Linebacker and setting demolition charges to deny the LZ to the enemy. They need pickup after mission completion."

Granger's expression steeled. "So your bird's shot to hell, your crew's exhausted, and now I have to risk another crew for a third run because Zaines decided to extend the mission?"

"Sir, with respect… Zaines is the man on the ground. He has the facts and knows the stakes. He wouldn't have stayed behind if it wasn't critical. Those soldiers in the Lineback would've been abandoned otherwise."

Granger studied her. "I saw the report on *Jack*. Engine three is gone. Engine two's coolant pump is failing. Your crew's been flying for sixteen hours straight." He paused. "Love, I'm not going to order you and your crew to fly back into that hellscape for a third attempt. But if you think *Jack* and your crew are up for it, I'll sign off. I need you and Green to tell me in writing *Jack* can do it, and that you both volunteer."

Love met his eyes. "Sir, we'll get it done."

"That's not what I asked. I need assurance from both pilots that bird is flyable and will survive a third trip. Are you willing to accept that level of risk? And more importantly, are you willing to risk your crew's lives on it?"

Love's chest tightened. Three lives on the ground. Four lives in her crew. But Zaines wouldn't abandon soldiers. She wouldn't abandon him.

"Yes, sir. We volunteer. All of us."

Granger held her gaze for a few seconds. "Get me that written confirmation from you and Green. If Ford says *Jack* can fly, and you two are willing to put your names on it, I'll authorize the mission."

"Yes, sir."

She turned and headed back to the flight line. Green met her at the *Jack*.

"Commander wants written confirmation we volunteer," she said. "You and me. Are you in?"

Green looked at the battered Osprey, then at the tactical display showing three blue icons surrounded by red. "Yeah. I'm in."

They signed the authorization on Green's datapad. Two signatures committing four lives to one more run.

Love climbed back into the cockpit. Ford's voice came through the intercom. "Engine detachment complete. Coolant pump flushed and refilled on engine two. Hydraulics patched. Missile pods loaded and armed. We're as ready as we're gonna get."

"How's engine two's pump looking?"

Ford hesitated. "Honestly? It's sketchy. Could last the whole mission. Could fail five minutes in. No way to know without tearing it down, and we don't have time for that."

"Good enough. Strap in."

Love started the engines. Three turbines spooled up. Engine two ran rough, a vibration she could feel through the stick. The coolant pump was struggling. She watched the temperature gauge. It climbed slowly but stayed in the green. For now.

She lifted off. Ahead, the night sky glowed orange where artillery was already pounding the LZ. Republic Reapers streaked overhead, their weapons lighting up the forest. The firebase's entire fire support network was focused on one crater. One extraction. Three lives. Love pushed *Jack* toward the fire.

Third time's the charm. Or the killer.

The LZ appeared through the smoke. The crater had transformed into an inferno. Artillery impacts stepped like fiery giants across the tree line. Air strikes had turned the forest into splinters. The bombardment was working and the red contacts on Love's tactical display were pulling back, seeking cover from the maelstrom. But they weren't retreating, just repositioning, waiting for the fire support to lift so they could close the trap.

And in the center, three blue icons still blinked. Zaines and his two operators, continuing the fight, still held their position against impossible odds.

Love brought the *Jack* in fast, with no cover this time. She dropped straight into the crater at full speed, engines screaming. Engine two's temperature gauge climbed into the yellow. The coolant pump was failing. Warning lights flashed across her instrument panel, and she ignored them all.

Blaster fire came from every direction. The artillery barrage had suppressed the enemy but not eliminated them. Zodark forces emerged from cover the moment *Jack* entered the crater.

Ford's gun went silent. "Gun's overheated. Weapon's down. Still breathing."

Torres kept firing with one hand. Love saw his other arm hanging wrong through the internal camera feed. He was operating the heavy magrail one-handed. Impossible. Yet he was doing it anyway.

Green worked the controls through smoke filling the cockpit. "Taking fire from all quadrants."

The three Deltas and several soldiers, no doubt those who were once trapped in the Linebacker, sprinted for the ramp. Zaines moved last, his weapon laying down covering fire. The Republic warriors with him bounded in pairs. An Orbot round caught Zaines in the back, the impact dropping him. His battlesuit absorbed most of the kinetic energy but the force was enough to put him on the ground, where he didn't move.

The two Delta operators grabbed their team leader and hauled him toward the Osprey, dragging him across ground that erupted with impacts. Zodark forces were rushing the crater now. The artillery barrage had lifted. The enemy knew this was their chance.

"All aboard. Get us out of here!" Ford yelled.

Love heard him moving in the back, securing the Deltas and a handful of other soldiers, and then closing the ramp.

Love pulled pitch and engine two died. The coolant pump had failed. The turbine seized from thermal overload. Thrust disappeared from the rear right engine.

Engine three was already gone. Now engine two was dead. The *Jack* was once again down to two engines.

The remaining engines screamed. The Osprey climbed through fire on half power and cleared the tree line by meters.

For half a second, she stared at her dead husband's picture, whispering to him, "Keep us in the air, Jack. Please. Get us out of here. Be my angel."

Engine one suddenly began vibrating. The mount wasn't seated properly. The bolts were loosening. Love felt it through the stick, a rhythmic shudder increasing with every second.

Firebase Redemption appeared ahead, two kilometers away. Love lined up for the landing approach. She nursed the throttle, coaxing the last bit of thrust from the dying engines. The vibration was violent now, shaking the entire airframe.

The vibration got worse. Engine one's mount was failing. The metal was coming apart.

One engine remained. Engine four. Rear right. Alone.

They fell. Two thousand meters of altitude between them and the ground.

Green frantically punched commands across the controls. Rerouting power. Dumping fuel. Anything to slow the descent. "Three hundred meters," he called. "One-fifty. One hundred."

Love pulled back on the stick.

The *Jack* hit the tarmac hard enough to shatter the landing gear. The contact drove Love against her harness and her vision whited out for a second. The Osprey's nose dipped, the tail lifted, and for a moment, they were balanced on the edge of flipping. They skidded forty meters before stopping. Metal screamed. Sparks flew. The hull plating tore against concrete. The sound was deafening.

Then silence.

And more silence.

Love's ears rang, her fingers still gripping the stick.

"Everyone out," Ford muttered. "Now." There was an urgency to his tone that took Love right out of her daze. There was a fire, and fuel was leaking. They needed out before *Jack* turned into a bomb.

Love popped the canopy and climbed out on legs that didn't want to hold her. Green followed, moving like an old man.

The ramp was already down as medics surrounded the bird. The Deltas hurried off, carrying Zaines between them. The master sergeant was conscious, his helmet off, and his eyes tracking Love as they carried him past. He gave her a slight nod. She'd gotten him out. That was what mattered. Ford limped down the ramp in a rush, one hand pressed to his side. Blood seeped between his fingers. A shrapnel wound.

Torres followed quickly, his right arm in an improvised sling. He'd operated a damn heavy magrail one-handed while the *Jack* fell apart around him. It was impressive. More than impressive. He knew it too, and gave Love a weak grin.

While they moved quickly away, she turned to see the *Jack* sitting broken on the tarmac, the engines dead, the landing gear collapsed. Hydraulic fluid pooled beneath the wreckage and fuel leaked from ruptured lines. The tail section had partially separated from the fuselage. Fire suppression teams sprayed foam across the hot spots, keeping her from exploding into a million trillion pieces of hot debris.

She cringed, remembering that the photograph of Jack was still taped to the dash. Then she inwardly smiled. That meant the Osprey would survive, because in no way would she let Jack get away with destroying the only picture she had of him. She'd haunt him in the afterlife.

It was good, then, and the bird would live, just like the Deltas. Just like her crew. All breathing. All alive. The mission board would

mark it as a success and the statistics wouldn't mention the Osprey
she'd nearly destroyed to make it happen.

Chapter 39:
Pod Five

Year 2099
Naval Space Force Station Salon-de-Provence
France, Earth

The simulator pod waited. Coop stood outside the titanium shell, watching other pilots climb into their units. Twenty-three candidates. All of them ready to prove themselves.

His pod looked nothing like the drone sim pods he'd operated for years. Those had been chairs with wraparound displays inside egg-shaped structures with neural synchronization. This was different. Yes, a full-body interface requiring neural sync, but a rounded pod, with holos in front, to the sides, and behind. You climbed in via a ladder to the top of the pod and then through a hatch where you plopped yourself onto the seat, slapped the helmet on, and then started the sim.

Commander Belmont appeared beside him. "Problem, Lieutenant?"

"Negative, sir." Coop straightened. "Just familiarizing myself with the equipment."

"You've logged over five thousand hours in drone pods. This is the same principle. Different execution." Belmont gestured toward the open hatch. "The interface reads neural patterns like the Orion sim pod, but this one translates thought into action a bit more."

Coop climbed into the pod, anticipation building. This was it. The moment he'd been working toward.

The interior smelled like new composites and electronics. Leather too. He settled into the pilot's couch, the padding conforming to his body. The neural helmet descended from above, with multiple contact points inside the helm pressing against his skull.

"Relax, Cooper," Belmont said from outside the pod. "The system reads better when you're not fighting it."

The interface activated. The familiar tingle of neural connection sparked across Coop's scalp, that weird sensation of something foreign touching his thoughts. He'd felt this countless times in drone sim pods.

The pod's systems came online. Holographic displays materialized in a 360-degree arc around him, tactical data streaming across his visor. Flight controls responded to his hands. Left gripping the throttle, right on the stick.

The simulation loaded. It would be a simple atmospheric flight through a canyon system. No combat. No stress. Just fly the route without crashing.

Coop's left hand advanced the throttle. The simulated engines responded, the virtual fighter accelerating smoothly. His right hand pulled the stick, banking into the first turn. The aircraft responded. He grinned.

It's working. Holy hell, it's actually working.

Years of drone piloting kicked in. Throttle control. Stick pressure. The subtle movement of thrust and lift that kept aircraft flying. The neural interface read his intentions, translating thought into action faster than manual inputs could manage.

The canyon walls blurred past. Coop navigated the turns, keeping the fighter between the stone walls.

One turn at a time. Feel the aircraft. Become part of it.

The route demanded constant corrections. Banking left, then right, following the canyon's curves. The interface responded to his inputs.

He cleared the final turn. The canyon opened into a valley. Mission complete.

The simulation ended. The pod's systems powered down, the neural connection severing. Coop exhaled slowly, adrenaline still singing through his veins.

I flew. Actually flew.

The hatch opened and he climbed out to find Belmont waiting, tablet in hand. His expression gave nothing away. "Time?"

"Two minutes forty-seven seconds. Acceptable for initial qualification."

Acceptable. Not good. Not exceptional. But acceptable meant passing, meant continuing.

"Report to Pod Five tomorrow, 0600," Belmont said. "Next session adds combat elements." He paused, studying Coop. "Your drone experience is helping, but it's also creating bad habits. You're trying to fly like you're controlling from orbit. You're not. You're in the cockpit now. The g-forces are real. The spatial awareness is different. Your body is part of the weapon system."

Coop nodded, still processing the fact that he'd just flown something. "Yes, sir. I understand."

Belmont's expression softened slightly. "Tomorrow I'm going to stress you. Push your coordination past where you think it can go."

"I won't quit, sir."

"We'll see." Belmont walked away, leaving Coop alone beside the simulator pod.

That night, Coop lay in his bunk staring at the ceiling. The neural connection had left a dull ache behind his eyes. Neural fatigue from the intensity of the connection. He needed to get used to that again.

But he'd flown, and that mattered more than the pain.

The next morning brought the combat scenarios Belmont had promised. Coop climbed into Pod Five at 0545, ready. A good night's sleep and an evening workout had helped. The neural interface activated, and this time the connection felt cleaner.

Good. Getting better at this.

The simulation loaded. Red threat indicators blazed across his peripheral vision. Enemy fighters. Incoming missiles. Threat warnings screaming. Coop's heart rate spiked immediately. The pod's g-force simulation kicked in, pressing him into the seat as the virtual fighter maneuvered. He gripped the stick, focused, and rolled hard left. Warnings flashed across his HUD.

Stay calm. Flow with it.

He eased his grip and let the stick float in his hand instead of clenching it. The fighter responded smoother, his left hand working the throttle while the interface read his intentions, translating thought into action.

An enemy fighter appeared on his six, the threat warning shrieking in his helmet. Torpedo lock. Three seconds to impact.

Coop rolled right, his body responding to the g-forces the pod generated. His vision grayed at the edges.

Combat. Real combat simulation. This is what he'd trained for.

He kept the stick steady and pulled into a climb that would've crushed him if this were real.

The projectile tracked. Coop snap-rolled, breaking left, then right, executing evasion patterns. The seeker lost lock and streaked past, close enough that the proximity warning blared.

The enemy fighter followed. Coop reversed, a maneuver his drone days had taught him. He pulled hard, seven gs crushing him into the seat, his vision tunneling to a pinpoint. The virtual opponent couldn't match the turn. Coop's targeting system achieved lock, the reticle flashing green. Tone in his helmet. He squeezed the trigger and simulated magrail rounds shredded the enemy aircraft.

The fighter exploded in a bloom of orange fire that filled his forward display.

Splash one.

The pod's systems registered the kill. But three more fighters were inbound. Coop's focus sharpened. Three on one. Time to prove what he could do.

He banked hard, throttle wide open, and dove toward the deck.

The enemy fighters followed, thinking they had him cornered.

Big mistake.

Coop rolled inverted and dove, throttle to the firewall, heading for the deck. The g-forces crushed him. Nine g's. Ten. His vision went black. The pod's safety systems should've stopped the simulation. Didn't. Everything went dark.

Four counts in. Six counts out.

The tunnel vision cleared just enough. He was fifty meters above the ground, the simulated terrain screaming past at supersonic speed. Both enemy fighters had followed him down, trying to capitalize on what they thought was a panicked escape.

Coop pulled. Eleven g's. The inertial dampeners worked overtime to keep the g-forces from crushing him. Without them, he'd have been dead at nine. The technology bought him two more g's, maybe three, but even with dampening assistance, his body protested violently. The stick fought back against his grip. The fighter shuddered, trying to tear itself apart from the stress, or so it seemed from the constant shaking the pod was simulating. His vision narrowed and blood ran from his nose.

The aircraft came around. Barely. The two enemy fighters couldn't match the suicidal maneuver. One tried but plowed into the ground at Mach 1.2. Fireball. Flames licking toward the sky. The last fighter pulled up, trying to escape.

Too late.

Coop's targeting system locked. He didn't have time for guns, so he thumbed the missile release. Fox Two. The simulated Sidewinder leapt from his wing, tracking true. The enemy fighter dumped flares, chaff, everything. The missile ignored the countermeasures.

Direct hit.

The simulation ended.

Coop sat in the pod, breathing hard. Blood dripped from his nose onto the flight suit. The high-g maneuver had pushed him a little too far.

"Cooper." Belmont's voice came through the helmet speaker. "Exit the pod."

Coop took a moment to gather himself, then released the harness. "Acknowledged."

The pod's hatch opened and the helmet lifted away. Belmont's face appeared at the hatch, along with two medics.

"Let's get you checked out."

They helped Coop from the pod. He climbed out under his own power, though his legs felt like rubber. The medics steadied him to the deck. One of them shone a light in his eyes and checked his vitals, then wiped the blood from his face.

"Pupils reactive. Pulse elevated but stable. Minor epistaxis. He's OK."

Belmont stood beside Coop. "That was the stupidest flying I've ever seen."

Coop managed to nod.

"It was also effective." Belmont crossed his arms. "Three kills. You're done for today. Report to medical. Then to my office at 1400."

The medics escorted Coop to the medical bay.

Dr. Shelly Mark was waiting. Middle-aged and with the tired expression of someone who'd seen too many pilots push themselves too far, though she smiled when she saw him.

"Lie down."

Coop settled onto the exam table. She ran scanners over his head, conducting standard post-high-g checks.

"You pushed hard out there. Eleven gs will cause nosebleeds in anyone. It's normal." She pulled up holographic scans. "Everything looks good. No serious issues. You're healing well from your previous injuries. I can barely even see the old blaster wound scarring on your chest. The Gallentine treatments did excellent work.”

“So I’m cleared?”

“For now. But, Cooper, eleven gs is at the edge of human tolerance. Keep pushing like that and eventually something will give. Your body’s in good shape now, but don’t get cocky.” She handed him a towel for the nosebleed that had started again. “Standard procedure after high-g maneuvers. You’ll be fine.”

“Noted.”

“Good. Now get cleaned up. Belmont’s waiting for you at 1400. Don’t be late.”

Chapter 40:
Leading the Flight

Year 2099
Naval Space Force Station Salon-de-Provence
France, Earth

Four weeks had passed since that meeting at 1400. Belmont had been brief. "Acceptable progress…continue training…push harder." Coop had nodded and walked out with something he hadn't felt in months: part of the team.

Then this week came, week four, and it brought the reckoning.

But not in the way Coop had expected.

They kept him in the simulator pods. Day after day. More scenarios. More combat. More proving he belonged here. Coop climbed into Pod Seven, anticipation building in his chest.

When do I get into a real Phantom? When do I stop flying simulations and start flying actual aircraft?

The wait was killing him, but he understood. Every pilot had to prove themselves in the sims first.

He settled into the pilot's couch. His right hand found the stick smoothly. His leg responded perfectly as he adjusted the rudder pedals. No hesitation.

The neural interface activated. The connection was clean. Perfect. Like his brain had fully adapted to the interface.

The simulation loaded. Belmont's voice blasted through the helmet speaker.

"Today's scenario is different. You'll have wingmen, call signs Hellfire and Toad. Three Republic fighters against eight *Vulture*-class enemy craft. The engagement starts in atmosphere and transitions to orbital space. You're flight lead, Coop."

"Understood." Coop took a breath, then spoke into his mic. "Hellfire and Toad, this is Coop. Comms check."

"Hellfire, loud and clear," answered a woman's voice. Coop noted that she sounded confident.

"Toad here. Ready to tango." The second voice was male, young, and eager.

The simulation environment materialized. They were flying at low altitude, around twenty thousand meters. Scattered clouds. Enemy contacts rising from below, eight Vultures climbing hard, their distinctive profiles flying through the atmosphere.

"Contact. Nine bandits, low and climbing. Hellfire, take my wing. Toad, defensive position."

"Copy, Coop."

"Roger that, boss."

The Vultures accelerated. Coop watched their formation, and they flew well. They knew what they were doing.

Just like the old days—flying with Raven, Lucky, Ninja and Ghost Dog, with Strike leading us through the fire, and with Bear watching our backs.

The memory of his old squadron hit him. Even though some of them were dead, for a moment, with wingmen responding to his commands, it felt like they were still there.

"All elements, go vertical. We're taking this fight upstairs."

Coop pulled the stick. The simulated Phantom responded instantly with their afterburners ignited. The g-forces hit. Six, seven, eight. His vision grayed at the edges but didn't tunnel. He handled it perfectly.

Training's paying off, Coop thought. *Every sim is making me sharper.*

Hellfire and Toad followed, the three Republic fighters climbing through the atmosphere. Five thousand meters. Ten thousand. Fifteen thousand. The sky darkened and stars appeared, the curvature of Earth becoming visible below.

The Vultures pursued. They were faster in atmosphere and closing distance.

"Incoming missiles! Break and chaff!"

Coop rolled hard, dumping countermeasures. The simulated chaff bloomed behind him, a cloud of metallic confetti. The missile lost lock and detonated harmlessly.

But they were still ascending, the atmosphere thinning. The fighter's engines screamed as they transitioned from air-breathing to rocket mode. The g-forces changed. There was no more lift from wings, just pure thrust now. The sensation shifted, that weird feeling of leaving atmosphere, like falling upward.

Coop breathed through the disorientation. Four counts in. Six counts out.

The stars blazed with no atmosphere to scatter their light. They were pure, hard points of white fire against absolute black.

"We're in space. So, switch to reaction control. Toad, watch your thrust vectors."

"Copy."

The Vultures emerged from atmosphere seconds later. Eight sleek killers, their weapons hot, their formation perfect.

"Hellfire, break left and engage. Toad, stay with me."

"Roger!"

"On your six, Coop!"

Coop rolled. In space, the maneuver felt different. No air resistance and simple, pure inertia. The Phantom spun like a top as he fired maneuvering thrusters. The fighter reversed course quickly.

Two Vultures dove at Hellfire. She engaged, her guns spitting tracers that didn't arc like they did in atmosphere. Straight lines, perfect ballistic paths.

"Hellfire's engaged! I've got two on me!"

"Toad, support Hellfire. I've got the others."

"Copy!"

Coop faced six Vultures. They spread out, trying to bracket him. Classic space combat tactics without gravity to pull you down or air to slow you.

The first Vulture fired. Coop saw the cannon's flash and counted the time, judged the range, and then fired his thrusters. The rounds passed where he would've been.

Remember the training. Space combat is chess, not dogfighting. Every move costs fuel. Every maneuver changes your orbit.

He targeted the closest Vulture. Fox Two. Missile away. In space, the rocket motor burned brightly.

The Vulture tried to evade, and fired their thrusters. Changed vector. But the missile tracked and in three... two... one... the fighter erupted in a bloom of fire and broken, charred metal.

"Target neutralized!"

Five Vultures remained on Coop with two more engaging Hellfire and Toad.

The enemy adjusted and came at him from multiple trajectories. High, low, and lateral, trying to force him to choose which threat to counter.

Coop did neither and went retrograde. He fired his main thrusters in reverse, killing his forward velocity. The Phantom stopped in space. Just hung there.

The Vultures shot past, their momentum carrying them forward. They'd been expecting him to evade, not stop.

Coop rotated. Fired. Railguns. One Vulture took hits across the cockpit. Atmosphere vented. The fighter spun, out of control, and broke into hundreds of pieces.

"Two bandits down!"

Four left.

"Coop, I'm hit! Losing pressure!" Toad yelled, panicked.

Coop checked his tactical display. Toad's fighter was venting, and in the process, tumbling, too.

"Toad, eject!"

"Negative! I can save it!"

"Eject now! That's an order!"

A pause. Then: "Ejecting."

Toad's fighter exploded moments after the ejection pod separated safely.

Now only two Republic fighters against seven Vultures.

Just like the old days—outnumbered, outgunned, but not out-skilled.

"Hellfire, status?"

"I've got two on me. Can't shake them."

"Hold on. I'm coming."

Coop burned hard, using precious fuel to change his vector. The four Vultures that had been chasing him followed. He led them toward Hellfire's position.

"Hellfire, on my mark, reverse thrust. Full burn."

"Copy."

Coop watched the geometry, and waited, and waited. The Vultures were closing and were almost in position.

"Mark!"

Hellfire's fighter reversed. Coop dove under her, the Vultures following. They passed each other in space. Coop rotated and pressed his trigger while Hellfire did the same.

The four Vultures found themselves between two guns, caught in a crossfire. Coop's rounds tore through one. Hellfire got another, down two enemy craft in less than five seconds.

"Splash three and four!"

Five Vultures left, but those were adapting and spreading out, making themselves harder to bracket.

Coop's fuel was low. Hellfire's too. And five against two were still bad odds.

"Hellfire, we need to even these odds. You see that debris field from Toad's fighter?"

"Affirmative."

"We're going to use it. Follow me."

Coop burned toward the expanding cloud of wreckage. Twisted metal, frozen atmosphere, and chunks of composite armor spinning in zero gravity.

The Vultures followed.

Coop dove into the debris field and fired his thrusters in random intervals, dodging spinning fragments at the same time. All to use the wreckage as cover.

The Vultures tried to follow, and two of them took hits from debris. One lost an engine. The other's cockpit shattered.

"Fifth kill confirmed... sixth kill confirmed!"

Three left. Coop and Hellfire emerged from the debris field, and Coop noticed the remaining Vultures appeared cautious now, each moving away in erratic patterns, as if completely caught of guard for a second before moving back into formation.

"Hellfire, I'm out of missiles. You?"

"Same. Guns only."

"Make it matter."

The three Vultures came at them together and Coop didn't try anything fancy. He flew straight at them. Head-on. Pure, utter, satisfying aggression.

The Vultures fired and Coop fired back. Space lit up with flashes, rounds crossing in the void.

One Vulture burst into flames before extinguishing in the vacuum of space. That one was Hellfire's kill.

Two left.

Coop's fighter shuddered. Hits. Damage warnings. But he kept firing and sent his shots across the lead Vulture's nose. The fighter broke apart.

One left.

The last Vulture broke off and tried to run. Burned hard for distance.

Hellfire chased it, her guns speaking fast and far. After one hit, then two, the third killed the Vulture, tearing it apart.

"That's all eight! Mission complete!"

The simulation turned to black and Coop sat in the pod, breathing hard, exhilarated. His hands were steady. His vision clear. He'd flown a great mission.

I did it. Flew a full space combat mission. Led a flight through atmospheric-to-space transition under fire and won.

The hatch opened and Belmont stood there, and for the first time since Coop had met him, the commander was smiling.

"Eight kills. No losses except Toad, who panicked. You led your flight through an atmospheric-to-space transition under fire and won." He jotted on his tablet. "That was textbook flight leadership, Coop."

Coop climbed out of the pod. "Thank you, sir."

"Tomorrow, you'll get your wish. Tomorrow, I'm clearing you for actual flight training in a Phantom." Belmont paused. "You've proven yourself in the sims, Cooper. Time to see what you can do in a real cockpit."

Coop stood there, processing the words. Tomorrow. A real Phantom.

He nodded at Belmont. "I won't let you down, sir."

"I know you won't, Coop." Belmont walked away.

Coop looked back at the simulator pod and thought of Raven and Lucky. Ninja and Ghost Dog. Strike and Bear. And the rest of his old squadron.

Unlike some of them, he wasn't dead. He was Coop, and just getting started.

Chapter 41:
Pod Seven to Phantom

Year 2099
Naval Space Force Station Salon-de-Provence
France, Earth

Standing in the ready room at Naval Space Force Station Salon-de-Provence, Coop stared through the reinforced glass at the F-42C Phantom waiting on the tarmac. It'd been three months of training in sim pods, and today, the trainer aircraft looked smaller than he'd expected.

Commander Belmont finished the briefing. "Standard atmospheric circuit. Three touch-and-gos. Return to base. Questions?"

Nobody spoke. The other pilots in his class watched Coop with expressions he'd learned to read over the past months. Some curious. Some skeptical. A few competitive. Everyone wanted to prove themselves the best in the class.

"Cooper," Belmont said. "You're up. I'll be monitoring from the ground control pod."

Coop's surprise must have shown on his face because Belmont added, "Don't look so shocked, Lieutenant. Normally you'd fly with Lieutenant Commander Sharlow, Lieutenant Arnaud, or Captain Duchamp monitoring from the control pods. They handle most of the initial dual instruction flights. But I asked for this one specifically." He paused. "It's rare for me to monitor dual flights anymore. Administrative duties and all that. But I want to see firsthand how you handle actual flight. Your sim performance has been exceptional."

Coop grabbed his helmet and walked toward the door. Behind him, someone muttered something about the old man flying again. He kept walking.

The Mediterranean sun hit him hard on the flight line. Heat shimmered off the tarmac in waves making the distant hangar seem to float. The F-42C Phantom sat gleaming, seventeen meters of composite armor and thrust vectoring. The single-seat cockpit was standard. Belmont would monitor from a ground control pod with full telemetry feeds and the ability to override Coop's controls remotely if necessary.

Don't screw this up, he thought. *Bear, help me out, pal.*

The crew chief waited by the ladder, a grizzled master sergeant whose nametape read "Ricker." He nodded. "She's all yours, Lieutenant. Preflight's complete. Fuel's topped, systems green across every board you can imagine. Commander's already done his walkaround."

"Thank you, Chief."

Ricker grinned. "First dual flight in the program?"

"First ever."

"With the old man himself monitoring, no less." The crew chief patted the ladder. "This bird's forgiving. Treat her right, she'll bring you home. And don't worry. Commander Belmont's got your back from the control pod. He can take over remotely if things go sideways."

Coop climbed into the cockpit. The single-seat layout felt intimate, just him and the machine. He settled into the pilot's couch, the padding conforming to his body.

The neural interface settled against his skull when he put his helmet on. He closed his eyes, felt the connection establish. The pathways routed perfectly, signals flowing smoothly. He ran through the preflight checklist.

"You've got the aircraft, Cooper," Belmont's voice came through the intercom. "I'm monitoring your telemetry from my pod. Full override capability if you need me, but this is your flight. Show me what you can do."

"Yes, sir. I have the aircraft."

He keyed the radio. "Salon Tower, Phantom Two-Four, ready for departure."

The controller's tone came back immediately. "Phantom Two-Four, Salon Tower. Winds zero-niner-zero at four knots, altimeter three-zero-one-two. Cleared for takeoff, Runway Two-Six. Maintain runway heading, climb and maintain one thousand five hundred feet."

"Phantom Two-Four cleared for takeoff, Runway Two-Six. Runway heading, climb to one-five-hundred." Coop's voice stayed steady despite his heart beating faster than a race car's piston.

He advanced the throttle. The engines responded beneath him, building power. The vibration traveled through the airframe into his seat, his hands, his chest. Real thrust. Real physics. Not simulation anymore. The F-42C Phantom rolled forward, acceleration pressing him into the seat. The nose lifted and the wheels left Earth.

He was flying, and what a rush.

"Nice rotation," Belmont said through the comm link. "Smooth on the controls. Keep it coming."

"Phantom Two-Four, contact Departure. Good luck."

"Departure, Phantom Two-Four passing six hundred for one-five-hundred."

"Phantom Two-Four, Departure. Radar contact. Climb and maintain one thousand five hundred feet, turn left heading two-six-zero. Report level."

Coop banked left, feeling the aircraft respond to his inputs. The coordination felt natural, smooth. "Two-Four turning two-six-zero, climbing to one-five-hundred."

The Provençal countryside spread below. There were olive groves and limestone cliffs his great-great-grandfather had once flown over. Terraced vineyards stepped down hillsides. The mistral wind carved patterns in the Mediterranean haze. Somewhere down there, Presley Paul Cooper had trained with French pilots during a different war.

"Phantom Two-Four level one thousand five hundred."

"Phantom Two-Four, roger. Cleared for the overhead break. Report initial."

Coop's excitement built. The overhead break. High-speed pass down the runway at three hundred knots, pull into a tight break turn, roll out on downwind. Standard carrier break procedure adapted for training. One of the most satisfying maneuvers in aviation.

Just fly, Coop, he told himself. *Just fly.*

He pushed the throttle forward. The F-42C Phantom accelerated hard, the speed building fast. Four hundred feet, three hundred knots. The runway appeared ahead, streaming beneath him.

"Phantom Two-Four, initial."

"Two-Four, roger. Cleared for the break. Report downwind."

Coop counted landmarks. Three seconds. Two. One.

He rolled hard left and pulled, four g's slamming him into the seat. His vision grayed at the edges but he held steady, breathing through it. Four counts in, six out. He rolled out on downwind with the runway off his left side.

"Good break," Belmont said. "Textbook execution. You're handling the g-forces well."

"Thank you, sir."

Breathing hard now. Heart racing. But flying.

"Phantom Two-Four, downwind, touch-and-go."

"Two-Four, roger. You're number one. Cleared for the option."

Coop focused completely, every sense engaged.

His hands found the rhythm. The aircraft responded smoothly. He completed the turn, clean and controlled.

"Perfect turn, Cooper. Well done."

"Phantom Two-Four, turn final. You're cleared touch-and-go."

"Two-Four, final, touch-and-go."

He lined up on final approach. His hands moved with confidence. The runway centerline appeared in his HUD and he followed it down. Throttle back. Nose up. Feeling for the ground.

The wheels kissed the runway smoothly, exactly as briefed. He advanced the throttle immediately for the touch-and-go, the F-42C Phantom accelerating back into the sky.

One down.

"Excellent landing, Cooper. That was textbook perfect."

"Thank you, sir."

The exhilaration ran through him. This was real. He was actually doing this.

He climbed back into the pattern, his confidence building with each second. The second circuit went even smoother. His hands were steady on the controls.

"Phantom Two-Four, looking good. Cleared for touch-and-go number two."

The second landing came perfectly. He was exactly on centerline, exactly on speed. The F-42C Phantom touched down and lifted off again.

Two down.

"Outstanding," Belmont said, and Coop could hear the approval in his voice. "You're a natural at this, Cooper."

Coop gave himself a moment of satisfaction. The training was paying off. All the work, all the determination, leading to this moment.

He banked into the third circuit.

"Phantom Two-Four, be advised winds now one-zero-zero at one-five knots, gusting to two-zero. Crosswind component approximately one-two knots. Cleared for the option."

Coop's focus sharpened. Crosswind landing. The real test.

"Cooper," Belmont said. "Crosswind landing is always challenging on first flights. But I've seen your simulator work. You can do this. Remember your technique. Wing low into the wind, opposite rudder. I'm here if you need me."

"Yes, sir. I've got it."

The third approach brought the challenge that would define him.

Tower's voice crackled through his helmet. "Phantom Two-Four, winds now one-zero-zero at one-five knots, gusting two-zero. Crosswind component one-two knots right quartering. Cleared to land full stop."

Coop set up the approach, focused and ready.

His left hand worked throttle while his right gripped the stick. Steady. Controlled.

"Two-Four, final, full stop."

"Roger, Two-Four. Wind check one-zero-five at one-eight, gusting two-one."

Getting interesting, he thought.

The wind hit hard on short final, a gust shoving the F-42C Phantom right of centerline. Coop applied left aileron and right rudder, the crossed controls feeling natural to him. He made the correction well, bringing the aircraft back to centerline.

"Phantom Two-Four, good correction. Looking good."

Coop felt Belmont's confidence through the comm. Watching from the ground pod, but not worried.

Every instinct told him this was right. This was what he was meant to do.

Left aileron. Right rudder. The Phantom crabbed through the air, nose pointed into the wind while the fuselage tracked the runway centerline.

Fifty feet. The gust hit again, harder. Coop added power with his left hand, cross-controlled with his right. Forty feet. Thirty. The runway rushed up.

At the last moment, he kicked right rudder to align the fuselage with the runway. The main wheels touched simultaneously. Perfect. He held the stick neutral, let the nosewheel settle as airspeed bled off.

The landing was flawless. Textbook crosswind technique despite the gusts.

"Outstanding, Cooper." Belmont's voice carried genuine pride in it. "That was as good a crosswind landing as I've seen from anyone, let alone a student on their first flight. Absolutely outstanding."

"Phantom Two-Four, outstanding work. Exit right, contact Ground."

Coop grinned. He couldn't help it. He'd just greased a crosswind landing on his first flight, and with Belmont monitoring from his pod. "Two-Four, roger. Contact Ground."

He switched frequencies while rolling clear. "Salon Ground, Phantom Two-Four clear of Two-Six."

"Two-Four, Ground. Taxi to the ramp via Alpha."

"Alpha to the ramp, Two-Four."

As they taxied in, Belmont spoke over the intercom. "Cooper, I want you to understand something. I've been instructing pilots for years, military and nonmilitary. I've flown with Academy hotshots, veteran combat pilots transitioning to new platforms, and everything in between. What you just did was exceptional airmanship from start to finish. Perfect break, perfect pattern work, and that crosswind landing was as good as it gets. You should be proud."

Coop's throat tightened. "Thank you, sir."

"I asked to fly with you today because your simulator performance suggested you'd be one of the best in this class. You just proved it. You belong here, Lieutenant."

The jet spooled down with a dying whine. Coop popped the canopy, yanked off his mask, and sucked in the hot ramp air that tasted of jet blast. The yellow-shirted crew chief raised his thumbs and a single finger, pointing at the tie-down spot like he was parking a pickup.

Coop climbed down the ladder feeling like he could take on the world. Belmont emerged from the ground control facility across the tarmac, helmet tucked under one arm, walking toward several people under the squadron awning.

Sharlow, Arnaud, and Duchamp stood twenty meters off under the squadron awning, sipping coffee and pretending they weren't watching. Nobody moved. Nobody clapped.

Belmont didn't look up. "OK, Coop—0600 tomorrow, ride two. Steep turns and stalls." He held in a grin. "Try not to puke in my jet."

He turned and walked off, boots crunching on gravel, g-suit flapping half-zipped.

Sharlow lifted his coffee cup in a lazy salute while Coop stood by himself beside the jet, exhilarated. Twelve minutes later, he grabbed his helmet bag, told the crew chief he'd be back for the forms, and started the walk to his quarters.

He made it to his room riding the high of his first flight. He closed the door and sat on his bunk replaying every moment.

The exhilaration wasn't fading. This was real. He'd done it.

At 0200, Coop found himself in the base library, alone. He'd tried to sleep but his mind wouldn't stop replaying the crosswind landing, the way his hands had moved perfectly, the feeling of the Phantom responding to his inputs. And Belmont's words continued to play in his mind: "You belong here."

The holographic display showed rotating F-11A Gripen specifications in detail.

The manned starfighter represented everything he'd been fighting for. Actual combat spacecraft capable of engaging Zodark forces in the black. Altairian-Human hybrid technology. The Republic's first human-operated starfighter designed to fight where drone links had failed.

He scrolled through the technical data.

Offensive systems: six Joint Advance Tactical Missiles. Twin rotary magrail guns capable of sustained fire rates that would shred enemy armor. Four laser blasters for close-range engagement.

Defensive suite: ECM/ECCM electronic countermeasure systems. Automated flare and chaff dispensers. Sand-water antimissile system. Four antimissile drone interceptors that could swat incoming ordnance before it reached the hull.

He kept reading—engagement envelopes, thrust-to-weight ratios, combat radius with and without external tanks, maximum g-loading—every technical detail his focused mind could absorb.

His excitement kept him going. He kept scrolling, kept memorizing, kept preparing for a future that was now inevitable.

Each specification reinforced what Belmont had said. The manned fighter program wasn't about perfect coordination. It was about making the right decisions when everything went wrong. About fighting battles that required human judgment and adaptation. About going where drones couldn't.

The library's lighting dimmed as the automated systems entered night mode. Coop barely noticed. He kept reading. Kept absorbing. The Gripen's specifications burned into his memory. Weapons loadouts, defensive capabilities, the hybrid technology that made this starfighter different from anything humanity had fielded before.

Coop's exhaustion finally caught him. His head dropped forward and he dreamed immediately.

Bear sat in a Gripen's wingman position, that crooked grin he always had on his face. He gave Coop a thumbs-up like this was always the plan.

Coop woke with his forehead still pressed against the holodisplay. The dream felt different this time—a vision of what was actually coming. Bear's approval still burned in his mind, real as the controls he'd gripped during the crosswind landing.

He sat back slowly. A smile broke across his face. This was really happening. Not someday. Not maybe. Actually happening.

He'd completed his first dual flight, and executed a perfect crosswind landing on his first try. He'd even earned Belmont's approval—the commander who rarely flew with students anymore. He'd passed the first major milestone in a program that would put him back in combat.

His father would be proud. Every Cooper who'd come before would be proud. He'd taken their legacy of aerial combat and dragged it into the stars through sheer determination and skill.

Coop touched the display one more time, his fingertips tracing the Gripen's outline in the holographic field.

I'm going to fly you. Going to fight in you. Going to prove I belong among the best.

Chapter 42:
Charleston

Year 2099
Decimomannu Air Base
Sardinia, Earth

The bus from France to Sardinia took fourteen hours, winding through mountain passes where snow still clung to peaks in late March. Coop pressed his forehead against the window, watching villages blur past. The other pilots on the bus did the same. Nobody talked much.

Sardinia appeared at sunset, the island rising from the Mediterranean. The Republic had built its advanced fighter training facility on the coast, runways extending toward water where Roman galleys had sailed two thousand years ago. Coop shouldered his duffel and followed the others off the bus, breathing salt in the air.

A lieutenant checked their orders and pointed toward the barracks. "Chow at 1800. Briefing at 1900. Tomorrow starts at 0530, so get squared away tonight."

The briefing room was like every other command space Coop had ever been in: the smell of industrial floor sealant mixed with energy drink residue and the faint, acrid bite of overheated coolant lines running behind the walls.

Major Simon Drummond stood at the front. "You've got eight weeks to qualify in the F-11A Gripen," he said. "That's ground school, simulators, dual instruction, solo progression, and weapons qualification. Most programs take twelve weeks. You don't have twelve weeks. The fleet needs pilots yesterday."

He gestured at the screen behind him. A Gripen rotated in on the holographic display, its hybrid design showing Republic and Altairian technology merged together into something ready to kick butt and take names.

"Half of you will wash out in the first three weeks. The rest?" He paused. "The rest will deploy to active squadrons. Questions?"

Nobody raised a hand.

"Good. Ground school starts at 0600. Don't be late."

The next four days were intense—classroom instruction from 0600 to 1800, systems, limitations, and emergency procedures. Coop

303

absorbed the information flood. He took detailed notes, asked sharp questions, and stayed engaged through every session.

He showed up early. Took notes. Asked questions when clarity was needed.

Day five brought cockpit familiarization.

The F-11A Gripen sat on the tarmac. Coop walked the preflight inspection with the others, Drummond calling out each inspection point.

"Left intake. Check for FOD, damage, proper alignment. Right intake. Same check. Nose gear strut, tire pressure, torque links. Main gear..."

The walkaround took twenty minutes. Every panel. Every seam. Every surface that could kill you if it failed.

Then Drummond gestured to the ladder. "Cooper. You're up."

Coop climbed up and settled into the cockpit, just like he did in the trainer jets. And like the jets, the seat fit like it had been molded for his body. Controls were positioned where his hands naturally fell. Displays oriented for combat operations.

"Find your ejection handle," Drummond said from the ground.

Coop's left hand found it between his legs. It was yellow and black striped.

"Circuit breaker panel."

Left console. Rows of breakers. Coop scanned them, memorizing positions.

"Emergency oxygen."

Right side. Green handle.

Drummond ran him through every system. Every switch. Every control. Thirty minutes in the cockpit, hands moving across panels.

Week two brought the simulators.

Coop climbed into Pod Two, the neural interface crown settling against his skull. Connections established and the cockpit materialized around him.

"Basic handling," Drummond's voice came through the helmet. "Start-up checklist, taxi, takeoff, pattern work. Don't crash."

Coop worked through the start-up. Battery on. Avionics. Engines. The simulated Gripen came alive around him, systems responding to his inputs.

He taxied toward the runway, the simulated Mediterranean spread out below, impossibly blue.

"Decimomannu Tower, Coop One-Two, ready for departure."

"Coop One-Two, Tower. Winds two-six-zero at eight, runway two-four, cleared for takeoff."

Coop advanced the throttle and the Gripen accelerated. He pulled the stick and the nose lifted, the wheels leaving virtual ground.

He was flying.

For real.

The first landing attempt was rough. Coop came in too fast, too high—too aggressive.

"Again," Drummond said.

The second attempt wasn't much better. Coop floated halfway down the runway before touching down, then couldn't stop before running out of concrete.

"Again."

Third attempt. Fourth. Fifth.

On the sixth try, Coop greased it. The wheels kissed the runway. Smooth. Clean.

"Acceptable," Drummond said. "Tomorrow we add emergencies."

Week three started with dual flights.

The real Gripen sat on the ramp, morning sun turning its hull into a brilliant shine. Coop walked the preflight with Drummond watching every move. Left intake. Right intake. Nose gear. Main gear. Every panel. Every check.

"Get in," Drummond said.

Coop climbed the ladder and settled into the cockpit. Drummond would monitor from the ground control pod with full telemetry feeds and override capability.

"I've got remote control from the ground pod," Drummond's voice came through the helmet once Coop was strapped in. "Follow along on the controls. Feel what I'm doing through the stick inputs."

They taxied, Drummond controlling the aircraft remotely while Coop's hands rested lightly on stick and throttle, feeling the inputs transmitted through the flight control system.

The takeoff pressed Coop into his seat. Four g's. His vision grayed slightly but he stayed focused.

"You've got the aircraft," Drummond said, releasing remote control.

Coop's hands closed on the controls and the Gripen wobbled. He overcorrected, pitching the nose up too hard.

"Relax," Drummond's voice stayed calm. "Small inputs. Let the aircraft fly itself. You're just guiding it."

Coop eased his grip and relaxed his shoulders. The Gripen steadied.

"Better. Now give me a thirty-degree bank to the left."

Coop rolled left but gave it too much stick. The bank steepened to forty-five degrees.

"I'm taking control," Drummond said, overriding from the ground pod. The Gripen smoothed out immediately. "You're fighting it, Cooper. Stop thinking like a drone pilot. You're not sending commands to a machine thousands of klicks away. You're in the machine. Feel it. Flow with it."

They flew for an hour with Drummond demonstrating through remote control, and Coop attempting.

"Not bad for a first flight with a Gripen," Drummond said on the ground. "But you've got a long way to go."

The dual flights continued. Day after day. Week after week.

Flight three: Basic aerobatics. Loops. Rolls. Coop's spatial awareness worked overtime during the rolling maneuvers, processing orientation changes quickly.

"Clean flying, Cooper," Drummond said.

Flight five: Formation work. Coop flew wing on another Gripen piloted remotely by Drummond from the ground, trying to hold position three feet off the lead aircraft's wing. He made the small corrections, holding formation tight.

"Excellent work," Drummond said.

Flight seven: Emergency procedures. Drummond failed systems randomly through remote override. Engine fire. Hydraulic failure. Electrical problems. Coop worked through the checklists, processing them quickly.

"Good responses," Drummond said. "But emergency procedures need to be automatic. Muscle memory. We'll run these until you can do them unconscious."

Flight ten: high-g maneuvering. Drummond commanded aggressive maneuvers through the ground control link, pulling the Gripen through turns that crushed Coop into his seat. Six g's. Seven. Eight. Coop handled it well, breathing through the pressure.

"Good g-tolerance," Drummond said. "You're handling eight g's cleanly. That's solid performance."

By flight fifteen, something clicked.

Coop rolled into a turn without overthinking it. He manipulated the controls. Left hand on throttle, right on stick, small inputs, and flowing with the aircraft instead of fighting it.

The Gripen responded extremely well.

"Now you're getting it," Drummond said.

Week five brought the moment Coop had been anticipating. It was his first solo.

Drummond stood on the tarmac, arms crossed. "You've logged eighteen monitored flights. Today you fly completely solo. No remote monitoring, no override capability. You're going to fly the pattern. Three touch-and-goes, full stop on the fourth. Keep it simple. I'll be watching from the tower, but the aircraft is one hundred percent yours. Get in."

Coop walked the preflight alone. Left intake. Right intake. Nose gear. Main gear. Every check committed to memory. He climbed the ladder and again, settled into the cockpit, completely by himself with no remote link active.

Coop ran through the start-up checklist. Battery. Avionics. Engines. The Gripen came alive around him. And like every time, he found the controls. Left hand finding the throttle. Right hand on the stick.

"Decimomannu Tower, Coop One-Two, ready for departure, first solo."

"Coop One-Two, Tower. Winds two-five-zero at nine knots, runway two-two, cleared for takeoff. Chase One is airborne and has you in sight. Contact Departure on button four. Good luck, Lieutenant."

Coop glanced up. An F-11A circled overhead. His safety chase. Standard procedure.

He advanced the throttle and the Gripen rolled forward, accelerating. The nose lifted and the wheels left the Earth.

He was flying, actually flying, and all alone.

The Mediterranean went wide and far below, and a gorgeous blue he was at awe with no matter how many times he witness that stretch of water. Coop banked left, turning downwind.

"Coop One-Two, you're cleared for the option."

Coop turned base, then final. The runway appeared ahead. He adjusted power and pitch and the Gripen descended toward the numbers.

The wheels touched concrete and directly after, he added power, taking off again.

Touch-and-go number one, and it went as clean as could be.

He flew the pattern again. Second landing. A third. Each one building confidence.

The fourth landing came and went, and Coop taxied to the ramp and shut down the engines.

Drummond met him at the ladder. "Acceptable. Tomorrow we start tactical training."

Week six brought weapons employment.

Coop flew to Whiskey-Four-eight airspace, a restricted range over open water. Drummond's tone burst through from Range Control.

"Coop One-Two, Range Control. Target drone inbound, your twelve o'clock, twenty kilometers. You're cleared to engage with guns. Call your tally."

Coop's tactical display painted the target, a small drone simulating an enemy fighter.

"One-Two, tally target."

He rolled toward the intercept and the targeting reticle appeared on his HUD. He flew the intercept geometry and the reticle settled over the target. He squeezed the trigger.

The magrail guns fired. Tracers reached out and the drone darted to the side, but it was too late as the drone exploded into hundreds of fiery pieces.

"Splash one," Coop transmitted.

"Good kill," Drummond said. "RTB for debrief."

Week seven brought the advanced scenarios.

Coop climbed into the Gripen at 0530. Again, a real aircraft fully loaded with real weapons, and with it, a real mission profile.

"Today's different," Drummond had said in the briefing. "You're going orbital. Intercept profile against simulated targets in space. This is what you've been training for."

Coop ran through start-up. Taxied. Took off. The Gripen climbed through scattered clouds, five thousand meters. Ten thousand. Fifteen thousand.

"Coop One-Two, you're cleared for orbital transition. Point your nose at the sky and give me full throttle."

Coop pulled the stick back and advanced the throttle to maximum. The Gripen's hybrid propulsion transitioned from air-breathing turbines to plasma drives. Acceleration built. Four g's. Six. Eight.

Earth's curvature appeared below. Blues and greens giving way to black space. The transition felt like being born into something new, experiencing space from inside a cockpit instead of through camera feeds. Granted, he'd been in space before, in shuttles, in large vessels, but never as the pilot manually driving the actual ship.

"Contact," Range Control transmitted. "Six bandits, bull's-eye zero-nine-zero for sixty, medium, hostile. You are weapons free, training rules apply. Call your targets."

Coop's tactical display illuminated with six red contacts designated as simulated Zodark Vultures in standard intercept formation. A double-vic spread at forty thousand meters, advancing at combat velocity. The lead pair held center position while flanking elements staggered high and low. At the same time his drone training and flight training kicked in, so did his TASC training, flooding his consciousness with pattern recognition, threat assessment, and target priority calculations that felt both learned and instinctual.

"One-Two engaged, targeting group lead."

He rolled sixty degrees port toward the nearest threat, his left hand working across the power distribution panel to shunt energy from auxiliary systems to weapons capacitors, while his right hand worked the stick through a barrel roll bringing him onto an intercept trajectory. The targeting reticle settled over the lead Vulture, painting it with the targeting laser as the firing solution went solid green.

Fox Two. Simulated missile away.

The first Vulture exploded in simulated flames and broken metal, its icon fragmenting into debris scatter on his display.

"Contact destroyed."

Two more Vultures broke formation and dove toward him from his high six o'clock position, accelerating hard to force him into their overlapping engagement. Coop cut throttle to sixty percent and pulled into a vertical climb, the hybrid propulsion system compensating instantly as the inertial dampeners absorbed the eight-g transition. He emerged above both attackers, inverting his fighter at the apex of the climb to maintain visual contact.

After calculating firing solutions, he fired dual missiles. Both Vultures died within three seconds, their icons winking out as simulated warheads found their marks.

The remaining three scattered into evasive patterns, breaking hard in different vectors before reforming into a kill box designed to leave no escape.

Coop recognized the tactic immediately. A thousand drone engagements against similar formations flashed through his mind. His TASC training identified their positioning, calculating the angles and timing, while his fighter pilot instincts provided solutions his conscious mind hadn't fully articulated yet.

He flew like two different people occupying the same cockpit. The incredible targeting of a drone operator married to the spatial awareness of a natural pilot, pulling from somewhere deeper than training, somewhere that felt like genetic memory.

The fourth Vulture crossed his nose at point-blank range. Less than three hundred meters. The enemy pilot executed what should have been a deflection shot. Coop fired and the sim registered catastrophic damage to the Vulture's reactor section.

"Holy…" someone muttered over the tactical frequency, the transmission cutting off as whoever it was remembered comm discipline.

Coop pursued the last two contacts as they broke in opposite directions. He pulled nine-g turns to stay inside their turning radius, the flight suit's pressure bladders inflating hard against his legs and abdomen to keep blood in his brain. He kept the stick steady, breathing through the pressure in sharp, controlled exhalations.

The fifth Vulture tried breaking away vertically, climbing at maximum thrust while deploying countermeasures. Coop anticipated the maneuver before it fully developed, reading the enemy pilot's energy state and predicting the escape vector. He fired before the enemy completed his turn, the missile tracking through the chaff dispersion to find its target.

A cloud of flames for a second before the vacuum of space extinguished the explosion.

The sixth Vulture ran, diving hard toward the outer engagement zone boundary and burning maximum thrust. Coop chased for two minutes, his Gripen's superior acceleration closing the gap steadily despite the Vulture's head start. His targeting reticle was just settling into firing parameters when Range Control's voice returned.

"Terminate simulation. RTB for debrief."

Coop brought the Gripen around in a sweeping two-hundred-seventy-degree turn, pointing its nose back toward Sardinia Base. The starfighter descended through the engagement zone boundary.

The Gripen touched down smooth. Coop taxied to his assigned spot and shut down the systems.

The crew chief met him at the ladder. "Nice flying, Lieutenant. Also, you've got a priority personal comm waiting in the ready room."

Coop climbed down and pulled off his helmet. "Thanks, Chief." He walked toward the ready room, still riding the adrenaline from the engagement. Inside, other pilots clustered around display terminals, conversations creating a staticky background noise.

A corporal near the communications station waved him over. "Lieutenant Cooper? You've got an active holo link on terminal three. Civilian origin, Charleston, South Carolina."

Coop's stomach tightened. Charleston. Only one person would be calling from there.

His mother. He should have called her much sooner, really. But between recovery, training, and clawing his way back into flight status, he'd let it slide. She'd understand. She always did. That was the problem, though, wasn't it? She never really pushed, never really demanded, so it was easy to let contact slip, and all too often. Unlike his father, who'd made his disappointment crystal clear, his mom had simply… waited. Always the patient one. Patient the way she'd been with his dad, waiting for her ex-husband to change when he never did. She was always the hopeful one, and yes, a bit strict with her words maybe, but never with her actions.

He moved to terminal three and tapped the accept button. His mother's face materialized above the holoprojector, life-sized and clear despite the distance. She sat in her kitchen, afternoon light streaming through the window behind her. She had that expression, equal parts worried and annoyed.

"There you are," she said. "I've been waiting ten minutes."

"Sorry, Mom. I was flying."

"Flying." She leaned closer, studying his face. "You look exhausted. Are they feeding you enough?"

"I'm fine."

"And I had to learn you're in Sardinia from your father." Her eyes narrowed. "You couldn't call your own mother?"

Coop blinked. "Wait. Dad told you?"

"He called two days ago. First time in… I don't know… years." Her expression shifted, uncertain. "Just to tell me where you were. That you'd made it to advanced fighter training."

"He talked to you?"

"Barely, but yes. Why would I lie about that? Anyway, he sounded… I don't know. Proud? Not something I'd ever seen in him." She shook her head. "You couldn't call your own mother and tell her yourself?"

Coop felt heat creep up his neck. "I wanted to surprise you. I've got leave when I graduate. I was going to come home and—"

"Surprise me? Blake, you've been gone for months. And you thought you'd just show up like you'd been out getting groceries?"

"Well, no… I—"

"I'm your mother. I deserve better than secondhand updates from your father of all people. Do you know how long it's been since I've seen you in person?"

"No, Ma."

"I've kept track. It's been eight years and eleven days. But, regardless, you really coming home?"

"For a while before my assignment."

"And you'll stay for a while?"

"Maybe two weeks if I can?"

"If you can? No, it's a must. I insist. Tell them I insist." Her expression turned serious. "But after that… you're deploying into combat again, aren't you?"

Coop hesitated. "Eventually, yeah."

She closed her eyes briefly. "I'm terrified. But you should have heard your father. He's so proud. You could have taken the medical discharge. Instead, you fought your way back, he said." Her eyes started to get misty. "Just promise me you'll be careful."

"I promise I'll do everything I can to come home."

"In one piece."

"Yes, ma'am."

She nodded. "Good. So, when you come home, can you promise two weeks?"

"I'll comm with exact dates once I know."

"You'd better. And, Blake? I love you. So much."

"I love you too, Mom."

"Now go rest. You look like you haven't slept in days."

"Only two," he said, grinning.

"Smart aleck." But she was smiling too. "Don't make me wait too long to see you."

"I won't."

The hologram dissolved, and Coop sat for a moment, staring at the empty space. His father had called her. After years of silence between them, his dad had reached out just to tell her where Coop was.

He didn't know what to make of that. Didn't know if he wanted to make anything of it. But somewhere in the back of his mind, a question formed that he'd have to deal with eventually.

He stood. Tomorrow would bring more training, more steps toward flying in the war.

But tonight, he'd sleep easier knowing his mother was proud of him, even if she was terrified for him. Even if she didn't say she was proud, he could hear it in her voice.

He'd make it home. Give her that time of knowing exactly where he was and that he was safe. Then he'd deploy. But first, he'd see his mom. It was the least he could do.

Chapter 43:
Nine Months Ready

Year 2099
Planet New Eden
RNS *Poseidon*

Nine months had transformed Task Force 27 "Frontier" from a collection of ships into something Lee believed would become legendary. The RNS *Poseidon* hung in moorings at New Eden Orbital Station, her hull shining brightly under the station's arc lights. Around her, thirteen other Republic vessels occupied their assigned berths. Four Decatur-class frigates. Two heavy cruisers. One battlecruiser. Three cruisers for escort and patrol. Two support vessels. Every ship had been through the grinder—tactical simulations, joint operations drills, emergency response scenarios, and coordination exercises, throwing everything at the crews, everything they had. And it created one of the best forces Lee had ever witnessed.

At the moment, Lee stood on *Poseidon*'s bridge, watching cargo shuttles on the main holo ferry the final supply pallets from the station's warehouses. The bridge felt different after nine months splitting time between orbital operations and planetside briefings. Smaller somehow, though nothing physical had changed.

Nine months in command, Lee thought, *and it still surprises me how the space contracts when you're not looking.*

Outside the viewports, massive transfer cranes maneuvered containers filled with everything a task force would need for a two-year deployment: ammunition, spare parts, medical supplies, food stores, reactor fuel, and a thousand other necessities. The logistics alone staggered the imagination. Fourteen ships operating independently from Republic supply lines for twenty-four months required planning that made even major fleet operations look simple by comparison.

Lee caught himself. *That's overboard. But still, the work that's gone into this operation has been immense.*

"Captain." Rhom approached from the XO's station. "Final manifest from Station Ops. We're at ninety-seven percent capacity across all storage bays."

"The missing three percent?"

"Reserve ammunition for the magrails. Station commander says the shipment's still at the Yards. Manufacturing backlog. ETA is forty-eight hours."

Lee pulled up the inventory on his own display. They had enough for sustained combat operations, but the reserve stocks gave them flexibility for extended engagements. The task force wasn't scheduled to deploy for another five days—plenty of time. "Inform Admiral Costello. We'll wait for the full load."

"Aye, Captain." Rhom made a note on his pad. "Also, Captain Sato requested a meeting before we deploy. Something about formation adjustments."

"When are we scheduled?"

"At 1800 hours aboard *Invincible*, sir."

"Confirm it."

Rhom nodded and returned to his station. Lee watched him move with growing confidence. *Good. The guy's impressed the heck out of me.* The XO position had swallowed lesser men, but Rhom had adapted. He wasn't Sato, and never would be. But he brought his own strengths to the job. Eventually, they'd develop their own rhythm, intuiting each other's decisions almost before they were even thought, just like Lee and Sato once did on this bridge.

Across the bridge, Phillips monitored electronic warfare feeds at his console. Rodriguez coordinated with the supply shuttles. MacGregor's voice drifted up from engineering, running diagnostics on the reactor systems. After nine months of constant training and preparation, the crew operated like butter, smooth and melted into sync.

Lee's comm lit up. "Captain Lee, this is Colonel Bonny on the *Saratoga*."

"Go ahead, Colonel."

"Sir, we've completed the final combat drop simulation. All platoons green across the board. My people are ready."

"Casualties?"

"Simulated losses were within acceptable parameters. Six percent on the hot drop scenario, three percent on the cold insertion. The C100s performed as expected."

Lee pulled up the simulation data. Bonny's soldiers had improved steadily over the past two months, learning to coordinate with naval fire support and fighter cover. The C100 combat synthetics added a dimension to their operations that traditional infantry couldn't match. Eight feet of armored combat platform didn't care about fear or exhaustion.

"Good work, Colonel. What about Colonel Garfield's division?"

"*Bunker Hill* finished their run an hour ago. Similar numbers. Gary's people are solid."

"Appreciated. We'll have a final briefing tomorrow at 0900, all senior officers."

"We'll be there, sir. Bonny out."

Lee terminated the connection and turned back to the viewport. The station's lights reflected off *Invincible*'s hull three berths away. Sato's battlecruiser looked ready for war, her weapons systems calibrated, her armor plates fresh from the yards.

Nine months ago, she'd been a newly promoted captain learning to command her first ship. Now she led one of the most powerful vessels in the task force with the same competence she'd brought to every assignment Lee had ever given her.

The student became the master in her own right.

Lee had watched her command *Invincible* through simulation after simulation, making calls that improved on his own tactical thinking. She didn't need his advice anymore, not really. During the joint exercises last month, she'd proposed a formation adjustment that increased their combined point-defense coverage by nineteen percent. Lee had adopted it for the entire task force without modification.

Yet their dynamic hadn't disappeared, just transformed into something different. Once a mentor, always a mentor in some way. Lee had learned that truth from watching Sato develop her command style. He'd also learned it from a dead man, Captain James Oldendorf, who somehow still mentored him through all the things Lee remembered the man saying over the years.

Advice still flowed between Lee and Sato, but now it moved both directions. She'd comm him with tactical questions, and he'd offer perspective. He'd ask her opinion on formation adjustments, and she'd provide insights that came from her unique position commanding a battlecruiser. The relationship had matured from teacher-student into something closer to peers, though the foundation of trust built over years of partnership remained unshakable.

"Sir." Rodriguez looked up from her station. "Message from Admiral Costello. He's requesting your presence at Station Command at 1600 hours."

Lee checked his chrono. Two hours. "Acknowledged. Inform the admiral I'll be there. Comm Captain Sato and reschedule for 2000 hours."

"Aye, sir."

He took a final look at the task force arrayed before him. Fourteen ships. Fighter squadrons, bomber wings, assault transports. Medical facilities, logistics support, repair capabilities.

Two months ago, two *Intus*-class Medium Orbital Assault Ships had arrived: RNS *Saratoga* and RNS *Bunker Hill*. Each carrier brought three thousand, one hundred and twenty soldiers, nine hundred and thirty C100 combat synthetics, and forty C200 medical units organized into two Orbital Assault Divisions. Lee had integrated them into Task Force 27's training regimen immediately, running simulation after simulation until the coordination between naval and ground forces became second nature.

The OAD commanders—Colonel Carole Bonny on *Saratoga* and Colonel Gary Garfield on *Bunker Hill*—proved as competent as their reputations suggested. They understood the complexities of orbital insertion, close-air support coordination, and the precision required to getting thousands of soldiers planetside while hostile forces tried to kill them.

The joint exercises had been brutal and necessary. Naval captains learned how to position their ships for optimal fire support during ground operations. OAD officers learned how naval assets could shape the battlefield before boots touched dirt. The fighter squadrons— F-97 Orions, B-99 bombers, and AS-90 ground-attack craft—practiced orbital bombardment patterns until the timing became clockwork.

The logistics officer's voice crackled through the bridge speakers. "Captain, final ammunition pallets are secured in magazines three and seven. Primary magrail penetrator stocks loaded and accounted for. Missile inventory at one hundred percent across all launch systems."

Lee acknowledged the report, watching through the viewports as the last cargo shuttle detached from *Poseidon*'s port loading bay. Similar operations proceeded across the task force. Frigates taking on their allotments. Cruisers filling their holds. The assault carriers loading enough supplies to sustain ground operations for months.

The planning documents had run to thousands of pages. Everything from toilet paper to plasma torpedoes.

Around the orbital station, cargo handlers in EVA suits guided containers through vacuum using maneuvering thrusters. Automated systems verified inventory against manifests. Inside *Poseidon*, Chief MacGregor's engineering teams ran final diagnostics on every critical system.

Reactor performance: optimal. Drive systems: green across the board. Weapons systems: fully functional. Life support: operating within normal parameters. Communications arrays: tested and verified.

Two years was a long time to operate without yard support. Every system needed to be perfect before they cast off.

Out there in the deep black, Lee mused, *perfection's the only thing keeping us alive.*

"Captain." Rodriguez turned from her station. "Admiral Costello's office confirms your 1600 meeting. Conference room three, station command level."

"Acknowledged."

Lee checked his chrono again. Ninety minutes. Enough time to review the final personnel assignments and grab something resembling food from the officer's mess.

His comm chimed. MacGregor's voice, rough as always. "Cap, we've got a fluctuation in the starboard fusion manifold. Nothing critical, but I want to run a full diagnostic before we deploy."

"How long?"

"Four hours if we strip it down proper. Two if you want me to cut corners."

"Strip it down. I want it perfect, Mac."

"Aye, Cap. We'll have her singing by morning."

Lee terminated the connection. Mac never reported problems unless they needed fixing. The man had kept *Poseidon* running through battles that should have killed them all. If he wanted four hours, he got four hours.

Outside the viewport, *Invincible* sat in her moorings. Sato would be running her own diagnostics, checking every system twice. She'd learned that from him during their years together. *Never trust the*

*automated reports. Walk the ship. Talk to the chiefs. Know your vessel
like you know your own body.*

Lee sat for a moment and thought about Rass. Nine months
away from the front lines had bothered him initially. Part of him
believed his place was there, leading ships against Zodark positions,
pushing the offensive deeper into enemy territory. The guilt had kept
him awake some nights during the early training period.

Many times he shook his head, thinking, and thinking. Always
something similar to *good officers dying while I ran simulations in safe
orbit around New Eden.*

But intelligence briefings told a different story.

The Rass operation had proceeded better than expected.
Republic and Primord forces had secured orbital supremacy within
months. Ground operations cleared Zodark strongholds systematically,
rooting out the remaining insurgency. The three-century occupation
was ending.

They hadn't needed him to make it happen.

Command meant accepting that the mission continued whether
you were there or not. The Republic had depth now. Experienced
officers who could execute difficult and complicated operations
without his participation.

Task Force 27, Frontier, represented different strategic thinking.
Not invasion, but of targeted intervention. The Pharaonis threat in the
Tully sectors required finesse, not overwhelming force.

*My experience with joint operations and hybrid tech makes this
the right mission for me,* he told himself. *Even if part of me misses the
straightforward clarity of fleet engagements. Out there, beyond the
established front lines, we'll be writing new doctrine with every
decision.*

"Sir." Rhom faced Lee. "Final crew assignments for your
review. We had three last-minute transfers. Medical reasons, family
emergencies. Station personnel found replacements, but you'll want to
sign off."

Lee took his datapad, scanning the names. Two engineering
techs and a weapons specialist. Their replacements showed solid
service records. Nothing that raised concerns.

He signed the authorization.

"Also, Captain Sato sent a message. She wants to discuss the forward screen formation before the admiral's briefing tomorrow."

"Tell her we'll cover it at 2000 hours tonight."

"Aye, sir."

Lee handed back the pad and returned his attention to the viewport just as his comm chimed again. Admiral Costello's aide. "Captain Lee, the admiral is ready for you early if you're available."

Lee checked the time. Fifty-nine minutes ahead of schedule. *Costello doesn't call people in early without reason.*

"On my way."

He stood, straightening his uniform. Rhom looked up from his station, question in his eyes.

"You have the bridge, Commander. Call me if Mac finds anything else that needs fixing."

"Aye, sir."

Lee walked to the lift, the bridge sounds fading behind him. The doors slid open. He stepped inside.

"Station Command Level," he said.

The lift began its descent, separating from *Poseidon*'s hull. Through the transparent walls, the orbital station sprawled in every direction. Docking arms, defensive platforms, the massive fuel depot cylinders, repair yards where ships hung in skeletal frameworks. New Eden filled half the sky beyond, a blue-green jewel against the starlit black.

Home. For now.

In five days, they'd leave it behind. The Tully sectors waited, light-years away. Zodark and Pharaonis activity had been escalating for months—raids, interdictions, deaths.

Task Force 27 would provide security.

The lift reached the station, magnetic clamps engaging with a solid thunk. Lee felt the subtle shift as station gravity took over from *Poseidon*'s artificial spin. The doors opened onto a bustling corridor.

A lieutenant commander stepped aside, saluting. "Captain Lee."

Lee returned it and kept moving. The admiral's office was three sections forward, past the tactical operations center and the communications hub. He could see the entrance now, two Marine guards flanking the doors, a waiting area where a young aide sat at a desk.

The aide looked up as Lee approached. "Captain Lee. The admiral is expecting you. Please go right in."

Lee nodded and walked past the guards.

The door opened.

Admiral Costello stood at the central holotable, studying a star chart. The Tully sectors glowed in amber with dozens of systems, hundreds of possible routes, infinite variables.

The admiral looked up.

"Captain. Thank you for coming early." He gestured at the holotable. "We've received new intelligence from the Tully. It changes things a bit."

Lee stepped forward, his eyes already analyzing the chart.

And so it begins.

Chapter 44:
Elite Tier

Year 2099
Decimomannu Air Base
Sardinia, Earth

Coop arrived at the briefing room at 0458 hours—early enough to claim a seat in the back row where he could watch the other candidates filter in. Sixteen pilots from the original class of thirty-two remained. The rest had washed out over eight weeks of failures.

Lieutenant Revale entered at 0458, two minutes early, still managing to look like he owned the place. The man had talent; Coop would give him that. Revale had scored in the top three on every evaluation. He just couldn't shut up about it.

"Heard they're throwing adaptive scenarios at us," Revale said to no one in particular as he dropped into a seat near the front. "Real-time difficulty scaling based on performance metrics."

"That's the rumor," someone replied.

Coop stayed quiet. He'd learned that lesson in the first week when talking too much about his TASC background had painted a target on his back. The other candidates saw him as the combat veteran drone pilot trying to prove something. They weren't entirely wrong.

Major Drummond entered at exactly 0500 hours. The room went silent.

"Good morning." Drummond said this in that way of someone who'd said the same words a thousand times to a thousand different students. "Today's final evaluation will test everything we've drilled into your heads for the past two months. Orbital insertion. Multiple threat engagement. Electronic warfare countermeasures. Fuel management under combat stress. Emergency procedures."

The holographic tactical display flickered on behind him, showing a complicated mission scenario with multiple threat vectors and civilian elements. Coop leaned forward slightly.

"Each of you will fly solo," Drummond continued. "The scenario adapts to your performance. Graduated difficulty levels designed to push you to your absolute limits. Some of you will face relatively straightforward engagements. Others will get scenarios that would challenge veteran pilots with five years of fleet experience."

Revale shifted in his seat. So did half the room. Thing was, Coop didn't.

"Scoring criteria are as follows." Drummond pulled up a matrix on the display. "Weapons employment effectiveness. Tactical decision-making. Situational awareness. Energy management. Survivability. Minimum passing score is seventy-five percent. Anything below that results in recycling to the next training class or outright elimination, depending on the deficiency."

Seventy-five percent meant you could fail an entire category and still graduate if you dominated the others. But that assumed you didn't catastrophically fail multiple areas. The scoring was designed to identify specialists and generalists, to see who could survive when their strengths got neutralized.

"Your scenarios are classified until you enter your cockpit," Drummond said. "No advance preparation beyond the fundamentals we've been drilling. No study groups. No tactical discussion. You get in your bird and you fly. Questions?"

Silence.

"Good. First launch is at 0630. Dismissed."

****

The Gripen waited on the flight line. Coop ran his external preflight check at 0620, touching through the familiar inspection points. Everything felt right.

He climbed into the cockpit at 0628 and started the preflight sequence. Reactor initialization. Avionics power-up. Flight control check. Weapons systems verification. Each step completed with the muscle memory of forty-eight training flights over eight weeks.

The scenario loaded at 0631.

MISSION CLASSIFICATION: ELITE

SCENARIO: DEEP SPACE INTERCEPT--CONVOY PROTECTION

HOSTILE CONTACTS: MULTIPLE

COMMUNICATIONS: DEGRADED

WEAPONS STATUS: MALFUNCTION RANDOMIZED

Elite tier. The highest difficulty classification available. Something settled in Coop's chest…determination and focus. This was the scenario they gave to candidates they wanted to see excel. The exact type of mission separating the competent from the exceptional, the survivors from the heroes.

"Gripen Four-Four, you're cleared for launch," the tower controller said.

"Four-Four copies. Cleared for launch."

The Gripen screamed off the runway and climbed toward orbit on a pillar of fusion fire.

Coop transitioned to orbit at 0638 and immediately picked up eight hostile contacts on an intercept vector with a civilian refugee convoy. The convoy consisted of three distinct elements spread across fifty thousand kilometers of space. His primary mission was protection. His secondary mission was survival.

"Gripen Four-Four, be advised you have eight bandits inbound on the convoy. Designate targets Alpha through Hotel."

"Four-Four copies eight bandits."

Eight against one with three separate convoy elements to protect. They formed a dispersed attack pattern. Two pairs high and low with four strung out in a ladder formation between them. They were using vertical space in three dimensions, forcing Coop to defend across multiple planes simultaneously. He analyzed it all in under two seconds: the high pair would draw his attention while the ladder climbed toward convoy element one.

He rolled inverted and burned perpendicular to their approach vector, creating an angular velocity problem that forced them to adjust. Targets Alpha and Bravo took the bait, breaking from the high pair to intercept him. Coop let them commit, then executed a displacement roll, rotating his fighter ninety degrees while translating laterally using differential thrust. The maneuver put him outside their turning radius while maintaining his own firing solution.

He fired two missiles. Both tracked clean through the black and both targets died in brief orange blooms the vacuum snuffed instantly.

Then his weapons panel lit up red.

PRIMARY MISSILE SYSTEMS OFFLINE

GUNS ONLY

Guns only against six remaining fighters while protecting a refugee convoy across fifty thousand kilometers. A smile pulled at his lips. They wanted to see what he could do when the easy options disappeared.

The four-fighter ladder had reached convoy element one. Target Charlie held the lowest position, approximately eight thousand meters below the civilian ships. Coop dove hard, building velocity until his airspeed indicator showed numbers that made his g-suit inflate against his legs and abdomen. He came in on a pure vertical approach, using Charlie's blind spot directly beneath the fighter's engine bells.

At two thousand meters, Coop executed a cobra flip, killing forward velocity with reverse thrust while rotating his nose up through ninety degrees. The maneuver put him tail-forward for three seconds, bleeding speed while bringing his guns to bear. Charlie never saw it coming. A three-second burst caught the Zodark in the reactor section. The simulated fighter came apart in a cloud of flames that his sensors registered as a confirmed kill.

Now, only five were left.

Targets Delta and Echo had reached convoy element two and were executing a helical descent pattern, spiraling down toward the civilian ships. Standard antifighter doctrine called for head-on engagement, but head-on against two fighters meant gambling on who died first.

So, he burned perpendicular to their spiral, building velocity in a straight line, taking him twenty thousand kilometers past convoy element two. Then he killed thrust entirely, letting momentum carry him ballistic while he rotated his fighter through 180 degrees. When Delta and Echo passed his position, he was flying backwards relative to them but on a parallel course with firing solutions on both.

The convoy's mass created a sensor shadow, masking his approach. The civilian ships' hulls blocked the Zodarks' targeting radars just long enough for Coop to light them both up. Delta died first, a two-second burst through the cockpit. Echo broke hard when his wingman exploded, but broke directly into Coop's guns. Another two-second burst and Echo joined his partner in the debris field.

Three bandits remained. Targets Foxtrot, Golf, and Hotel had bypassed convoy elements one and two entirely, burning straight for element three with the kind of single-minded focus that meant they'd identified the most valuable target. Probably a hospital ship or transport carrying children. The scenario designers liked to add emotional weight to tactical decisions.

Coop checked his fuel. Thirty-eight percent remaining. Enough for the intercept and atmospheric reentry with maybe two percent margin. Maybe.

He burned everything he had.

The intercept took four minutes of sustained maneuvering, requiring constant thrust vectoring. Foxtrot flew a randomized jink pattern, changing velocity and vector every eight to twelve seconds. Golf used a vertical spiral climb while Hotel executed something Coop had only seen in classified threat assessments, a tumbling attack run rotating the fighter end-over-end while maintaining course.

Coop targeted Foxtrot first because the jinking pattern was predictable in its unpredictability. He calculated the timing intervals, recognized the pattern after four cycles, and fired on where Foxtrot would be rather than where the fighter was. An eleven-degree deflection shot required leading the target.

The burst caught Foxtrot amidships. The fighter tumbled, trailing debris, and exploded four seconds later.

Golf's spiral climb was beautiful and suicidal. The maneuver burned massive amounts of fuel. Coop didn't chase the spiral. He projected when the fighter would have to straighten out and positioned himself along the future vector.

When Golf's fuel state forced him to abandon the spiral, Coop was waiting. A four-second burst turned Golf into expanding debris fragments.

Target Hotel was still tumbling.

The maneuver was called a "death blossom" in fighter pilot slang, a desperation move sacrificing precise targeting for maximum defensive value. Hotel couldn't hit anything while tumbling, but Coop couldn't hit him either. The fighter's rotation rate made targeting solutions impossible for the half second required to achieve guns lock.

Unless Coop matched the rotation.

He rolled into a tumble, synchronizing with Hotel's spin rate, using reaction control thrusters to maintain rotational velocity while closing the distance. His inner ear protested. His vision grayed at the edges from the g-forces and disorientation, but he stayed focused, breathing through the stress.

But his guns stayed locked on Hotel.

The chase lasted ninety seconds and burned his fuel down to twenty-two percent. Coop's vision tunneled, but he forced it back through breathing technique and focus. At eight hundred meters, his targeting reticle achieved a solid lock.

He fired.

The burst caught Hotel through the center mass. The tumbling fighter's rotation carried it through the stream of magrail rounds like meat through a grinder. The explosion lit up Coop's cockpit displays with radiation warnings.

"Gripen Four-Four, all hostile contacts neutralized. Convoy is secure."

"Four-Four copies."

Then his thruster control went to hell.

STARBOARD MANEUVERING THRUSTERS OFFLINE

RECOMMEND EMERGENCY ATMOSPHERIC RE-ENTRY

Coop checked his fuel again. Eighteen percent. Not enough for a controlled orbital descent with failed thrusters. He'd have to come in ballistic and hope the Gripen's heat shielding held.

He oriented for reentry and committed.

The atmosphere hit him hard. The Gripen shook. His damaged thrusters made the fighter yaw left, and Coop compensated with reaction control thrusters, burning fuel he didn't have. The heat shield glowed cherry-red through the cockpit displays.

The yaw forced him into a corkscrew descent that added rotational energy to his velocity vector. He couldn't stop the spin without thrusters he didn't have, so he used it instead, timing his reaction control bursts to turn the uncontrolled rotation into a controlled spiral that bled velocity through increased atmospheric friction.

The Gripen's hull temperature climbed past safety limits. Alarms screamed warnings about structural stress and heat damage. Coop ignored them and focused on keeping the nose oriented downward through the rotation. If the fighter went sideways at this speed, it would tumble and break apart.

He rode the edge of control all the way down. The spiral tightened as air density increased, and Coop used the last of his reaction control fuel to flatten the descent angle in the final thirty seconds.

The Gripen touched down at 0720 with two percent fuel remaining and smoking landing gear.

He'd just flown forty-two minutes of sustained high-stress combat maneuvering and survived.

****

Major Drummond's office was much smaller than the briefing room. More personal.

Coop sat at attention while Drummond pulled up the telemetry data. Every maneuver appeared on the screen. Every weapons employment. Every decision made during those forty-two minutes.

"Let's review your scoring," Drummond said.

The matrix appeared.

WEAPONS EMPLOYMENT: 96%

TACTICAL DECISION-MAKING: 94%

SITUATIONAL AWARENESS: 98%

ENERGY MANAGEMENT: 91%

SURVIVABILITY: 97%

OVERALL SCORE: 95.2%

Drummond let the numbers sit there for ten seconds before speaking.

"Highest final evaluation score in this squadron's history," he said. "You want to tell me how you anticipated target Charlie's position before it appeared on your tactical display?"

Coop met his eyes. "Formation doctrine analysis, sir. The Zodarks fly predictable patterns. Once I identified their formation structure, I could predict where the next fighter would maneuver."

Drummond closed the file. "The Republic needs pilots who can perform consistently at excellent levels, Cooper, not pilots who occasionally perform at genius levels and then crater when the pressure exceeds their limits." He paused. "The question now becomes whether you can maintain this standard under actual combat stress rather than controlled training scenarios."

Coop's expression remained confident. "I can, sir."

"Your performance over the past eight weeks has been exceptional. You've demonstrated not just skill, but the kind of tactical thinking and adaptability that separates good pilots from great ones." Drummond's expression softened slightly. "You're also the best natural pilot I've seen in a long time."

The silence stretched.

"You've graduated, Lieutenant Cooper," Drummond said.

Coop stood, saluted, and walked out of the office with his head up. Against all odds, he'd graduated.

The Coopers simply didn't quit.

Chapter 45:
Wings and Scores

Year 2099
Decimomannu Air Base
Sardinia, Earth

The hangar lights turned the concrete floor into a mirror. Sixteen pilots stood in formation, dress uniforms crisp, shoulders back.

Major Drummond stood at the podium, flanked by Commander Belmont and the base commander. Behind them, the silhouette of an F-11A Gripen caught the overhead floods.

"Lieutenant Marcus Revale."

Revale marched forward, heels striking the deck. Drummond read from the datapad.

"Final evaluation score: eighty-two percent. Weapons proficiency: eighty-four. Tactical decision-making: seventy-nine. Energy management: eighty-five."

Solid scores. Competent. Revale stood at attention while Drummond pinned the wings to his chest, right above the left breast pocket. Revale saluted, turned, and returned to formation.

The ceremony continued. Lieutenant Warren: eighty-five percent. Lieutenant Choi: eighty-seven. Lieutenant Mbeki: eighty-six. Each pilot stepped forward, received their wings, and returned to the formation. The scores clustered between eighty-two and eighty-eight. Respectable numbers. Combat-ready pilots.

"Lieutenant Blake Cooper."

His boots felt like they weighed fifty pounds each. The walk to the podium stretched forever and ended too soon. Drummond looked at him with respect.

"Final evaluation score: ninety-five point two percent." Drummond's tone carried across the hangar. "Weapons proficiency: ninety-six. Tactical decision-making: ninety-four. Situational awareness: ninety-eight. Energy management: ninety-one. Survivability: ninety-seven."

Silence settled over the formation, and Coop heard someone shift their weight behind him.

"Highest graduation score in squadron history."

Drummond accepted the wings from his aide. Small things. Metal and enamel, maybe an ounce total. He pinned them to Coop's chest, fingers working the clasp.

The weight crushed him.

Nine months of fighting my injuries. Months before that in rehab, learning to walk without dragging his right leg. Dealing with the tremors in his hand and sometimes in his entire arm. The cramps. The pain. Ten years before that, starting this whole damn journey. Bear's face flashed through his mind, then Weber's, then the faces of the soldiers on Ridge 248 who'd never made it off that rock, his mates in the Jolly Rogers squadron.

These wings mean I'm volunteering to do it again, he told himself.

To fly toward the guns, to put himself between the enemy and whatever they wanted to destroy, and to maybe die in the black, frozen and alone, fighting an enemy that had been subjugating the galaxy since before he was born.

Drummond extended his hand. Coop shook it. The major's grip was firm.

"Congratulations, Lieutenant."

Coop saluted, turned, and walked back to formation. He felt eyes on him the whole way, and some of those looks carried respect, and others carried something sharper.

The ceremony concluded with the base commander's remarks about duty and honor and the proud tradition of the fighter pilot.

"Fall out. Dismissed."

Pilots came to attention briefly, then the formation broke. Pilots clustered in small groups, comparing notes, making plans for the celebration at the base club. Coop headed for the door.

"Cooper."

He twisted around to see Belmont standing alone near the Gripen, hands behind his back.

"Sir."

"Walk with me, Lieutenant."

They moved through the hangar, past maintainers prepping birds for tomorrow's training flights. Belmont stopped at the nose of the Gripen and looked up at the cockpit.

"You know what I see when I look at you?"

"Negative, sir."

"A pilot who earned his wings." Belmont nodded. "Not despite your injury. Because of how you handled it."

Coop said nothing.

"The others may talk, so let them. In whatever way they do, positively or negatively in your direction." Belmont turned to face him. "You proved what you needed to prove. To me. To yourself. To your family. To the Republic. That's what matters."

"Yes, sir."

Belmont nodded once before telling him he earned every ounce of graduating and then walked away.

Coop stood alone in the hangar for a long time. *Top score. Squadron history.* He smiled for a moment.

The next day, the assignment briefing started at 0900 hours in the base operations center. Sixteen pilots, back in service uniforms, assembled while a captain from personnel distributed datapads. Encrypted orders. Algorithmic assignments based on scores, aptitude, squadron needs, strategic priority. Each pilot thumbprint-authenticated receipt, standard security protocol.

Coop powered on his datapad and opened the file.

ASSIGNMENT ORDERS

TO: LT Blake Cooper, Republic Navy Fighter Corps

FROM: Bureau of Personnel, Fighter Wing Assignments

EFFECTIVE: 15 May 2099

ASSIGNMENT: 13th Fighter Wing, New Eden Station

MISSION PROFILE: Defensive patrol, training operations, system security

DEPLOYMENT CLASSIFICATION: Noncombat

LEAVE STATUS: 14 days PCS leave authorized

REPORT DATE: 28 May 2099

He read it three times. *New Eden. Training missions. Noncombat.*

Around him, the room erupted in voices, pilots comparing orders.

"203rd Wing, *Gallipoli*. Holy crap, that's Rass."

My old ship, Coop thought. *Revale gets my old ship.*

"I got the *George Washington*."

"Carrier assignment. RNS *Saratoga*."

Revale's voice cut through the noise. "Cooper, where'd you draw?"

Coop looked up. "Thirteenth Wing. New Eden."

The room went quiet.

"New Eden?" Revale's expression shifted. "That's garrison duty."

"Training missions and patrols," Choi added.

"Safest posting in the Republic." Mbeki pushed out his lower lip. "Easiest assignment. Medical history probably flagged him."

There it is. The truth nobody wants to say to my face.

"Nice." Revale powered off his datapad. "Well, Cooper, you did good, but I don't imagine you're OK with that."

Before Coop could reply, the captain from personnel cleared his throat. "Assignments are final. Questions can be directed to your squadron commanders upon arrival. Dismissed."

The pilots filed out, heading for whatever plans they'd made to celebrate more. Coop stayed in his seat, staring at the datapad.

Logical. Reasonable. A garrison assignment made perfect sense given his medical history. Time to adapt to operational flying without getting shot at, which would be a gradual progression toward combat readiness if the war escalated. The Republic was investing in his long-term potential.

Smart move.

Safe move.

He powered off the datapad and left the operations center.

****

The barracks were empty. Everyone else had gone to celebrate yet again. Coop sat on his bunk and pulled out his grandfather's journal. He stared at his for a few minutes, and decided not to open it. Instead, he set it on the footlocker.

His new wings sat in their presentation case on the desk and he got up, walked over, and took them out and pinned them to the wall above his bunk, right next to the photo of Bear.

New Eden. Training missions. Defensive patrols. I'll be OK.

His classmates would deploy to actual combat. They'd face real Zodarks, real Orbots, real danger, real tests of everything they'd learned. Revale would fly from the *Gallipoli*, Coop's old ship. Choi would run convoy escorts through contested space. Mbeki would fly CAP over carrier groups in active war zones.

And I'll fly training routes.

The guilt settled in his chest like a stone. *I spent eleven thousand hours hunting enemy drones through virtual battlespace, coordinated fire missions that killed thousands on Ridge 248 and at moon, Nightfall, flew drone missions for years and years during the war, and then got injured and eventually graduated top of my class when everybody around me said I couldn't even fly again. Now I get the easy assignment while everyone else goes to war.*

But underneath the guilt ran something else, something he didn't want to acknowledge.

Relief.

Finally, some time to rest from the constant action. The thought of actually facing Zodark fighters, of watching his wingman die, of dying himself in the dark expanse, it put a big rock in his stomach. At least, for now. In time, he knew that would change, but right now, taking somewhat of a break by being in constant action, well, it felt right.

Coop lay back on his bunk and stared at the wings on the wall. The metal caught the light from the hallway.

His datapad showed seventy-two hours until departure. Fourteen days PCS leave authorized before reporting to New Eden.

He pulled up his mother's contact information. Maybe he could convince her to move to New Eden. It was worth a shot.

Still, he'd get to see her before shipping out. To tell her about the wings. About making it through. About becoming the pilot the Coopers would be proud of, even if the assignment is garrison duty.

Coop set the datapad aside and closed his eyes.

The wings stayed on the wall, watching.

Chapter 46:
The Vanishing Fleet

Year 2099
Planet New Eden
RNS *Poseidon*

The room was crowded. Three intelligence officers clustered around the holo-table. A signals analyst stood by the viewport, tablet in hand. A commander from Fleet Intelligence leaned against the wall, arms crossed.

Costello looked up. The admiral worked his jaw tight, his eyes harder than Lee had seen them in months.

"Captain, close the door."

Lee did. The lock clicked behind him.

"Show him," Costello said.

The senior intelligence officer, a lieutenant commander named Jargas, activated the holo-table. The display came to life. Star systems appeared, and trade routes glowed green on the holo, and Republic monitoring stations pulsed white.

Red icons clustered near the Serpentis system border.

"Three days ago," Jargas said, "we detected increased fleet activity here." He highlighted a sector near the Trrahan frontier. "Standard patrol patterns. Nothing unusual. Pharaonis raiders, mostly frigates and destroyers. Six ships total."

Lee moved closer. The red icons drifted along established routes.

"Yesterday morning." Vargas swiped the display. The time stamp changed and the red icons multiplied. "Seventeen Pharaonis vessels. Mixed composition. Cruisers, battleships, support craft. They rendezvoused here." He pointed to a point in deep space, far from any stargate. "No settlements nearby. No strategic value. Just empty space."

"Staging area," Lee said.

"That's what we thought." Jargas swiped again. New icons appeared. These were darker red, almost crimson. "Then these showed up."

Lee's hand tightened on the table edge. "Zodark."

"Twelve heavy cruisers. Two battleships. One carrier." Vargas zoomed in. The Zodark ships sat in formation with the Pharaonis fleet.

The room went quiet. Lee stared at the display. Zodark ships that would be better off fighting Republic forces at Rass were here, light-years and light-years away, meeting with Pharaonis raiders.

"How long ago?" Lee asked.

"Thirty-six hours. They held position for approximately four hours. Then—"

Vargas swiped. The icons vanished.

Lee blinked. "What happened?"

"Unknown. Our monitoring stations tracked them, then lost contact. No FTL signatures. No debris fields. No energy spikes. They were there." He gestured at the empty space. "Then they weren't."

Costello pushed off from his desk. "We thought it was a sensor malfunction, so we sent a recon drone to the coordinates. It arrived two hours ago."

The holo-table updated. Drone footage played. Empty space. No ships. No wreckage. Just stars and void.

"Nothing," Costello said. "Like they were never there."

Lee studied the display. All those ships. Pharaonis and Zodark, working together. Then gone.

The door chimed. A lieutenant burst in, tablet clutched in both hands.

"Sir, we just got confirmation from Station Theta-Nine. The contacts were real. Three separate sensor arrays tracked them."

Costello spun toward her. "And now?"

"Gone, sir. All of them. No projected course. No FTL trails. They're just… not there."

Lee's stomach dropped. He looked at Jargas. "Play the timeline again."

Jargas replayed the sequence. Eight ships became twenty-five. Zodark reinforcements arrived. They held formation, and then… nothing.

"That's impossible," someone muttered.

Lee frowned. "Apparently not."

The holo-table chimed with new data streaming in. Jargas pulled it up. His face went pale.

"What?" Costello demanded.

"Station Delta-Seven just reported multiple contacts near the Serpentis gate. Pharaonis signatures. Estimate…" He paused, recalculating. "Estimate ten-plus vessels."

"Ten?" Lee leaned over the display. "From where?"

"Unknown, sir. They weren't there an hour ago. Now they are."

The room erupted. Officers spoke over each other, theories flying. Stealth technology. Sensor ghosts. Hidden bases they obviously weren't aware of.

Costello raised his hand. Silence fell.

"Options?"

A commander stepped forward. "We need more intelligence. Send recon drones to all suspected coordinates. Map their movements. Figure out where they're going."

"How long?" Costello asked.

"Days. Maybe a week."

"We don't have a week." Costello looked at Lee. "Your task force deploys in three days. If these ships are moving toward Tully space—"

"They could be dug in before we arrive," Lee finished.

Another beep. Jargas pulled up new data. His expression darkened.

"Sir. Station Gamma-Four reports losing contact with monitoring outpost Echo-Seven. Last transmission indicated multiple unidentified contacts approaching their position."

Lee felt his pulse quicken. "When?"

"Forty minutes ago. We're trying to reestablish—"

The holo-table updated. A monitoring station icon turned red, then gray.

"Echo-Seven is offline," Jargas said quietly. "That's the third station in two weeks." He turned to Lee. "They're not just raiding anymore. They're clearing a path."

Lee studied the star chart. The destroyed monitoring stations formed a line, a corridor leading straight toward Tully space. Toward Serpentis. Toward the stargate network that connected three allied territories.

"They're preparing an invasion route," he said.

One of the commanders nodded. "Destroying our early-warning network and eliminating our ability to track their movements. By the time we realize they're coming—"

"They're already there." Costello crossed to the viewport. New Eden floated below. "Captain Lee, your assessment?"

Lee looked at the display. All those ships, location unknown, and some near Serpentis. Monitoring stations going dark. The Tully sectors spread before them.

Every instinct screamed to leave as soon as possible.

He thought of his crew. Nine months of training. Integrated formations with the Altairians. Simulations and drills and endless preparation. They were prepared, though they might need the Altairians for support after arriving.

"We go, sir." Lee met Costello's eyes. "Now. Because waiting means they're already where we need to be."

Costello studied him. The room held its breath.

"Agreed. Contact Captain Sato and the rest of the task force captains. Full briefing in one hour. Captain Lee, you'll present the intelligence data."

"Yes, sir."

"And, Lee?" Costello's expression was grim. "Your task force is all we have in position at the moment. As of right now, we only have Altairian support of twelve ships, and we won't be able to get reinforcements for at least two weeks. If this goes bad—"

"Understood, sir."

Lee left the office. The corridor outside was bright as he walked toward the lift, his mind racing.

Twenty-five ships. Maybe more. Zodark and Pharaonis, coordinating. Advanced enough to disappear from Republic sensors for some odd reason.

The lift descended as Lee checked his chrono—1347 hours. Three days until deployment became six hours. Maybe less.

He thought of Sato on the *Invincible*. Rhom on the *Poseidon*. MacGregor in engineering. Phillips at the EW station. Thousands of crew members across the task force, preparing for a mission that might have just turned into something big already.

The lift opened and Lee stepped into the docking bay. The *Poseidon* sat in her berth, running lights glowing. Crew members moved across the deck, loading supplies, running final checks. They looked confident. Ready.

Lee crossed the deck. A cargo loader rumbled past, hauling ammunition crates. A maintenance team worked on a frigate's sensor array. Everything normal. Everything routine.

He climbed the *Poseidon*'s gangway. The ship whirred around him, alive with power and purpose and everything that made the Republic what it was today.

Commander Rhom met him at the airlock. "Sir. How was the meeting?"

Lee looked at his executive officer. Rhom had earned his position, proven himself in nine months of training.

"Assemble senior staff in the briefing room," Lee said. "Fifteen minutes."

"Yes, sir." Rhom paused. "Is everything all right?"

Lee thought of those vanished ships along with the destroyed monitoring stations. His task force deploying into unknown danger with incomplete intelligence and no backup. Thing was, he'd done it before, and with success, and he'd do it again.

"No, Commander. Everything is not all right."

He walked toward his quarters. The corridor was quiet. He passed crew members who nodded, saluted, went about their duties. They trusted him, believed in him, and would follow him to their death. Heck, they'd go to hell for him if ordered.

Lee entered his quarters and sat at the desk and pulled up the intelligence data on his personal terminal.

His door chimed.

"Enter."

Rhom stepped inside. Behind him came MacGregor, Rodriguez, Phillips, and the other department heads. They filed in, filling the small space. Their faces showed curiosity. Concern. Not fear.

Lee stood. "We're deploying in six hours. Not three days. Six hours."

The room went still.

"Intelligence has detected a major enemy fleet movement. Pharaonis and Zodark forces, working together. They've recently destroyed three monitoring stations and disappeared from our sensors.

We don't know where they are. We don't know where they're going. But we know they're moving toward Tully space."

He pulled up the holo-display. The red icons appeared, then vanished. His crew watched in silence.

"Our mission hasn't changed," Lee continued. "We're still deploying to the Tully sector. Still coordinating with the Altairian task force, if needed. Still protecting the stargate network. But now we're doing it against an enemy that's playing some games with us right now, and just before we deploy. We need to stop those games."

The main display showed Task Force 27's composition. Fourteen Republic ships. Twelve Altairian vessels. Twenty-six total against an enemy of unknown size.

The odds weren't good. But they never were.

Lee thought of his crew. His ship. The mission ahead. And in six hours, Task Force 27 would leave New Eden and into FTL to hunt those ships down.

Chapter 47:
Squadron History

Year 2099
Victory Base Complex
Emerald City, New Eden

The Gripen flew through New Eden's atmosphere at Mach 2. The stick felt solid under Coop's hand. No tremor. No spasm. Just clean response and perfect control.

Below, Emerald City sprawled across the coastline. Completed towers shined in the morning sun. Construction zones marked the edges where Synth builders worked through the night. Residential districts spread inland like circuit boards etched into wilderness, if that made sense.

It did to Coop.

"Flight, this is Peewee. Maintain formation spacing. We're three minutes from the transition zone."

The squadron commander's voice came through all nice and calm. Coop checked his tactical display. Shadow held position on his wing, close enough to see the pilot's helmet through the canopy. Carbine maintained high cover. Matchstick brought up the rear.

"Copy, Lead," Shadow said. "All green on my end."

Coop keyed his mic. "Coop is good."

The cities blurred past below. Coop's mother flashed through his mind. Three and a half weeks ago, standing in her Charlotte apartment. Her eyes filling with tears when he'd shown her the wings.

"Are you sure about this?" she'd asked. "After everything that happened?"

He'd told her the truth, that he wasn't sure about anything except that he was a pilot and pilots fly.

What surprised him was what came after. His mother agreed to move to New Eden, and accepted his financial help without the pride that had kept her trapped in that apartment for years. She admitted that she'd been running from his father's ghost the same way Coop had been.

The formation banked east over construction zones. Agricultural operations transformed barren valleys into farmland below, and Coop adjusted his throttle and maintained position.

The transport from Earth had carried six pilots fresh from Decimomannu. All of them were wearing new wings and carrying that nervous energy of warriors heading to their first duty stations. The knowing looks when they'd learned about his assignment to the 13th Wing still burned.

Garrison duty. Safe posting. Medical red flag.

The weeklong transit had given him time to study New Eden's strategic significance. It was the first successful distant colony and also held a massive civilian population nowadays. This place was a symbolic importance to the Republic. Plus, it was relatively safe compared to Rass or Intus or the contested systems where the real war raged.

Sky cars darted between tower complexes below. Civilian traffic, normal life—the kind of thing people on Rass would kill for someday, as the fighting between the Zodarks and the allied Prims and Earthers still raged. Who knew when that place would finally find some peace?

Commander Shula had been waiting when Coop reported three days ago. The man had read his file and knew about the infamous Ridge 248, like it seemed everybody had, and it was getting all too annoying to Coop. The guy also knew about his time on Nightfall, his TBI, his years as a drone operator, and the nine-month fight to get back in a cockpit.

"Prove you can fly," Shula had said.

Four words. No sympathy. No doubt. Just the challenge.

Then came Chief Roby in the maintenance hangar. The old crew chief's eyes had widened when he'd read Coop's nameplate.

"You related to Henry Cooper, call sign 'Hank'?"

"My father."

Roby had studied him for a long moment. "Nah, are you serious?"

Coop dipped his head. "As a tower clearance."

"Well, I'll be… I knew him during the Great War. Good pilot. Brave as hell. Also haunted by every man he couldn't save. I can't tell you how badly that wrapped around your father. It consumed the poor guy. I'm sure you noticed that growing up."

"I did."

Shadow's fighter pulled closer. Perfect formation spacing. Now, garrison duty didn't mean flying with washouts. The 13th Wing drew some of the best pilots, no doubt. Every member of this squadron had seen real combat in some way, shape, or form.

The altimeter climbed. Coop watched the numbers tick up while Roby's words from this morning echoed in his head.

"Your father was one of the bravest pilots I ever knew. Also one of the most broken. Don't make his mistakes, kid. Don't carry ghosts."

It hit Coop hard, because he was doing just that, carrying the dead, such as Bear, such as Weber. Would he turn into his father? It shook Coop to the core, and he vowed, right then and there, to get counseling, to do something to ease the pain of loss, instead of burying it all down far deep where it would eventually come up like a noose around his neck later, growing tighter and tighter and tighter.

The Gripen's engines hummed with power. The formation began its climb toward upper atmosphere.

Coop's mother had called last night. The house sale had gone through faster than expected. She'd sounded lighter. Younger. Like buying that place had lifted weight she'd been carrying since the divorce.

"Are you making friends?" she'd asked.

"The squadron's solid."

"Are you taking care of yourself?"

"Yes, Mom."

He'd told her about Shula's no-nonsense approach. About Roby's connection to his father. About the way the other pilots had welcomed him without asking about his medical history or why someone with his scores had drawn a garrison posting.

Hearing himself describe it made him realize he'd found something resembling home.

The sky darkened as they climbed through thirty thousand meters.

"Flight, this is Shadow. Transition to vacuum protocols."

Coop punched in the prespace checklist without conscious thought. Muscle memory and healed neural pathways working in harmony. Good. That would always be good. Diesel had got him through the worst and put him in a position to succeed. He couldn't thank the man enough.

Matchstick and Carbine held their positions as the formation punched through the last wisps of atmosphere. The subtle shift when the engines transitioned from air-breathing to pure thrust. Then they were in space.

The void opened up around them. New Eden curved below, blue-green and beautiful, just like Earth. Orbital defense platforms floated in their designated positions and Republic Navy ships maintained patrol patterns—cruisers and battleships and frigates and the massive bulk of a carrier that dwarfed everything else in orbit.

Coop's chest expanded. Hell, practically exploded.

Pure exhilaration flooded through him as the Gripen responded to his inputs with zero atmospheric resistance while stars burned with unwavering clarity in every direction.

"Coop, how you doing back there?" Peewee asked.

Coop activated his mic. "Like I was born for this."

"Copy that. Welcome to the show."

The formation spread out. Five fighters maintaining security over humanity's first successful distant colony.

Coop thought about Ridge 248, calling fire on his own position, Li's leg torn open by shrapnel, Crawford jury-rigging equipment with trembling hands, and Weber dying in the first hour.

He thought about Bear, the Jolly Rogers squadron, and his eleven thousand hours or more in a drone cockpit fighting a war from thousands of kilometers away.

All of it had led here. To this moment, to this cockpit, and to these wings he'd fought so hard to earn. Here, in space, where the only thing between him and the infinite was a few centimeters of composite armor and the choice to keep flying, was exactly where he belonged.

Shadow's tone boomed through the tactical net. "Coop, you seeing this traffic?"

Coop checked his sensors. Three civilian transports inbound from the stargate. Standard approach vectors.

"Got them."

"Roger. Keep an eye on the middle one. Navigation's a little sloppy."

Coop focused on the transport in question. The pilot was drifting outside the designated corridor. Not dangerous yet. But worth watching.

"Think he's new?" Carbine asked.

"Or drunk," Matchstick said.

"Stow it," Peewee said. "Coop, you want to give them a gentle reminder?"

Coop switched to the civilian frequency. "Transport Victor-Five-Niner, this is Republic Fighter Coop. You're drifting outside your approach corridor. Recommend course correction to bearing one-seven-three."

A pause. Then a sheepish voice. "Copy, Coop. Correcting now. Apologies. New navigator."

"No problem, Victor-Five-Niner. Welcome to New Eden."

The transport adjusted course and Shadow chuckled over the squadron frequency. "Nice touch with the welcome."

"Figured they were nervous enough already."

"You're learning fast."

The patrol continued. Hours of flying patterns and watching sensors while maintaining some sort of readiness for anything. Protecting the civilians below who went about their lives without thinking about the fighters overhead.

Boring work, but essential.

Coop looked at New Eden below. Underneath the cloud cover, there were the cities and the farms and the millions and millions of people building lives in the aftermath of the war that once occurred here, and amid the war occurring all around the galaxy.

Maybe this was exactly where he needed to be.

Chapter 48:
The Photograph

Late 2099
FOB Redemption
Planet Rass

Love stood alone beside the Osprey *Jack* at Forward Operating Base Redemption, nine months into the Rass campaign. The photograph of her husband Jack rested in her hands, worn at the edges from handling.

Around her, the firebase had evolved. What started as temporary positions had calcified into something permanent. There was an expanded perimeter, reinforced bunkers, and maintenance facilities that actually functioned most of the time. Outside, the war continued its slow grind. They were mopping up now, hunting down scattered Zodark holdouts across the planet. Tedious work. Dangerous work. But it meant they were winning.

The Primords would reclaim their world eventually and the forests would regenerate, and nature's wounds would heal.

Right now, though, flying over Rass meant watching a planet bleed. Each time they dropped bombs or set off explosives or put lasers and magrail rounds into boulders, hills, valleys, trees, and animals, it pushed the planet's ecosystem back miles and miles.

Love leaned against the *Jack*'s hull. The bird bore nine months of scars, just like planet Rass. Chief Walzi's team had rebuilt the transport twice. Fresh welds showed exactly where the fuselage had separated during that Delta extraction all those many months ago. With it all came new engines, new landing gear, and new hydraulics.

But the photograph still lived, taped to the instrument panel when it wasn't in her hands. And the "Vivere Pugnare Alium Diem" plaque still hung in the cabin.

Some things you didn't replace.

Ford approached, carrying two cups of actual coffee. Real coffee, not the synthetic garbage from the mess. He only did this when he wanted to talk.

He'd healed from the wounds he took during the Delta extraction. Mostly. He moved with a hitch now that he pretended wasn't there. Love pretended she didn't notice.

They both gravitated to the *Jack* during downtime, the bird having become more than a transport. The Osprey was proof they'd survived.

Ford handed her a cup and leaned against the hull beside her. They stood in the comfortable silence of people who'd flown together through hell and kept the door open behind them.

"Walzi's team is going to install another starboard gun," Ford said.

"I saw the work order."

"It'll happen tomorrow morning. Can't wait to test it."

"I bet." Love sipped her coffee. "The port engine still running hot?"

"Within tolerances. Walzi thinks it's the fuel mixture. He's adjusting the ratios."

"Good."

They talked shop—engine performance, hydraulic response, and the reinforced hull plating Walzi wanted to install next week—technical conversation that kept them from talking about anything that mattered.

Love tucked the photograph into her flight suit pocket but kept one hand there, fingers resting against it.

She noticed that Ford noticed, but he didn't comment.

She supposed throughout all the time they'd spent together, all those years had taught him when to push and when to let silence work.

"Williams would've loved the new gun mounts," Ford said after a while.

Love nodded. "Yeah."

"Hawthorne too. And his crew."

They counted the dead the way pilots always did. By name, by face, by the specific missions where everything went wrong despite everyone's best efforts.

"That extraction in grid two-nine," Love said. "Second Platoon."

"The one where the LZ collapsed."

"Lost four soldiers before we could get them out."

Ford stared into his coffee. "That corporal. The one from Texas."

"Bratton."

"Bratton. Right."

They stood quiet for a moment.

"Coop made it off-planet," Ford said.

"I know. We heard the news together, remember? He's on Mars. Medical facility there."

"Last I heard, he was heading somewhere else. Don't know where."

Love raised her brows. "You heard that?"

"I did."

"Well, as long as he's breathing, I'm happy."

"Ditto," Ford agreed.

Love allowed herself a small measure of satisfaction. Coop had survived his deployment with Alpha Company. He'd walked off Rass alive, though battered, barely alive. That counted for something in a campaign that ate up soldiers like they were french fries.

"Zaines sent a message last week," Ford said. "His team's rotating back to New Eden."

"All of them?"

"All eight. Walking, talking, breathing."

Love smiled despite herself. "We did good work that day."

"Damn right we did."

Ford shifted his weight, that hitch in his movement visible for just a second. He cleared his throat. "So, I've been thinking about the stargate network."

Love rolled her eyes. "Here we go."

"No, listen. You know about the Dogon tribe? West Africa, way back?"

"Ford—"

"They had detailed knowledge of Sirius B. A white dwarf star invisible to the naked eye. Did you hear that? Not. Visible. Described its fifty-year orbital period centuries before modern astronomy confirmed it." Ford warmed to his subject. "They claimed amphibious beings from the Sirius system visited Earth and shared astronomical knowledge. Now we've got stargates connecting star systems, and Sirius has… I don't know… how many gates in its network?"

"So, you think ancient aliens taught a tribe in Mali about stargates." It wasn't a question, it was a statement of disbelief that even Chief would believe such a thing.

"I'm saying the strategic placement isn't random. Someone planned this network. Maybe the Dogon weren't making it up."

Love shook her head. "We know it was planned. Everyone knows it was planned."

Chief shrugged. "Oh, yeah. Misspoke, but you see what I'm getting at."

"Yeah, that maybe these Dogon were good astronomers and a rich oral tradition of myth and storytelling. Something to keep them from boredom, kinda like an ancient version of Shakespeare."

"You're no fun."

"I'm realistic."

"Same thing," Ford said, but he was grinning.

This was their ritual. Ford's ridiculous theories gave their minds something to chew on besides command stress and the faces they couldn't save. The banter felt normal. Felt human. Most of all, it felt like proof they hadn't lost themselves completely.

"What about the Primords?" Love asked. "They've been using stargates for centuries. You think they're connected to your Dogon tribe?"

"Maybe."

They finished their coffee in quiet, except for the mechanics all around working on transports, Reapers, and Orions.

"You thought about what comes after?" Ford asked.

Love tensed. "After what?"

"After Rass. After the campaign ends. After we're not flying combat missions every day anymore. When you end your time with the Republic military?"

"No."

"No?"

"Planning beyond the next mission feels dangerous." Love stared at the Osprey's hull. "Like tempting fate."

"We've been here nine months. War's winding down. Eventually there's going to be an after."

"Winding down? Could take years, Ford."

"True."

Ford leaned forward, though subtly. "Still, you thought of what you'd do?"

"Negative."

Love pulled the photograph from her pocket again. Jack's face looked back at her, frozen in a moment before he died, before everything went wrong and sideways.

"I don't know what after looks like," she said.

"Neither do I."

"But you're thinking about it."

Ford nodded. "Yeah. I'm thinking about it."

Love studied the photograph a moment longer, then tucked it away.

"Tomorrow's mission board will have new assignments," she said.

"Always does."

"And we'll climb back into the *Jack* and do it again."

"Until we don't have to anymore."

She sighed. "Well, you wanna have dinner?"

He grinned. "I'm starving."

"Green and Torres will be there, no doubt. Be good to talk about something besides fake alien myths."

"Fake?" This time Ford rolled his eyes. "You're like the Catholic Church, dismissing Galileo. 'The Earth doesn't move, heretic!'"

"Holy heck, Ford. Are you seriously comparing yourself to Galileo?"

"Why not? You're playing the Inquisition pretty well."

Love chuckled. "All right, that's it. This is officially ridiculous. Let's go get chow before I excommunicate you."

They pushed off from the Osprey and headed toward the operations center together. Behind them, through the open ramp, the "Vivere Pugnare Alium Diem" plaque caught the fading light.

A promise kept for years and years.

A promise they'd keep for however many more it took.

Chapter 49:
The Hunt Begins

Year 2099
Planet New Eden
RNS *Poseidon*

The RNS *Poseidon* pulled away from New Eden Orbital Station. Thirteen Republic vessels fell into formation around her, maneuvering into predetermined positions. The orbital station receded on the main viewscreen, the massive docking arms and defensive platforms shrinking against New Eden's blueish curve.

Lee sat in his command chair, arms crossed.

The *Invincible* took position off *Poseidon*'s starboard quarter, her battlecruiser dwarfing the frigates flanking her. Lee studied the vessel on the main display. Sato commanded that ship now. He knew she led her crew with the same competence she'd brought to every assignment he'd ever given her. The sight stirred something within, pride mixed with the bittersweet recognition that their partnership had transformed into something different but no less valuable.

She'd earned her command through fire and blood and endless hours of proving herself worthy. So, the *Invincible* was hers now, and she'd use it well.

"All ships report ready for departure, Captain," Rodriguez said from her station. "Formation integrity at ninety-eight percent."

"Traffic control confirms our corridor is clear," Reynolds added, while tapping inputs across his navigation console. "Jump coordinates locked and verified."

Lee glanced at Rhom, who sat at his XO console, monitoring every station's data points. His new second-in-command had settled into the role over the past nine months, learning when to speak and when to simply execute orders. It was different from Sato's approach, but effective in its own way.

"Rhom, ship status?"

Rhom checked his displays. "All departments report ready, sir. Engineering confirms reactor output at optimal levels. Weapons systems hot. Point-defense grid online and tracking."

"Sensor array calibrated and functioning," Baldry reported. "Full spectrum coverage established."

Lee keyed the shipwide comm. "All hands, this is the captain. We're departing New Eden for the Tully sectors. Our mission is to locate and neutralize hostile forces threatening allied space. We've trained for nine months. You know your stations. You know your jobs. Do them well. Lee out."

He closed the channel and looked at Reynolds. "Take us out, Lieutenant. Standard departure vector."

"Aye, sir. Maneuvering thrusters engaged."

Poseidon moved forward. Around them, the task force maintained formation, each ship holding position with minimal correction burns.

Lee watched the orbital station fall away, the blue-green orb of New Eden visible beyond it.

Nine months ago, he'd arrived here as a commander. And now, he was departing as a captain leading fourteen warships into hostile space.

"Captain, we're receiving formation updates from the Altairian contingent," Rodriguez said. "Commander Gandolly reports his twelve vessels are in position and ready to proceed."

"Acknowledge. Transmit our jump time. They're authorized to execute on their own schedule."

"Aye, sir."

The bridge settled into the normal rhythm of departure operations. Lee listened to the quiet chatter between stations until MacGregor's voice crackled over the engineering channel, confirming power distribution to the FTL drives. Rhom coordinated with the weapons department, ensuring all firing solutions remained updated as the formation shifted. Reynolds plotted micro-corrections to their trajectory, accounting for gravitational influences from New Eden's moons.

"Clear of the gravity well," Reynolds announced. "All ships report clear for FTL transition."

"Formation status?" Lee asked.

"Tight and clean," Rodriguez said. "The *Invincible* is exactly where she should be. So is everyone else."

Lee permitted himself a small smile. Sato would accept nothing less than perfection from her crew. She'd learned that from him, though she'd added her own style to it, her own understanding of what command required.

The student had become the master of her own ship.

"Sir, receiving final clearance from New Eden Command," Rodriguez said. "We are authorized for FTL departure."

"Acknowledge clearance. All ships, prepare for jump." Lee settled deeper into his chair. "Helm, engage FTL drives on my mark."

Reynolds punched in commands on his interface. "FTL drives spooling up. Thirty seconds to full power."

The bridge lights dimmed slightly as the massive energy requirements of the FTL system drew power from the reactor. The deck vibrated, a sensation always preceding the transition. Around the task force, space itself started to warp as fourteen Republic vessels prepared to punch through reality.

"FTL drives at full power," Reynolds reported. "All ships confirm ready status."

Lee looked at the viewscreen one last time, at New Eden hanging in the darkness behind them. Then he gave the order that would begin their mission in earnest.

"Execute jump."

The FTL drives engaged. Reality twisted. Space compressed and stretched simultaneously as *Poseidon* punched through the barrier between normal space and the quantum tunnels allowing ships to cross light-years in days instead of centuries. The main viewscreen went dark for half a second before the navigation computer compensated, displaying the swirling vortex of distorted starlight marking their passage through dimensions beyond human perception.

Around them, the rest of Task Force 27 made the transition, their forms warping and elongating in the visual distortion before settling into the eerie stability of FTL space.

The journey to Tully space had begun.

"Jump successful," Reynolds said. "All ships accounted for. No anomalies detected."

"Time to destination?" Lee asked.

"Seven days at current velocity."

Lee stood from his chair. "Commander Rhom, you have the bridge. Standard watch rotation. Alert me if anything changes."

"Aye, sir. I have the bridge."

****

It'd been seven days in FTL, and at the moment, Lee walked to his quarters after his stint on the bridge. Crew members stepped aside as he passed.

His quarters were modest for a captain commanding a task force: there was a desk, bunk, small head, and a terminal for classified work.

He sat at the desk and pulled up the intelligence reports, reading them again although he'd already committed most of the details to memory.

The memories came anyway.

The Academy was another lifetime, though he could still remember the faces of his classmates, young officers full of conviction and untested courage. He'd been one of those spirited cadets, ready to take on the world and take down the bad guys in the galaxy, before Oldendorf showed him what command really cost.

Lee had once been a lieutenant assigned to the *Kentucky* under Captain James B. Oldendorf, learning what leadership meant when the man showed him through example rather than lecture, and absorbing lessons about sacrifice that no classroom could teach. He'd watched Oldendorf make decisions, saving lives and costing others. Now he understood that command meant living with those choices every day.

He recalled taking the conn when Oldendorf died on that shattered bridge, along with the vessel's XO. Zodark vessels closed in for the kill then, like they always did, and at the time, half the senior staff was dead or dying. The terror of responsibility had crushed down while he gave orders that would either save the ship or condemn everyone aboard.

They'd survived.

Barely.

But they'd survived.

There was the patrol duty in the asteroid belt near Mars afterward where he learned to command without a mentor watching over his shoulder. He made mistakes and fixed them before they killed anyone. It allowed him to grow into the role one crisis at a time, and at a much faster pace.

Then there was the *Poseidon*.

He remembered the invasion at Intus, where he'd fought alongside Primord forces to retake their world from Zodark occupation. He'd flown recon missions into contested space, hunting Zodark supply lines and raiding convoys. At Rass, his battle group had destroyed seventeen orbital platforms and lost seven crew members including Witkowski. He'd spent nine months preparing this task force for deployment into hostile territory with incomplete intelligence and no backup.

His parents would probably never know what he'd become.

Separated by the choices he'd made when leaving their religious community, he had chosen service over faith as they defined it. Not as he would. To him, it was the opposite. He'd decided to walk the path God had laid out for him, not the one where he sat idly by while others protected humanity. That distance between his family and him used to hurt. Right in the heart and gut, simultaneously. It all used to make him question whether the path was worth the price of their approval.

But sitting here in his quarters aboard a heavy cruiser he commanded, leading fourteen warships into potential combat against enemies who'd demonstrated tactical sophistication beyond previous assessments, Lee knew the answer.

He was proud of what he'd built. Proud of the officer he'd become through all those years of struggle and growth.

Before him, the terminal displayed star charts and fleet movements, along with tactical assessments and probability matrices. Lee studied them until the patterns burned into his mind. The Pharaonis raiders had been coordinating with Zodark forces, establishing forward positions near the Serpentis stargates. A myriad of confirmed vessels had vanished from Republic sensors three days ago, and new contacts appeared near monitoring stations that subsequently went dark.

Whatever waited in Tully space had been planning this operation for months while the Republic scrambled to respond.

Lee ran simulation after simulation on his personal terminal. Dozens of potential scenarios. None particularly encouraging. The enemy could coordinate across species lines. They could conduct operations that avoided detection. There was something to it that he, and the rest of Command, was missing. And he'd find out exactly what that was.

Task Force 27 would face every ounce of it with fourteen ships and whatever support the Altairians could provide.

He studied the star charts until he could navigate them in his sleep, memorizing stargate positions and monitoring station locations. Calculated response times and engagement ranges. Prepared his mind for the mayhem coming when theory met reality.

Today was the seventh day, but beforehand when the days passed in FTL transit, Lee maintained a routine. He appeared on the bridge for each watch change, reviewed department reports, and conducted drills keeping the crew sharp. Rhom handled daily operations with increasing confidence. Rodriguez managed communications. Reynolds plotted contingency navigation routes for every scenario Lee could imagine. Baldry refined sensor protocols for detecting stealthed vessels.

MacGregor reported from Engineering that the reactor was performing beyond specifications. The weapons department ran firing drills until every gun crew could hit targets in their sleep.

The task force was ready.

Lee exhaled and stood. It was time. He exited his quarters and walked to the bridge thirty minutes before scheduled FTL reversion.

The crew had already begun pre-emergence protocols: securing stations and bringing weapons systems online. Rhom stood from the command chair as Lee entered.

"Captain on the bridge."

"As you were." Lee settled into his chair. "Status?"

"All ships report ready for reversion," Rhom said. "Weapons hot, sensors active, defensive systems standing by."

"Time to reversion?" Lee asked Reynolds.

"Twenty-eight minutes, sir. Emergence coordinates confirmed. We'll drop into normal space at the last known position of the enemy fleet."

"Tactical plot?"

Rhom brought up the display on the main viewscreen. "We'll emerge here, at the center of a search grid. Frigates will deploy to outer positions, establishing a sensor net covering two hundred thousand kilometers. Heavy cruisers maintain central position for rapid response. The *Invincible* and her escorts will patrol the upper quadrant."

"Time to full sensor coverage?"

"Twelve minutes after emergence, assuming no contact."

Lee studied the plot. If the enemy was still in the area, they'd find them. If not, they'd expand the search until something turned up.

"All hands, this is the captain," he said over the shipwide comm. "We're about to emerge in the sector where a combined Pharaonis-Zodark fleet was last detected. We don't know what we'll find. Stay sharp. Trust your training. Watch your sectors. Lee out."

Lee watched the chronometer tick toward zero, his palms resting on the arms of his command chair.

"Thirty seconds to reversion," Reynolds announced.

The bridge lights brightened as the FTL drives began their shutdown sequence. Lee felt disorientation as reality reasserted itself, the universe snapping back into its proper configuration after seven days of quantum displacement.

"Reverting to normal space in three… two… one… mark."

The viewscreen flared white. It then resolved into a star field of normal space.

Poseidon dropped out of FTL with the rest of Task Force 27, fourteen Republic vessels materializing in formation as their sensors swept the surrounding void.

"Sensor sweep active," Baldry reported. "Scanning all frequencies."

Lee leaned forward, eyes on the tactical display as it populated with data.

Empty space stretched in every direction.

Peaceful darkness unmarked by ship signatures or energy readings.

"Contacts?" he asked.

Baldry typed across his console. "Negative, sir. No vessels detected within sensor range. No energy signatures. No debris fields. Nothing."

The tactical display remained clear.

Just stars.

Billions of them, all scattered across the black. Ancient light from distant suns. Nebulae glowing faintly in the deep. The vast cathedral of space stretching endlessly in all directions.

Empty.

Beautiful.

And one hell of an infinite space.

Lee sat back in his chair, studying the viewscreen. The enemy fleet had vanished without a trace, but they were out here somewhere. Hiding. Planning. Waiting. And Task Force 27 would find them.

"All ships, commence search pattern," Lee ordered. "Standard grid deployment. Frigates to outer positions. Cruisers maintain formation. The *Invincible* takes high patrol. Sensors active, weapons hot. Find me those ships."

"Aye, sir," Rhom acknowledged.

Around them, the task force began to move. Frigates peeling off to establish the sensor net. Cruisers maintaining central position. The *Invincible* climbing to high patrol with her escorts. Fourteen warships spreading across two hundred thousand kilometers of space, hunting an enemy that had done the vanishing act.

The search had begun and Lee kept his focus on the stars because somewhere out there, the enemy waited, and he would find them. No matter how long it took. No matter how far they'd run.

Task Force 27 had come to the Tully sectors to do a job, and they'd see it through.

The Republic needed this mission to succeed. The allied worlds needed protection. The crew needed to prove themselves worthy of the trust placed in them.

And Lee needed to show that nine months of preparation had forged something extraordinary from fourteen ships and the people who crewed them.

He settled deeper into his command chair, his hands again steady on the armrests, his eyes on the holo where stars burned in the endless dark.

"Begin the hunt," he said.

And the task force moved into the black.

Chapter 50:
Lexington Orders

Year 2099
Victory Base Complex
Emerald City, New Eden

Three months had passed since Coop first flew with the 13th, and the squadron had become something he hadn't expected: a family. Commander Shula ran debriefs the way snipers zero their rifles, dissecting every patrol, every intercept, every decision made in the black. Peewee led by example, his calm voice over the tactical net a steadying force when situations got complicated. Shadow flew like she'd been born in a cockpit, her spatial awareness bordering on other worldly. Matchstick brought humor to everything, somehow making even the most routine patrols entertaining. Carbine reminded Coop of Bear sometimes. That same easy confidence, that same willingness to take the shot when others hesitated, that silliness and over joking that got him both in trouble and laughs, all in one.

They and all the others in the squadron had accepted Coop without question—or so it seemed—judging him only on what he could do right now, not on where he'd been or what he'd survived.

The blaster fire that had torn through his chest during the Ridge 248 extraction still showed up on medical scans, permanent scar tissue mapping the Zodark energy weapon's path through muscle and bone. But Diesel's relentless physical therapy had rebuilt what the enemy weapon had destroyed, and Dr. Drexler's counseling had helped him process the guilt that came with survival. The medical nanites and stem cell technology had done the rest, knitting together damaged tissue until he could breathe without pain, run without his chest seizing, fly without wondering if his body would quit at a critical moment.

The morning briefing started at 0700 hours sharp and Coop took his usual seat in the back row while the squadron filtered in with datapads. Chief Roby appeared in the doorway before Shula arrived, catching Coop's eye and nodding toward the maintenance office.

Coop followed him out, wondering what had the old crew chief wanted.

"Got news this morning," Roby said, pulling up a classified message on his datapad. "New battleship commissioning next month. RNS *Lexington*. They're assembling a carrier group around her for deployment." He paused, studying Coop's face. "Word is they're pulling fighter squadrons from across the Republic. The 13th is on the short list."

Coop felt something settle in his chest. Not fear exactly. Recognition. The easy posting was ending. Garrison duty was temporary. To Coop, it always had been.

"When do we find out for sure?" Coop asked.

Roby shrugged. "Could be days. Could be hours. Fleet Command's been scrambling to get the *Lexington* operational ahead of schedule. They need more capital ships on station like… yesterday." He looked at Coop with the same expression he'd worn when talking about Hank Cooper—Coop's dad—during the Great War. "You ready for this? Real combat, not training patrols."

Coop touched the challenge coin in his flight suit pocket. Bear's coin. The one constant companion through every trial since Nightfall.

"As ready as I'll ever be."

****

The briefing room fell silent when Commander Shula entered at exactly 0700 hours, his expression giving nothing away as he pulled up the morning's agenda on the holographic display. Patrol assignments appeared first. Standard security patterns over Emerald City and the agricultural zones. Nothing unusual.

Then Shula cleared his throat.

Coop knew from the subtle shift in the commander's posture that something significant was coming.

"Fleet Command transmitted deployment orders at 0530 this morning," Shula said, his voice carrying across the room. "The 13th has been selected for carrier group assignment aboard the RNS *Lexington*. Commissioning ceremony is in four weeks. We deploy for combat operations against Zodark forces threatening Republic supply lines."

The room erupted in voices. Some excited. Some apprehensive. All processing the reality that their garrison posting had just transformed into a combat deployment.

Peewee grinned like someone had handed him the keys to a new fighter. Shadow's expression remained neutral, but she checked her datapad automatically, no doubt already thinking three steps ahead. Matchstick let out a low sigh, and Coop couldn't tell if he was excited or worried. Carbine caught Coop's eye and nodded once, a silent acknowledgment that they'd both known this was coming; it had been something they'd discussed in private on more than a few occasions.

Shula waited for the noise to die down before continuing.

"This is what we've been training for. The tactical scenarios we've been running were preparation for exactly this type of deployment. Fleet Command doesn't pull squadrons for carrier group duty unless they believe we can handle whatever we encounter out there."

He looked around before continuing, "The *Lexington* will be the centerpiece of a battle group tasked with securing shipping lanes and providing fire support for ground operations on Sumer, the home world of the Sumerians in the Qatana System. Our job is what it's always been: maintain air superiority, protect our assets, eliminate enemy fighters before they can threaten Republic forces."

Shortly after the briefing concluded, Coop walked out of the briefing room and headed straight for the flight line, needing to feel his Gripen's hull under his hands, needing the confirmation that this was real and happening.

The morning sun turned New Eden's sky brilliant blue. Construction crews worked in the distance where new residential districts were rising from the wilderness. His mother had called last night from her new house, excited about the neighborhood, about the community she was in, about finally feeling like she belonged somewhere. She'd asked if he was happy.

He'd told her the truth. A resounding yes. And now he was leaving her once more. It was hard to swallow, but at the same time, she'd understand. This was his life, this was his passion.

The 13th Wing had given him purpose beyond survival, beyond proving he could still fly despite the injuries that had nearly killed him. They'd given him brothers and sisters who judged him only on what he brought to the fight, and nothing more.

Deployment to a combat zone changed everything.

But maybe that's exactly what he needed. A chance to put the training to real use, to honor Bear's memory by doing the job they'd both signed up for.

The Gripen sat in its hardened shelter, maintenance crews running checks on systems Roby's people had babied for three months. Coop ran his hand along the fuselage, feeling the composite armor that stood between him and the vacuum, thinking about his career and every mission that had led him here.

His chest didn't ache anymore where the Zodark blaster had torn through his vest. The stem cells and nanites had done their work, rebuilding tissue the old medical technology would have left scarred forever.

Dr. Drexler's voice echoed in his memory, something she'd said during their last session before he'd shipped out to Earth all those many months ago: "*Survival isn't the end of your story, Lieutenant. It's just the beginning of the next chapter.*"

Coop pulled Bear's challenge coin from his pocket one more time. Studied the worn metal. The edges smooth from months of handling.

On Ridge 248, he'd thought his story ended in blood and blaster fire.

In the hospital on Mars, he'd thought it ended in rehabilitation and medical discharge.

At Decimomannu, he'd thought it ended watching others fly missions he thought he'd performed worse on.

But standing here on the New Eden flight line with his Gripen behind him, Coop finally understood what Dr. Drexler had meant.

The story didn't end.

It just kept going.

New chapters. New missions. New brothers and sisters to fly with.

He pocketed the coin and turned toward the ready room where the 13th Wing waited.

Four weeks until the *Lexington*. Four weeks until the next chapter began. And this time, he was ready to write it himself.

****

Brandon and I hope you've enjoyed this short spinoff series from our main Rise of the Republic series. This story continues with book four of the main series, *Into the Chaos*. The characters we followed in this series return in the final three books of the main series, which are available in all formats. If you happen to have read the Battles of the Republic series without reading the main series, you can pick up the action starting with *Into the Stars*.

This has been an exciting series to write. It has spanned six years and seventeen books (when we include the spinoffs). To answer some of your questions about whether there will be additional books in this series… yes, I plan to continue this series in the future, likely advancing it further in the timeline. Old scores still need to be settled. If you would like to stay up to date on new releases and receive emails about any special pricing deals we may make available, please sign up for our email distribution list. Simply go to https://www.frontlinepublishinginc.com/ and sign up.

As a bonus, if you sign up for our mailing list, you will receive a dossier for the Rise of the Republic Series. It contains artwork of the ships we've written about, as well as their pertinent stats. It will really help make the series come to life for you as you continue reading.

As independent authors, reviews are very important to us and make a huge difference to other prospective readers. If you enjoyed this book, we humbly ask you to write up a positive review on Amazon and Goodreads. We sincerely appreciate each person that takes the time to write one.

We have really valued connecting with our readers via social media, especially on our Facebook page https://www.facebook.com/RosoneandWatson/. Sometimes we ask for help from our readers as we write future books—we love to draw upon all your different areas of expertise. We also have a group of beta readers who get to look at the books before they are officially published and help us fine-tune last-minute adjustments. If you would like to be a part of this team, please go to our author website, https://www.frontlinepublishinginc.com/, and send us a message through the "Contact" tab.

We also have free additional content available on Patreon, at https://www.patreon.com/c/frontlinepublishing/membership . We spent quite a bit of money on artwork to accompany the series, which you can find on Patreon. We do share quite a bit of content within the free tier, and paid subscribers will have access to even more. As the writing business changes and evolves, this has become a new way for us to connect with our audience.

Abbreviation Key

AA	Anti-aircraft
AI	Artificial Intelligence
AO	Area of Operation
ASAP	As soon as possible
BDA	Battle Damage Assessment
BP	Blood Pressure
CAP	Combat Air Patrol
CAS	Close-Air Support
CHU	Containerized Housing Unit
CIC	Combat Information Center
CMO	Civil-Military Operation
COMSEC	Communications Security
CPR	Cardiopulmonary Resuscitation
CPT	Captain
DZ	Drop Zone
ECCM	Electronic Counter-Countermeasures
ECM	Electronic Countermeasures
EENT	End of Evening Nautical Twilight
EMCON	Emission Control
ETA	Estimated Time of Arrival
EWO	Electronic Warfare Officer
EVA	Extra-vehicular Activity
FOB	Forward Operating Base
FSB	Fire Support Base
IFF	Identification Friend or Foe
FAE	Fuel-Air Explosives
FLIR	Forward-Looking Infrared
FTL	Faster-than-light
HUD	Heads-up Display
JAG	Judge Advocate General's Corps
JATM	Joint Advanced Tactical Missile
KIA	Killed in Action
LIDAR	Light Detection and Ranging
LT	Lieutenant
LZ	Landing Zone
MRE	Meals Ready-to-Eat

OIC	Officer in Charge
OPFOR	Opposing Forces
QRF	Quick Reaction Force
R & D	Research and Development
REDCON	Readiness Condition
RNS	Republic Naval Ship
RON	Remain Over Night
RPG	Rocket-propelled Grenade
RTB	Return to Base
SAM	Surface-to-Air Missiles
SEAD	Suppression and Destruction of Enemy Air Defenses
SIGINT	Signals Intelligence
SW	Sand and Water
UV	Ultraviolet
VTOL	Vertical Takeoff and Landing
WFJ	Wideband Frequency Jamming
XO	Executive Officer

THE END